BALANCE OF POWER

Copyright © 2017 by David Archer.

All right reserved.

Without limiting the rights under copyright reserved above, no part of this publication may be reproduced, stored in or introduced into a retrieval system, or transmitted, in any form, or by any means (electronic, mechanical, photocopying, recording, or otherwise) without the prior written permission of the author of this book.

This is a work of fiction. Names, characters, places, brands, media, and incidents are either the product of the author's imagination or are used fictitiously. Any resemblance to actual events, locales, or persons, living or dead, is coincidental.

This eBook is licensed for your personal enjoyment only. This eBook may not be re-sold or given away to other people. If you would like to share this book with another person, please purchase an additional copy for each person you share it with. If you're reading this book and did not purchase it, or it was not purchased for your use only, then you should return it and purchase your own copy. Thank you for respecting the author's work.

Published by: David Archer

Get David Archer's Starter Library FOR FREE

Sign up for the no-spam newsletter and get two introductory novella's, two introductory audiobook's, and advanced discounted links to new releases, all for free.

Get Instant Access To Everything By Clicking Here.[1]

1. http://www.davidarcherbooks.com/sign-up

PROLOGUE

The bar was rather busy for a Thursday night, but that didn't seem to bother Jimmy Morgan. After all, there was a band playing and plenty of lovely young ladies to watch him with their drooling eyes. He could have any of them, he knew, with no more effort than a flick of a beckoning finger. Wealth and power, he had determined, were the greatest aphrodisiac of all, and he was their master.

"This is how the world works now, Ralphie," he said to the boy sitting beside him. "It's like being the king around here, you know? I'm the guy everybody wants to please and nobody wants to piss off." He tilted his bottle toward the boy and smiled. "High time they all start to understand that makes you the prince. They'll give you the same respect and obedience they give me, but you have to make them fear you, too. I won't be around forever, so you're going to have to make your name just as big as mine before that happens."

Ralph Morgan was Jimmy's son, and despite the fact he was only nineteen, he had a bottle of beer in his own hand and was sipping on it slowly. Moments earlier, when a sheriff's deputy had walked through the door, he had grinned and raised the bottle in salute to the law enforcement officer. The deputy had only grinned back and waved before stepping up to the bar to chat with the bartender for a moment.

"They already do, Pa," the boy said. "How you think I get away with dating the mayor's daughter? Ain't because he thinks I'm some preacher's kid. He knows damn well I'm in her pants, and I don't know how many times I've brought her home drunk, but he still smiles and pats me on the back whenever I come to pick her up. That ain't all because of you. These people know I ain't a man they want to piss off."

Jimmy laughed loudly. "Well, you gotta keep it that way. The more arrogant and cocky you are, the more the people around here will want to kiss your ass. And that's going to get even better now that you're gonna be running one of the shows for me. Think you're ready for that?"

Ralphie shrugged. "Just tell me what you want me to do," he said. "I ain't afraid of nobody or nothing."

"Yeah, I know, and I've been thinking about what to let you take over. We make a hell of a lot of money in a lot of different ways, and I'm thinking you need to head one of them up for me. Got any preference?"

"Nah," Ralphie said. "Just put me wherever you want me; I'll do you right proud."

Jimmy made a show of pretending to think it over, but he'd already made a decision. Jimmy Morgan ran many different criminal enterprises throughout most of Northwest Arkansas, everything from drugs to prostitution to murder-for-hire, and there wasn't a cop, fed, or judge anywhere in the region who would dare try to touch him. Figuring out where to put his son hadn't been a bit difficult, since the boy was definitely a chip off the old block.

Jimmy had gotten started himself when he had inherited his father's junkyard in the small town of Berryville, Arkansas. The old man had been a drinker and had gotten behind the wheel after a dozen beers too many. The car drifted into oncoming traffic and met a gasoline tanker truck head-on. The resulting explosion had left both drivers dead and a half-dozen others severely burned. Lester Morgan had been only forty-two years old, and Jimmy was only eighteen, but suddenly the whole business was his.

The day after they buried what was left of Lester, Jimmy went to the yard and looked at it through fresh eyes. He'd been working there since he was twelve and knew the place inside out, but it suddenly dawned on him that almost all of the cars were more than fifteen years old. Sure, there was a market for the parts, but Jimmy knew there was more money in later-model stuff. When the bank released the business accounts to him, he planned to start buying newer wrecks at the insurance auctions, but then he found out that his father had blown an awful lot of money. There was barely enough in the bank for him to cover payroll for more than a couple of weeks, but that wasn't going to stop Jimmy.

Jimmy had been a star of the football team and knew just about everyone close to his age within fifty miles. Some of them, he knew, were what his mother referred to as "morally challenged." As long as there was money in it, there were half a dozen guys who would do just about anything. Jimmy laid off all but two employees and worked twelve-hour days himself for a couple of months to build up his working capital, then went looking for some of his buddies on a Saturday night.

Come the following Monday evening, a number of nearly new cars were driven through his gates and into the big old barn they used for a garage. The boys who drove them in jumped out and grabbed tools, so that by the time the sun came up those cars were nothing but parts, all neatly labeled and put into their proper place in the part of the barn they called the warehouse. Cutting torches took care of what was left of the bodies, slicing and dicing and obliterating vehicle identification numbers, and then the pieces were tossed into the big scrap dumpster outside.

In less than a year, Jimmy's yard was known as one of the best places to buy late-model parts in the entire area, and he'd made enough money to allow him to make plenty of legitimate buys, but he wasn't about to give up the huge profits he was making with stolen vehicles. The local cops knew what he was up to, but Jimmy was never bashful about sharing the wealth. As long as the cars were coming from outside the area, a little grease on the palms of law enforcement meant that he would be left alone, and his crews would not be convicted of anything worse than joyriding if they were caught.

That was the same year he was paid a visit by his county prosecutor, Roger Anthony, a man who was known to be a lot more concerned about reelection and maintaining his own power base than enforcing the law. Anthony brought along the county sheriff; Sheriff Redford liked money as well, but he didn't like the punks who were selling drugs in his county. Jimmy had a big enough crew, the two of them suggested, to run them out of the county and take the operation over. For a small percentage—say, 15 percent—Anthony and Redford would make sure Jimmy and his people were able to operate without interference.

By the time he was twenty-one, Jimmy Morgan was a multimillionaire. While there were plenty of rumors about his involvement in the crimes, Redford and the local prosecutors were in on the whole thing, so no charges were ever filed against him. When the feds caught wind and tried to set up their own investigation, Redford and his deputies kept them confused and on wild goose chases that left Jimmy standing high and dry. The money it cost Jimmy, in his opinion, was money well spent.

Over the next couple of years, the operation continued to grow. Through his crew, he managed to find and entice a number of lovely young ladies who were more than willing to negotiate for their affections and move into prostitution. Anthony and the sheriff were more than happy to take another "small percentage" of the new enterprise, and even approached their counterparts in a couple of the neighboring counties and found them just as amenable. Jimmy's operation spread out, and he grew even more wealthy.

But then a new local city cop started trying to make trouble. Officer Clayton had gotten wind of Jimmy's operations and was well aware that most of his fellows were on the take, but this young officer had integrity. After learning quickly that Jimmy was well protected, he contacted an uncle who was with the FBI and launched an investigation of his own.

By that time, though, Jimmy had reached the level of being essentially untouchable. His crew was extremely protective of him, the way a man might protect a goose that laid golden eggs. The slightest rumor that a federal prosecutor was considering charges was enough to cause something unpleasant to happen to the prosecutor or someone they loved. It was never anything fatal, but the message was loud and clear: leave Jimmy Morgan alone, or things will get much worse in a hurry. No amount of security seemed to be able to prevent these occurrences, so they were quite sufficient in deterring further attempts to prosecute Jimmy.

Officer Clayton's involvement in the attempts to take Jimmy down came to light when the office of a federal prosecutor was ransacked one night and word got back to Jimmy. He fumed about it for a couple of days, then went to Sheriff Redford.

"You need to find some way to shut that kid down," Jimmy had said.

"Shut him down?" Redford asked. "From what you're telling me, it needs to be permanently. This little shit knows way too much; he knows I've been working with you. If he's gotten any evidence together, sooner or later there's going to be a federal DA who will come after us."

Jimmy grinned at him. "Then we need to make sure that doesn't happen."

At three o'clock the next morning, fire alarms rang out. Officer Clayton's house, where he lived with his wife and baby daughter, was already engulfed in flames by the time the trucks arrived. Three badly burned bodies were recovered, and the following day Clayton's uncle arrived. He stormed into the sheriff's office and demanded cooperation in his intent to hang Jimmy for the fire, but then he did a strange thing. He went back to his hotel room, where he apparently decided to take his own life.

He had died from a single gunshot to his right temple. The medical examiner, after a brief chat with Redford, didn't hesitate to rule it a suicide, despite the fact that the man had been left-handed.

After that, even the feds tended to stay away from Jimmy Morgan. Jimmy's reach grew and grew, until he was the de facto king of more than half a dozen Northwest Arkansas counties.

Now he looked at his son and smiled. "Let me ask you a question," he said. "I know you been moving some goods for us, and you been doing pretty good at it. The trouble is, you're young, and kids tend to do some pretty stupid things from time to time. You ain't been using any of those drugs, have you, Ralphie?"

Ralphie gave him a look that questioned his father's stupidity. "Aw, hell, no," he said. "You think I don't see what that crap does to people? I like keeping my brain fully functional, thank you."

Jimmy nodded, his smile getting even wider. "That was one of the first things I figured out when I started taking over the drug business around here. We sell this shit, we sell it to every dumb bastard out there who doesn't care what it does to his life, but we ain't stupid enough to use it. If you can keep that in your head, I think maybe that's the place to start you out. You been working with Ronnie Sneed while he's been running that operation, but there's other places I could use him. I want you to start taking over the business from him tomorrow morning. Couple months, I'll move him plumb up to the main office, get him out of your hair."

Ralphie grinned and held up his bottle, clinking it against his dad's. "I like that," he said. "I think I've come up with a few ideas that might expand that operation quite a bit. Pot and meth are good products, but there are some others I think we've been neglecting. Heroin, some of the synthetics, they even got liquid pot now you can use in one of those e-cigarette things. Somebody around here is selling that stuff, might as well be us. Right?"

Jimmy gave him a thumbs-up. "Good thinking," he said. "Just do me a favor and check with Ronnie about it first. Make sure there isn't a reason he's been letting it slide. I'm not saying it's not a good idea—just make sure it won't cause us any problems before we do it."

"No problem," Ralphie said. "I'm out to make us richer, not cause us any trouble."

Jimmy went back to looking over the girls, trying to decide which one he wanted to take home for the night. He had never married Ralphie's mother, and she had decided to split back when the boy was only ten. Trying to take Jimmy's son when she did so was the mistake that cost her her life, but only Jimmy knew that, and her body had gone up in smoke when a pile of old tires "just happened" to catch fire a couple of days later. As far as Ralphie knew, his mother was living on the West Coast somewhere. He even got a birthday card from her that first year, but his belief that she had deserted him had hardened his heart against her. He wanted nothing to do with her, so the question of her whereabouts never came up.

Jimmy looked up as the bell over the door tinkled and a tall blond man walked in. The guy looked tough, and he carried himself like he might have been a soldier at one time or another. Jimmy instantly recognized the possible threat. Rival gang leaders from around the state had tried more than once to have Jimmy killed, which is why the tables around him were filled with armed rednecks. Each and every one of them was watching the new guy just as closely as Jimmy, but they started to relax when he sat down at the bar and ordered a beer.

Jimmy looked over and caught the eye of Scott Forney, who headed up his security detail. "Any idea who that might be?"

Forney shook his head and slowly got to his feet. He walked over to the bar and sat down beside the blond-haired man, then motioned for the bartender to come over. When she did, Forney ordered a beer of his own and turned to the stranger.

"Hey, man," he said. "Ain't seen you around here before. You new, or just passing through?"

The big man shrugged. "That all depends," he said.

"Yeah? Depends on what?" Forney asked.

The blond man turned and looked him in the eye. "Depends on whether or not I find work. My sister lives here, and she seems to think this is the ideal place for me."

Forney grinned at him. "Really? And who is your sister?"

"Katie Madison," the big man said. "Well, Kate is what she goes by around here, but I've always called her Katie. I'm Rex Madison, by the way." He extended a hand, and Forney shook it.

"Scott Forney," he said. "Kate Madison, huh? I didn't even know she had a brother. Don't think she ever talks about you."

"Yeah, well, there's a reason for that. See, up until not long ago, I was a guest of the federal government down in Beaumont, Texas. Black sheep of the family, you might say. Katie always tried to keep me under wraps—I guess it doesn't do a girl's reputation much good to have a brother doing time in a fed joint. I've been out a month, but I can't deal with all the probation crap back in Ohio, so Katie suggested I come give it a try here. Just got in this morning."

"Federal time always has probation attached to it," Forney said. He watched the man's face carefully while he was talking. "Bloody Beaumont, huh? Is it as bad as they say? I've heard stories about somebody dying there every week."

Rex shrugged. "Ain't really like that, but it's bad. I've seen both guards and inmates end up dead in the riots, and I saw a guy get his throat slit just for looking into another man's cell. You learn real quick to keep your eyes on the floor right in front of you all the time. Somebody thinks you're looking at him, it's like waving a red flag in front of a bull."

Forney nodded. "So why was you there?"

"Because Uncle Sam doesn't like it when one of his DEA boys gets his head blown off. We had one who got into a little operation we had going back in Cleveland, but he slipped up and got found out, and then he got dead. They couldn't prove who did it, so they just wrapped us all up, conspiracy bit. I did most of five years over that."

"Man, that sucks. What kinda dope?"

Rex laughed. "You name it," he said. "Meth, crack, X, heroin, pot, and anything else you can imagine. As long as there was a market, we were selling it."

Forney leaned close so that their shoulders were almost touching. "So, tell me," he said in a stage whisper, "you have anything to do with that fed? Him getting his head blowed off?"

Rex had his bottle up to his lips, but he turned and glanced at Forney out of the corner of his eye. "Now, come on," he said. "If I did, would you really expect me to admit it to somebody I just met? And would you even believe me if I said I did it?"

Forney shrugged and chuckled. "Hey, man, 's just you and me talking. I ain't gonna say anything to anybody else."

"Cool," Rex said, "and I'm not gonna be stupid enough to tell you anything that could possibly send me right back to Bloody Beaumont, dig?"

Forney laughed and sat up again. "So what kinda work you looking for?"

Rex turned and looked him in the eye. "Kind that makes me a hell of a lot of money."

CHAPTER ONE

"Okay," Allison said, "there is no way I'm going to let you marry that girl without a proper wedding. We can do this quick, but after all she's been through, we're going to do it right." She turned and looked at Jenny. "Let your boys take care of Randy; I'm sure they can keep an eye on him for a while. I want you to take Sarah out to Supply and tell Martha I said we need a wedding dress by tomorrow morning. She's probably got dozens of them out there, and she's got the staff who can make any alterations it might need. Think you can handle that?"

Jenny jumped to her feet, squealing and clapping her hands like a little girl. "Yes! Oh, yes!" She hurried across the room and grabbed Sarah by the hand, pulling her to her own feet. "Come on, girl, we've got to get you all set up for your big day. First we'll go pick a dress, then we'll get your hair and makeup—I'm thinking extensions, give you back that long, beautiful hair. That work for you?"

Sarah put a hand to her head and rubbed it through the short stubble on her scalp, all that was left of her blonde locks after her ordeal. "Can they put extensions in hair this short?"

"Of course they can—it's called superglue. Then it's off to get you some really racy stuff for your honeymoon. We'll make you so hot even Noah is gonna melt!"

Sarah's face turned red, but she was smiling as Jenny led her out the door.

Allison got up and walked over to a table at the side of the room, picked up a pen and paper, and scribbled something down. She turned and handed the note to Noah.

"This is the number of the pastor at my church," she said. "Don't worry, he knows exactly who we are and what we do, but he's genuinely a man of God. Tell him I said he's performing a wedding tomorrow afternoon, and all he's gonna want to know is what time."

"Thank you," Noah said.

"No problem. Now, you go get the marriage license and make whatever preparations you need, while Donald and I take care of the guest list."

"Guest list?" Noah's eyes actually got wider. "What have you got in mind?"

"Noah, Noah," Allison said. "Almost everyone in the organization knows who you are. If you're getting married, most of them are gonna want to be there. Deal with it."

Noah shrugged. "Yes, ma'am," he said. He got to his feet, followed by Neil and Marco, and headed out the door.

He called the pastor, Reverend Walton, and related Allison's message. As she had predicted, his only response was to suggest that they hold the service at 4:00 p.m., followed by a reception in the church's dining hall immediately after.

"Reception? Should I arrange catering?" Noah asked.

"Don't worry about it," Reverend Walton said. "I've got a dozen ladies in the congregation who think cooking and baking is their calling from God. They'll be more than happy to make sure there's a feast ready."

"But I don't even know how many people are coming," Noah said. "Maybe you should give Allison a call. I think she's taking care of all that."

"Don't worry, I shall. You just go on and get ready for the biggest day of your life. And by the way, it wouldn't hurt anything to see you and your new bride in our pews now and then." The line suddenly went dead, and Noah stared at his phone for a moment before putting it back in his pocket.

Noah and Sarah had ridden to the debriefing in the Corvette, but Neil and Marco grabbed him when they got to the garage and stuffed him into the shotgun seat of the Hummer. "Dude," Marco said, "you're getting married tomorrow. It is therefore an absolute necessity that your friends kidnap your butt and drag you off for a bachelor party. Since the list of your friends is topped by me and Neil, we get the honors."

Noah turned in the seat so that he could look at both of them. "The last thing I need in the world is a bachelor party," he said. "Just take me down to the courthouse. I have to get the marriage license before anything else."

"We're going, we're going," Neil said. "But if you think you're getting out of a bachelor party, you're crazy. I mean, come on, how often are we going to get the chance?"

Noah stared at him for a moment, then shrugged. "Okay, I guess. As long as it involves a steak and no dancing girls."

"What? No dancing girls?" Marco almost shrieked. "Dude, the dancing girls aren't for you, they're for us."

Noah turned around and looked him in the eye. "No dancing girls," he said.

Marco sputtered a couple of times but then finally gave in. "Fine, no dancing girls. Can we at least have a keg?"

"As long as we do it at the house," Noah said. "I can barely deal with Neil's driving when he's sober; there's no way he's driving after a keg."

Neil drove out of the garage and down the street to where the courthouse sat, and he and Marco waited in the Hummer while Noah went inside. They had been waiting for about twenty minutes, with Marco texting furiously on his phone, when Jenny and Sarah suddenly pulled in and parked beside them. Sarah got out of the car and headed inside while Jenny rolled down her window and leaned out. "Seems both applicants have to sign for the marriage license," she said. "We were just about to start looking at wedding dresses when Noah called, so we had to run back to the car and fly down here. Why is it you guys can never figure out what's got to be done before you start?"

"Because then we'd be girls," Neil said. "Real men don't read directions, don't ask for directions, and never let a lack of understanding stop them from at least trying to accomplish their goals."

Jenny's jaw dropped as she stared at him. "Oh my goodness," she said, "an honest man. Neil, I may have to just marry you."

Neil's eyes went wide, and his mouth opened three times, but no sound came out. Marco leaned forward and clapped him on the back.

"Dude," he said, "you're really turning into a ladies' man, aren't you? What would Lacey say?"

Jenny burst out laughing. "Relax, Neil, I'm only kidding. You're sweet, but you're way too tall."

Marco scrambled across the back seat and leaned out the window. "Hey, I'm not that tall," he said.

Jenny rolled her eyes at him. "You're also way too old for me," she said. "I like my men a little younger." She winked at Neil once and smiled. "You're just about the right age, though, Neil. Maybe I should reconsider."

Neil rolled up his window and turned on the stereo. Jenny and Marco both burst out laughing.

It was only about five minutes later that Noah and Sarah came out of the building. Sarah held up the marriage license and waved it in triumph. "We actually got it," she said. "Can you believe it?"

"If I didn't believe it, I wouldn't have driven like a maniac to get you here in time," Jenny said. "Now, get your butt in the car—we have shopping to do."

Sarah turned quickly and grabbed Noah, kissing him lightly before getting back into Jenny's car. The two girls drove away, each of them holding up a hand and waving goodbye.

Noah shook his head and got back into the Hummer. "Hey," he said, "what kind of things am I supposed to be doing to get ready for a wedding?"

"You got a tux?" Marco asked.

"Yeah."

"Then you're good. Now, we go eat and drink and make merry, for tomorrow you get wed. You can buy her flowers on the way to the church tomorrow afternoon." He slapped the back of Neil's seat, and the skinny kid threw the Hummer into gear and they were off.

Their next stop was at Kirtland Liquors, where Marco arranged for a tapper and two kegs of beer. It took him only a few minutes to get them, and then Neil helped him load them into the back of the Hummer. Marco got back in, and Neil drove them to Walmart.

"Guys, we can't eat that much," Noah said, as Marco tossed T-bones and strip steaks into the shopping cart. Neil had another one that was already half-full of fresh corn, baking potatoes, pull-apart rolls, and red Solo cups.

"We can with enough help," Marco said. "I might have sent out a few invitations to the party."

Noah looked at the stack of steaks. "Forty-seven of them?"

"Probably not that many," Marco said. "But Willie and Ross can probably eat two or three apiece, and Mr. Jackson loves to eat. We don't want to run out, right?" He tossed in a couple more and pushed the cart toward the front of the store.

Once everything was paid for and loaded into the Hummer, they headed for Noah's house. The drive from Walmart took almost half an hour, and Noah was surprised to see a couple dozen vehicles parked in his yard. Someone had decided not to wait for the kegs, and there was a cooler full of beer on Noah's picnic table.

"And there he is, gentlemen," shouted Wally. "Camelot, we all want to offer our congratulations." Someone shoved a can of beer into Noah's hand, and he raised it along with everyone else.

"Thank you," he said. "I appreciate all of you coming. Let me get the grill fired up and we'll start the corn and potatoes."

"Oh, no," Marco said, "you're the guest of honor. Neil, help me get the grill set up."

Someone had the foresight to bring folding chairs—Noah figured it had to have been Wally, and he was right—so he sat down in one as Neil started the grill, and Marco recruited a couple of men to help them set up the beer tapper. They had to open the garage and run an extension cord out to plug it in, and then a young man named Gary, who had once given Noah some competition in the PT course, opened the back of his Chevy Trailblazer to expose the giant speakers and cranked up the stereo.

The party was on.

OUT AT THE SUPPLY DEPOT, Sarah felt like she had won the lottery or maybe like she was actually Cinderella. Martha did indeed have a number of wedding dresses, along with just about any other kind of clothing you could imagine. More than one mission had been carried out by someone pretending to be part of a wedding party, and Jenny herself had once used such a disguise.

"I've got to say this is a first," Martha said. "We never used one of these for an actual wedding before." She had been showing Sarah different dresses, but suddenly she got a gleam in her eye. "Wait just a minute," she said. "I think I know just the one for you."

Fifteen minutes later, Sarah stood in front of a bank of mirrors and stared at herself. The beautiful white dress she was wearing fit like it had been specially tailored for her, and the lace and embroidery on it was some of the most exquisite she had ever seen. She almost had tears in her eyes as Martha and Jenny showed her the veil and tiara that went with it, and instantly agreed that it was the perfect dress.

Martha carefully packed it into a box and handed it to Jenny, who insisted on carrying it out to the car. "Now we've got the dress, it's time for all the other goodies. I already called my hairdresser and told her the situation, so let's go there first."

Sarah got into the car and looked at Jenny as she slid behind the wheel. "I can't believe you're doing all this for me," she said. "I mean, you barely even know me."

Jenny looked her in the eye and reached over to squeeze her shoulder. "Let me tell you something," she said. "The thing that got me into this life was when my little sister was murdered. When that happened, all my dreams and plans of how I was going to help her with her wedding went up in smoke. Now, I just spent the better part of a week with your guy, taking on some of the most dangerous people in the world because he wasn't going to let you get away. He may get away with telling everyone else he's an emotionless robot, but that sucker don't fool me at all. Any girl who can get through that iron curtain he's got wrapped around his emotions is a girl who is worth knowing. Maybe I don't have my own little sister, but you'll do."

They each pretended not to see the tears that were barely holding back, as Jenny started the car and headed toward the hair salon.

Hair extensions are nothing new; they've been around since the time of the Egyptians. Unfortunately, there hadn't been a lot of advancement in the technology since then, either. Sarah had to sit for almost three hours while two hairstylists worked to give her back her long blonde hair. The result, on the other hand, was outstanding, because once the hair was in place, it was so beautifully styled that Sarah had trouble believing she was looking at her own reflection in the mirror.

Jenny dragged her out of the salon, and they headed for the mall, where major name stores awaited. Sarah's new shoes came from JCPenney, a new purse came from Dillard's, and an assortment of negligees were chosen at Victoria's Secret. By the time they left the mall, most of the day had passed.

"Okay, I'm starving," Jenny said. "You have a choice: we can go to Applebee's or Ruby Tuesday. Which will it be?"

"It doesn't really matter," Sarah said, "but this time you're going to let me pay."

"Woo-hoo," Jenny said. "If you're buying, there's a steak and a margarita in my future. Let's go."

"Sounds good to me," Sarah said. "Where are we going?"

Jenny laughed. "Someplace I don't think you ever even heard of," she replied. "There is a club set up especially for those of us who work on the teams. It's called the Assassin's Club, and just being on Team Camelot makes you a member automatically. It's where I go when I want to get drunk, because you don't have to worry about being careful not to say too much."

The Assassin's Club was located in the Restricted Area, which most of the local residents thought was part of a military base. Both girls had to show their IDs to the guards at the gate, but instead of following the road toward R&D like usual, Jenny turned off onto a winding side road that went up into a heavily forested area. The Club came into view a couple of minutes later, a big, square nondescript building with dozens of cars in its parking lot.

"Everybody inside has a security clearance high enough that you don't have to pretend you're just some normal girl. Even the bands that play here are made up of people from within E & E, and most of them are pretty good. Ready to go have some fun, let your hair down?"

Sarah grinned nervously, but she nodded. "Just don't let me get so drunk I do something stupid," she said.

"Now, where's the fun in that? Don't worry, all we're going to do is drink and dance and have a good time. And don't worry about any of the guys in here giving you a problem; they all know exactly who I am."

Sarah followed Jenny through the door and was almost instantly surrounded by people she knew. Elaine Jefferson, Moose's former girlfriend, was there, along with Lacey Jackson, who was dating Neil, Noah's old friend Molly, and several other women she recognized from R&D, Supply, and other parts of the organization. They had just accepted seats at a big table with some of these ladies when a pair of hands landed on her shoulders.

"Well, it's about time you girls got here," Allison said from right behind her. "Let's get this party started!"

Sarah was never certain how they got back to Jenny's place and barely even remembered the argument about why she couldn't go home to Noah's house that night, but the hangover she had the next morning explained both. Apparently, Jenny had kept the margaritas coming until the bartender cut them off, and then somebody—neither of them remembered who—had given them a ride, while someone else drove Jenny's car home.

CHAPTER TWO

Noah's bachelor party ran on until well past midnight, despite the fact that it had started in the early afternoon. He woke at just after ten the next morning with a mild hangover of his own, and when he staggered out toward the kitchen for coffee, he found someone sleeping on every conceivable piece of furniture and many spaces on the floor.

He stepped carefully over those and found a relatively clear path to the kitchen. Neil, who Noah vaguely recalled had passed out fairly early, was sitting at the table with a cup of coffee in front of him.

"It's pretty fresh," he said. "Grab a cup and sit down."

Noah did exactly that and then looked at the tall, skinny kid. "Just how stupid did we act last night?"

"I'm not too sure," Neil said. "The last thing I remember was you telling the story of how your parents died for about the fifth time." He looked at Noah through bleary eyes and pointed a finger in his face. "Did you know that when you're drunk, you're just as emotional as anybody else? You were crying the whole time you were talking about it."

Noah blinked. "I remember that," he said. "I just don't remember what I was feeling at the time."

"That's because you keep it all suppressed. Someday, boss, all those emotions you keep buried are going to erupt like a volcano. I just hope it doesn't happen at the wrong minute, because it'll either get you killed or make you kill everyone else around you."

Noah shrugged. "I'll cross that bridge if I ever find it," he said. He took a big swig of his coffee and smacked his lips. "This is good, thanks."

"No problem, I needed it myself. How did I end up in the bathtub upstairs, anyway? Somehow, I bet that was Marco."

"It was. He took you in there so you wouldn't be in the way. People were stepping on you."

The two of them sat and drank a couple of cups apiece, as various people slowly began to regain consciousness. The coffee maker was refreshed several times to accommodate them all, but most of the men offered congratulations to Noah once again and then headed for their own homes to sleep it off for a while. By noon, it was only Noah, Neil, and Marco, and the three of them decided it was time to eat something, so they headed for the Sagebrush Saloon. For once, Neil didn't object to accepting a ride from Marco, even though it meant climbing into the narrow back seat of his late-model Mustang.

The hostess led them to a table, and it was only a minute before Elaine, her eyes bloodshot, smiled down at them. "What'll it be, guys? And before you make any smart-ass comments, you don't look a whole lot better than I do. I take it you all partied pretty hard last night?"

"We're not talking about it," Neil said. "What happened to you?"

"I toasted the bride one time too many. Jenny and Allison cooked up a scheme to get a bunch of us out to the Club, and we danced way too long and hard." She grinned at Noah. "I think Sarah had the time of her life, but we kept her out of trouble."

"Thank you," he said. "I'm sure it meant a lot to her for you to be there."

"Yeah, well, she would've been there for me, if it was my party. Coffee?"

"Coffee, yes," Noah said, "and I'll have a western omelet."

"Almost sounds good," Neil said. "I think it might even stay down. And yeah, coffee."

"Make it three times," Marco said. Elaine nodded and walked away.

The food arrived in a fairly short time, and the three of them ate rather quickly. By the time they were finished, the hangovers were faded to the point they could think, and they headed back to the house to start getting ready for the wedding. It was almost one o'clock by that point, so they had only three hours.

Noah went to his room to shower and shave, then opened his closet and pulled his tuxedo out of the plastic bag that protected it from the elements. It had been in the house since the day he moved in, but he had never worn it before. It fit perfectly, confirming his suspicion that it had been specifically tailored for him once he had accepted the job and been approved by Doc Parker.

Meanwhile, Neil and Marco had started cleaning up around the house. By the time Noah came out, it didn't look nearly as much like a natural disaster had struck it. Noah thanked them and then asked them to sit down at the table with him.

"I've never even been to a wedding," he said without preamble, "but I've read enough books to know that there are certain traditions. One of those is the best man, and I've been thinking about that." He looked at Neil. "You've been with me since the first week," he said. "I would be honored if you would be at my side today."

Marco laughed and slapped Neil on the shoulder. "See? I told you he'd pick you." He looked at Noah and rolled his eyes. "He's been hoping you would ask, but somehow he thought you were going to choose me. I told him that wouldn't make sense, since I'm new on the team. You picked the right man for the job, boss."

Neil gave Noah a sheepish grin. "It really should be Moose, if he was here," he said. "But I'll do my best to make you proud."

"I know you will," Noah said. He reached into his pocket and withdrew a small box, then opened it to show that it contained a pair of wedding rings, one for Sarah and one for him. "I bought these when I got Sarah's engagement ring. I want you to hold them for me, until it's time."

Neil swallowed hard, then took the box from Noah. He looked at the rings for a moment and then closed it, slipping it into his pocket. "I'm going to go over to the trailer and get changed," he said.

"Yeah, I've got to run home and change, myself," Marco said. "See you at the church, okay, boss?"

"I'll be there."

Alone for the first time that day, Noah suddenly remembered that he hadn't made honeymoon arrangements, so he went to the living room and picked up the laptop they always kept there. He googled various resorts and finally settled on one in Cancun, Mexico. He purchased a two-week package and scheduled their flight, which would leave Denver at just after midnight.

He went back into the bedroom and packed his own clothes, then got out another suitcase and packed some things of Sarah's that he knew she liked, including her favorite toiletries and perfumes. He left some room in the bag because he knew Jenny had planned on buying her some things, then wondered if he should have bothered at all. He shrugged and dug out their passports. It seemed a little strange to see their own official names on the passports they would use, for once.

He set the bags in the living room and took out his phone. It was a weekday, so he called Allison's office with the intent of leaving word for her about where they would be going. He asked for her voice mail but was surprised when she picked up the line.

"Speak," she said, "but not loudly. Noah, this is the first hangover I've had in twenty years. And just so you know, your new bride is a lightweight. She can't hold her margaritas very well."

Noah's eyebrows went up. "I shall bear that in mind," he said. "I was calling to let you know where we'll be going on our honeymoon. I decided on Cancun."

"That's a beautiful place," Allison said. "I want you guys to go down there and have fun, put everything else behind you for a while.

And frankly, Noah, this may do her more good than all the therapy in the world."

"I think so, too," Noah said. "She needs the security, and our getting married will offer her validation for her feelings. That's something she's been lacking, and the trauma she's been through makes it critical that she has it."

Allison was quiet for a moment, and then he heard her chuckle. "I take it you studied psychology somewhere along the line?"

"No," Noah said. "Just human nature. It's not that hard to figure out if you really pay attention."

"I'll bear that in mind. Anyway, shouldn't you be getting ready for your wedding?"

"I've been ready for an hour. Just been taking care of a few details, packing clothes for the trip, that sort of thing. Don't worry, I'll be at the church in plenty of time."

With some effort, Noah managed to stuff the luggage into the back of the Corvette, making sure to leave Sarah's bag accessible. He took another walk through the house and turned off lights, made sure all the windows and doors were locked, then walked across the yard to Neil's trailer and knocked on the door.

He wasn't surprised when Lacey answered it, already dressed and with her makeup perfect. "He's almost ready," she said. "He told me you asked him to be your best man. I think that's sweet of you, and sort of fitting since Sarah asked me, Elaine, and Jenny to stand up with her."

Noah shrugged. "He's the closest friend I've got," he said. "There was no one else I could even consider."

Lacey stepped aside to let him into the trailer, and Noah looked around. He'd only been in it a couple of times since Neil moved in, shortly after Noah was recruited. He looked around and realized that a lot of the decorative touches he saw were probably from Lacey.

"Place looks nice," he said.

"It does now," she replied. "If I had left it up to Neil, it would still look like a reject from a Southern trailer park. Of course, that's what he grew up in, so it probably seemed like home to him."

"I remember," Noah said. "That was why he wanted to rent it from me. It reminded him of the one he grew up in. It still looks better, though."

"That's because she wouldn't let up until I said it was okay to redecorate," Neil said, coming out of the bedroom. He didn't have a tuxedo, but the suit he was wearing was perfectly acceptable in Noah's opinion.

"It's getting close to time," Noah said. "I don't know what else I need to do before the wedding, but I'm open to suggestions."

Lacey giggled at him. "Buddy, all you got to do is show up," she said. "Everything else will fall right into place, trust me." She cocked her head to one side and looked at him closely for a moment. "So, tell me," she said. "What really brought this on? Sarah has been dreaming of marrying you for months, but she never believed you'd ever really go for it. What changed?"

Noah looked at her, his expression as blank as always. "I came to realize that, no matter how different they might be, I do have some kind of genuine feelings for Sarah. I can't stand the thought of not being with her, and anytime she's in danger, it's like I can't breathe properly until I get her back and know she's safe. I don't know what love is supposed to feel like, but I think that description might fit, at least to some degree."

Lacey's smile got wider. "Don't think you're different because you don't know what love is supposed to be like," she said. "I've come to the conclusion that none of us know that until it slaps us in the face and says, 'Here I am,' you know what I mean?"

"I think I do," Noah said, noticing that Lacey didn't look at Neil as she made the comment. A quick glance at Neil showed Noah that the skinny kid was keeping his own eyes averted from her.

Noah's intimate familiarity with human nature told him instantly that this was a relationship that was coming to its end. Lacey had been very good for Neil, but the young man had been going through some changes over the last couple of months, and Noah had noticed that he seemed more confident, more independent. Maybe he didn't need the emotional security of having a girlfriend as badly as he once had.

"Well, anyway," Neil said, "it's time to get on the way. I know it's only a quarter of three, but it's probably a good idea for you to get there early, let the preacher tell you what all you have to do and everything."

Noah nodded. "I agree. By the way, Sarah and I will be going to Cancun after the wedding. We'll be gone for two weeks, and I'm hoping it'll do her some good."

"It will, Noah," Lacey said. "I know it will."

Noah walked back across the yard and got into the Corvette while Neil and Lacey climbed into the Hummer. The big SUV followed the sports car out the driveway and down the curving road to the highway, and then Noah turned toward Kirtland and the next big change in his life.

CHAPTER THREE

"It was a beautiful wedding," Allison said as she hugged Sarah. "Sorry I broke down and cried, but you're about as close to being a daughter as I'm ever likely to have, and I hope you know just how lucky you are to have found so much happiness despite the line of work we're all in. I never had time for a personal life, myself. I'll probably end up dying old and alone, with a house full of cats."

The wedding had gone quickly, and the reception had lasted only an hour and a half. By the time the toasts and roasts were over, and everyone got a chance to congratulate the happy couple, it was just six o'clock. Allison, Marco, and Neil were the last three in line, and the two men were shaking Noah's hand as if they were trying to keep it from going with him.

"Molly caught up with me at the reception," Neil said. "She's already got some ideas on this dummy file we want to feed the mole, so I'll start working with her on that tomorrow. It should all be done and ready by the time you get back, and maybe we can find out just who it was that... Well, you know."

"I do," Noah said. "I'm looking forward to finding out just who it is, but I want to bring him or her in, not kill them. I'll be counting on you guys to help me do that."

Both Marco and Neil nodded. "We're in," Marco said. "Whoever it was, they need to pay."

Allison shoved the two of them toward Sarah and reached out to pull Noah into a hug. He accepted it gracefully and even managed to return it to some degree.

"Don't be thinking about the mole while you're gone," Allison whispered into his ear. "Concentrate on her. Parker and I both agree that will be the best possible medicine to give her at the moment."

"I'm planning on it. As far as I'm concerned, this place doesn't even exist for the next two weeks. Of course, should anything happen, you know how to reach me."

"Yes, but I also know how to handle things without you. This is your honeymoon. I don't plan on interrupting it, not for anything."

With the farewells all said and the good wishes of everyone they knew, Noah led his new wife out of the church and to the Corvette. She had managed to change out of the wedding dress a few minutes earlier, and Noah had traded the tux for his usual jeans and polo shirt. Some of the girls had taken care of getting Sarah's new clothing into the suitcase for her, so they were ready to go.

It wasn't until they got around the corner of the church that Noah saw the strings of tin cans and the big "Just Married" sign that were affixed to the back of his car. Sarah started giggling, but Noah simply raised an eyebrow and opened the passenger door for her. Once she was inside, he walked around the front of the car and slipped in behind the wheel, started it up, and let the cans rattle along behind as he headed toward the interstate.

The sign and the strings lasted just long enough to make it through town before falling away, and then Noah let the Corvette have its head as he turned onto I-70 toward Denver.

"Your hair looks fantastic," Noah said. "I can't even see how they put it on."

"One of the personal benefits of the miracles of modern science," Sarah replied with a smile. "I'm glad Jenny thought of it. It hadn't even occurred to me that extensions might work, but the girls she took me to knew what they were doing." She looked over at him and shook her head, as if in wonder. "Noah? If I'm dreaming, don't pinch me. I don't want to wake up."

"It's not a dream," he said. "You're not having second thoughts, are you? It's a little late to decide you don't want to be married."

"Bite your tongue," Sarah said. "Noah—you don't realize just how much this has meant to me. I understand you're not like other men, but just the fact that you admit to having feelings for me at all, that's amazing. For you to say you love me and actually ask me to marry you? To me, that's almost a miracle." She chuckled. "Did you know that I used to have these mental arguments with myself, where I would pretend that I was trying to talk you into getting married? I must've come up with a thousand logical arguments, good reasons why us getting married would be a good idea, but I never told you any of them because I never believed you'd really want to."

Noah smiled at her, and her own eyebrows went up as she realized that the smile was genuine. Seeing Noah Wolf with an actual smile on his face that wasn't contrived was something that didn't happen often.

"I think I had to figure it out for myself," he said. "And this was definitely the right decision for me."

They made it to the airport without any problems and in plenty of time to get through security for their flight. Noah had repeated to Sarah his intent to leave E & E behind them for the next two weeks and required her to promise to do her best to do the same. It hadn't been difficult to get her to agree.

The flight itself was uneventful, and both of them slept through almost all of it. They woke as the plane was descending and were surprised that it took them only a few minutes to collect their baggage. The handlers in Mexico seemed to be more on the ball than the ones back in Denver, and Noah carried all three bags from the carousel to the car rental counter.

The Jeep Noah rented was nice, and the GPS on his phone directed him to Omni Cancun Resort, where he had booked their rooms. After the flight and time involved renting the car and driving, it was just after 7:00 a.m. when they arrived. The desk clerks happily checked them in, and they went up to their room on the fourth floor to get some rest before setting out to enjoy the activities the resort offered.

They did go to sleep, but it was more than an hour later. Sarah was determined to make love to her husband for the first time before sleeping again.

For the next two weeks, Noah and Sarah Wolf felt like they were in paradise. Between time on the beach and the many activities available, Sarah saw Noah's genuine smile several times. Noah rented a personal watercraft, and they went out to explore the islands off the coast. They went scuba diving several times and marveled at the incredible variety of beautiful fish, took a drive down the coast to visit a Mayan pyramid, swam in the wild with dolphins, and spent a fair amount of time shopping for souvenirs.

Sarah, it seemed, had a list. She had found a pad and paper in the hotel room and made a list of all the friends back home she wanted to bring a gift for, and she enlisted Noah's assistance in choosing them by taking him into the biggest tourist mall she could find.

"Okay, first is Neil. What on earth could we bring back for Neil?"

"Neil? I'm trying to think of what sort of thing he might like. I mean, his big thing is technology and gadgets."

"Good point," she said. She looked at the brochure she had been given when they entered the mall and suddenly smiled. "They actually have a store here called Spy Gear, can you believe that? Let's go see if there's anything there he might like."

They spent an hour looking through all of the high-tech gadgets available in the store and finally settled on a small flying drone that held a camera that could transmit video back to a smartphone. It had a number of special features that included infrared, night vision, and other things, and Noah agreed that Neil would have a blast with them.

For Lacey, Renée, and Elaine, Sarah chose items of clothing that she thought each of them might like. Lacey got something that looked like an incredibly long scarf, but when it was wrapped and tied just right became a jumper. When a salesgirl demonstrated it on a mannequin, Noah's eyebrows went up half an inch, and he ordered a second one for Sarah.

Elaine and Renée each got a simple Mexican skirt with a peasant blouse, the type of thing that many of the local women were wearing. Sarah thought they would love them, and Noah thought she was probably correct.

Jenny, on the other hand, proved to be a bit more difficult to buy for. Sarah looked at a lot of different clothing, but then Noah took her by the hand and led her into a different store, one that specialized in edged weapons. He pointed at a set of blades that looked like the ones Wolverine had in his hands, but Sarah shook her head.

A moment later, however, she announced that she had found the perfect gift. It was a necklace with a large carved turquoise cross, but when it was twisted just right there extended a three-inch, double-edged blade made of some sort of superceramic material. The edge was guaranteed forever, and the label assured the buyer that it could be worn right through a metal detector without setting it off.

Allison got a silver desk set, and they bought Donald Jefferson a set of silver cuff links, since most of his shirts seemed to need them.

Finally, they were down to Marco. "I don't know him well enough to even guess what he might like," Sarah said. "Any ideas?"

Noah thought about it for a moment and then led her into another store. After browsing for a few minutes, the two of them agreed on a large beer mug that commemorated the Mexican hero Pancho Villa. At some point in the past, Noah had heard him mention an admiration for the former bandit who helped to liberate his country.

Some of their best times, however, were spent just lounging at the pool at the resort. There was actually a bartender set up at the level of the water, so they could swim right up to the bar and sit on a submerged stool to enjoy a margarita or a cold Modelo, and it didn't take long for Noah to realize what Allison meant about Sarah being a lightweight. By the time she finished the second margarita, Sarah was ready to tell everyone in earshot just how happy she was to have married the love of her life.

Both of them were taking video with their phones, and Noah hired a local photographer a few times to capture footage of them at various activities. While he could personally remember almost every detail of each experience, he knew that Sarah would like to look back on these days at some point, and he already planned to have Neil compile all the video into some home movies they could watch from time to time.

Nothing, however, lasts forever. Two weeks can seem like a lifetime when you are just beginning it, but the last day always seems to have come too quickly. It was finally time to head back to the real world, and Noah and Sarah said goodbye to the new friends they had met. This included a couple from Australia, another from England, and their favorite waiter at one of the in-house restaurants, who had actually invited them to come to his home and meet his family one evening. They had taken him up on it and spent several hours gathered around a simple fire pit while Roberto, the waiter, playfully scolded his nine children for the antics they were using to catch the attention of the *gringos*. Sarah thought the children were adorable, especially the two smallest ones who were still in diapers, while Noah seemed to be a source of excitement for the older ones. The boys thought his tall, blond, muscular frame must mean he was some sort of hero, while the girls simply thought he was gorgeous.

It had been a wonderful trip, and the memories they were taking away from it would be cherished forever, but it was finally time to leave. Noah drove them back to the airport and turned in the Jeep, and an hour later the plane lifted off to bring them home to Kirtland.

When they arrived at Denver International, Noah was quickly reminded of his observation about Mexican baggage handlers being more efficient. It took almost an hour and a half to retrieve their bags, and then the Corvette refused to start; apparently, one of the doors had not shut all the way and a light was left on, so the battery was dead. Noah caught one of the security officers, who was willing to give him a jump, and they were finally headed for home.

It was almost midnight by the time they got there, but Noah wasn't quite finished yet. He told Sarah to wait in the car for a moment while he checked something, then went to the front door and opened it before going back to the car and swinging her door open. She took his hand and stepped out, and then he swept her up into his arms and carried her to the house and across the threshold.

Once they were inside, he set her on her feet and turned her to face him, and she threw both arms around his neck to pull him down for a kiss.

"Welcome home, Mrs. Wolf," he said.

CHAPTER FOUR

Noah was up the next morning with the sunrise, and Sarah was up by the time he finished his shower. He opened the bathroom door and was immediately pulled into a hug, and that turned into a kiss. A few minutes later, Sarah went to get her own shower while Noah dressed and headed for the kitchen. By the time she joined him, he had managed to make quite a mess by spilling coffee grounds on the counter.

"You want to let me take that over?" Sarah asked.

Noah looked at her and actually managed a small grin. "Neil says my coffee isn't as good as yours, anyway," he said. She giggled at him as she pushed him aside, cleaned up the mess, and dumped out the coffee he had made. A few minutes later, the coffee maker was happily purring away, and she waited until it was almost done before pouring a cup for each of them.

Then, it was time for breakfast. "I was thinking," Noah said, "we might run down to Charlie's for breakfast."

"No way, José," Sarah said. "You've gone and made an honest woman of me. The least I can do is make breakfast for my husband, right?"

Noah wasn't about to argue, and it wasn't long before waffles and eggs were sitting on the table in front of each of their chairs. They sat down to enjoy breakfast together, and even though they had done so many times before, it seemed like a first.

"I suppose we need to check in," Noah said. "Let's face it, the Dragon Lady knows we're back by now. We need to see what's on the agenda."

Sarah nodded, and Noah picked up his phone from where he had laid it on the table. He dialed the number for Allison's office and asked for her when it was answered.

"About time you got back here," Allison said as she came on the line, but he could hear the smile in her voice. "Remember what I said about being able to handle things without you?"

"Yes," Noah said hesitantly.

"Well, I did. Unfortunately, it meant sending two other teams out to do something you could handle alone, but that's life. How's Sarah doing?"

"I'm fine," Sarah said. "He's got you on speakerphone, so don't try to finagle him behind my back."

"I wouldn't dream of it," Allison said. "Seriously, Sarah, how are you feeling?"

"If you're asking whether I've gotten over being captured and tortured, the answer is yes. Honestly, Allison, I think I'm ready to go back in the field whenever you need us to."

"Noah?" Allison asked. "What's your take on that comment?"

"She seems like the same old Sarah to me," Noah said, "but I'll admit to the possibility of being biased, or only seeing what I want to see. I think it wouldn't hurt for her to spend some time with Doc Parker, just to be sure."

"Oh! Noah, you traitor! Allison, don't listen to him. I'm fine, I really am."

"Hrumph," Allison said. "This is one time I'm going to take his advice. Parker is available this morning, so take her on out there, Noah. Drop her off and go have some coffee or hang out with Jackson or something, but give them a couple of hours together. After I hear back from him, then I want both of you to come by my office this afternoon. Let's say around two o'clock, okay?"

"Yes, ma'am," Noah said. The line went dead, and he turned to Sarah. "Babe, don't get upset. This is just a precaution, nothing else.

Remember, you went through some pretty serious trauma. The last thing we need is for you to be holding stuff in that might come back to haunt us later."

"Yeah, yeah, I know," Sarah said grudgingly. "I don't feel like there's any real problems, though. I mean, I can think about what happened without feeling like I want to cry anymore."

"Yes, but that could simply be a matter of getting used to the memories. Talking to Doc Parker isn't going to hurt a thing."

"Fine," Sarah said. "Then let's go get it over with. And if he says I have to start therapy, I might just shoot the old man myself."

They cleaned up the kitchen quickly and headed out to the car. Noah slid behind the wheel of the Corvette and hit the key, but all it did was click. "Battery must have gone bad," he said.

"No problem," Sarah said, "we haven't taken my car anywhere in a while, anyway." They got out of the Corvette and walked over to her Camaro, and Noah held the driver's door open for her. She slid in, and then he walked around and got into the passenger side.

Getting to Dr. Parker's office took only a few minutes, and Sarah tossed Noah the keys as she got out of the car. He climbed out and walked around to give her a kiss, then spent almost a minute getting the seat back far enough for his longer frame and adjusting the mirrors. Two hours, Allison had said, and Noah thought her suggestion to visit Mr. Jackson was a good one. After two weeks of relaxation, a heavy workout would do him good.

He got to the physical training facility just as another group was about to take off, and Jackson invited him to run along. E & E's idea of physical training involved few of the standard exercises; instead, every person who might end up in the field was put through a parkour course, running and using obstacles in their way to help them get where they were going even more quickly. Most of the people in this group were newbies, so Jackson was happy to have Noah set the pace for them.

Noah was glad he got to set the pace, as well. Most of the time when he ran with one of the groups, it was one of the regulars who was leading, and a few of them were capable of giving Noah a serious workout just trying to keep up with them.

This time, he took off at slightly more than a leisurely jog, just enough to make the rest of the group work a bit. The route they took normally went through a bit of the forest and into downtown, where they might run right through the middle of office buildings at times, and Noah had been known to run across the tops of desks more than once. Today he decided to take it a little bit easier and just let his followers get a good taste of working up a sweat.

That didn't mean it was going to be a picnic, though. He took them up fire escapes, across buildings, had them jump down onto semitrailers and into dumpsters and a dozen other stunts that most of them had never dreamed they might have to try. Each run usually lasted about an hour and a half, and by the time they got back to their starting point, a few of the stragglers were at least a mile behind.

"You lost a couple," Jackson said. "Are they going to survive?"

"They'll be along shortly," Noah replied. "I took it a little easy on them, but some of them are going to need a few weeks of exercise before they're ready for the whole course."

Jackson threw back his head and laughed. "That's what I've been trying to tell them," he said, "but they keep insisting they're ready for anything I can throw at them. That's why I jumped at the chance to throw you. How was the honeymoon?"

"Pretty great, but now I have to try to get back in shape. I think you'll be seeing me often for the next couple weeks."

Jackson nodded. "Cool. I'll put together a group for you to lead. How about mornings, say around ten?"

"I'll be here." Noah wiped his face down with the towel Jackson handed him, then turned and walked back to the car and drove back toward Parker's office. Sarah was still inside when he arrived, so he sat in the car and waited.

It was almost twenty minutes later when the door opened and she stepped out of the building. Noah's first glance up at her told him that she had been crying, but he wasn't surprised. Parker had a knack for seeing right through any attempt you might make to hide feelings or problems, and there was little doubt in his mind that she had been in some stage of denial over what happened to her. Parker would have seen that and forced her to face it. He got out of the car and was waiting when she reached him, and pulled her into his arms.

"I hate him," she said softly. "Why is it he always has to be right?"

"What happened, babe?" Noah asked.

She simply held on to him for a moment, with her face buried in his shoulder, but then she looked up into his face. "I wasn't letting myself remember," she said. "I was telling myself that it wasn't as bad as it really was, and that's not good, I guess."

"No. You have to feel what happened; you have to accept the pain and the fear and everything else that came with it. Those things have to become completely real to you before you can honestly put them behind you, but they'll also become a part of who you are. This is why I thought it would be good for you to come and see him."

Sarah looked at him for a moment and then stuck her tongue out at him. "Then I hate you, too, even though I love you. Come on, I'm hungry." She walked around the car and got into the passenger seat, so Noah got back in behind the wheel and they drove down to Charlie's for lunch, instead of breakfast.

Lunch at Charlie's was never something that happened quickly. Every order was prepared individually so that the food was always as fresh as possible. Both of them ordered burgers and fries, and by the time they were finished eating, it was time to head for Allison's office.

Luckily, the office was just down the street a few blocks. Noah drove them into the underground garage, and they rode the elevator up.

Allison's secretary simply pointed toward the conference room when she saw them, so they waved and went inside. Allison and Mr. Jefferson were there waiting, along with Neil and Molly.

"Parker says you're going to be fine," Allison said to Sarah, "but he thinks it would do you good to come in once a day for a week or two." She turned and looked at Noah. "Jackson says you're going to be working with the newbies for a while, in the mornings, is that right?"

"Yes, ma'am, ten o'clock every morning."

"Good. I'll tell Parker to keep that same slot open for Sarah." She turned to Jefferson. "Go ahead."

Donald Jefferson simply pointed at Molly, and she got to her feet.

"Okay," she said. "With Neil's help, we've come up with a plan to smoke out the CIA mole. We've created a dummy file on you, Noah, one that incorporates just enough truth to make it convincing, such as some of your legitimate missions and after-action reports, but everything else was created. We've given you a personal history completely unlike the real one, down to living parents. There is a couple in Texas who had a son who would be around your age, and who was beaten to death in prison after being sentenced to death for a couple of gang-related vengeance murders. They're pretty deeply involved in drug trafficking, so we built the file to show that you were actually their son, recruited from prison and your death faked. He was exactly the kind of person we sometimes recruit, so it's believable."

Noah nodded slowly. "So, the idea is to let the mole think that threatening them will secure my cooperation?"

"Yes," Jefferson added, "and of course, it will. At least as long as it takes for us to identify him or her, you'll pretend to be doing exactly what he wants. Now, we're hoping that we built in enough traps that it will expose the mole as soon as he tries to contact you, but we may have to let him see cooperation to some degree."

"I can do whatever I need to," Noah said. "It's absolutely critical that we identify and catch this person."

"I agree completely," Allison said. "Originally, I wanted you to simply identify and terminate the mole, but we need to find out just how much damage has been done to national security before that happens. It's imperative that this individual be taken alive."

"I'd come to the same conclusion," Noah said. "We need to find out everything we possibly can about what he or she has been doing, who the contacts are, everything." He looked at Neil and Molly, then turned back to Allison. "How soon are we putting this into play?"

"Immediately," Allison said. "We expect it to take some time before any contact is actually made with you, so the sooner we launch the plan, the better. Randy Mitchell is still under absolute observation, but Doc Parker is convinced that he wants to fully cooperate. Let's face it, you're probably the only chance he's ever got for getting out from under this monster's thumb."

"Where is Mitchell now? If he's not going out into the field with his team, it might look..."

"He is," Jefferson said. "Team Cinderella was sent out on a mission eight days ago, and they're due back today or tomorrow. Everything went according to plan, and Mitchell was contacted twice by the mole, both times to respond to questions about what happened in China. Our mysterious mole seems to have stepped up his efforts to track you down, Noah, and so we hope this will play right into our plans. The day after Team Cinderella returns, Mitchell will 'inadvertently' gain access to a file archive—a fake one, of course—where copies of active files are kept against the threat of data loss or compromise. He'll manage to copy your file onto one of those little gadgets that plug into a computer and will hold it until he is contacted again."

"At which time," Molly went on, "he'll let the mole know he has it and offer to trade it for his own freedom and the safety of his sisters. We decided on that ploy, rather than have him ask for money, because it would be more in character. He has followed the mole's orders all along only because of the threat against those girls, and has protested each time that he wanted out. Something this big, it would look fishy if he simply asked for money instead."

Noah nodded. "Absolutely, that makes sense. So, once that's done, all I have to do is wait for the mole to use whatever means you set up to contact me. How will that happen?"

"What we anticipate," Molly said, "is that one or both of your fake parents will probably be threatened, and you'll receive a message about it. The message will probably tell you that they will be killed if you don't cooperate, and will undoubtedly include a way for you to respond. It's the way you should receive the message that we hope will lead us back to the mole, though. Neil?"

"We studied the prison file on the guy who supposedly became Noah Wolf, and he was something of a car nut. We built you a series of profiles on different automotive forum sites, all of them tied to an email address we created for you. We also planted tracking bugs into the software on every one of those websites, so when a message is sent to you through one of them, the bug will go looking for the hard IP address of the computer it was sent from. Trouble is, there are ways to mask the IP of an originating computer, so we also gave them all a bug that will attach a hidden file to any message you send in response. That hidden file will hijack even the most secure email server and send us back a message containing the IP address of any computer he uses to view it. We'll also be recording your phone and everything that goes into or out of it."

"And there's no way he can get around that part?" Noah asked.

"Well, I could, so we have to assume that it's possible. If all of our little bugs fail, then it will be up to you to find some way to make this character meet you face-to-face."

"Wait a minute," Sarah put in. "I thought Randy was supposed to demand a face-to-face meeting in order to turn over the file."

"We had thought of that before," Molly replied, "but both Neil and I are afraid it would seem suspicious. The last thing we want is for the mole to cut off contact with Randy, because he's the only one we know for sure is under his thumb."

Sarah glared at her. "So instead, we're going to put Noah in danger? What if China or whoever the mole is working for decides they want Noah dead?"

Allison leaned toward Sarah and caught her attention. "Sarah, Dr. Parker runs our own version of the FBI's criminal profiling division. Based on everything we know about the mole, we've come to the conclusion that we're dealing with an analyst, not a field agent. This person is probably a career intelligence analyst who has become disillusioned, so he's likely to be in his late fifties or early sixties, probably approaching retirement. This isn't someone who would ever attempt to take on somebody like Noah."

"No, he'd just send someone he's already controlling, somebody who might have a chance of getting it done."

"Which is why," Allison went on, "Noah is going to be under constant guard until this is over. That's already begun, by the way; Teams Unicorn and Hercules have had you both under surveillance since you arrived back at the airport last night. You won't see them, but one of them is on duty and watching at all times. If a meeting is set up, they'll be there."

"Sarah," Noah said softly, "this is our best chance to get the bastard who sold you out. Trust me, baby, if it comes down to a shootout, I'm going to walk away alive."

CHAPTER FIVE

The meeting ended, and Noah took Sarah home, stopping along the way at an auto parts store to pick up a new battery for the Corvette. Neil and Marco showed up a few minutes later, Marco with his girlfriend, Renée, in tow. She and Sarah disappeared into the kitchen for some girl talk, while the three men changed the battery and stood around talking.

Noah looked over at Neil. "Lacey coming?"

Neil's face became a scowl. "No," he said bitterly. "We, uh, we sort of went our separate ways."

Noah nodded. "I had a feeling that was coming," he said. "You doing okay?"

"Hey, yeah, I'm fine. She just had too many issues for me."

Marco chuckled. "What that translates to, boss," he said, "is that our little boy is growing up. Lacey seemed to think he was supposed to let her hold on to his balls and ask for them anytime he wanted to do something out of her sight."

"Shut up, Marco," Neil said. He turned and looked at Noah. "It wasn't exactly like that, but she definitely has control issues. She wanted me to try to get transferred off the team and over to R&D or data analysis. You believe that?"

Noah looked at him. "Would that be something you'd want?"

"Oh, hell, no," Neil said. "You are not getting rid of me that easily! Noah, I—I was scared to death when all this started, but even though it gets to me sometimes, I belong on this team. I don't know what I'd do without you, without Sarah, even without this big dumb lug over here." He hooked a thumb at Marco.

"Good," Noah said. "I'm not ready to give you up, either. This team is my family, now, so I'm glad you're sticking with us."

In the kitchen, Sarah and Renée were talking about Sarah's honeymoon, and both girls were smiling.

"After you guys left," Renée said, "Marco actually asked me if I would want us to get married."

"Oh, my gosh," Sarah said, gushing. "What did you say?"

"I—I said I'd have to think about it. I mean, he's on a team; every time you guys go out, I have to wonder if I'm ever going to see him again."

Sarah nodded. "Renée, I understand what you're saying," she said, "but isn't that a reason to have whatever happiness you can? I mean, if you love him. Or have you guys not gotten to that point, yet?"

Renée shrugged and looked down at the bottle of root beer Sarah had given her. "I honestly don't know," she said. "Marco isn't real big about talking about his feelings, and I'm not completely sure about my own. I mean, I like him a lot, and there's nobody else I want to be dating, but..."

Sarah smiled and patted her hand. "One day at a time," she said.

A little while later, all of them gathered in the kitchen while Sarah made dinner, her own particular favorite, lasagna. Noah had broken out some beer and wine coolers, and they turned it into a small "Welcome Home" party for the honeymooners. They sat and talked together through dinner, then played a few hands of rummy and followed that up with Monopoly. It was after midnight by the time the party ended and their guests went home.

Noah helped Sarah clean up, and then the two of them went to their bedroom and cuddled together until they fell asleep.

The following morning, they rose at seven thirty to shower and get dressed for the day, then drove into town to the Waffle House for breakfast. The Waffle House had only opened recently and was staffed almost entirely by civilians who knew nothing of E & E, so they kept their conversations to mundane things while they ate. The service was good and the food was better, and they lingered as long as they could over coffee after they finished eating.

At last, though, it was time for Sarah to make her appointment with Doc Parker, and Noah dropped her off. She leaned through his window to kiss him goodbye, and then he drove on over to the PT area.

Jackson, true to his word, had a group of twenty people waiting. He led Noah up in front of where they were lounging around and called them to attention.

"All right, people, listen up," he said loudly. "This is Noah, and he's going to be your group leader for a few days. He's going to push you a little harder than you been used to, but he won't overdo it. Just follow him no matter where he goes, and do your best to keep up. If you get lost, just find your way back here and wait, got it?"

They all agreed that they understood, and Jackson turned them over to Noah. He smiled at them all for just a moment and then turned and started running without saying a word. It took all of them a moment to realize what was happening, but then they all took off after him.

Noah veered into the forest and followed a path for about three hundred yards, then suddenly cut to the right and leapt up onto a stump. He used it to launch himself a bit higher, caught an overhanging branch, and swung himself forward so that he landed on his feet five yards farther. When he hit the ground, he started running again and heard a number of frustrated sounds behind him as various members of the group missed the branch or simply fell.

He stopped and looked back to give them a moment to catch up, then turned and sprinted off again. The group did their best to follow, although several of them started cursing him when he ran up an inclining tree and used it as a launching pad to jump across a small creek. A few of his group landed in the water, but this time he didn't stop to wait until he came out of the forest on a two-lane road.

Once they caught up, he took off running again, this time following the road. This particular road was the one that led into Kirtland's industrial area, which had built up around some small factories. A few of them had gone out of business recently, and Noah chose one of those buildings as part of his run.

This particular building was only two stories tall, but the inside was one large open expanse. It had been occupied by a company that made steel structural members for many of the buildings in town, and there were many pieces of equipment that had been left behind. Noah made a flying leap through a broken window and then ran up a flight of stairs to a catwalk that spanned the building. When he reached the top, he stopped and looked back to make sure the others were following, but as they started up the stairs he took off again, running the length of the catwalk to the other side of the building and jumping from it onto the top of a movable storage bin, then down to the floor.

There were numerous machines still in place, and he used them to vault across the massive room, jumping over some and sliding under others, while others yet helped him to make sudden turns. By the time he got to the front corner of the building, his group of trainees was scattered all around it. He stood and watched as they figured out where he had gone, then caught up with him. This time, he waited until they had all gathered around.

"You've got to try to keep up," he said. "If you end up in the field, it's highly unlikely your team leader will be able to stop and check on you. Each of you would have your own job to do, and your entire team is counting on you to do it. Nobody can stand around and wait for you to catch up."

"Geez, man," said one of the men, a guy about Noah's age. "We're trying—can't you give us a break?"

"No," Noah said, and then he turned and took off running. He went through a door and across what had once been the lobby of the offices, then into a storeroom that he knew had a broken window. The window wasn't very big, so he had to dive through it, then roll back up to his feet outside. Once again, he stopped and waited.

The man who had complained was the first one through the window after him, and he also dived through. The rest followed, although the last three ended up climbing out, gasping for breath.

"We'll take a five-minute break," Noah said. He pointed to a shady area just a few yards away and walked over to sit down on a fallen log. The rest of them gathered up around him, most simply dropping to the ground and breathing heavily.

"Thanks, man," said the guy who had spoken before. "Some of these folks just aren't ready for this much exertion."

"That's why it caught me off guard when you spoke up in there," Noah said. "I noticed you weren't really having any problems keeping up with me. Are you just thinking of them?"

The man looked around at the stragglers and grinned, then turned back to Noah. "Nothing so altruistic," he said. "See the brunette? She was one of the ones who climbed out at the last. I guess I'm just a little bit sweet on her."

Noah looked at the girl, then turned back to the young man. "Nothing wrong with compassion," he said. "But I wasn't kidding when I said they'll all have to keep up if they end up in the field. That's what this training is all about, getting them ready. What's your name?"

"I'm Darrell, Darrell Kowalski." He extended a hand, and Noah took it.

"Noah Wolf," he said, and Darrell's eyes suddenly went wide.

"Noah Wolf? As in, like, *the* Noah Wolf? Man, you're just about all we hear about. Almost every instructor we've got talks about you."

Noah shrugged. "I didn't know," he said. "I just do my job, and right now that job includes running all your asses off."

Darrell rolled his eyes. "Yeah, well, we spent all yesterday afternoon hearing about how you took out Adrian, the assassin in London, and probably saved the monarchy from being discontinued. The day before that, it was all about how you tracked down that guy Andropov, who almost wiped us all out last year. They all seem to think we should be imitating you or trying to be you."

Noah shook his head. "They shouldn't do that," he said. "I'm not the only team leader, and I don't even think I'm the best. I've worked with one other who's every bit as efficient as I am, and maybe more so."

"Really? Can I ask who?"

"Cinderella. I'm sure you'll hear about her sometime soon."

"Cinderella? You mean, there's a woman who's actually an assassin?"

Noah nodded, knowing that everyone in the group would already have enough security clearance for the things he was saying. "Yes, and she's a very nice person when she isn't supposed to kill you." He got to his feet and walked away, offering an occasional word of encouragement to some of the people who seemed to be having the roughest time.

When it was time to go again, he started off across the Industrial Park and picked up the backstreet that led into town. The rest of the run went fairly easy, as he simply took them through alleys and streets and up the occasional fire escape. When he was at home, Noah ran the PT courses two or three times a week to keep himself in shape, so he knew all of them fairly well. It paid off as he showed this new group several different ways to get down off tall buildings without getting hurt.

Ninety minutes after they started, Noah led the group back to Jackson. The tall, former military instructor grinned at him as he brought them to a halt, and almost all of them dropped to the ground once again.

"You didn't lose any?" Jackson asked.

"Not this time," Noah said. "But they should know that tomorrow I'm not going so easy on them." He pointed Darrell out to Jackson. "That guy there? He kept up with me no problem, but he was always looking out for the slower ones. He claims it's because he likes one of the girls, but I get the feeling he's just the compassionate type. He might make a good instructor for the newbies."

Jackson held up a tablet and poked a couple of buttons on it, then smiled at Noah. "He hasn't been assigned to any particular job yet," he said. "I'll bear your suggestion in mind. He could be an asset to my department."

Noah clapped Jackson on the shoulder and turned around to the group. "Okay, you all did pretty good. Tomorrow I'm not going to take it quite as easy, though, so be ready with your heart in it. If you don't feel you can handle it, don't be afraid to tell Mr. Jackson, and he can put you back in a newbie group for a couple more weeks. See you all tomorrow."

He turned and jogged to the parking lot, before driving off to pick up Sarah.

Once again, he had to sit in the car and wait for a little while, but at least she wasn't crying when she came out this time. Noah started to get out, but she waved for him to stay seated and walked around to open her own door. As she got into the car, she leaned over and grabbed his face with both hands and pulled him down for a kiss.

When she pulled back again, she sat there staring into his eyes for a long moment. "You," she said, "are the best thing that has ever happened to me."

Noah simply looked at her for a few seconds, and then he smiled. "Ditto," he said. He shifted the car into gear and headed for home.

They got to the house and heated up a frozen pizza for lunch, then settled into the living room to watch some TV. Sarah handed the remote to Noah, and he chose a recent science fiction movie. They both enjoyed it, and when it ended, Noah let Sarah choose the next one. Her pick was a romantic movie, and the two of them enjoyed it just as much.

Just as that one was ending, the doorbell rang and Noah got up to answer it. He opened the door and was surprised when Jenny and all three of her team shouted, "Welcome home!"

Noah stepped back and let them in, keeping his eyes on Randy Mitchell the whole time. Jenny reached up and tapped his cheek to get his attention. "You can relax," she said. "He's honestly doing everything he can to make up for the things he did wrong. He was absolutely ready to play his part, and we were just informed that it begins tomorrow."

"No problem," Noah said, "but I'm not sure how Sarah is going to react."

"Yeah, well, that's the thing," Jenny said. "We brought him along because Doc Parker said she needs to face him and learn to forgive him. Now, I'm not normally all that much into forgiveness, but he and I have had a lot of chances to talk the last couple weeks. You should ask him why he was afraid to come forward and tell us what was going on."

Noah nodded and let them all into the living room. As he had expected, Sarah smiled when she saw Jenny, but the smile froze on her face as soon as Randy stepped into the room.

Surprisingly, though, she didn't say a word at first. She motioned for all of them to sit down and asked if anyone wanted something to drink, then got up and went to the kitchen. She was back a few minutes later with a pitcher of iced tea that she had made earlier in the day and several glasses, and made a point of pouring one for each of them, including Randy.

When she had reclaimed her seat beside Noah, he decided to take the bull by the horns. "Randy," he said, "I'm supposed to ask you why you never came forward and asked for help when the mole contacted you. Would you explain?"

He nodded. "Yeah, and Jenny said this might be a show-and-tell, so I brought along some visual aids." He reached into a pocket of his shirt and pulled out a stack of photographs that he passed over to Noah.

Noah flipped through them with Sarah looking over his shoulder. Each photo showed a young girl, both of them probably in their early teens, and each had a set of crosshairs drawn over the face. There were a total of nearly twenty photos.

"Those pictures were taken over the course of about a week, and some of them—the ones that show them sleeping—were taken right inside my parents' home. The point they make is pretty simple: no matter what happens, this guy can get to my sisters. When I saw those, and I should mention that he had me on the phone when they were handed to me by some street punk, I took him very seriously when he said that if I told anyone what was going on, they would be dead." He looked down at the floor for a moment, then looked back up at Noah. "I know that I'm supposed to forget everyone from my past, but the truth is that this hit me on an emotional level I just couldn't handle. I was already in high school by the time they were born, so I kind of helped raise them. There was just no way I could turn my back and let something like that happen to them, but I do realize now that I should have gone to Jenny."

"Damn, Skippy," Jenny said. "If you had, we probably would have got this bastard by now."

Sarah took the photos from Noah's hand and looked through them again. After a moment, she looked up into Randy's eyes.

"I never had a sister," she said, "so I can't claim to know exactly what you felt when you saw these, but I think I can understand what you mean when you say it hit you on an emotional level. Look, I'm not happy about what you did, especially after what it put me through, but I'm not going to hold it against you. Apparently Jenny has decided you're worth saving, and I gather Allison thinks so, as well. I'll let go of this—this anger—but it might be pretty hard for me to completely trust you again."

"I understand," Randy said. "I probably would've shot me myself, if I were in your shoes. But I appreciate you letting me at least try to explain."

"Okay, so are we all good now?" Jenny asked. "Good, that crap is out of the way. Now, tell us about the honeymoon!"

Noah glanced at Sarah, who nodded, and then he got up and left the room for a moment. When he came back, he spent a couple of minutes connecting his computer to the TV, and then they all sat around watching the raw footage he had shot while they were in Cancun. All of them laughed at some of the more comical moments, such as when Sarah was standing in the surf and was knocked down by a wave, or when Noah was feeding one of the dolphins and it decided to take a nip of his finger.

But then there began the oohs and aahs when they saw the underwater shots of all the beautiful fish and plants through which they swam, and the many videos taken at the Mayan temple and other locations. The evening turned out to be enjoyable, and they finally decided to drive on out to the Sagebrush for dinner.

CHAPTER SIX

The next day was a Saturday, and Sarah and Noah had invited Jenny, Elaine, Neil, Marco, Allison, and Donald Jefferson out in the afternoon. Noah fired up the grill for burgers and hot dogs, and Sarah drove into town to pick up potato salad, coleslaw, and french fries that she would heat up in the oven inside, as well as stocking them up on beer and soft drinks.

Neil set up a portable screen and a video projector, and they watched the honeymoon videos once again, this time with an audience of their closest friends, and everyone enjoyed them. By the time the food was ready, they had already seen most of it, and so they settled down at Noah's picnic tables and lawn chairs to eat.

And then it was time for Sarah to pass out the gifts they had brought back. She recruited Noah to help, and they went into the house and came back with packages she had wrapped only that morning.

"Okay," Sarah said, "there was no way I was going to someplace as fantastic as Cancun and not bring back something for all our dearest friends, so we've got presents for each of you. Anybody who doesn't like what we brought you, you're disowned. Everybody got that?"

"We got it," Marco yelled. "Just make like Santa, okay?"

Sarah decided to present the gifts to the women first, though she had left Lacey's gift hidden in her closet. Since she and Neil were no longer an item, she figured it would be best to meet up with Lacey privately to give it to her.

"Okay, Elaine," Sarah said. She handed Elaine the package, and everyone laughed as Elaine ripped it open like a child at Christmas.

When she saw the lovely Mexican skirt and blouse, her face lit up in a huge smile.

"Renée is next," Sarah said. "Renée, I haven't really known you long enough, so I got you the same thing as Elaine. I hope that's okay." Renée ripped the package with as much enthusiasm as Elaine had shown and made it clear that she was absolutely delighted.

"All right, now for Allison." She handed Allison a box, but the boss lady opened it a little more delicately than her predecessors had done. When she saw the beautiful desk set inside, and then realized it was made of genuine silver, she was just a little bit overwhelmed.

"Oh, it's lovely," she said. "It's going on my desk first thing Monday morning."

"Jenny, it's your turn," Sarah said. The box she handed Jenny was smaller, but the look of pure delight on the little woman's face was priceless, especially when Sarah demonstrated how to extend the blade. Jenny's eyes took on a mischievous tone, and she announced that she would never go anywhere without the cross again.

Sarah smiled and then turned to Neil. Noah handed her a box, and she passed it to the skinny kid. Neil acted more like a child at Christmas than any of the ladies, and when he saw the drone inside the box, he jumped to his feet and let out a whoop! "These are awesome! I love it," he said, showing his gift to everyone.

"Mr. Jefferson," Sarah said, "since you always wear cuff links, we got you a set." Jefferson broke into a huge smile of his own at the sight of the silver cuff links with black onyx stones.

"And we can't forget Marco," Sarah said. "I actually didn't have the slightest idea what you might like, but Noah picked something out. I hope it's okay." She took the box from Noah's hands and passed it to Marco, and he jumped to his feet as Neil had when he saw the mug. "Pancho Villa," he shouted. "*Mi amigo*! Oh, man, he's like my all-time hero."

"Pancho Villa?" Neil asked. "Wasn't he like some Mexican bandit or something?"

"Well, yeah, for a little while," Marco said. "But he was a lot like Robin Hood. He really did take from the rich and spread the money around to the poor, but then he figured out that the Mexican government was corrupt and started his own army to help in the revolution. Mexico never would have overthrown the corrupt government and discovered real liberty if it wasn't for him."

"Dude, you're from the bayou in Louisiana. Why in the world would Pancho Villa be your hero?"

"Because my great-grandmother was actually his cousin." He held the mug up beside his face. "Can't you see a resemblance?"

Neil squinted at him. "Yeah, I think I can," he said. "I think you both have the same big mouth."

Marco made an obscene gesture, and everyone laughed.

The party continued until well past sundown, but finally people began heading toward home. First Marco and Renée, then Elaine, followed by Allison and Mr. Jefferson, until only Neil and Jenny remained.

"This was a blast," Jenny said. "Thanks so much for inviting me, you guys, and I absolutely love the necklace." She looked over at Neil. "So, Neil," she said, "how come you didn't bring your girlfriend tonight?"

Neil scowled. "Lacey and I kind of broke up," he said. "It was fun while it lasted, but she was too much of a control freak for me."

Jenny's eyebrows shot up. "Really? I'm sorry to hear that. Can I ask what it was that caused the problem?"

"Yeah, she wanted me to quit the team and try to get some kind of office job downtown. I told her there was no way I was going to do that, and she said it was her way or the highway, so I opened the door for her. I liked her a lot, but I'm just not the kind of guy who can handle letting a woman be in charge all the time."

Jenny sat back in her lawn chair and stared at Neil for a moment, and Sarah watched Jenny. She'd seen the look on Jenny's face before and instantly recognized it. Jenny, for all she was one of the toughest women in the world, was honestly attracted to skinny Neil. Before Jenny could speak, Sarah jumped up out of her chair and grabbed her by the hand, dragging her into the house.

"What do you think you're doing?" Sarah asked when she got Jenny alone. "That kid is like my little brother. You're not gonna..."

"Relax, Sarah, sweetie," Jenny said. "Didn't you hear what he was saying? He broke up with Lacey because she was too bossy, right?"

Sarah narrowed her eyes and looked at Jenny closely. "Yeah. So?"

Jenny let out a sigh. "Let me tell you something," she said. "This job, I love it, because it lets me let out all this violence and rage inside of me. Without it, I'd probably end up in real trouble, and there wouldn't be any Allison to come and rescue me, you know what I mean?"

"Yeah, I think I do. But, about Neil... Jenny, you've got to understand that while he may see himself as a tough guy, he's really pretty much a softy. Every time he has to use a weapon, every time he actually has to kill someone, he spends hours crying about it. He's just not as tough as you are."

"Sarah, he doesn't have to be. See, I have to go out there and run my team with an iron fist. I can never, ever let them see any kind of weakness, or I'll lose their trust and their respect, and then they won't be there when I need them." She sighed deeply once again. "When I come home, though, all I really want to do is leave that behind. See, I can go out there and be Ms. Tough Bitch on the job, but that's not who I really am."

"It's not?" Sarah asked. "You sure have everybody else fooled, then."

Jenny chuckled. "Comes with the job, right? We have to be who-ever we have to be in order to do what we have to do, but like I said, that's not who I really am. Who I really am is a girl who would love to have a man simply take charge, somebody I can cook for and take care of and lavish a lot of love on, but most of the guys I meet only see me as Cinderella. Neil doesn't want a girl who's bossy and dominant, and I want a guy who will let me be the submissive I am on the inside. Would it really be so bad if he and I were to get together?"

Sarah opened her mouth to say something but then closed it. She tried once more, but still, nothing came out.

Jenny came and put her arms around Sarah and pulled her close. "Like I said, you can relax. If there is one man in the world who is absolutely safe from me, it would be the one guy that I think could accept me for who I am and still insist on putting his foot down when I get annoying."

"And you think maybe Neil is that guy?" Sarah asked.

Jenny shrugged, and then they both began giggling. "There's only one way I'll ever know, right?"

Sarah fought down her giggles as much as she could, then pulled back and looked Jenny in the eye. "Okay," she said after a few seconds, "but I need you to understand one thing. I'm pretty protective about Neil. If you hurt him, you'll have to be more scared of me than anyone you've ever faced out there in the field. You got that?"

They stared at each other for a few seconds and then both began laughing so hard they could barely stand. They were still laughing when they rejoined the two men outside.

The four of them sat around and talked for another half hour, but then Neil said he was tired and would see them all later. He got up and walked across the yard to his trailer, and then Sarah told Noah about the conversation she and Jenny had had.

Noah only shrugged. "They're both adults," he said. "If Jenny's serious and wants to be able to let down her guard at home, I think Neil is the kind of guy who could appreciate that. My only concern would be if the two of you got into a fight. Jenny, you live with violence almost every day. Are you sure it wouldn't come out if you were arguing?"

"I'm sure, Noah," Jenny said. "I've had a couple of boyfriends since I've been here, but it never worked out. They were either too scared of me to tell me what they thought, or they wanted a mama to tell them what to do, and neither one of those things is going to work for me. I'm not saying Neil is the right guy for me, I'm just saying I like him. He's tall, he's good-looking, he's close to my age, and I really get the feeling that he could handle having a submissive girlfriend. Of course, that doesn't mean he's attracted to me—he might not be. I'm not going to go chasing him, but I might make a point of letting him know I wouldn't turn down a chance at a date."

Noah looked over at Sarah. "I can't say I see any harm in it," he said. "This life has plenty of risks in it, but they're both aware of what those risks can be. As long as it didn't interfere in either team, I don't see a problem."

"Unless she gets it in her head to try to steal him away from our team," Sarah said. "There's no way I..."

"Hey," Jenny said, "let's just put that problem to bed right now. You guys have a good situation, now that you're married and still working together, but there's no way in the world I could have a guy I was dating on my team. It would just be too confusing. You don't ever have to worry about me trying to steal him away."

"Well, that pretty well takes away my last objection," Sarah said. "Just remember what I told you, all right?"

Jenny smiled. "I won't forget," she said as she got to her feet. "Oh, speaking of forgetting, I almost forgot something important. I'm supposed to let you know that Randy sent word to you know who that he's got the information you know who has been after. The asshole insisted on having it delivered digitally, but he did agree to let Randy off the hook in exchange for it."

"Then I should hopefully be hearing from the mole one day soon. Thank you."

"Just relaying the message. See you guys later." She walked away and got into her car, and Noah and Sarah were alone.

The two of them got up and gathered up the leftovers, then picked up all the trash and threw it into the big can that sat beside the garage. They carried the food inside and put it away in the refrigerator, then headed for bed.

Sunday broke bright and sunny, and the air was warmer than usual for late fall. The happy new couple spent most of the morning in bed, but then Noah decided to take the boat out one last time for the year. While he went down to get it ready, Sarah made them sandwiches and loaded soft drinks into a cooler with ice and brought it all down a few minutes later. Noah already had the boathouse door open, so he helped her climb aboard and then fired up the engine and backed it out onto the lake.

Air that felt warm on land was considerably cooler over water, and it wasn't long before they both were wearing windbreakers. Noah let Sarah take the helm for a while, and she shoved the throttles forward to their stops. The boat shot ahead, its bow rising as it planed across the water, and she laughed as she enjoyed the wind in her face.

"We need a faster boat," she yelled over the engine noise and wind.

"Why? This one does pretty good."

"Because I love to go fast!"

They raced around the lake for a while and then found a quiet spot to stop for their lunch. Fish were jumping out of the water all around them, and Noah commented that he wished he'd brought his fishing tackle.

"We can go back and get it, if you want," Sarah said, but Noah shook his head.

"No, I'm just enjoying being out here with my wife," he said.

Sarah giggled and smiled at him. "Mmmm, I love the sound of that."

They stayed out on the water until it was getting close to dinner-time, then headed back in and put the boat away. Neither of them felt like going out for dinner, so they microwaved some burritos and opened the bag of chips, then settled in front of the TV once again.

The rest of the week seemed to pass by quickly. Their mornings were spent with Sarah at Doc Parker's office, while Noah ran his group of new recruits. In the afternoons, they tended to simply stay home, and when they got tired of watching movies, they decided to explore other hobbies. Noah took Sarah out to the big barn, where he was gradually restoring an old Ford pickup truck that had come with the place, and wasn't terribly surprised when Sarah enjoyed getting greasy with him. After all, she had grown up around cars and probably knew as much about them as he did.

And then everything changed. On Friday morning, Noah received an email that included several pictures of the couple who were supposedly his parents. Each of them had crosshairs drawn over the faces, and Noah knew that the mole was making his move.

Sarah was looking over his shoulder, and she instantly took off out the door. She was back only a couple of minutes later, and Neil arrived less than a minute after she did, carrying his own laptop.

"We have contact," Noah said. "These are the same kinds of photos that Randy Mitchell got. No doubt in my mind this came from the mole in the CIA."

Just as he said those words, the computer chimed the arrival of another email. This one contained only a telephone number, and Noah stared at it for a moment.

Neil took out his cell phone and used its camera to snap a photo of the computer screen, then set it to record video and pointed it at Noah. Noah nodded and took out his own phone, then dialed the number.

"Tell me who you are," said a digitally distorted voice that answered the phone. Noah sat silently for a moment, then said, "Camelot."

"It's good to see that you are not a fool, Camelot," the voice said. "I gather you received my little gifts?"

"If you're referring to the pictures of my mom and dad, yes. You want to tell me who you are and what this is all about?"

"Who I am is not important," the voice said, "other than that you know I am the one to whom you will answer from now on. If you fail to do what I ask or in any way attempt to defy me, if you tell anyone about this contact, your parents are dead. If you look closely at those pictures, you'll know that I can reach them at any time I choose. You wouldn't want anything bad to happen to them, now, would you?"

Noah hesitated, making it seem that he was honestly thinking it over. "No," he said simply. "Now what do you want?"

"I want you to understand that you belong to me now," the voice said. "I want you to know that there is absolutely nothing you can do to stop me, and that failure to obey my orders will result in the death of one or both of your parents. Do you understand that?"

"Yeah, I understand, but I need you to understand," Noah said, sounding nervous. "Do you have any idea who I work for? If they ever find out..."

"I know exactly who you work for, and I know exactly who you are. The only way your employers could ever learn about this contact is if you tell them, so you need to be more afraid of yourself than of me. I'm certainly not going to reveal anything about it, and the messages I sent you will vanish from the servers any second now. There's no possible way you can prove this conversation ever took place, because even the number you dialed is untraceable. After we get off the phone, it will revert to being the private number of a doctor in Alabama."

"Then what was the point of all this? What good is it for you to threaten me if..."

"The point is that you know what you must do. I will contact you when I need your services."

The line went suddenly dead, and Neil stopped recording. Noah looked up at him.

"So, were your bugs able to trace the email origin?"

Neil opened his computer and woke it up, then started tapping on the keys. He stared at lines of data that streamed across the screen, then suddenly struck the table with his fist.

"It was bounced too many times," he said. "We didn't get enough data to trace it back."

Noah nodded. "Then we wait for him to contact me again. Neil, we don't discuss this on the phone with anyone. I need you to go to Allison's office today and let her and Jefferson know about this one. You probably ought to get hold of Molly, too."

Neil nodded as he closed his computer and stood. "I'll head that way right now. It's always possible he left some kind of trail when he hacked that phone number, too. We'll try everything we can think of." He walked out the door.

Noah leaned back in his chair and looked at Sarah. "Well, the plan seems to be working. For now, we just keep on acting as normal as we can. Let's get ready for our usual morning routine."

Sarah smiled sadly at him. "I guess the honeymoon really is over, isn't it?"

CHAPTER SEVEN

The rest of the day and the weekend passed with no further development, and Noah and Sarah continued acting as if nothing had happened. Nothing about the mole was ever discussed over telephones, and it was considered too risky for members of the team to keep making appearances at the office.

On Monday, Doc Parker was brought up to date and became part of the information relay. The next time Noah was contacted by the mole, Sarah would tell Parker, who would then visit Allison. This way, since Parker was often in and out of the offices, it was less likely anyone would pay any attention, while Allison and Jefferson were kept fully in the loop.

It wasn't until that Thursday that Noah heard anything further. He received another email message from the same automotive website, but this one contained only a phone number, a different one. With Sarah beside him, he took out his phone and dialed.

The same distorted voice answered. "I have a job for you," it said. "Do you understand what will happen if you refuse?"

"Yes, I do, dammit," Noah said, sounding angry. "But you need to understand that I can't jeopardize my job, and I won't betray my country."

"You will do whatever I tell you to do," the voice said, "or your father will suffer the consequences. There is a man in your organization who is aware that you would be working with me. This makes him a danger to both of us, and so I want you to eliminate him. He should not be hard for you to find, and I'm certain you will be able to take care of the situation. His name is Randy Mitchell, and just in case you feel some kind of loyalty to him, you should know that he was the one who gave me your identity. He must be eliminated within the next forty-eight hours. I will make contact with you again after that is done."

The line went dead. Noah looked at Sarah. "I've just been ordered to kill Randy Mitchell within the next forty-eight hours."

Sarah's space took on a crestfallen expression. "Oh, Noah," she said. "How do you plan to handle this?"

"I'm leaving that up to Allison. It's possible she'll tell me to go ahead and do it, but I want it to be her decision."

Sarah nodded. "Yeah, really. Well, I'll tell Parker this morning. Forty-eight hours isn't a lot of time, so hopefully they'll get back to you pretty quick."

They got dressed and headed out to their usual morning, with Sarah visiting Doc Parker and Noah taking his group of trainees for yet another run. He had been pleased to note that no one had dropped out of his group when he gave them the chance, and they were all managing to keep up with him to some degree.

When the run was finished, he drove back to pick Sarah up as usual, but she stepped out the door and motioned for him to come inside this time. He climbed out of the car and followed her in, and she led him into Parker's office.

"I have a secure line to the main office," Parker said without preamble. "Allison wants to speak with you." He picked up the handset of a wireless phone and handed it to Noah. "She's already on the line—go ahead."

Noah put the phone to his ear. "Camelot," he said.

"About time," Allison said. "Sarah filled me in on your phone conversation this morning. I'm a little concerned about how to handle this, to be honest. We know that he had Randy, and apparently he had the girl in North Korea, under his thumb, so it's quite possible he's got someone else within our organization. In fact, it's almost certain, so it's doubtful he'll believe you if you simply tell him it's done.

The problem is that we have no idea who else might be tied to this bastard, so it won't be easy to fake Randy's death."

"I agree," Noah said. "He'll have someone who can absolutely confirm Randy's death, and for all we know it could be someone in the morgue."

"Exactly. I just hate the idea of having to kill him after he's done everything he possibly could to help us bring this son of a bitch down. Any ideas?"

"Assuming the mole does have someone else inside, I don't know how we could actually fake his death in a way that wouldn't be found out. The only other possibility would be to eliminate him, or appear to, in such a way that there isn't a body to examine. I've got no idea how to do that, but if I come up with one I'd need Marco and Neil in on it. The only problem with that would be how to make it convincing."

Allison was quiet for a couple of seconds, then spoke. "Do what you can. I don't want to lose Randy right now, not if we can avoid it. But, Noah, if you can't come up with a foolproof way to fake it, then he is expendable. It's absolutely imperative that you gain the mole's confidence, even if it means you have to eliminate Randy." The line went dead, and Noah handed the phone back to Parker.

The old psychiatrist looked into Noah's eyes. "I could hear most of that," he said. "I don't know the details, but there's more than one way to make someone appear to be dead, even allowing the body to be examined, but still let them survive it. Talk to that whiz kid of yours—he's got a mind like a walking encyclopedia. If anybody can figure it out, I'd bet on him."

Noah nodded. "That was going to be my next move. I've heard of things like that but usually just in movies. I figure if there's really a way to do it, Neil would be the one to find it."

He turned to Sarah. "Let's go," he said to her. "I've got to move fast if I've got any chance to pull this off and get away with it."

Parker said nothing more as they walked out of his office, and they were in the car and moving only seconds later. "Tell me exactly what you think of Renée," Noah said suddenly. "Can she be trusted?"

Sarah looked at him, her eyes wide. "Renée? I don't know her all that well, but she seems pretty nice. Well, as nice as anyone connected to this outfit can be, anyway. Why?"

"Because she works at R&D, and I'm probably going to need some things from out there. Trouble is, I can't go out and ask for them, so I need someone on the inside there. Call Marco and tell him we're playing cards tonight and to bring her along. Try to let him know, without coming out and saying it, that it's absolutely urgent they show up. I'll get hold of Neil when we get back home."

Sarah looked at him for another moment, then took out her own cell phone and punched the icon for Marco. He answered after a couple of rings.

"Marco, it's Sarah," she said brightly. "Hey, listen, Noah and I want to play some cards tonight. Do you think you can convince Renée to come along? It'd really mean a lot to us to have another couple there, and you guys are our favorites."

"Yeah, we were planning on getting together tonight, anyway. Want us to bring anything?"

"Just be sure you both come," Sarah said. "We really, really want to play."

"Well, then put some beer in the fridge. Oh, hey, what time?"

"How about six? I'll have dinner ready by then, okay?"

"Six o'clock," Marco said. "We'll be there."

"He says they're coming," Sarah said to Noah. "I think he caught the hint that it was important."

Noah nodded but didn't say anything. When they got back to the house, he stopped the Corvette beside Neil's trailer and walked up to knock on the door.

"Hey," Neil said as he opened it. "Everything okay?"

"I have to come up with a way to make it look like I killed Randy Mitchell. I've got Marco and Renée coming over this evening, and I'm hoping to recruit her to help us get anything we might need out of R&D. I need you to come help me figure out a way to pull this off."

"Right now? No problem, I was just loafing anyway. I'll grab my computer and be right over."

Noah got back into the car and drove over to his own house, and Neil was walking across the yard as he and Sarah opened the door. The three of them went in and sat at the kitchen table, and Sarah put on a pot of coffee.

"Okay," Neil said, "I was actually kinda dozing on the couch when you knocked. Did you say we have to kill Randy, or make it look like we did?"

"We need to come up with a way to make it seem like we did, but it's possible the mole has other people within our organization who will be trying to verify. What I need to do is come up with something that will convince anybody that he's dead, but without actually killing him. If we can't come up with an answer, then I'll be forced to put him down for real."

"Well, considering what he did to Sarah, I'm not going to lose a lot of sleep if that happens. Why are we going to any effort to keep him alive?"

"Neil," Sarah said, "the guy was blackmailed into doing what he did. If he'd done it for money, I'd probably volunteer to blow his head off myself, but all he was trying to do was protect his little sisters. As much as I hate what happened, I can understand why he did what he did."

"Besides which," Noah said, "Allison thinks he's still an asset. She'd prefer not to have him eliminated at this point, if we can come up with a way."

Neil rubbed his hands over his face, then looked at Noah again. "So, what are we thinking? Car bomb, maybe? Take him out on the boat and give him some concrete overshoes?"

"Maybe nothing so drastic. In movies, they sometimes have a drug or something that makes people appear to be dead. Is there actually such a drug?"

Neil's eyebrows went up. "Well, yeah," he said. "It's pretty tricky stuff to use, though. Tetrodotoxin is what it's called; it comes from the livers of puffer fish and the venom of the blue-ringed octopus. Just a minute, let me look it up." He turned to his computer and started tapping on the keys. A moment later, he turned it around so Noah could see the screen.

"It takes an extremely small amount to completely paralyze a human body to the point where the person would appear to be dead. No detectable pulse, no detectable respiration, body temperature starts dropping—the only problem is that there's a very fine line between 'he looks dead,' and 'oops, he really is dead.' I don't think there's ever been any kind of study on just what the dosage should be to get the effect you're looking for."

Noah stared at the screen for a moment, then looked up at Neil. "This is what's so frustrating about having to be careful who knows what we're up to," he said. "If this were a sanctioned mission, I'd just go out to R&D and ask Wally. I'd be willing to bet someone out there knows exactly what dosage we should use."

"And they probably have some in a refrigerator out there," Neil said, nodding. "Which, I suppose, is why you're hoping to corrupt Marco's girlfriend tonight, am I right?"

"Yes. When we invited them over, I hadn't really come up with an idea, but I was almost certain I'd need something from Wally's department."

"But why involve Renée?" Sarah asked. "Why not just go to Allison and see if she can get it for you?"

"No," Neil said, "Noah is right. The Dragon Lady, if our mole has people inside, would be the main one he'd want them to watch. How often does she go out to R&D? The answer is just about never, because she doesn't go into the field."

"Well, only when she's going out to recruit someone, anyway," Noah said. "No, the smaller the group that knows about this, the better. I'm taking the chance that Renée can become an unofficial member of the team, at least while the mission is to take down someone like this."

"Okay, I guess," Sarah said. "I just wish we knew her a little better. I mean, if it was Elaine I wouldn't hesitate, but we haven't really spent that much time around Renée yet."

Noah looked at her for a moment, then turned to Neil. "Can you tap into her cell phone? If there's even the slightest chance she's been corrupted by the mole, then she'd almost certainly try to send some kind of message to him that she's coming over here tonight, wouldn't you think?"

Neil rolled his eyes. "I could do that in my sleep," he said. "Anybody got her number? I can use that to get her ESN, and then my computer can record every call or text or email, or anything else she does on it."

Sarah gave him the number while he called up the program he would use, and it took him less than half a minute to have it all set up. He looked at the screen for a few seconds, then broke into a big smile.

"Check this out," he said. "She's got an app on her phone that already records every call, every text, every single keystroke. There's about three gig worth of data stored, which would probably be about the last two weeks or so. I'm setting up a search algorithm to look for anything suspicious in it right now."

"How long will it take?" Noah asked.

"That much data? Probably an hour or so, but it'll tell us if there's any kind of increased risk to letting her in on this. I can't say for certain that not finding anything would mean she was clean, but I think it might give us a general indicator."

"Then do it. We need every indication we can get of who we can and cannot trust."

"It's running. Now, here's a question for you. Assuming we find some way to make Randy look completely dead without actually killing him, how are you going to get him to cooperate? I'm pretty sure he's smart enough to realize that a slight miscalculation in the dosage might make him enter ghosthood a lot earlier than he wanted to."

Noah blinked. "Why would you expect me to let him in on the secret? If it did scare him, he just might go running straight to the mole to try to talk him out of it. That would ruin everything we're trying to do." He shook his head. "If we can get our hands on the drug, my next move is to find a way to deliver it without him seeing it coming. It's got to be as much a surprise to him as to everyone else. Absolutely everyone outside of our small group has to think he's dead."

"Then what's going to happen to him?" Sarah asked. "I mean, he's gonna be lying in a morgue in some kind of coma, right? How do we make sure he doesn't get buried alive?"

"That's a good point," Noah said. "I'm probably going to have to find a way to make his body disappear. We can't bring anyone else in on this, so it would be strictly up to me." He looked at Neil. "I'm assuming there's a way to wake him up?"

Neil shrugged. "Epinephrine, probably. I'll see if I can find anything on the dark web about this. If anybody has ever used this stuff, that's where I would find it." He turned back to his computer and started tapping on the keys.

Noah and Sarah sat and watched in silence as Neil worked his magic. Page after page of data rolled across his monitor, and the skinny young man's fingers almost flew over the keyboard. He kept at it for more than twenty minutes without taking his eyes off the screen, then suddenly asked, "You guys got anything for lunch? I'm starving."

Sarah's eyes went wide and then rolled sideways, but she got up and opened the refrigerator. It was a matter of only a few minutes to make sandwiches out of leftover steak and pile potato salad onto plates, and she set one at each of their places. Neil reached out and picked up his sandwich without appearing to even look at it first, took a huge bite, and then smiled.

He chewed quickly and swallowed, then said, "I got it. TTX, tetrodotoxin, isn't enough by itself, but a highly unethical and illegal study done by the Russians in the 1960s found that a cataleptic state—completely indiscernible from death, but from which the victim will awaken—can be induced by the injection of one milligram of TTX along with twenty milligrams of haloperidol for every forty-five kilograms of body weight. That equals about a hundred pounds, so somebody weighing 150 pounds would need roughly one and a half times that dose. The victim will be completely without signs of life, even though heart rate and respiration are still present, but faint, for up to thirty-eight hours. And no, there is no need for an antidote. The victim will slowly increase respiration and heart rate in the last couple of hours and should regain mobility around the same time." He looked up at Noah. "One of the more interesting things they found was that the victims are usually wide awake and fully aware of their surroundings the whole time, but simply incapable of doing anything to let anyone else know what's happening to them."

Noah considered all this information for a moment. "So, what you're telling me is that Randy would be completely aware that he was being pronounced dead, but he wouldn't be able to speak or move his eyes or anything else. Right?"

"That about sums it up, yeah."

"But it won't actually kill him?"

"Well, not if you can believe the Russians. Remember, it was their military doctors who conducted these experiments."

"Then it would work. How hard is it going to be to get hold of the second ingredient, assuming we can even get our hands on the first?"

"Well, if you were schizophrenic, you'd probably have it in your medicine cabinet. I'd lay odds Doc Parker probably keeps a big bottle of it somewhere around his office."

Noah blinked. "Well, him we can trust. Let's find out if we can get our hands on the tetro-whatever, then we can ask him about haloperidol in the morning. If nothing else, he can probably figure out a way to get me some of it."

"Undoubtedly," Neil said. "That only leaves the question of the vector. How do you intend to inject Randy with it, if you're not going to let him in on the plan?"

"Well, I've been giving that some serious thought. How long does it take for the paralysis to set in?"

"According to this article, between seventeen and forty-six seconds. After that, the victim is completely cataleptic. He can't move, he can't speak, he can't so much as open his eyes, or close them, for that matter."

"Then I'll have to get to him when he's completely alone, where no one else can possibly overhear, and then I'll explain it to him right after I give him the shot. It'll be too late for him to decline to participate, but at least I can warn him about what he's about to go through."

"Okay, and then you've got about thirty-six to thirty-eight hours before he gets back on his feet and is really, really pissed off. Most of that time, he's probably going to be in the morgue. How do you plan to get him out without tipping anyone off?"

"Actually, I've got an idea on that. As an E & E operative, he pretty much belongs to the organization. Every once in a while, I've heard, R&D uses cadavers in testing some of their equipment. I'm going to find out from Renée how they go about it, but I would bet it's just a matter of the Dragon Lady approving a requisition form for a corpse."

CHAPTER EIGHT

Since they were going to be discussing sensitive issues, Noah decided to forgo the grill and have dinner inside, and asked Neil to do whatever he could to make sure no one could possibly overhear them. Neil grinned and jogged over to his trailer, coming back a few minutes later with a couple of small suitcases.

The first one he opened contained a device that could detect any type of radio signal, the same sort of device used by other federal agencies in sweeping for bugs. It took him less than ten minutes to pronounce the house completely clean, and then he opened the other case.

Inside that one was the drone that Noah and Sarah had bought for him, equipped with a GoPro camera that was set to infrared. "This baby you got me is fantastic," he said. "When it gets closer to dinnertime, I can use this to scan the area and make sure nobody is close enough to be aiming any type of listening device at us."

Sarah went all out, making pot roast with potatoes, onions, and carrots, while Noah and Neil made a run to the store to pick up beer, soft drinks, and snacks for after dinner. They were back in plenty of time, and at her insistence, both men helped Sarah give the house a thorough cleaning.

Marco and Renée showed up a half hour early, so they all sat out on the rarely used patio, just off the kitchen. Noah, Marco and Neil opted for bottles of beer, while the girls each took one of Sarah's raspberry wine coolers.

Marco was watching Neil, who was doing something with his phone. "What are you up to over there, Neil? Texting some new girl?"

Neil only grinned and shook his head, but a moment later he looked up at Noah and said, "Boss, the only heat signatures within half a mile, other than us, seems to be a coyote and a couple of rabbits. I've also checked the house again for any new radio signals. We're all clear, boss."

Marco and Renée glanced at one another, then Marco looked at Noah. "Boss man? Something going on?"

Sarah spoke first. "Renée, how high is your security clearance?"

Renée's eyebrows rose half an inch, but she didn't hesitate. "I have Q clearance," she said. "Everyone in the offices at R&D has to have it. Why?"

"Because the matters we are about to discuss would certainly be classified top secret, and probably with a restricted designation," Noah said. "Do you know anything about the circumstances surrounding Sarah's recent capture by the Chinese?"

"The circumstances surrounding it? All I know is that she was captured by someone during a mission and ended up in the hands of the Chinese interrogators. Is there something more?"

"Actually, there is. The fact of the matter is that a member of another team had been subverted by a CIA mole, and Sarah was targeted specifically because she is on my team. The Chinese, it seems, are doing everything they can to identify me, so when the mole found out where she was, he arranged for her to be grabbed and sold to China."

Renée turned and looked at Sarah, her eyes even wider. "Oh, my God," she said. "Sarah, I didn't know."

"That's because we've been keeping it pretty secret," Sarah said. "Don't worry about it. I'm actually okay."

"Part of the reason it's been so secret," Noah went on, getting Renée's attention again, "is that a decision was made at the main office to use that operative against the mole. He was given a file that seems to be about me, even though it's completely fabricated, and has passed it off. The idea was to set a trap to catch the mole if he tried to contact or subvert me, but it didn't work. He's using some false information in the file to blackmail me into doing what he wants, and I have to do everything possible to convince him I'm playing along."

Renée was nodding. "And I guess you need some kind of help from me, which means you need something from R&D but don't want to go through official channels. Am I right?"

Marco cleared his throat and touched Renée on the arm. "Before this goes any further," he said quickly, "I had absolutely no idea this was going to happen tonight."

Renée smiled at him. "It's okay, Marco," she said. She turned back to Noah. "So? How can I help?"

"The mole has ordered me to kill that same operative. The problem with that is that Allison believes the man is salvageable and still an asset. I've gone over this with her, and if there's no other way, then I'm to go ahead and terminate him, but we're trying to find a way to make it appear that he's dead and then cover up the fact that he's not."

Renée nodded slowly. "Maybe a bombing? Blow up his car and make it seem like he was in it?"

Noah shook his head. "I had actually considered that gambit, but there needs to be an actual death certificate, and a body that someone—assuming the mole has subverted others inside our organization—could examine. Neil came up with an idea, but we'd have to get hold of something called..." He looked at Neil.

"Tetrodotoxin, TTX."

"Is there any possibility that R&D would have some?" Noah asked.

"TTX? Yeah, as a matter of fact. One of the labs is actually working on something that involves it, but I don't know what."

"What about haloperidol?" Neil asked quickly. "Any of that out there?"

Renee's eyebrows suddenly lowered, and she looked at Neil suspiciously. "Yeah," she said slowly. "I handle the requisition forms, and that's something else the same lab is working with. Did you already know that?"

"No, but TTX and haloperidol are the magic mixture the Russians came up with for making someone seem to be dead, and that's what we're trying to do. When you said a lab was working with TTX, I just naturally figured they might be working on the same idea."

"Okay, I guess that makes sense." She turned to Noah. "So you want me to get this stuff for you, right? Let me ask you this—how soon do you need to have it?"

"I'm supposed to make sure Randy is dead within the next thirty-eight hours or so," Noah said. "This is the only chance he's got to survive this thing, so the sooner, the better."

Renée looked into his eyes for a moment, then nodded as if coming to a decision. "Well, as it happens, I occasionally work late, with Wally's authorization. What that means is that I happen to have in my possession a set of keys, and I'm listed with security as having twenty-four-hour access to the facility. Now, the problem is that I can't just walk into one of the labs and take something out, because I don't have the kind of pass that opens the lab doors."

Noah sighed. "What about tomorrow morning? Is there any way you could..."

"Hold on, I wasn't finished," Renée said, holding up a hand to stop him. "There is somebody who does have a lab pass, and it just happens to be my roommate. Her name is Mary, and if I asked her to, she'd go out with me and get what you need."

"The problem with that," Noah said, "is that we don't know who we can trust. The mole could have any number of people in the organization that report back to him. Frankly, I'm sticking my neck out pretty far just talking to you about this."

Renée sat and looked at him for a moment, chewing her bottom lip. "Okay," she said at last, "there's one other thing I can think of. How do you feel about Wally himself? Would you be okay with him being in on this?"

Noah's eyebrows went up a quarter of an inch. "Actually, I would," he said. "I gather you're thinking of a way to make that happen?"

"Yes. Wally's an incredible genius, and while he rarely takes credit, most of the things our labs come up with start out as a doodle on his desk pad. He and I are also very old friends, since we were both recruited from the CIA when Allison set up E & E. If I just gave him a call and told him I need him to meet me at the office for something important, he'd drop whatever he's doing and meet me. Once we're inside I can tell him what you need, and there's no doubt in my mind he'll get it for you and let me bring it back."

Noah looked at Neil. "Can you tell her exactly what it is you're going to need?"

"Yeah, of course," Neil replied, "but this may be better than we ever dreamed. They probably already have the correct formula worked out. I can write up a note she can give him, and I'm pretty sure he'll know what to send back. But, Noah, what if Wally has been compromised?"

"Wally has probably the highest access of anyone outside the main office," Noah said. "If the mole had somehow managed to compromise him, I suspect finding me wouldn't have been a bit difficult. Write your note—this is a go." He turned to Renée. "Why don't you call him now and set up a time? The sooner, the better. Dinner can wait."

Renée grinned and nodded, then took out her cell phone. She dialed the number and listened for only a moment. "Wally? Hey, listen, it's Renée. I've gotta run by the office for a few minutes, and there's something I'd like to talk to you about. Would you mind meeting me out there? Twenty minutes? Actually, I'd need a little more than that. Let's make it's about thirty minutes, is that okay? Okay, great, I'll see you there."

She turned to Noah. "Okay, it's set. I can be back here in an hour and a half with what you need in hand."

Noah nodded. "All right," he said. "We'll hold dinner for you."

Marco shrugged and shook his head but followed Renée back out to his car. The two of them drove away, and Noah felt Sarah wrap her arms around him from behind.

"I hope this wasn't a mistake," she said softly. "We're letting a lot of people in on secrets that were supposed to stay within our small group."

"Wally's good," Neil said. "Noah is absolutely correct. If somebody was pulling Wally's puppet strings, they wouldn't need anybody like Randy. The only real risk in this ploy is using Renée, but I doubt she's even in a position that would be of any benefit to the mole."

Noah suddenly turned and looked at Neil. "You just made an extremely good point," he said. "I wonder what it was about Randy that put him in the mole's sights."

Neil shrugged. "You know, now that you mention it, I'm not sure anybody has even asked that question."

"SO," RENÉE SAID TO Marco as they drove toward R&D. "You really didn't know about this before we got there?"

Marco shook his head. "No, I didn't. I had an idea that they wanted to talk to you about something, but I never would've guessed it was this. Honey, I'm not sure, but this could blow up in your face. You sure you want to get involved?"

"Wally is probably Noah's biggest fan," she said with a grin. "Even if I wasn't getting him involved now, I would have confessed about this to him in the morning just to cover my own ass. Trust me, he'll bend or break any rule to help Noah, even if that means taking risks for himself. You'll see. Just come on in with me when I talk to him."

Marco made a face and rolled his eyes. "Like you thought I'd let you do this on your own? If it blows up, I want you to know that I'll be right there beside you in the firebox."

Wally was already waiting when they pulled in, sitting on the hood of his classic 1966 Riviera. He slid off the hood as they parked beside him, then led the way to the door and used his keys to open it.

Once they were inside, he turned and nodded toward Marco, then looked at Renée. "Okay, sweetheart," he said with a smile. "I figured it was something pretty important if you wanted me to come out tonight to talk to you in a secure environment. What's going on?"

"Ah, nothing much," Renée said. "I just need you to help me steal some top secret material out of one of your labs."

Wally's smile didn't even flicker. "Far out," he said. "Who we gonna kill?"

Renée burst out laughing. "Actually, the idea is to avoid killing someone." She gave Wally a quick rundown of the situation and Noah's plan, ending with Neil's idea about using the chemical mixture that would make Randy appear to be dead. The note Neil had written got his attention for a moment, then Wally took out a disposable lighter and set it aflame, dropping it into the dirt around a potted plant.

Wally laughed as he did so, rubbing his hands together with childish excitement. "Wow, this is awesome! Yeah, no problem, let's go get it. And, by the way, Jake and Clancy have already perfected the dosage and blended it into a single formula. The stuff hits in about forty-five seconds, and then the only things that continue working are the involuntary muscles, the heart, diaphragm, stuff like that, but they're so slow that it takes some extremely special medical equipment to even detect. Give it to someone while they're hooked up to normal monitors, and they go flatline almost instantly."

Wally was leading the way through the labyrinthine hallways as he spoke, and they arrived at a door a minute later. Wally used a key card to open the door and invited the two of them inside.

Despite the fact he was considered simply an R&D supervisor, almost all of the projects his shops and laboratories worked on stemmed directly from ideas of his own, and the scientists and engineers that worked under him filed daily reports. Wally was almost always up to speed on everything they were doing and spent enough time wandering from one lab or shop to another that he was intimately familiar with all of them. His key card opened a secure cabinet in this one, and he reached in and quickly extracted a single vial.

He handed it to Renée and then opened another cabinet to retrieve a sterile syringe with a hypodermic needle. "You'll need this, too," he said. "That dose should work just fine; it's calculated for a male between 160 and 200 pounds. If I remember Randy correctly, he's about 180. That should keep him in zombie land for about thirty-five hours, maybe a little less."

Marco nodded. "Sounds about right. Gotta tell you, Wally, this is pretty cool of you."

Wally chuckled and waved in dismissal. "Oh, don't be silly," he said. "I know what's going on with the whole mole situation, so anything I can do to help Camelot find that bastard, I'm willing to do. And don't worry about repercussions later, Renée. I can handle it. There won't be any problems. Now, you kids better run along and get that back to Noah. And tell him if there's anything else he needs, just to send you after it. You'll get it."

He locked the lab as they left and walked with them to the exit door. As they stepped outside, he waved and then got back into his car and drove away.

"You were right," Marco said to Renée as they got into the car. "That was easy."

"I was pretty sure it would be. Wally likes to hang out in my office sometimes, and Noah is one of the things he's always talking about. Like I said, Wally is his biggest fan."

"Sounds like it. I thought for a moment he was gonna insist on coming along to the party. Not sure how well that would have gone over, you know?"

Renée chuckled. "Yeah, not so well. Wally's a genius at the logistics end, but I've heard some of the crazy ideas he has come up with as plans for carrying out various missions. Sometimes they get a little wacky, and I'm being generous."

They got back to Noah's house and recounted their adventure to him, passing off the vial and hypodermic. Noah put them into a cabinet in the kitchen and thanked them both.

"Okay, mission successful," Neil said. "That means it's time for dinner, right?"

"You'd be ready for dinner five minutes after you finished breakfast," Sarah said to him with a laugh.

"Nope, not true," Neil replied. "Gotta have lunch in there somewhere. Can't pass up lunch."

Neil, Marco, and Renée sat down at the table while Noah helped Sarah carry over the food and refresh their bottles. A moment later they sat down to eat, and they all agreed that Sarah's pot roast was some of the best they'd ever eaten.

"Renée," Noah said at one point, "there was one thing I forgot to ask you about earlier. Assuming this works, we're going to need to make Randy disappear afterward. If he survives, he'll end up with a new identity, but we don't want to take a chance on him being buried at the local cemetery. What's the procedure for R&D to requisition a cadaver?"

"Oh, that's easy," Renée said. "I'll just tell Wally in the morning that we need a couple of bodies for one of the labs, which is actually true, by the way. Then I'll make sure he arranges to grab Randy's body in the deal. Once they come to us, there's no further record of them. When our lab is done with the body, we have our own crematorium, and the ashes just get dumped somewhere. Don't worry, I'll take care of all that for you in the morning, as soon as the word goes out that he's dead."

When dinner was over, Renée helped Sarah clear the table while Noah got out their Monopoly game. The five of them played until well past midnight, and it was clear that Neil was winning by the time they finally gave it up. They all said good night to each other, and then Marco and Renée drove away.

Neil turned to Noah as Marco's taillights disappeared. "Figured out how you're going to handle it yet?"

Noah sensed Sarah's eyes turning to look at him as well, and he nodded. "If it were a real kill, it would happen at a time when I could get the victim alone. Randy lives by himself in an apartment somewhere in Kirtland. Think you can find me the address?"

Neil just looked at him for a few seconds, then nodded. He turned and walked back into the house and set his computer back onto the table. A few seconds later, he pointed at the screen. "Renaissance Apartments, corner of Eighteenth and Manchester. He's in apartment 4C, northeast corner. That's the far back corner of the building, nothing under it but an alley. Only security cameras in the building are down in the front lobby, where the mailboxes are, and on the parking lot which sits just to the west of it."

Noah nodded. "Good. That makes it easier." He turned to the cabinet and retrieved the vial and needle. "I wish I knew whether or not he's home alone right now. I don't suppose there's any way you can check that, is there?"

Neil grinned. "As a matter of fact," he said, "Molly and I were given access to the server that holds all of his activity recordings. Remember the little transmitter that was implanted under his skin? Every so often it uploads everything it records to a server so it can keep recording even more. Uses a speech-to-text algorithm to give us transcripts we can search through. Give me a few minutes to look through his last few hours and I can tell you."

His fingers flew across the keyboard for a few seconds, and then words began to fill the monitor in front of him. He typed in a time code and then studied the transcripts in front of him for about three minutes.

"He's at home alone," Neil said finally. "Last recording was about half past ten, when somebody left his place after visiting for a while. He said he was tired and was headed for bed then, so he's probably safe in dreamland at the moment." He looked up at Noah. "I just had a thought," he said. "You know Randy has this recorder embedded in him. It's supposed to let us track everything he does and says. What happens if somebody who reads the transcripts is already corrupted? You can't explain to him what's going on."

Noah nodded. "If anybody who can see those transcripts was under the mole's thumb, none of this would be happening. He would have known the file was fake and that we were setting a trap, so he never would have bothered trying to contact me at all."

"Still," Neil said, "I think it would be a good idea if anything you said never ended up in the transcript. It's set to do its next upload at 6:00 a.m. All you have to do to prevent it is take his phone—that's how it connects to the server."

Noah ran a hand over his face. "I wish there was a way to let him sleep through the next day and a half. I can't imagine this not being traumatic for him, but hopefully he'll come through it okay."

Neil scoffed and rolled his eyes. "Since when did you suddenly become compassionate? Personally, I don't care if he's traumatized for life, not after what he did to Sarah."

"It's not compassion," Noah said, looking at Neil quizzically. "Allison feels like Randy still has value to the organization. Because of that, I hope this doesn't ruin him."

Sarah, who had been sitting at the table staying quiet, suddenly reached over and touched Noah on the cheek. "It's okay," she said. "I won't say I've completely gotten over it, but it helps to know that he was forced to do what he did." She winked mischievously. "But don't think I'm not going to be glad he suffered a little bit, all right?"

"I understand," Noah said. "All right, there's no sense wasting time. I'm heading over to Randy's, now."

"Hey, hold on," Neil said. "When we're out on a mission, you've always got the team to back you up, but this time you're going to be on your own. What happens if one of the local city cops pulls you over, and then Randy gets found, you know, sort of dead in the morning? I know Allison could make the problem go away, but the mole might find that a little suspicious, don't you think?"

"I thought about that, and I'll be careful. I won't give them any reason to pull me over."

"Okay, yeah, that's all well and good," Neil said. "Even better, though, is they never see you at all, right?" He reached into a pocket and pulled out two small plastic boxes. Each of them contained what looked like a Bluetooth headset for a cell phone, but Noah recognized them instantly as some of the special communicators they had used on different missions. As small as they were, they operated through cell towers and could communicate over just about any distance, while a full charge in their batteries would last nearly seventy-two hours. "Don't give me that look," Neil said. "Wally knows I don't always turn in all the goodies he gives us, and he let me hang on to a couple of these. I've kept 'em charged up and ready, just in case we need 'em, and I had a feeling tonight was going to be the night."

Sarah reached over and picked up one of the headsets. "So, what? You're gonna keep track of the cops and let Noah know how to avoid them?"

Neil grinned, and there was something wicked about it. "Hey, I want to have more fun than that. I'll just make sure they're busy somewhere else, whenever he's moving. Something simple while he's going into town, but as soon as he says he's ready to head back out, I'll set off alarms in a couple of the banks on the far end of town from the apartment building. Every cop and deputy around will be focused on those, and I can hack the few traffic cams in town to make sure they don't get a look at him, either."

Noah nodded and took the headset from Sarah, slipping it onto his ear. "Let's do this," he said.

CHAPTER NINE

Noah's Corvette, while not flashy, was probably the only one of its kind in the Kirtland area, so he decided to drive his old Ford pickup into town. At least half of the farmers in the area had one similar to it, so any witnesses would only see it as "one of those old farm trucks." He left it in a dark corner of the parking lot at the grocery store three blocks from Renaissance Apartments and made his way into the alley behind it.

"Okay, I'm at point one," he said.

"You're good," Neil's voice said in his ear. "Local yokels are checking out a power outage over by Alley Town; they'll be busy for ten minutes or so."

"All right," Noah said. "I'm moving to point two."

Noah moved down the alley to where it met the cross street and paused. At a little after 2:00 a.m., there wasn't really any traffic on the streets, but he didn't want to risk being seen if he could avoid it. He stopped at each intersection where the alley met a street and watched for a minute or more before crossing and continuing.

It took him almost ten minutes to cover the distance, and then he was standing in the alley just underneath Randy's fourth-floor apartment window. "I'm at the lower goalpost," he said, letting Neil know that he had reached the building. "Checking out entry routes."

"Ten four," Neil said. "Let's go silent until your exit."

"Acknowledged," Noah said.

The fire escapes were a modern style that couldn't be reached from ground level, but a quick leap up onto a dumpster allowed Noah to throw himself upward high enough to catch a window on the second floor. He scrambled for a moment, then got onto the ledge of the window and managed to crab sideways until he got to the fire escape. From that level, there were stairs that led all the way up the side of the building.

Randy's apartment didn't have a window that opened directly onto the fire escape. There was a door that opened onto it from the main hallway, but it could be opened only from the inside with an alarm bar, which meant that Noah had to climb into the window of a neighboring apartment. He carefully checked the window for signs of an alarm system and didn't find any, so it was the work of only a few seconds to slide a knife blade between the upper and lower panes and flip the security latch. The window, which was fairly new, slid up silently, and Noah peeked inside to find himself entering the bedroom of a small child.

He moved as silently as he could, stepping over the sill and carefully, slowly, letting his right foot make contact with the floor. There was something under his heel, and he adjusted his foot to come down off it as he looked down, then realized that it was a small toy car. He brought the other foot in and positioned it carefully as well, then turned and closed the window behind him. He latched it again, then moved slowly and silently toward the door.

The door was not completely closed, a precaution many parents take so that they can hear a child cry in the night. Noah reached for the knob and began to pull it slowly open, ready to stop instantly if the hinges were to make any noise. His luck held, though, and he was able to step into the hallway and pull the door back to its not quite closed position. He passed what must be the master bedroom, its door also slightly ajar, and then moved into the living room.

The apartment's front door was secured with a dead bolt, but there was a knob on the inside that allowed it to be turned. Noah opened it and pulled the door slowly toward himself, relieved once again when it made no noise, then stepped into the main hallway and shut it behind himself. Randy's apartment door would be the next one on the left down the hallway, and he moved quickly toward it.

A careful examination of the door showed that it was also locked with a dead bolt, but part of Noah's training had involved handling locks. He withdrew a set of picks from his pocket and had the dead bolt and doorknob both unlocked in less than a minute. He turned the knob carefully and stepped quickly inside, shutting the door behind him and securing both dead bolt and doorknob once again.

Like most agents, Randy would likely be a light sleeper. Noah needed to be as silent as possible if he wanted to reach the man without waking him. The apartment was a mirror image of the one he had entered through, a two-bedroom flat with a living room, kitchen, and bathroom. It was no trouble for Noah to figure out which bedroom would most likely be the master, and he was relieved to find the door standing half-open.

Randy, of course, being a childless bachelor, wasn't so concerned about modesty. A quick glance through the door showed Noah that the man was sprawled across the bed on his back, sleeping the way a man does when he feels safe in his own home.

Noah moved as if he were in slow motion, taking one step every two to three seconds as he made his way toward Randy. The slightest sound, he knew, the slightest vibration, could be enough to wake the other agent and result in a fight that could force him to kill. His goal at that moment was to keep Randy alive, and he didn't want to risk failing over a simple misstep.

Finally, after several agonizing seconds, he stood beside the bed where Randy Mitchell lay. He withdrew the hypodermic and filled it from the little glass vial, thumped out the tiny bubble of air, and dropped the bottle back into his pocket. In one smooth motion, he leaned forward, pressing a hand to Randy's mouth as he stabbed the needle into the flesh of his pectoral muscle and drove the plunger home.

Randy's eyes flew open and his hands came up, but the shock of being awakened by an attack had disoriented him. Noah yanked out the needle and dropped it on the floor, then gathered Randy's hands into his own free right and clutched them to his chest as the potent drug took effect. The struggle lasted only a dozen seconds before Randy started to lose muscle control, and after twenty seconds Noah was able to let go. Randy's arms dropped to the bed beside him, barely able to move, and his eyes seemed to glaze over just a few seconds later.

Noah felt for a pulse and found none. He knew, of course, that this was the direct effect of the TTX in the mixture, but something about it still struck him with a sense of awe. There was no sign of breath or heartbeat in Randy Mitchell, and yet he was—hopefully—still alive.

He leaned over Randy and looked into his open eyes. "The mole took the bait and contacted me," he said softly, "and his very first order to me was to kill you. I didn't want to do that, so the drug I've just used on you will make you appear to be dead for the next thirty-six hours or so. During that time, Allison will make sure you're set up with a completely new identity, because the Dragon Lady isn't done with you yet. I know this is going to be frightening, but hold on. You'll get through it."

Noah watched his eyes but saw absolutely no sign that Randy had either heard or understood anything he had said. The possibility that the dosage had been lethal after all crossed his mind, but he had been authorized to kill Randy if there was no other way. He decided he would have to simply wait and see whether it had worked, so he picked up the hypodermic and slipped the safety cover back over the needle before dropping it back into his pocket.

The struggle had been so brief that nothing in the bedroom had actually been disturbed. Noah glanced around for a moment and saw Randy's iPhone on the nightstand at the opposite side of the bed, plugged in and charging. He stepped quickly around and picked it up, yanking the plug out of the wall and shoving both charger and phone into a pocket before leaving the master bedroom and moving into the second.

He opened the window and looked down, but it was a sheer drop of four stories. Situated on the back corner of the building, there was only an alleyway at the ground level, and nothing close that Noah could use in making his way down. He closed that window and turned to the one on the perpendicular wall and looked out.

Another sheer drop, but four feet to the right was a drainpipe from the gutters that ran around the top of the building. The pipe was made of cast aluminum and was about eight inches in diameter, a series of connecting sections about four feet long. Each section was flared at the top so that the section above it fit neatly into the flare, and the whole thing was connected to the building with sturdy steel brackets on each section.

Noah climbed out the window and stood on the edge of its ledge, holding on to the upper frame of the window with his fingertips as he closed it. Once that was done, he carefully stood on the ledge and focused on the drainpipe, then swung his body hard into a flying leap. He caught the lip of an upper flange of the pipe with his hands and then managed to get his feet on the one just below.

The pipe was too close to the building to allow him to wrap his arms or hands around it, so his descent consisted of simply sliding down each section until he met the flange of the next. There were three sections to each story of the building, so the trip to the ground took him all of a minute.

"I'm out," he said softly. "On the ground outside the building, preparing to head back."

"Roger that," Neil said. "Operation Diversion in twenty seconds."

Noah looked around carefully and made sure that no one had seen him, then began moving just as stealthily through the alley as he had before, making his way back to his pickup. He hung back and watched the truck for a full minute from the cover of a bush, just to be sure no one was watching it closely, and that's when he heard the sirens.

While he stayed out of sight, Noah saw four squad cars roar past on the way to investigate at least three different bank alarms going off. He waited an extra minute to see if any others might be passing by, then walked calmly over and climbed in behind the wheel.

"I'm rolling," he said.

"You're good to go," Neil replied. "Every cop in the county is headed for the banking district. There's nobody between you and home base, so we'll see you in just a bit."

"Roger, out," Noah said as he put the truck in gear and drove sedately out of the parking lot.

The ride across town and out the country roads to his place took nearly forty-five minutes, and both Neil and Sarah were waiting at the barn as he pulled the truck inside. He and Neil swung the doors closed, and the three of them walked back into the house.

"He definitely looks dead," Noah said. "I couldn't detect any sign of life at all."

"That's the idea," Neil said. "If the stuff works as advertised, he's probably having about one barely detectable heartbeat every twenty seconds or so, and respirations would be so minute that normal medical equipment wouldn't even pick them up. I guess the chemicals suppress the metabolism just enough that the oxygen he does get is enough to prevent any significant physical damage."

Sarah was standing beside Noah in their kitchen, her arms wrapped around his waist and her cheek against his chest. "I gotta say," she said softly, "I know we don't want him to really be dead, but there's a part of me that's feeling some relief right now. Whether he lives through this or not, either way seems like a fitting punishment for what he's done."

"Yeah," Neil said, nodding. "I would imagine that he's going to spend the next day and a half just wondering if he's even alive. According to all the literature, brain activity is pretty suppressed by TTX. There won't be any detectable signs of brain activity, but he's supposedly going to be at least marginally aware of everything that happens to him. I think that's gotta make the victim wonder if it's possible to be aware of your surroundings after you die, right?"

"That's what I mean," Sarah said. "Either way, fitting punishment."

"Well, all we can do now is wait," Noah said. He withdrew Randy's iPhone from his pocket and handed it to Neil. "You want to make sure nobody can find this?"

Neil grinned and used a tool from his pocket to remove the back and take out the battery, then popped out a second part. "Most people don't realize that this little gizmo has a capacitor in it that can keep the GPS working for up to four hours after the battery is removed. Right now, nobody in the world could find this phone. We can pass it off to Mr. Jefferson when the time comes. I'll keep it hidden until then." He rubbed his eyes and reached out to pat Noah on the shoulder. "I'm going home to get some sleep, boss," he said. "I've got a hunch things are going to get busy in the morning."

Neil turned and walked out the front door, and Noah took Sarah's hand and led her toward the bedroom. They stripped and got into the bed and curled up together, and then Sarah suddenly began crying.

Though he had no idea how she was feeling, Noah understood that some part of her was experiencing a mixture of relief and guilt at the thought of Randy's suffering. He tightened his arms around her and let her weep.

NOAH WOKE AT JUST BEFORE 8:00 a.m. and was already showered and dressed by the time his phone rang. The caller ID told him that it was Allison, of course.

"Camelot."

"Something I thought you should know, Camelot," Allison said. "I just got the word that Randy Mitchell was discovered dead in his apartment this morning. It seems nobody had been able to get him on the phone, so Jenny went by to check on him. Oh, and I got a cryptic email from Wally this morning saying that somebody seems to have made off with something special from his department last night."

Noah nodded, even though she couldn't see him. The way she was praising things told him that she was fully aware of what Noah had done, and that Randy was probably not dead after all.

"I'm sorry to hear that," Noah said. "Any idea what happened to him?"

"No, but it doesn't really matter. I just thought you'd like to know since your team worked with his, recently."

"Well, he was a good agent. What happens to him now?"

"Well, we don't go into autopsies and such on our own people, simply because they are all expendable in any case. Funny thing, though, Wally's email also mentioned that they are in need of a few cadavers for research purposes. Seems to me that Randy would volunteer, if he was able, don't you think?"

"I think that would be an admirable idea," Noah said. "It's still a pity, though. Randy seemed like a pretty decent sort."

"He had his good days," Allison said. "Hopefully, this trip out to R&D will allow him to have a few more before he's done."

The phone went dead, and Noah slipped it back into his pocket. He had been standing in the bedroom when it had rung, and he glanced over his shoulder to see Sarah sitting up in the bed.

"Jenny found Randy's body already this morning," he said, "and Wally sent Allison an email that clued her in on what's going on. He also added a request for cadavers for testing uses, so that's where Randy is going. I'm sure Wally is going to have his people take care of him until this wears off, and Allison will probably have his new identity all set up by then."

Sarah looked at him sleepily but nodded. "So now we just wait for the mole to contact you again?"

"That's the plan. Somehow, I don't think it will be long."

Sarah nodded and fell backward onto the bed again. Noah left her to get a little more sleep and went to the kitchen to make coffee.

Neil tapped lightly on his back door about ten minutes later. "Saw your kitchen light come on," he said. "Any word yet?"

"Yeah," Noah said. "Allison called. Jenny found Randy's body this morning, and Wally found a way to let Allison know what's happening. As soon as they get done with the body at the morgue, it'll be going out to R&D as planned."

"Awesome. How bad is the coffee?"

Noah poured them each a cup and sat down at the table with Neil. Neil took a sip and made a face that said it wasn't too terrible.

"So, now we wait again? See what the mole thinks about all this?"

"Yes. Hopefully, Randy's death will look realistic enough. The only thing I'm concerned about is that he might wonder why the body disappeared so quickly. According to Renée, though, it's not uncommon for the bodies of our personnel to end up out there, so it might not be all that surprising to him."

They sat and talked for a few minutes, and then Neil followed Noah into the living room. Noah logged on to his computer, but there was no message waiting from the auto website. He logged off again, and the two of them were simply sitting there when Sarah came out of the bedroom, still dressed in one of Noah's T-shirts.

"I just called Doc Parker," she said, "and said I had a rough night and didn't feel like coming in today. He said that was okay, so you might want to let Jackson know you won't be coming. It feels like a good day to just stay home."

Noah nodded and took out his phone, but before he could dial Jackson's number, it rang. The caller ID told him that it was Allison calling once more.

"Camelot," he said.

"Briefing at eleven. We have a mission, and I think this one calls for your particular abilities." The line went dead.

Neil's phone went off a few seconds later, and he got the same message. Sarah hurried back to the bedroom to grab her own and found a missed call from Allison, so she called back quickly and was told the same thing.

"So much for taking it easy," she grumbled. "What time is it, anyway?"

"It's almost nine," Noah said. "We've got a little time."

Sarah nodded and wandered into the kitchen, coming back a moment later with a cup of coffee of her own. She sat down beside Noah on the couch and leaned against him.

"Hold me," she said, and Noah put an arm around her. She snuggled in against him and closed her eyes for a few moments, then opened them again and took a sip of her coffee. "I thought they were going to leave us inactive for a little while."

"Parker must have given you a clean bill of health," Noah said. "I don't know what the mission is, but Allison said it needed me. We'll play it by ear, like always."

Sarah picked up the remote and turned on the television, flipping channels until she found a talk show she liked. The three of them sat there and watched it, and when it ended at ten she got up and went to get dressed.

Neil waited until she was out of earshot and looked at Noah. "Boss? You really think she's ready for the field again?"

"That isn't my call," Noah said. "I have to assume that Parker feels like she is, and I trust Allison to help me keep her out of harm's way. We'll just have to handle it however is necessary."

Neil shook his head. "Well, I'll do my best to keep my eye on her whenever you're not around."

Noah looked at him, and the faintest ghost of a smile crossed his face for a split second. "Thank you," he said. "I genuinely appreciate that."

CHAPTER TEN

The three of them rode together in Neil's Hummer to the briefing and found Marco pulling into the garage just ahead of them. When they had entered the elevator together, Marco looked over at Noah.

"Guess you heard the news about old Randy, right? Bit the dust last night, I hear."

"Yes," Noah said. "I understand it was a shock to everyone who knew him."

Neil and Marco both had to stifle their laughter, but a quick glare from Sarah was enough to do the trick. By the time the elevator opened, both of them wore the sober faces of men who had just learned of the passing of a friend.

The doughnuts were in place like always, and each of them grabbed one as they entered the conference room. Allison and Donald Jefferson were already waiting, with Molly sitting in a chair off to the side.

"It's good to see you all," Allison said. "Sarah, how are you feeling?"

"I think I'm doing okay," Sarah said. "The nightmares haven't bothered me since the first few days, and I can tell you that Noah has made sure to give me plenty of good memories to focus on." She smiled at her husband.

Allison nodded at Noah. "I'm sure he has," she said. "Unfortunately, we had a request come in for an elimination that requires Noah's ability to blend into any situation. This one is domestic, down in Arkansas. There is an organized crime ring that is impossible to break up, and the DOJ, in cooperation with DHS, has decided that its leadership needs to be removed."

"The Department of Justice?" Neil asked, his voice high-pitched. "They actually ask for assassinations?"

"On rare occasions, yes," Allison said. "Since we began operations, however, this is only the third such request we have forgotten. Does that surprise you, Mr. Blessing?"

"Well, yeah," Neil said. "Scares the hell out of me, too. It was the DOJ who came after me when I hacked into the bank; I never would've believed they might just have me killed."

"They wouldn't," said Donald Jefferson, a slight grin on his face. "American domestic anticrime organizations like the DOJ, FBI, and such will only resort to elimination when they become absolutely convinced that there is no possible way to successfully prosecute a dangerous offender. In this case, the targets run a regional organized crime ring that is so tightly controlled and loyal that they have been unable to develop any clear evidence that would stand up in court. In many such situations, they can be completely aware of who the offender is, even the types of crimes he may have ordered or even participated in, but knowing this and being able to prove it are two entirely different things. Courtroom procedures require a level of confidence in the evidence that goes far beyond what may seem obvious to an investigator. Defense attorneys, especially those who can command multimillion-dollar fees, are very good at convincing juries that the evidence isn't what it appears to be, and witnesses can be frightened or eliminated. As a result, many organized crime figures have been arrested many times, but never convicted."

"That's not the exact problem in this case, however," Allison went on. "Jimmy Morgan, the top man in this organization, is an extremely intelligent man who chose to turn his intellect toward building and expanding multiple criminal enterprises. His control extends to almost every form of organized crime, including drugs, prostitution, theft, fraud, extortion, murder—you name it, and he's into it. In the past twenty-four years, sixteen different federal prosecutors have been, shall we say, dissuaded from pursuing charges against him. This is a man who has never even been arrested, and those who work for him never do more than a few days in the county jail and a little probation. The corruption in his domain reaches into every law enforcement agency and prosecutor's office in nine counties in Northwest Arkansas."

Noah cocked his head to one side. "If he's that powerful, then he's got people working for him who consider themselves almost as powerful. Won't eliminating him simply invite one of them to step into his shoes?"

Jefferson picked up a remote and a picture appeared on the screen behind him. "This is Jimmy Morgan," he said. "He's forty-two years old and the de facto king of a large part of Northwest Arkansas. His organization refers to itself as the Morgan Mafia, and an interesting tidbit of trivia is that four different forays by big-city mob figures to try to take over have only resulted in a couple of dozen dead mobsters. Even the Sicilian mob is staying out of the area. We were contacted for a sanction because there have been reports over the past few months that Morgan is working with potential terror groups, using his operations to bring terrorists and materials into the country. He's apparently unconcerned with what they might do, as long as they agree to stay out of his domain."

"And he's dumb enough to believe them?" Marco blurted out.

"Apparently, he believes he can control them, and possibly with good reason. Several known terror operatives have turned up dead in different places around his domain. They seem to have a tendency lately to get out of that part of Arkansas as quickly as they can." He clicked the remote and a picture of a younger man appeared. "This is Ralph Morgan, Jimmy's only child. As the heir apparent, it's expected that he'll be groomed to take over, and it appears he'll be starting soon with one of the divisions already running. He's known to be just as ruthless as his father, and it's no secret that the entire community of Berryville, Arkansas, where they live, is pretty much terrified of the boy. He and a few of his cronies have either beaten or intimidated other local teenagers numerous times, and Ralph is believed to be responsible for at least two suspicious deaths. With the upbringing he's had, he'd probably be even more likely to work with terror cells than his father, which makes him an even greater risk to national security."

"Damn, and he ain't nothing but a kid," Marco said. "Sounds like he might be all set to take over if his daddy disappears."

"That's exactly how the FBI and DEA see it," Allison said. "And there are probably a dozen of his father's lieutenants who can step in if both of them are gone, and that's why we feel we need Team Camelot on this one. It's not a single elimination but may involve up to a couple dozen people. We've asked Molly to work with us on developing a basic mission plan, and she's the one who decided that you're the only team to handle this one. Molly?"

Molly leaned forward in her chair and looked at Noah for a second, then glanced at Sarah. "I'm really sorry to have to send you back into the field so soon," she said, turning back to Noah, "but I've been studying everything about the Morgan Mafia for the last couple of weeks and they're just too tight and secured for anything but a single operative in a blitz hit. That single operative, Noah, has to have your unique ability to focus. Anything else would lead to mistakes that would expose the mission and doom it, and the team sent out on it, to failure."

She glanced at Allison, who nodded, then went on. "This is not going to be a quick or easy mission. Noah, you're going to have to go into deep cover and infiltrate the organization. Successfully eliminating this threat to American security is going to mean getting yourself into the top ranks and being able to identify all of those capable of keeping it going once the heads are cut off. I'm estimating that, with your particular skill set and abilities, this will take anywhere from two to five months. At that point, you will have to develop a plan for eliminating them all within a very short time frame, probably within the span of just a few hours. Since it is highly unlikely that an opportunity to do so will present itself naturally, you will almost certainly have to orchestrate it."

"Whoa, whoa, wait a minute," Sarah said. "Noah is going to have to go into this outfit and stay there for several months? How are we supposed to operate like that?"

"I've laid out a basic plan, but Noah will want to refine it," Molly replied. "He will have to appear first, alone. That will allow him to make the first steps in infiltrating the organization. Once he has begun to do so, since he's coming in as an outsider, it won't be that surprising that his wife—you, Sarah, of course—comes to join him. When you do, your brother will come along with you. That will be Neil, of course, playing the nerdy computer geek. Marco will arrive separately, and it will be up to Noah to arrange a situation that will let the four of you live close and spend time together. Neil will be responsible for intelligence and security, and I'm confident he can handle both. Marco is perfectly suited to pose as someone Noah could recruit into the organization or introduce to it, hopefully giving him an ally within its ranks."

"What about identities, characterizations? If I'm supposed to infiltrate a criminal organization, I'm going to need a background that fits. It's going to have to stand up to scrutiny, especially if they have corrupt cops who can check out our backstories."

Molly nodded. "Of course, and we've already begun working on that. Noah, you're going to be posing as a man named Rex Madison, who was recently released from federal prison where he served time on drug-related charges. The real Rex Madison died about five years ago in an accident, but we've reconstructed his history because he had a sister named Kate who happens to work for the FBI. She's been in deep cover in Arkansas on this case for almost three years, but she's not part of the criminal operation. She's there only as an observer, though she has become pretty well-known in the area. Using her brother's identity gives you an excuse for suddenly appearing in the community. When I asked her about it, she agreed almost instantly."

"But you said her brother actually died. Wouldn't there be public records of that, people back where he grew up who would know it, that sort of thing?"

"Kate and Rex grew up in a small city in Ohio, Zanesville. Absent father, workaholic and alcoholic mother, not a real good situation. Kate was apparently determined to make something of herself and ended up in the FBI. Rex, on the other hand, had a lot of problems through his teens and even did some time in juvenile detention centers. When he turned eighteen, he left town and never went back. Both of their parents are dead, Kate hasn't been there in years herself, so when he was killed in a motorcycle accident she didn't even bother to put a notice in the local newspaper there. Since she hadn't talked to him in a long time, it wasn't hard for us to wipe out the real history of his last few years and create the prison record."

"What prison was I supposed to have been released from?" Noah asked. "I'll need to do some pretty serious research on it."

"Noah," Allison said, "do you remember Gary Mitchell? He was the acting coach who helped you get prepared for the Adrian operation?"

"Of course," Noah replied. "He works in ID development."

Allison nodded. "Yes, that's him. Well, according to your history, Rex Madison was released just a little over a month ago from the federal prison in Beaumont, Texas. As Molly said, we've altered all of his records throughout every database in order to establish that prison record. Gary helped develop the background you'll be using and is preparing a crash course for you on how to become Rex Madison."

"Does Noah look like this guy?" Sarah asked. "What if somebody actually knew him?"

"Rex and Noah would have been about the same size and age, and their photos do resemble one another. We've replaced every known photograph of the real Rex with one of Noah, and we've established that there is almost no possibility that anyone in the Morgan Mafia could ever have known him. Should such a situation arise, Noah will simply have to bluff his way through or eliminate the problem."

"Okay," Sarah said, though it was obvious she wasn't happy about it. "What about me? Did Rex actually have a wife?"

Donald Jefferson waved a finger in the air to get her attention. "No, but he does now," he said. "Marriage records were dated a week after his release from prison, showing that he married his high school sweetheart, Angela Holcomb. You'll also be given some extensive coaching. Since you may actually be in deep cover for some time, it's very important that you internalize the backstory that we've created for you. When you show up in town, it's very likely that they'll run at least a cursory background check on you, as well." He grinned at her. "It also makes it allowable for Noah to call you once in a while until you get there. I had a feeling you might like that."

Sarah smiled at him. "Thank you," she said.

"Same goes for Marco and Neil," Allison said. "All three of you will be coached just as heavily as Noah on your identities. Neil, you get to keep your first name. You'll be Neil Holcomb, and your background suggests that you're so immersed in video games that most of the world never even notices you. You dropped out of school at sixteen and earn your living as a game master on one of the big role-playing games on the internet. In public, Noah will treat you like a pain in his ass."

She turned to Marco. "Marco, we're going to use your Louisiana bayou upbringing. Your name is Aubrey LeBlanc, so let that old Cajun accent out. Aubrey, according to records, was also just released from the same prison where Rex served his time. In fact, the real Aubrey LeBlanc was released two weeks ago and promptly got himself killed his third night of freedom. We constantly scan for stories like that, and since he had no family and very few friends, we immediately killed all the news on it and commandeered his identity for this mission."

"Oh, *cher*," Marco said, "I be de best old gator from de bayou, you don' need no worry 'bout dat! But what about dem boys back in de prison, dey gon' know I ain't him."

Allison grinned. "Yeah, that's what I'm talking about. Don't worry about other inmates at Beaumont. Aubrey did most of his time in solitary, and that's where he and Rex met. Gary will help you guys develop your characters, as well. Marco, you will be going in about a week or so after Sarah and Neil arrive."

"As for equipment," Jefferson said, "you can visit with Wally this week and get whatever you need. Anything that might seem unusual should probably come in with Neil. Just let Wally know, and he can have it disguised as some of Neil's computer gear or something."

"Noah," Allison said, "this is a very important mission, so you'll be going in about a week from today. The next several days are going to be very intense, so think very hard about what you might need when you talk to Wally." She turned to Molly. "Do you have anything else to add on this?"

Molly shrugged. "Yeah, one thing," she said. "One thing we know about the Morgan Mafia is that they do have some way to monitor phone calls. In order for us to have a secure line of communication, we're going to be using Neil and his computer. Neil, have you ever played online RPGs?"

Neil blinked, then nodded. "Sure," he said. "Every computer nerd plays sometime. Hell, I still do."

"Good," Molly said, "because we've got one set up of our own. It's called *Target List*, and it's based, naturally, on using assassination as a political tool. I'll coach you in it because you can communicate with other players in the game, just like in most of the other ones. I'll give you code names for the people Noah will be dealing with, and we can discuss them as if they were targets in the game. It's highly un-likely anyone would think to check your game communications, but it's even more unlikely they'd be able to interpret them into what we are really saying to each other. You'll be listed as a game master, so that will be your employment. And just for the record, making this look real means that there are some ads out on Google about it, so there are civilians who will be playing, lots of them. Like all of these games, players can set up their own teams and allow others to join them. I'll be running one of those, with you as my game master. My team is called the Rampagers, and it's actually a room full of players based right here at Neverland. That way, there will always be some-body online that you can talk to, somebody who can relay informa-tion to me or up here to the main office."

Neil was grinning. "That is an incredibly awesome idea," he said. "It's so freaking awesome I should have thought of it first."

Molly stuck out her tongue at him. "Hey, you're smart, but you ain't got nothing on me. You and I will start working on getting you familiarized with it first thing tomorrow morning."

Allison leaned forward slightly and looked at Noah. "Okay, then," she said. "Noah, tell us about what's going on with the other mission."

Noah leaned forward in his seat. "Last night," he said, "I recruit-ed Marco's girlfriend, Renée, to help with that situation. She works out at R&D and was able to get Wally to help her get a drug that I needed. I went to Randy's apartment and managed to get inside while he was sleeping, then injected him with that drug. It causes a complete paralysis that is almost cataleptic; it makes the victim appear to be completely dead, with no signs of life, even though he's still alive and relatively conscious. After I injected him, I explained what was happening so that he might not be quite as terrified as I'm sure he probably is anyway, but I honestly couldn't tell you whether he was still alive when I left him. Now I'm simply waiting to see if the mole accepts his death."

"Jenny found him this morning," Allison said, "and she was convinced he was dead. She called it in, and we sent an ambulance to pick him up. At the morgue, he was certified dead, but since I had already been tipped by Wally, I just authorized his body to be sent out to R&D to be used for research purposes. Wally called me an hour later to confirm that the drug worked. Randy's alive, but it took some specialized equipment to be certain."

"Good. Any idea what you'll do with him after this?"

"He'll probably end up getting a new face and name and going right back to Team Cinderella," Allison said. "Parker is convinced that he is loyal to Jenny and won't ever allow himself to be blackmailed again. He's done so much in helping Jenny as part of her team that I'm reluctant to take him away for good."

"Is she aware that he isn't really dead?" Noah asked.

"Not yet, but she'll be coming in for a briefing later today. I'll be explaining it to her then."

"We will not allow her to share this with the rest of her team, however," Jefferson said. "The sad fact remains that we do not know who else might be compromised within our organization. At this point, we have confidence that the few people who are aware of the situation are still free of any risk, but that small group cannot get any larger."

"I have a question," Noah said. "What do I do if the mole contacts me while I'm on mission?"

"I'd say you do whatever you can to cooperate," Allison said. "The idea is to draw him into a position that will allow us to identify him.

You can't do that if you don't keep his confidence. That being said, it may well be impossible to keep him happy without blowing your cover. Somehow I doubt he expects you to bend over for him, but try not to burn the bridge. As fragile as it is, it's all we've got."

"Understood," Noah said. "On the other hand, if anybody taps my computer, they could conceivably see the messages I get from the car forums. Should I keep logging into them?"

"I thought of that," Molly said quickly. "I've added a subroutine to all of those websites that will relay those messages to Neil through the game system. He can let you see them when you get a chance, or you can work out a code so he can relay them to you by text message."

"That'll be easy," Neil said. "I've already got one in mind."

"Also," Allison went on, speaking to Noah, "you'll be keeping your own cell phone number for this mission. That way, if the mole were to decide to call you, he'll get through." Allison glanced around at their faces, then nodded once. "I think that covers most everything," she said. "Kate Madison has been thoroughly briefed on what's going on. She will appear to be somewhat hostile to you at first, but that's because she never talked about her brother. The hostility is to avoid it seeming odd that a brother turns up all of a sudden, but she'll be referring to you as the black sheep of her family. Her position will be that she only offered you the chance to come to town because she once promised her mother she'd try to watch out for you. You won't be socializing with her a lot at first, but she's been instructed to become friendlier once Sarah arrives."

Noah got to his feet, and the rest followed suit. "All right," he said. "I think we should start with the acting coach. How soon can I go to see him?"

Allison grinned. "He's expecting you in an hour."

CHAPTER ELEVEN

The tight time schedule meant that Noah had to jump out of the Hummer when they got back to the house, give Sarah a quick kiss, and drive off in the Corvette. He remembered the way to the ID Development building and was glad there was a shortcut he could take. It was a winding country road, but it was well paved and the Corvette was built to handle the curves. He made it just in time, although the guard at the security gate in front of the building actually jumped when Noah skidded to a stop in front of him.

"Noah!" The man behind the desk seemed genuinely delighted to see Noah walk into his office. "I was honestly excited when they told me I was going to be working with you again. How have you been?"

"I'm fine," Noah said as they shook hands. "I got married since I saw you last."

Gary Mitchell chuckled. "Yes, I heard. Seems you're the first team ever to involve a married couple, and the rumor mill went crazy throughout the entire organization. I understand a couple of other teams are exploring some possibilities along that line."

"Well, I wish them the best. Where do we start?"

Gary paused for a second, then remembered that Noah didn't think like most people and wasn't as much into small talk. "I've been studying the history they've manufactured for you, and it's quite extensive. Most of what we're going to do is simply rehearse you in details of the background for your character. You'll need to know all the answers and be able to come up with them quickly if questioned. There is enough information in public records to allow someone to check you out, and you need to know every detail."

"Right, I understood that. How do we proceed on this?"

Gary grinned. "Have you ever been hypnotized?" he asked.

"Actually, yes," Noah said. "It was during my psych evaluation when I was being court-martialed, before I was recruited. The psychiatrist said I was a perfect subject, because of my level of concentration."

"That's excellent. One of the techniques I've been using lately to help prepare our agents for deep cover missions like this is to put them under and then simply play a recording of the information they need to learn. Two or three sessions are usually enough to embed the information deeply, and while it won't change who you are at all, it will enable you to recall that information instantly when you need to be in character. Would you mind?"

Noah shrugged. "Not at all," he said. "I'm open to anything that helps me accomplish the mission."

Gary rose from his chair and had Noah follow him into another room, this one much smaller. There was a recliner in the room, and he told Noah to take a seat, then stepped back out himself. A moment later, Noah heard Gary's voice come over a speaker on each side of his head in the recliner.

"Now, the most efficient method of trance induction we found is to simply have you relax in the chair while I play a recording. This is an advanced hypnosis technique that uses rapid redirection of your concentration, so you'll find yourself becoming slightly disoriented. At that point, we can induce the trance and begin the session."

Noah didn't reply, and a moment later he heard Gary's voice begin to speak softly. Initially, it was simply instructions to relax, but then there were several phrases that seemed almost nonsensical. Relaxing in the chair with his eyes closed, Noah began to feel that he was being gently buffeted from side to side, and then he heard Gary tell him to sleep.

At that point, a new recording began to play. This one was more like a second-person narrative, however, as if the speaker were trying to remind Noah of facts from his past.

"You are Rex Madison. You were born twenty-six years ago in the town of Zanesville, Ohio. Your father was Charles Madison, who worked as a bricklayer for several different construction companies as you were growing up. Your mother was Carolyn Madison, a nurse. You have one sister, Katherine, who is two years older and whom you have always called Katie. You attended Grant Elementary school in Zanesville, followed by Webster Middle School and Zanesville High School. Your father was a construction worker who was often gone, and you and your sister were forced to fend for yourselves since your mother worked many long hours and was often drunk when she was at home. This led you to a troubled youth, and your first arrest came when you were thirteen years old. The charge was theft of a motor-cycle, but it was dismissed and you were released to the custody of your mother. You were arrested again two months later for posses-sion of marijuana with intent to distribute, your first foray into deal-ing drugs. You spent three months in a juvenile detention facility for that crime and were then released. You were arrested again only one month later for the same charge, and this time you spent a year in the same facility. Upon your release, you were offered the opportunity to join a local gang and began your true criminal career. You dropped out of high school at sixteen and continued with the gang, dealing drugs and gradually moving into other areas of crime. You were ar-rested several more times over the next few years, but the charges did not stick until five years ago, when a DEA agent that had infiltrat-ed the gang was found dead of a single gunshot wound to his head. You, along with several other members of the gang, were arrested and prosecuted for conspiracy to operate a continuing criminal en-terprise. Several of you accepted a plea bargain in return for a shorter sentence. You served five years in the federal prison at Beaumont, Texas."

The voice droned on for more than an hour, with no visible sign from Noah that he was hearing anything. When it ended, however, and Gary gave him the command to waken, Noah was able to respond instantly to a series of questions that had been prepared.

"Where did you attend elementary school?" Gary asked him.

"It was Grant Elementary, back in Zanesville," Noah said.

"When did you have your first run-in with the law?"

"Um, back when I was thirteen. I ripped off some guy's motorbike and took it for a joyride. Charges got tossed out, though."

Gary fired questions at him for a half an hour, then shook his head and grinned. "You are probably the most natural actor I have ever met," he said. "I fed you a bunch of dry facts, and you have already developed a personality to fit them."

Noah nodded. "I've always been able to do that," he said. "When I was a kid, I had a friend who figured out what was wrong with me and told me that I would have to be able to pretend to be normal unless I wanted to get locked up somewhere. I learned to watch people and try to act like them. Now, when I think of the character I need to portray in a mission, I usually base it off someone I knew or studied back then. Rex Madison reminds me of a guy I grew up with, so I've automatically adopted his personality for this."

"Well, your perception is amazing. I've actually seen video of Rex Madison, some old police interviews, and you're coming across so much like him right now that it's blowing my mind." He stood up and stretched. "I think that's enough for our first day. Let's start again tomorrow morning around nine, and we'll go for a longer session. Tomorrow we'll be talking about particular instances in your life, things that are on record in different places. They'll be useful if the people you're dealing with check you out and then want to compare what they learn with the things you say."

"Nine o'clock," Noah said. "I'll be here."

The two men shook hands, and Noah left the building, then headed over toward R&D. He wasn't sure what kind of equipment he might need and wanted to sit down and discuss some possibilities with Wally. R&D was only half a mile from ID Development, so it took him only a couple of minutes to get there.

The security guard on the gate checked Noah's ID and looked closely at his face, then waved him inside. He parked in front of the building and got out of his car, then walked inside and went through a second security check of his ID. Once the guard there was satisfied, he picked up the phone and notified Wally that Camelot had arrived and wished to see him.

Seconds later, running footsteps could be heard coming up the hallway, and Wally burst into the lobby. "Camelot!" he yelled, sliding to a stop just in front of Noah. He grabbed Noah's hand and pumped it up and down, clapped him on the shoulder, and told him to come on down to his office.

It was the first time Noah had ever entered Wally's office, and he was mildly surprised to find it looking more like a workshop. There were several tables inside, each of which was just about covered with scribbled notes or handmade cardboard or plastic models of things the intelligent man had thought up. There was one small desk and only two chairs, both of which looked like rejects from someone else's office.

Noah sat in the one beside the desk while Wally sat down in the other. "Camelot, what can I do for you?"

"Are you aware of the mission I'm going out on?" Noah asked.

Wally nodded excitedly. "Yes, yes, Allison told me about it. This is gonna be exciting. I don't suppose you've got any ideas yet, ideas on how you want to handle things?"

"Not really," Noah said. "I only just learned about the mission this morning, and I've just had my first training session on the character I'll be using. I really wanted to pick your brain a bit. The way I understand it, there may be as many as a few dozen people I'm going to have to eliminate. I'm hoping you might be able to come up with some kind of techno-wizardry to help me accomplish this."

"Wow, so many? And from what I gathered, you're gonna have to bide your time a while and then take them out pretty much all at once, right?"

"That's how it sounds."

Wally leaned back in his chair and looked up at the ceiling, steepling his fingers under his chin. "A big bunch of people, and they all have to die at around the same time, but you may not be able to get them all together in one place. Wow, this is going to be a tricky one. Let me think, let me think."

Noah sat quietly for almost ten minutes while E & E's resident evil genius let his brain consider the problem. Except for the slow and steady rise and fall of his chest, there was no other sign that Wally was even alive, let alone aware that he had a guest in the office.

Suddenly, Wally sat forward again and clapped his hands together. "I've got one," he said. "Remember the 3-D printer I gave you once? The one that can make just about anything out of some super-high-powered explosives?"

"Yes, and I'd thought about that myself. Is it still available?"

"Oh, hell, yes," Wally said. "You're the only team who has actually used it, but you did so with such great success on that mission that I actually had a couple of extras built. We also found ways to make its products even more functional. For example, we added some designs into its database that are extremely useful, like cell phone cases, pens, sunglasses, belt buckles, lots of stuff that you could make and give to people. You give somebody a pen—it looks like something fancy you could buy in a store, but it's really just a case made of our explosive with all the guts from a real pen inside. Or you give them a pair of sunglasses, then when the time comes it explodes and takes their entire head off. And the new detonator uses a microburst of radio waves to set it off—it's basically just a microchip. Tiny." He rubbed his hands together gleefully. "Of course, you can also make bigger things. The latest version fits into a footlocker-sized case, but the top comes off and all four sides fold down, so the actual device expands to the point that you can make something as big as the fender of a small car. I think it's up to four and a half feet by two feet by three feet, something like that."

Noah looked thoughtful for a moment, then nodded. "I definitely want that," he said. "Allison suggested that anything you send me should be disguised as some of Neil's computer equipment. Is that possible?"

Wally burst out laughing. "Neil is a computer geek," he said. "You know who buys fancy 3-D printers? Computer geeks. I doubt anybody would really think much about him having one, even a big expensive one like this. Allison says you're gonna be there for a while, right? All you gotta do is have him make lots of things you can give away to the people you want to eliminate. Oh, and those new microdetonators actually receive cell signals, now, so you can let them wander around for weeks and then set them all off at once by simply sending the proper detonation code. The code is an encrypted string of characters—the odds of them being set off accidentally would be like the odds of a black hole opening on the earth and only capturing one person. About as close to impossible as you can imagine."

"Wait," Noah said. "You mean, I could have Neil make stuff that I could give to these people, things they might keep with them all the time, and then set them off all at once? If it uses cell signals, what's the range limitation? How close do I have to be to set them off?"

"Noah, you could be at the South Pole. The detonation transmitter is built into a special satellite phone. You dial one number, and every detonator that has been activated will receive the signal. If you have programmed them all to a single detonation code, they all go off at once, no matter where they are in the world. As long as there is a cell signal that can reach them, they're gonna go boom!"

Noah stared at the geeky, balding man for a couple of seconds, then nodded. "That might just be the answer," he said. "What other kind of ideas would you have?"

Wally grinned, and Noah had a sudden mental image of a shark. "Well, let's think about it," Wally said. "You're going to be dealing with criminals, and most of them are probably going to be armed. What about guns? We've got one of the 3-D printers set up here, and it can make perfect replicas of any gun. They would actually work, actually fire, and yet the entire frame would be made of explosives. The detonator would be embedded in a thick part, so it would go off when you sent the signal. The one I send with Neil could make them, too."

Noah nodded but almost seemed to frown. "That could be good, but I was actually thinking of something not related to the printer," he said. "Would you have any other ideas how I might approach the problem?"

"Oh, oh, I see," Wally said. "Well, the first thing that comes to mind is religion."

"Religion? I'm not sure I understand."

"Well, not religion *per se*," Wally said. "I'm thinking of something along the lines of a particular philosophy that you might introduce to this group of criminals. If we could come up with something that they would embrace, you could probably arrange to have the ones you want to target attend something like a meeting, maybe a training seminar. Get them into the habit, and then you would be able to gather them all together in one location."

Noah narrowed his eyes and thought about what Wally had said. "I think I see your point," he said. "I'm just not sure what kind of philosophy or idea might work. If you come up with any suggestions, please let me know."

"Oh, I will, I will. Wow, Noah, this is almost like I get to be part of your team. I get to help brainstorm a little bit and maybe help you come up with your plan. I don't think I've ever had the chance to do that sort of thing before."

"Wally, I suspect that if anybody can, it's you. I'll be looking forward to any ideas you come up with. I understand I'll be leaving a week from today, so I don't have a whole lot of time, but if you call, I'll come."

The two men shook hands, and Noah left the building, climbed into his Corvette, and headed for home. He didn't push the car as hard this time, but the shortcut still got him home in just over half an hour.

He pulled into his yard and noticed that Neil's Hummer was parked over at his house, rather than at the trailer. Marco's Mustang was sitting beside it, and he spotted Sarah, Renée, Marco, and Neil all sitting at the picnic table he kept in his front yard. He parked the car and got out and wasn't surprised when Sarah ran over to throw her arms around him.

"I missed you," she said. "Do you realize that, except for when I've been going to see Doc Parker, or when you had to go out last night, we haven't been apart for more than a few seconds since you found me in China?"

"Yes, I know," Noah said. "I've avoided that as much as I could."

Sarah looked up at him adoringly and slipped an arm up behind his head to pull him down for a kiss. He allowed their lips to linger on each other for a moment and then looked up at their guests.

"Something going on?"

"Not really," Sarah said. "I was kinda lonely, so Neil was hanging out with me, and then Renée got off work early and the two of them came over. Marco brought a big basket of fried chicken—are you hungry?"

"Now that you mention it, I am," Noah said as they walked toward the picnic table.

CHAPTER TWELVE

S arah let go of him and jogged into the house, coming back a few moments later with a bottle of beer. She handed it to him and then sat down at his side, snuggling as close as she could.

"How'd it go, boss?" Neil asked. "Are they pounding your new identity into your head?"

"It isn't that bad," Noah replied. "Gary's using a hypnosis technique. He put me under, then he played a recording that basically told me who I'm supposed to be and all about my new past. Rex Madison, at least the way we've manufactured him here, reminds me of some of the punks I knew back in high school. I didn't have any trouble slipping into the character."

Neil's eyes were big and round. "Hypnotism? I'm not too sure how I feel about that. I mean, somebody hypnotizes you, they can make you do all kinds of things you might not really want to do."

"No they can't," Noah said. "I actually read a lot about it a couple years ago. A person under hypnosis won't do anything they don't actually want to do. The reason that stage hypnotists can make people bark like dogs or hop on one foot, that kind of stuff, is because the people actually want to play along. There was a study done back in the late 1990s that found that most people who volunteer to be hypnotized on stage never really go under at all. They simply act the way the hypnotist tells them as a way to get their own few minutes of fame."

Renée was nodding. "I read the same thing, back in college. As far as hypnosis to help you learn things, though, there is a staggering amount of evidence that it's effective. I knew college students who used it on each other, especially when they were cramming for exams. It really seemed to work."

"Hypnotism," Marco said. "I don't know a lot about it, but it seems a little spooky to me."

"Hey, if it works, then it helps us stay alive," Neil said. "If Noah can handle it, I guess I can."

Noah turned his head suddenly, as a car seemed to be approaching the house. There were only a couple of other houses on his road, and it was rare for an unfamiliar vehicle to pass by, but he didn't recognize the sound of this one. When it pulled up to his driveway and turned in, all three of the men rose to their feet.

It was a brand-new Jaguar, and its windows were tinted so dark that they couldn't see in. Noah and Marco each moved toward the car as it stopped near the others, but then the driver's window rolled down and Jenny smiled at them as she held both hands up to be seen. "I'm unarmed," she called out with a smile. "I come in peace."

The men relaxed as she climbed out of the car, and a moment later they were all seated at the picnic table. Neil ran inside and came back with one of Sarah's wine coolers, passing it to Jenny, who had been introduced to Renée and was already munching on a chicken leg.

"Hey, this is good chicken," she said around a mouthful. She quickly swallowed and actually blushed. "Sorry about that, forgot my manners. This really is good, though. Where did you get it?"

"Marco made it," Renée said. "Hard to believe a macho hunk like this can cook, right?"

"Oh, I don't know," Jenny said. "I'm always sort of suspected he might have a feminine side."

"Hey," Marco said, "we don't need none of that. Ain't nothing feminine about this macho hunk!"

"Okay, okay, I was just kidding." She turned to Noah. "Noah, I wanted to come out and thank you. Allison explained things about

Randy, and I just wanted to say thanks for finding a way keep him alive. There was a short time there when I was ready to kill him myself, but once he confessed everything and we knew what was going on, I kinda got over it."

"No problem," Noah said. "But the one you should be thanking is Neil. He was the one who figured out how to use the drugs to convince everybody Randy was dead."

Jenny turned to Neil and gave him her nicest smile. "Really? Maybe I should have guessed. I tell you, Neil, the more I learn about you, the more I think maybe you're just the guy I've been looking for."

With the exception of Noah, the entire group chuckled when Neil turned pink. He lowered his eyes and said softly, "I just—Noah wanted me to find a way, so I—it was just the only thing I could think of."

"I understand Randy will be coming back to your team?" Noah asked, drawing the attention away from Neil.

Jenny looked at him and nodded. "Yeah," he said. "Allison says he's going to be out for a few weeks, getting a new face and identity, but that I'll get him back. He really has been a great help to me, and—well, something I've never told anyone other than the Dragon Lady and Donald is that Randy actually saved my life once. We were on a mission in Germany when something went wrong, and I was suddenly locked in a room with five really big guys who thought beating me to death would be great sport. When I didn't come out of the building when I was supposed to, Randy came in looking for me. He heard the commotion and kicked in the door, shot two of the guys himself, and that gave me a chance to grab a gun. I took out a couple more, and then Randy got the last one just as he was about to shove a knife in my back." She shrugged. "I don't think I've ever really thanked him for that, now that I talk about it out loud. I have to remedy that, when he gets back."

The six of them sat and chatted through the afternoon, but by five o'clock it was starting to cool off considerably. Sarah suggested they go inside so she could make dinner, but Marco and Renée begged off. There was a movie playing at the local theater they wanted to see, so they drove away a few minutes later.

Jenny agreed to stay, and so did Neil. They went inside and Jenny helped Sarah put together a medium-sized stack of sandwiches and potato chips; then they all went into the living room to watch a movie. Neil wanted to find something in the action genre, but Noah handed the remote to Sarah and told her to choose. The four of them settled on the couch that faced the big TV over the fireplace, with the men on the outside and the girls tucked into the middle.

Sarah chose a romantic comedy about a plastic surgeon who convinces his receptionist to pretend to be his ex-wife, part of a plan to persuade a beautiful younger woman to marry him. The four of them relaxed as they laughed at the antics on the screen, and somewhere along the line Neil realized that his arm, which had been on the back of the couch, had somehow ended up around Jenny's shoulders.

Sarah had been watching them out of the corner of her eye and caught Neil glancing down at the pretty girl beside him several times. Jenny seemed to be focused on the movie, but Sarah could tell from the way she was snuggled in under Neil's shoulder that she was enjoying the position. When Jenny glanced her way for just a second, the two of them shared a very small smile.

When the movie ended, Jenny said she needed to get home and get some sleep because she was going to have a big day. As far as locals knew, she was Randy's cousin, so she was making arrangements for his "memorial service." Publicly, it had been announced that his body had been cremated, but it had turned out that he had a number of friends in Kirtland. Noah, Sarah, and Neil all promised to attend the service the following evening, and Jenny rose to leave.

Neil decided he needed to go home at the same time. "I better get some sleep," he said. "I've got to get with Molly in the morning to start learning about this new game." He said good night quickly and followed Jenny out the door.

Alone together at last, Noah filled Sarah in on his hypnosis session, describing as much as he could remember of the induction method and then surprising her with his retention of the many details of Rex Madison's life that he had been fed. "Gary's planning to use the same technique on everybody," he told her. "I think it's going to be very helpful for all of us."

Sarah looked at him from under lowered eyelids. "But you're not confused about who you really are? I mean, you know your name is really Noah, right?"

"Yes, of course," he said. "It's not like I really remember all this stuff, it's just—any question that's directed to me about the life of Rex Madison is going to trigger a response from the information that's being embedded for that purpose. That's the whole idea of using hypnosis, so that we don't make an accidental slip that gives us away."

Sarah seemed to relax a bit. "I wonder if the FBI agent went under something like that," she said. "They said she'd been there like three years or something, right?"

Noah nodded. "Yes, but she's just an observer. From what I understand, she basically just keeps track of new stories and rumors about the outfit, and reports back to Quantico. Considering the fact that seven other FBI agents have met with suspicious accidental deaths in that area, I think she must be quite a courageous woman."

"It sounds like it," Sarah said. "Just remember, she's your sister."

Noah looked at her in confusion for a moment, then recognized the humorous look on her face and knew that she was teasing him. "You don't have anything to worry about," he said. "There's only one woman in this world for me."

The rest of the week was busy, as Noah spent eight hours each day with Gary. Sarah resumed her sessions with Doc Parker, Neil spent each day with Molly, and Marco practiced his reversion to his Cajun roots.

In the evenings, it wasn't uncommon for them all to get together at Noah's place. Since he lived out in the country with no nearby neighbors except for Neil, they all felt comfortable hanging out there. Marco and Renée showed up around dinnertime each evening, and Neil was usually already there. Sarah made dinner a couple of times, Noah fired up the grill twice, and Marco surprised them once with a huge pan of what he called "bodacious gumbo." Noah, Sarah, and Renée all agreed it was delicious, but Neil hadn't made it that evening.

He had mumbled something earlier about having a date, but there was so much going on that no one had actually paid a lot of attention. It wasn't until he came in late that night that they noticed Jenny's car following him and parking next to the Hummer at the trailer.

"Somet'ing going on dere," Marco said. "Looking like de boy done go sweet on dat girl."

"It'll be okay," Sarah said. "I already warned Jenny that if she hurts him, she's dead."

Marco looked at the expression on her face for a long moment, then nodded solemnly. "Dat be enough," he said.

Jenny's car was still there the following morning, as Noah and Sarah each prepared to drive away. As they started out the driveway, she came out of the trailer and waved with a big smile. Both of them waved back and then turned onto the road to head to their respective appointments.

As soon as Noah walked into Gary's office, the questions began. They continued throughout the day, only pausing as the two men went to lunch, but by three o'clock in the afternoon Gary pronounced Noah ready.

"I haven't been able to trip you up for the last three days," he said. "Considering that I know exactly where the weaknesses are in this background, if I can't do it, then I don't think anyone can. You have an amazing ability to actually become the character you're playing, and that blows my mind."

"Like I told you before," Noah said, "I've been doing this all my life. It was how I survived, so it became a habit."

"That just makes it even more amazing," Gary said. He got to his feet and extended a hand. "You've got your ID and everything for the mission. Noah, all I can do now is wish you the best of luck, but I think you've got this. You literally become Rex Madison, so I don't think you're going to have any problem with that part of the job."

Noah shook hands with him. "Thank you," he said, and then he turned to leave.

Since it was a little early, Noah swung by R&D and asked to see Wally again. Just like before, Wally hurried out and ushered him back into his office. "Camelot," he said, "good to see you, good to see you. Listen, I did a little more thinking about your mission. I still think the printed explosives are the way to go, but I came up with a few other little ideas on how you might put them to work."

"Okay, I'm listening," Noah said.

"Okay, okay, okay, here's what I think. We talked about you giving people presents, but what about selling stuff to them? Remember I was talking about guns? If you started trying to give these people guns, they might wonder what was going on, and that started me thinking that they might even wonder if you were giving them things like pens and sunglasses. But what if you weren't giving them anything? What if you just happened to have some really good deals on stuff they like?"

Noah lowered his eyebrows and cocked his head as he looked at Wally. "I think I see your point," he said. "Just about everybody likes a good deal, and especially if it's a bargain price on something they were planning to buy anyway. What you're suggesting, if I read you right, is that I can take orders for guns or whatever, then just have Neil make them?"

"Actually, no," Wally said. "I think we need to go ahead and send you one of the smaller printers, rather than the big one I had in mind. Instead, I took the liberty of setting up—well, I had somebody else set it up—it's a little company that looks like a brokerage; it can get you anything you want. Donnie Jefferson liked the idea, and we put it all together so it looks like it's owned by a guy that you did time with, somebody you'd be really close to. That way, you can tell people you can get them just about anything they want at real low, bargain-basement prices, and all you gotta do is find out what they want and make a phone call. I'll put a couple of people on that line who can look up real quick what it would normally cost, and then you can tell those people they can get it for like sixty or seventy or eighty percent off if they go through you. How much you price it to them doesn't matter—that's just the way to hook them into wanting it and being willing to go through you to get it. We use the big printers here to produce the items and overnight them to you so you can deliver and collect. It all looks legit, and nobody is wondering why you're playing Santa Claus all the time."

Noah was nodding. "Now I know why they call you a genius," he said. "Wally, this is brilliant. I think you just gave me exactly what I need." He leaned forward in his chair. "Now, you'll go ahead and set them up with detonators that will all go off at once, right? No matter what the item is, it will go off when I send the signal?"

"Exactly. No matter what it is or where it is, when you send the signal it goes boom."

Noah stared at him for a couple of seconds. "This is probably the way we're going to have to go," he said, "but it's bound to mean there's going to be some collateral damage. There is almost no chance that every one of these people will be alone when that signal goes out, so there's certain to be casualties other than the targets." He lowered his eyes and thought for a moment, then looked back up at Wally. "The explosive is extremely powerful, right? What if somebody was wearing like a necklace, with a chain made of this stuff?"

Wally reached inside his shirt collar and pulled out a gold chain with an eagle dangling from it. Each link of the chain was roughly an eighth of an inch in diameter, the loops made of gold-colored wire that was about as thick as a pencil lead.

"A chain like this, made with our product, would completely sever the head from the body," Wally said with a grin. "I think I see where you're going. Now, even that could possibly kill someone who was sitting or standing very close, but if they were more than four or five feet away they'd probably survive." He blinked. "They might be deaf or blind, or have one bastard of a concussion, but I think most people would live through it. Only the person wearing the chain would be certain to die."

"Okay. And what if I wanted some that wouldn't explode? What I'm thinking of is maybe coming up with some kind of an emblem for this Morgan Mafia, something that we could put on a chain that everybody would want to wear. What if a guy thought it was so cool he wanted to give one to his wife, his girlfriend? Could you make some that wouldn't blow up?"

"Of course, of course," Wally said. "Remember, this stuff is absolutely stable unless it's hit by our special detonator. That's the only thing that's going to create enough of the concentrated heat and the proper chemical reaction that sets it off. You can even burn it in a normal fire without it going boom. The only problem I can see is how you know the guy gives the right one to the wife or girlfriend, and keeps the loaded one for himself."

"We make two different designs," Noah said. "Maybe one is a little bigger than the other, something like that. Only actual members of the outfit get to wear the big one, and everybody else has to settle for the little one. We still run the risk that the wrong person might be wearing it when it goes off, but if this outfit is as disciplined and tightly controlled as they say, that's probably going to be a pretty small risk."

Wally clapped his hands. "And now who's the genius? I still wouldn't rule out selling them other things, though. From what Donnie and Allison have told me, it's pretty important this mission succeeds, even if there is some collateral damage. If one of these people left his necklace at home that day, he's still pretty certain to have his gun, right? Can't hurt if they both go off at the same time."

Noah nodded again. "You're right," he said. "I just personally prefer to limit nontarget casualties whenever I can."

Noah's phone rang suddenly, and he pulled it out to look at the caller ID display. The call was from Neil, so he answered it quickly. "It's Noah, go ahead."

"Neil, here," Neil said unnecessarily. "Hey, I was messing around with your computer and you got a message about the car you posted online, I guess. I've got a number for you."

The message was a code, telling Noah that there had been a message from the mole. "I'm just leaving R&D," Noah said. "Text me the number, and I'll give him a call."

CHAPTER THIRTEEN

It took Noah a little more than ten minutes to get out of the high-security area, and then he called up Neil's text message and tapped the number with his thumb. He heard ringing a moment later, and then the phone was answered by the distorted voice of the mole.

"It's about damned time," Noah said. "I did what you want—Mitchell is dead."

"I'm aware of that," said the voice. "I have another job for you. When can you get away from your associates for a couple of days?"

Noah thought quickly. He was scheduled to leave for Arkansas the following day, but keeping the mole happy might justify being a day or two late on his arrival there.

"Probably tomorrow," he said. "I'm supposed to be going out on a mission in a couple of days, but I can shake loose for a little bit. Where would I be going?"

"I have a situation in Texas that needs to be handled by someone with your talents. You will be going to Odessa. Can you manage to get a flight there without anyone knowing it?"

Noah hesitated, trying to give the impression that he was thinking about how to accomplish what the mole wanted. "Yes," he said after a few seconds. "I have some IDs that no one knows about. Sometimes I just need to get off the reservation for a little while, get off by myself, know what I mean?"

"Excellent. Get to Odessa and call this number again. It won't be active, but I'll be notified that you called it. You'll get a new number by text message immediately after, and we'll talk then."

The line went dead, and Noah put his phone back in his pocket. There was no doubt in his mind that the "situation" was going to

131

mean someone was supposed to die. Noah knew that he might have to actually kill the target, since the executive order that established E & E authorized its agents to use lethal force whenever necessary to complete an assigned mission. In this particular case, the mission was to identify the mole. If necessary, Noah would actually carry out an assassination on his orders in order to maintain the fiction that the mole was able to control him.

Somewhere in the background, Noah was aware, Molly and her team of brilliant people were trying to trace the messages from the mole. Unfortunately, he—or she, Noah reminded himself—was particularly adept at blocking every such attempt. Each message through the forum site came from an account that was inactive only seconds after the message was sent, and the IP address always led to a server that turned out to be a dead-end offshoot from the information superhighway. The phone numbers that came in the messages were always dead, basically nothing more than a redirect routine in some obscure third-world telephone company's computers. Once Noah dialed the number and the conversation ended, that number would vanish and almost certainly would never be active again, or else it would go back to being some mundane phone number with no connection to the world of espionage.

It occurred to Noah that identifying the mole was probably going to require some sort of initiative on his own part, sooner or later. The only question in his mind was how to go about it. No matter what he tried, there were going to be risks involved.

Sarah was home already, of course, her session with Doc Parker having ended before noon. She came out the door quickly when he parked the car in front of the garage, and threw her arms around him as he stepped out.

"What am I gonna do for the next week?" she asked. "How am I gonna handle you being gone, not being with you, and not even knowing what's happening to you?"

"I'll be fine, Sarah," he said. "I'm going to take it pretty easy at first, not try to push anything. I'm not going to give them any reason to suspect me. By the time you get there, I'll have us a house and everything. It'll be okay."

Sarah nodded, but he could hear the soft sniffles. He held her for a moment longer, and then they started toward the house.

"Hey, lovebirds," Neil called out. "Want some company?"

"Sure," Sarah called back. "Come on over. Where's Jenny?"

A scowl appeared on Neil's face. "She left this morning," he said. "Going out on a mission. Am I crazy to get mixed up with her? I mean, what am I going to do if she gets herself killed out there?" He realized instantly what he had just said, and his face registered embarrassment.

Sarah looked at him blankly for a moment, then forced herself to smile and shook her head. "No, you're not crazy," she said. "I've watched the two of you together this past few days, and I think you each give the other something you need. But, Neil, don't get too wrapped up in her just yet. I mean, you barely even know her. This might grow into something serious, but take your time. Don't rush it—I think that might be a mistake."

Neil just nodded and ducked his head, then followed them into the house. The three of them went to the kitchen and sat around the table, and that's when Noah looked Neil in the eye.

"You made me a promise," he said. "I'm going to hold you to it. When I leave tomorrow, I want you to stay over here with Sarah until it's time for her to come join me. I don't want her alone."

Neil nodded and started to speak, but Sarah cut him off.

"Noah! I don't need a babysitter."

"I know you don't," Noah replied. "But you might need someone to talk to, even just for simple conversation. Aside from that, Neil is going to be posing as your little brother. You two already have a pretty good brother-sister kind of relationship, but I think it might be a good idea to sort of practice it, especially now."

"I'll be over here," Neil said. "Don't worry. And, Sarah, to be perfectly honest I could use the company probably as much as you could. We can play cards and stuff, keep both of us from doing too much thinking right now."

Sarah gave him a mildly dirty look, but after a few seconds, she nodded. "I guess so," she said. "Besides, we both start our training with Gary day after tomorrow. I might need Neil to hold my hand through that; I've never been hypnotized. The whole idea kind of makes me nervous."

"You'll be fine," Noah said. "I promise you, it can't hurt you in any way. You come out of it feeling like you had a good night's sleep, but all of a sudden you know things you didn't know before."

There was an awkward silence for a few seconds, but then Neil broke it. "So, what time do you leave tomorrow?"

"I've got to go out to R&D and pick up some wheels first thing in the morning," Noah said. "Molly doesn't think the Corvette fits Rex's personality, so I'm getting a '69 Dodge Charger. It's one of those cars they built with ridiculous horsepower, but Molly believes it will help me fit in down there. After that, I'm supposed to hit the road by noon, but I'm going to have to make a detour. I received contact from the mole and have to fly down to Odessa, Texas, and contact him again from there. He's got something for me to do there, but I don't know yet what it is."

Sarah's eyes had gone wide as he spoke. "Have you told Allison yet?"

Noah shook his head. "Not yet. I don't want to do it over the phone, and it might not be smart for me to try to go see her right after getting that call. If he's got anyone watching, then anybody connected with me that goes to see Allison or Mr. Jefferson right after he makes contact with me could give our game away. My plan is to simply pick up the car like I'm supposed to in the morning and send them a message through Wally. I'll drive to the airport at Kansas City, fly from there to Odessa and take care of whatever he wants there, then fly back and head for Arkansas."

Sarah was quiet for a moment, but then she nodded. "And you'll be staying with your sister?" she asked, with emphasis on the last word.

"Yes, but not for long. Gary called and got her on the phone today, so I've actually spoken to her now. We played it just the way he wanted, with her grudgingly agreeing to let me come and stay with her for a few days while I look for work and a place of our own. When I get there, I have to check in with the federal probation officer in Fayetteville. His name is Craig Roberts, and he has no idea about what's really going on. After that, I'm pretty much on my own. The story is that Katie doesn't want me hanging around her place all the time, so I'll probably try to find a way to get connected to the Morgan Mafia while I'm looking to rent a house."

Sarah looked at him for a moment. "Have you seen a picture of her yet?"

Noah reached into his pocket and pulled out a wallet, then flipped through some photos inside until he came to a particular one. He held it out to Sarah, and she looked at it critically for a moment, then seemed to relax. "She looks okay, I guess," she said. "Kind of chubby."

"That's probably why nobody pays a lot of attention to her," Noah said. "I've read that a lot of female undercover agents tend to be moderately overweight. It makes them kind of invisible; nobody thinks they could be someone they need to worry about."

"I get that," Sarah said. "I'm just glad I look better than her."

Noah just looked at her for a couple of seconds, but then the sound of a car turning into the driveway made him rise and look out a window. "Marco and Renée," he said. "I don't want to say anything to them about the mole. We'll keep that between ourselves, until I get a chance to talk to Wally."

Sarah nodded, then got up and went to let them in while Noah looked at Neil and raised his eyebrows. "She means she doesn't think she needs to be jealous of your new sister," Neil whispered, and Noah nodded.

"I know," he whispered back. "I just don't understand why she'd be worried about it."

"That's because you don't understand women. You don't, not even a little bit."

The five of them decided to go out to the Sagebrush Saloon for dinner, since it was the last time they would all be together for quite some time. Neil rode with Marco and Renée, while Noah and Sarah followed in the Corvette.

The hostess met them at the door and showed them to a table. Sarah asked if Elaine was working, but the hostess frowned.

"I'm afraid not," she said. "Elaine quit a couple of days ago. I understand she's going to be working with her dad in his office, now."

"Well, that sucks," Sarah said as they took their seats. "I'm gonna miss her here."

"She probably quit because of us," Neil said. "Every time we came in, it kind of smacked her in the face that Moose is gone, you know? I guess quitting was easier than feeling that pain every time we came through the door."

"You're probably right," Noah said. "Most people who lose a loved one tend to sever ties with people they were close to. I suspect we'll only be seeing Elaine by chance or when it's unavoidable from now on."

Sarah looked at him for a moment but didn't say anything. When the waitress approached and passed out menus, she managed to smile again. They each ordered their favorites and enjoyed dinner together.

Afterward, since Noah was scheduled to be leaving in the morning, Marco and Renée invited Neil out for the evening. Noah urged him to accept, then took Sarah home to spend a quiet evening together. Instead of watching television like usual, though, the two of them sat and talked until midnight, and then made their way to the bedroom and simply cuddled.

When morning came, they rose together. Noah had already packed a bag for his trip and loaded it into the back seat of Sarah's car. For once, it would be Sarah dropping Noah off instead of the other way around. They made a quick stop at a fast-food place for breakfast and then drove out to R&D. Sarah kissed Noah goodbye as he grabbed his bag and got out of her car, and then drove carefully back toward Doc Parker's office. Noah pretended not to see the tears in her eyes.

He stepped into the R&D building, and the security guard checked his ID, just like always. Wally was actually waiting for him this time and led him back toward the automotive section as soon as security cleared him.

"Camelot," Wally said as they made their way down the central hall of the building, "you're gonna love this car! I told the auto shop to give you something that can help you accomplish your mission, and they went all out. Just wait till you see it; you'll know what I mean."

"Sounds good," Noah said. "Molly told me it's a Charger?"

"Yep, a '69, but with a few special options the Duke boys never had," Wally said. "Just wait, you're gonna love it."

They came to a large double door, and Wally led the way into the automotive garage, a cavernous room with a dozen different workstations. This is where the organization's cars were built and maintained, and it was put under Wally's supervision because some of the cars needed special capabilities, especially those used by the teams when they were on mission.

Wally waved, and a short man in mechanics' coveralls smiled and waved back. "That's Rodney," Wally said. "Rodney's my right-hand man in the automotive section. I tell him what I want; then I just turn him loose. In this case, I told him I wanted a car that could help you accomplish an extremely difficult mission and gave him the general parameters. Let's go see what he came up with."

Noah followed Wally over to where Rodney stood waiting beside a beautiful Dodge Charger that had been painted in a flat black. The windows were tinted so dark that it was almost impossible to see through them at all, and a chromed blower and scoop sticking up through the hood told Noah there was some serious power in its engine. Wally made the introductions, and Noah and Rodney shook hands.

"Okay, Rodney," Wally said. "Tell Noah what you built for him, here."

Rodney grinned as he looked at the car. "Well, you can see that it's a 1969 Dodge Charger, but it's been built for speed. It's powered by a supercharged and fuel-injected 540-cubic-inch hemi crate motor cranking out over nine hundred horsepower. I backed that up with a six-speed automatic transmission that's been built to handle it, and some bulletproof rear gears that will let you hit two hundred miles per hour if necessary, while still giving you enough off-the-line torque to leave just about any other car sitting still. I built it with a keyless ignition system, so everything is controlled by the remote." He handed Noah something that looked like a fancy cigarette lighter with a number of buttons on it. "We used the standard icons. You can see which button unlocks the car or locks it, opens the trunk—there is a safe in the trunk, by the way, one that is already programmed to your right thumbprint. But the car has one really special feature that I'm kind of proud of. See the button down there that has an icon that looks like a whistle? You push that button anywhere within fifty miles of that car, and it will come to you. It has self-driving capability built into it, even better than Google's, and you can even use it when you just want to relax and let the car do the driving. Just put in the address of where you're going, and a little icon of a driver will appear on the screen. If you touch the icon, the self-driving application turns on and you can kick back and get some rest. If you touch anywhere else, it just cancels it and leaves it under your control."

Noah nodded appreciatively as he opened the driver's door and tossed his bag into the back seat, then looked around the interior. Even there, he felt a sense of perfection, as if every aspect of the car had been carefully done by a master craftsman. "It's incredible," he said. "It ought to be in a museum somewhere."

"Why?" Rodney asked. "It's a car, not a statue. I built it to get you where you need to go and help you accomplish what you need to do. If people want to admire it, let them admire it at a hundred and fifty miles an hour, that's how I feel about it."

Noah's eyebrows went up a half inch. "Okay, then," he said. "Wally says it's got some other special features?"

Rodney grinned broadly and nodded. "Oh, boy, does it ever," he said. "The body is made entirely of Kevlar, rather than the normal sheet steel. Slide in behind the wheel, and let me give you the full tour."

Noah sat down in the car and looked over the dashboard and console.

"Wally said he wanted you to have a car that would help you accomplish your mission, sort of like James Bond and his Aston Martin," Rodney said, as he sat down in the passenger seat. "To me, that means he wants the car to have lots of features you can use to get things done or keep you safe. Slip your right hand down alongside the seat, and you'll find a row of buttons hidden down there. Go ahead, you need to know where they're at."

Noah reached down between the seat and the console and found the buttons Rodney was talking about. "Five buttons, right?"

Rodney nodded. "Exactly. Push the first button and watch what happens."

Noah looked him in the eye for a moment, then pushed the first button as he was told. A video display in the dashboard had been showing stereo and satellite radio controls, but suddenly it changed. It showed the scene directly ahead of the car, and Noah looked at it for a moment before turning back to Rodney.

"Touch the screen on something that moves," Rodney said.

Another technician was walking across the garage in front of the car, so Noah touched his image on the screen. Instantly, he was surrounded by two bright red concentric circles, with crossed lines centered over his body. The image stayed on him as he walked, keeping him centered.

"Crosshairs?" Noah asked.

"Yes," Rodney replied. "Tapping an item on the screen tells the targeting computer to lock onto it. Now, on the back of the steering wheel there's a button on each side—feel them? Those are the triggers: if you squeeze one while targeting is activated, the headlight doors open silently, and there's a small machine gun mounted on gimbals between the bulbs of the right headlight that will unload on whatever you targeted. It fires 9 mm bullets at fifteen rounds a second, and it's loaded with two thousand of them. It has a forty-five-degree field of fire and will keep firing as long as you squeeze the trigger."

Noah nodded. "That's pretty cool," he said.

"Now push the second button."

Noah did so and the crosshairs on the screen suddenly turned yellow. "A different weapon?"

Rodney grinned at him. "High-explosive rounds fired from a modified 12-gauge shotgun shell. It's like a mini grenade launcher, and the same trigger buttons are used to make it fire. The rounds are made from one of our proprietary superexplosives. There's a primer embedded inside that sets it off when it strikes the target. You only have twenty-four rounds, so use them sparingly. Next button."

Noah pressed the third button and an infrared image of the garage ahead was suddenly projected onto the windshield, complete with heat-generated images of the people working there.

"Forward-looking infrared radar," Rodney said. "It will show you thermal images, even through conventional walls, combined with computer-enhanced radar images. Lets you know where the bad guys are hiding and makes it possible to drive at night without lights. It gives you a very realistic view of what's ahead, but this can only be seen from inside the vehicle. As bright as it looks, nobody outside could see it at all."

Noah nodded. "I can see how that might come in handy," he said.

"Next button," Rodney said, and Noah pressed it. The video display suddenly showed a clear image of what was behind the car, and Noah could hear the audio through the speakers. "You have 360-degree video capability through a camera that pops out of the roof. Just touch the corner of the screen and you can rotate the camera all the way around. If you find something you want to zoom in on, just tap the center twice. If you want to record the video, just squeeze one of the trigger buttons on the steering wheel. The hard drive built into this car can handle several hundred hours of video, so don't worry about running out of space. When you push the button again or choose another one, the camera retracts and is invisible." Rodney pulled the seat belt around himself and buckled it. "Okay, let's take the car out for a drive so you can try the last button."

CHAPTER FOURTEEN

N oah buckled his own seat belt and reached up to start the car. It used a keyless ignition system that only required him to push a button, and then he put the car in gear and drove it out of the garage toward the test track behind the building.

"Take a couple of laps around the track," Rodney said, "just to get the feel of the car. Don't be afraid to put your foot into it; this thing can handle the curves and corners."

Noah drove onto the track and pressed down on the accelerator. There were no other cars on it, so he had it all to himself.

The Charger shot forward with enough acceleration to slam him back into his seat, and Noah could tell the engine was everything Rodney had said it was. The car eased through the first couple of curves, and then Noah drifted it around a corner at more than sixty miles per hour. Rodney was holding on to the door and the dashboard, but there was a huge grin on his face.

"That's it," Rodney said, "that's it. I knew you'd be able to handle this thing—you just got that look about you." He continued to hold on to the door and the dash as Noah made two complete circuits of the track, which was a little over two miles long overall.

As they came around to begin the third lap, lining up on a straightaway that was almost half a mile long itself, Rodney told Noah to push the last button. Noah did so, and suddenly the roar of the engine almost doubled in volume. The car launched forward again, and Noah saw the speedometer go from eighty miles per hour to over one fifty in just a few short seconds.

"Nitrous oxide?" Noah asked, but Rodney shook his head.

"Nope," he replied. "That last button kicks in a hidden super-charger that's built into the intake manifold. It's powered by a supersmall electric motor that runs on a four-hundred-volt lithium-ion battery. It's only good for about three minutes at a time, and then the battery needs about an hour of engine time to recharge. When it kicks in, this car can do about two hundred and twenty miles per hour, but not even this car can take any serious curves, not at that speed. Use it carefully, though, and you can drastically cut down travel time from one place to another."

Noah was easing down on the brakes, getting the car back under control. He was still going faster than he liked when he entered the first curve, but the car drifted like it was made for that purpose. By the time he reached the second curve, he was back down to a reasonable speed.

"Couple other features," Rodney said. "The body was handmade right here in our shop, out of carbon fiber and Kevlar. All of the glass is polycarbonate and almost half an inch thick, and there is a polycarb deflection shield between the grille and the radiator that lets plenty of air through, but nothing else. A fifty-caliber round fired at point-blank range will do a little damage, but anything farther away or smaller than that won't even scratch the paint." He chuckled, and Noah nodded appreciatively. "The tires are filled with a foam rubber that was developed for the space program. They can't go flat, and it would take an awful lot of bullets to even make one ride rough. Oh, and the gas tank is a thirty-gallon fuel cell. You could shoot holes in it with a machine gun and it would never explode. Just a little safety feature I thought might come in handy."

"I'm definitely impressed," Noah said. "Anything else I should know about it?"

"Yeah," Rodney said. "The built-in computer can tell you just about anything you want to know about the car. Tap the info button on the screen twice, and it will give you a readout that tells you how many rounds you have left in the weapons, the status of the super-charger's battery, and how many data files you saved. There's a USB port just under the display so that you can download those files to a computer if you want to. It also has an intelligent security system. Whenever you lock the car up, it automatically keeps track of any-body who gets within ten feet of it, watching them with about a dozen different sensors. As long as they only look it doesn't do any-thing, but if they touch the car they get a warning to back away. If anybody is stupid enough to try to break into it, they're going to find themselves in sleepy land from an electric shock. If the car senses that it's being hooked up to a wrecker or anything, it will set off an alarm that sounds like an air raid siren, call 911 and report itself be-ing stolen, and if somebody manages to drag it away from where you left it, then it will send you a text message with its GPS coordinates every twenty minutes after that. The only way anyone would get into the car is by crushing it first, so you should be able to get it back."

Wally was standing outside the garage when Noah pulled up be-side him, and reached out to open the door. "Well?" Wally asked breathlessly. "What do you think?"

Noah looked up at him. "It's awesome," he said. "My only ques-tion is how am I supposed to justify having a car like this? Even with-out all its special features, this is a car that very few recently released convicts would be able to afford."

"Allison will go over that with you," Wally said. "I'm supposed to tell you to stop by her office as soon as you leave here. I guess they made some changes to your character profile and want to go over them with you."

Noah nodded. "Okay. Got anything else for me here?"

"Nope," Wally said. "I think that's it. If you're comfortable with the car, then I guess you're ready to go."

Noah nodded, then reached out and shook Wally's hand. "Thank you again," he said. He closed the door and put the car back into gear, heading for the gate that was already rolling open for him.

It didn't take that long for him to make it into Kirtland, but that was partly because he was feeling out the power of the car. The digital speedometer in the instrument cluster was bouncing on one hundred and forty miles per hour on a couple of long straight stretches.

He parked the car in the underground garage and locked it with the keyless remote, then got into the elevator and rode up to Allison's floor. Her secretary, a new girl that Noah didn't recognize, told him that she was in a meeting and asked his name. As soon as she heard it, she went pale and told him to go right on in.

Allison looked up from her desk and smiled. "Camelot," she said. "I won't ask if you're ready for this mission; I know that you are. I just wanted to go over a couple of details with you before you took off."

Noah nodded and sat down in the chair in front of her desk. "Wally said you wanted to fill me in on how Rex Madison can afford the kind of supercar that usually only shows up in movies."

Allison chuckled but nodded. "Yes, and it was your pal Molly who thought of it. Her plan called for you having a powerful car that would draw a lot of attention, so I sent her out to Wally's to see what was available. She spotted that Charger and said that was ideal, so I told Wally to have his guys tweak it for you. Of course, Wally pointed out that the car was one that would cost a small fortune even without his special touches, so I told Molly it might not be practical. She insisted that it was the perfect car, though, so we had to do a couple of things with your character to make it fit."

She pulled open a desk drawer and picked up a thick package, holding it out for Noah. He took it and glanced inside to see a dozen large bundles of hundred-dollar bills.

"A lot of cash," he said. "How does this fit with me just getting out of prison?"

"Very well, actually. Remember that you spent almost all of five years locked away, right? Well, it turns out you were a pretty smart young drug dealer. According to financial records, you'd been investing money every month into a pretty healthy stock portfolio. That money sat there earning some very substantial returns the whole time you were locked up, and you cashed out shortly after you were released. Your investment had turned into almost a million dollars during that time, but you didn't waste time spending a lot of it. In that package is all the paperwork showing that you bought that Charger from a custom car builder for just over two hundred and fifty thousand dollars a week later. The cash in that package, about a hundred grand, is all you've got left after Uncle Sam and that car, so don't spend it all in one place."

Noah nodded, mentally inserting this new information into the matrix of his cover identity. "All right," he said. "I'm supposed to be finding someplace for us to live. Should I use it to buy a house?"

Allison shrugged and waved a hand in the air. "That would definitely make it look like you're serious about sticking around, so it's not a bad idea. Up to you in the long run—you might just want to rent something, maybe pay a year up in advance. That would still look good but wouldn't deplete your cash reserve."

"I'll see what's available and go from there," Noah said. "Anything else?"

"No, I think that's it. Anything on your end?"

"Yes. I finally got a call from that particular individual we've been trying to identify. He wants me to make a detour, fly down to Odessa, Texas, and handle something for him. I figure I'll drive to Kansas City and fly out of there tonight. With any luck, I can take care of whatever he wants and be back in KC within a day or two."

Allison looked into his eyes for a long moment, then nodded. "Do it," she said. "Unfortunately, we need him to think he's got you under his control, so go ahead and do it. I'm authorizing any kills you have to perform in keeping his confidence. Just remember, you're in deep cover. It won't be Noah Wolf who's doing the killing in Texas; it'll be Rex Madison. You cannot afford to be arrested under that identity."

"I won't be," he said. "Remember when we did the job in Missouri? I still have the Wyatt Wilson ID I used then. After the Andropov attack and everything we went through after that, I just never got around to turning it in. I'm going to use it for the flight and to rent a car in Odessa."

Allison turned to a computer on her desk and tapped on the keyboard for a moment, and then a slow smile spread across her face. "That's excellent," she said. "That ID has some data encrypted in its magnetic strip. If you get arrested, it will instruct the police to contact the state department, and we'll get you out in no time. It's still fully valid, so you shouldn't have any problems with it." She turned and faced him again. "Noah, I want you to be as careful as you possibly can in both of these missions. If I could send anybody else to Arkansas, I would, but I think Molly is right. You're probably the only agent we've got who could pull this off, especially if you have to stay there very long."

"I'll do what I can," Noah said. "Unless there's something else, I should get on the road."

"Yes, you should. How is Sarah handling this?"

"She's a little shaken up. We haven't really spent much time apart since I found her in China, but Neil is going to stay with her until it's time for them to come to Arkansas. I just want to get to Texas and get this task over with so I can get started on the real mission."

"Then get moving. I'll do my best to keep an eye on Sarah, as well."

She looked down at some papers on her desk, and Noah knew that he had been dismissed. He stood and walked out of the office, nodded to the secretary, and then rode the elevator back down to the garage. A moment later, the big Dodge Charger turned out of the garage and headed toward the highway that would take him to the interstate.

From Kirtland to the Kansas City International Airport was a six-hour drive, and Noah arrived at just before 4:00 p.m. He left all of his Rex Madison documents in the glove box, locked up the car in long-term parking, and carried his bag into the airport terminal. Fifteen minutes later he had learned that there were no nonstop flights to Odessa, and the shortest flight would have him arriving at three o'clock the following morning.

Noah walked away from the desk and googled private charter flights from Kansas City airport and then began calling the charter companies that came up. It took him half an hour to find a flight, but it was a Cessna business jet that could have him there in less than two hours. Fortunately, Wyatt Wilson's credit card was up to the task, and the little plane took off with Noah aboard a half hour later.

It was 7:30 by the time he made it to the car rental desk, and almost 8:00 by the time he had secured a new Chrysler. There was a Holiday Inn only a short distance from the airport, so Noah called ahead to reserve a room and then hit a fast-food drive-through to grab his dinner. By 8:45, he was in his room and dialing the number that had come in the last message.

There was no answer, but another number came to him in a text message. He tapped it with his thumb and the phone dialed it automatically.

"Are you in place?" The distorted voice sounded the same as it always did.

"I'm here," Noah said. "Now what you want me to do?"

"You will receive a message shortly that will contain names, an address, and a couple of photographs. One of them will be a photo of a family. The other will be something you might find useful. The mother is in a position to be of value to me, but she does not believe that refusing me will have any repercussions. I want you to convince her otherwise. At this point, I do not want you to terminate anyone, but I want you to make it clear to her that the lives of her husband and children are within my grasp. Do you understand?"

"Yeah," Noah growled. "Any particular way you want me to do that?"

Something that sounded like a laugh came through the phone. "I'm sure you can come up with something," it said. "Just make sure it's effective. Once you feel certain you have accomplished this for me, you can proceed to your mission in Arkansas."

If I were normal, Noah thought, *a chill would have just gone down my spine.* "You know about that, do you?"

The rumbling sound that Noah took for laughter came again. "Of course I do. I have people high enough in your organization, in every organization, to make sure I know just about everything I need to know."

The line went dead, and Noah simply looked at the phone for a moment before putting it down on the nightstand beside the bed. The mole knew about his mission, and Noah let that knowledge circulate through his mind.

This fact told Noah several things. First, it told him that the mole's statement that he had someone high in the organization was almost certainly true. It also told him, however, that that person was not privy to the current plan that involved letting the mole use Noah. If that information had been divulged, the mole would never have alluded to having a high-placed source, and Noah's fake family would probably be dead.

His phone signaled an incoming text message, and he looked at it quickly. The first photograph showed a man and woman in their thirties, standing behind two girls and a boy who looked to be in their early teens. The second photo showed the man, but the woman he was obviously enjoying was not his wife. He closed the message and held his phone for a moment.

He considered trying to place a call to Allison to relay the information about the high-placed source but decided against using his own phone for it. Instead, he finished the last of his french fries and carefully crumpled the shirt that was in the top of his bag. He used his phone to take a snapshot of the open bag and then left the room and made his way out to the rental car.

As far as he could tell, he was not being followed. He drove around for half an hour until he spotted a Walmart, then parked and went inside. The nice thing about Walmart was that you could always find a cheap, throwaway cell phone, no matter what time it might be. He bought two of them and the corresponding activation cards and took them back to his room.

It only took a few minutes to activate them, and then he used one of them to call Sarah. She answered on the first ring, and Noah could tell that she had been crying.

"Hello?" The sniffle in her voice was obvious.

"It's me," Noah said. "Are you all right?"

"I'm better now," Sarah said. "I thought you weren't supposed to call in until you got to Arkansas?"

"Well, it became necessary, so I figured I'd take the opportunity to call you, first. I need to get a message to the Dragon Lady, but I don't want it coming through anyone connected directly to me. Do you still have Elaine's number?"

"Elaine? Yeah, why?"

"I need to get a message to her father," Noah said. "That's the safest way I can think of."

"What is it? I'll call her as soon as we get off the phone."

"No, I don't want to take a chance that her phone records might be vulnerable. I'll use a throwaway to call her, and I think I can disguise my voice enough she won't know it's me. That way, if anyone finds out she relayed the message to her father, it won't lead back to you."

Sarah hesitated, but when she spoke again, he could hear a smile in her voice. "Okay, I guess that makes sense." She gave him the number and then asked how he was doing.

"I'm okay," he said. "You sound like you've been crying."

"Yeah, well, comes with being a girl. I miss you. I know it's only supposed to be a week before I see you again, but right now it sounds like forever."

"It won't be that bad," Noah said. "Try to keep yourself busy. Is Neil there?"

"Yeah, he's out in the living room. You caught me just after I got out of the shower. I figured I'd take advantage of the opportunity to do my weeping where no one could see me."

"Go back out and spend time with him. He's supposed to be your little brother, now, so get used to treating him like one. From what I've seen, older sisters always pick on their little brothers. That shouldn't be too hard, will it?"

She chuckled at him. "Oh, I'm already pretty good at it. We played rummy a little while ago, and I beat him five games straight. You should have heard him—he was whining like a big baby."

"Then go play some more. I like it when you laugh."

Sarah was quiet for a moment. "That's the first time you've ever said anything like that to me. Are you sure you're okay?"

"I'm fine, I promise you. I'm just learning to deal with the fact that you reach parts of me I thought were dead."

From the sound of her voice, the smile must have gotten a lot wider. "That's so sweet," she said. "I love you, Noah."

CHAPTER FIFTEEN

Noah felt the corners of his mouth twitch upward, and the sensation was so unfamiliar that he turned and looked at himself in the mirror on the dresser. He stared at his reflection for a moment and then said, "I love you, too."

Sarah giggled. "I love hearing you say that," she said, "even if..."

"I love you, Sarah," Noah said, cutting her off. "And in case you can't hear it, you actually just made me smile. A real smile—I mean, it actually caught me off guard."

"Noah," she said, and all of the mirth seemed to be gone from her voice. "As much as I've always wanted that to happen, now would not be a good time for you to suddenly get your emotions back. This mission—we need your Vulcan brain, babe. This is no time to go soft."

"Relax," Noah said. "I'm not feeling anything else, just something akin to pleasure when you said you love me. I've been like this so long, I don't think I can ever come completely out of it."

Sarah sighed. "Okay, but don't scare me like that. I worry enough about you as it is."

"I guess that comes with being married, or maybe with loving someone. I'm not sure I know how to worry, but I know that I think about you a lot when we're not together, wonder how you are, that sort of thing. Anyway, I need to call Elaine and get rid of these burner phones. You stick with Neil, and I'll see both of you in a week."

"Okay," Sarah said, "but do me one favor. Would you—would you say it again?"

"I love you, Sarah," Noah said. "I'll see you soon."

He ended the call and immediately took the sim card and battery out of the phone. He used his Swiss Army knife to break the sim card and then flushed it down the toilet before turning on the other phone and dialing the number Sarah had given him.

"Hello?" Elaine's voice sounded sleepy and cautious.

"Urgent, urgent," Noah said, affecting a European accent and raising his voice an octave. "Message for your father. Someone high in organization feeding information about missions to mole. Urgent, urgent."

"What?" Elaine sputtered, but Noah ended the call and immediately dismantled the phone. The broken sim card followed its fellow down the toilet, and the rest of the parts went into the pocket of Noah's leather jacket.

Noah went to the bathroom and took a quick shower, then climbed into bed. Two minutes later he was asleep.

Noah was awake before the late-autumn sun managed to light up the morning. He dressed quickly and left the hotel, dropping the remains of the throwaway phones into a trash can near the parking lot. He used the GPS on his own phone to get directions to the address from the text message he'd received the night before and pointed the Cadillac toward it.

The text message said that the target family was Jim and Caroline Dickinson and their children, Rachel, Amber, and Jimmy. It took him only twenty minutes to get to their neighborhood, still well before 7:00 a.m.

He cruised past the house, a nice-looking ranch-style in an open subdivision, and parked in the driveway of a house with a For Sale sign in front of it that sat only four doors down. He could see the front of the target's house clearly, but it was nearly an hour later when the garage door opened and a car backed out into the street. He used the zoom function of his phone's camera to ascertain that the car had only one occupant: the woman from the photograph. She turned the car in his direction and cruised past a moment later.

Noah watched for a few minutes more, and then a school bus stopped in front of the house beside the one he was watching. All three of the children came out at once, as did other children from several other houses on the block, and Noah sat there and took their pictures as they climbed onto the bus and rode away. Once the bus was out of sight, he started the Cadillac and backed out, then drove back to the target's house and pulled into the driveway there. He parked close to the garage door and in the middle of the driveway so that a car inside could not get past his own.

He stepped out of the Cadillac, walked up to the front door, and rang the doorbell. A moment later the door opened, and Jim Dickinson smiled out at him.

"Can I help you?"

"Actually, you can," Noah said, and then he reached out and took Dickinson by his throat, closing his hand tightly as the fellow tried to jump backward. Noah followed, kicking the door shut behind himself, and shoved Dickinson into a chair.

Dickinson sat there in shock, staring up at the big blond man who had seemingly attacked him for no reason. "What the..."

"Mr. Dickinson," Noah said, "I represent someone who is seeking to do business with your wife. Apparently, she has been resistant to the idea, and it's my job to remove that resistance." He held out his phone, showing the pictures he had just taken of the Dickinson children. "My employer wants your wife to understand that refusing to do business with him could be detrimental to the health and well-being of your family. Now, I'm sure you wouldn't want anything bad to happen to your children, would you?"

Dickinson managed to close his mouth, then swallowed hard. "No, no," he said quietly. "But I..."

"Frankly," Noah went on, "I don't want anything bad to happen to them, either. That's why I decided to have this private little chat with you. You need to make it clear to your wife that she needs to cooperate with my employer. You need to make it clear to her that if she does not, something very bad will almost certainly happen to one of those lovely children you just sent off to school. In order to make sure she gets the message, I've got to leave you with something that will be convincing."

Noah called up the second photo from the text message on his phone and held it in front of Dickinson's face. The man stared at it for several seconds, his eyes wide, and then he looked up at Noah again.

"I—that isn't..."

"I don't care who it is, and I don't care to hear whatever ridiculous explanation you're trying to come up with. None of that matters to me, but I showed you that photograph so that you would know that my employer can find out anything he wants to know. I need you to understand that if he can arrange to capture a photo of you in such a compromising position, then he can undoubtedly track you down no matter where you might try to go. This is to convince you that running away is not an option. Do you understand that?"

Dickinson nodded, not trusting his voice to speak.

"Now the point of this little exercise," Noah went on, "is to give you proper motivation. However, I also need to give some to your wife. Since we both agree we don't want anything bad to happen to your children, that means something bad has to happen to you."

With the speed of a striking snake, Noah reached down and took hold of Dickinson's right ear and then yanked back so hard that the ear was torn half off the man's head. Dickinson screamed and clapped his own hand over the injured ear, but his eyes never left Noah's face.

"Be absolutely certain you tell your wife exactly how you came to be injured, and then explain to her that this is nothing compared to what will happen to one of your children if she does not cooperate. And don't bother trying to notify the police or give them my description, because it probably won't be me the next time. It will be someone you've never seen, someone you'll never expect. Someone you won't see coming." He cocked his head and looked Dickinson in the eye. "I'm going to leave now," he said. "Do not move from that chair until you're certain I'm gone. If I see your face at the window or the door, I will put a bullet through your head."

Noah continue to face Dickinson as he moved toward the front door, then quickly turned and walked out. He got into his rented Cadillac and backed out of the driveway, then drove away at a sedate speed. There had been no sign of Dickinson's face at any of the windows he could see, so he didn't anticipate any immediate repercussions.

Noah drove toward his hotel and then stopped at a small cafe for breakfast. He sat at the counter because there was a television above it that was tuned to the local news channel. He ordered steak and eggs and was pleased to see that there was no mention of an attack on a local citizen when he finished eating a half hour later.

He drove back to the hotel and went up to his room, repacked his bag, and then googled for a charter flight back to Kansas City. He got lucky this time, because the first number he called had a plane and pilot that could be ready to go within an hour. He went down to the front desk and checked out, then drove back to the airport and turned in the car. He asked the clerk at the rental agency where he should go to catch a charter flight, and the young lady was happy to give him directions.

This time, the plane was a twin-engine turboprop model. The pilot was sitting in a lounge area just inside the building from the charter gate, and Noah had no trouble finding him.

"Are you Wilson? I'm John Babbitt, your pilot. Want me to take that bag for you?"

"I've got it, thanks," Noah said.

"No problem," Babbitt said. "Let's get going."

Noah followed him out to the plane and accepted the invitation to sit up front. He always enjoyed flying and had even taken the controls a few times when he was younger, flying with his grandfather before his grandparents decided he was just a little too strange. That experience had come in handy a few months earlier, when he had actually had to steal a plane and fly it out of China after rescuing Sarah.

Babbitt liked to talk, and Noah put on an act for the man, laughing at his jokes and pretending to believe some of the whopper stories the fellow told. He even managed to tell a few of his own, but Babbitt would have been shocked if he had known that Noah was telling the truth.

Talking made the flight seem shorter than it actually was, and the plane touched down at the Kansas City airport at just before noon. Noah thanked Babbitt for the ride and made his way out to the parking lot.

The Charger was sitting where he had left it, although there were a couple of men standing close by and staring at it. When Noah unlocked the door and opened it, one of them hurried over.

"Man," the fellow said, "that's got to be the most beautiful car I've ever seen. Is she fast?"

"You wouldn't believe me if I told you," Noah said, and then he slid in behind the wheel and shut the door. When he pushed the ignition button, the man standing just outside broke into a huge smile and waved as Noah backed out and drove toward the gate.

He paid for his parking and left the airport, getting back onto I-70 and driving on toward Kansas City proper. The airport sat about forty miles west of the city itself, but traffic was light and so it didn't seem to take very long until he had crossed into Missouri. His GPS directed him to turn south onto I-49 a few minutes later, and he was almost out of the city before he decided to stop for lunch.

He pulled into a McDonald's and ate quickly, then got back on the road. The GPS told him that he was only three hours away from his destination, and the road was clear. With his Wyatt Wilson ID tucked into a hidden compartment of his bag and the Rex Madison documents back in his wallet, Noah decided that being in character would mean breaking the speed limit. He pushed the car up to eighty-five and waved back at all the kids who smiled from the back seats of their parents' cars as he flew past.

Three hours later, Noah parked the car in the parking lot of the federal courthouse in Fayetteville, Arkansas. He had to walk all the way around the building to get to the front door, where a pair of federal marshals required him to show his ID, then empty his pockets and put his shoes and belt into a tray that rolled through an X-ray machine. Once that was done, he stepped through a metal detector and then was allowed to collect his things and put his shoes and belt back on.

The marshals directed him to the probation office on the third floor, and he rode the elevator up. When he stepped out, signs directed him to room 319, and the receptionist there asked him his name. Noah handed over the documents he had been given for this purpose, along with his driver's license.

"Oh, yes," the receptionist said, "Mr. Madison. Mr. Roberts is expecting you. Just have a seat for a moment, and he'll be right out."

Noah sat down in one of the chairs in front of her counter and waited only a moment before Craig Roberts stepped out and walked up to him. Noah rose to his feet as Roberts extended a hand.

"Rex Madison? I'm Craig Roberts, I'll be your new probation officer. I got all your paperwork a couple days ago, but I wasn't actually expecting you until tomorrow."

"Well," Noah said, with a bit of surliness in his voice, "I figured I might as well come on over and get this out of the way. My daddy always told me to take care of the unpleasant business first, because it makes everything else seem to go even smoother."

Roberts grinned. "Yeah, I heard you had a bit of an attitude. Come on back to my office, and let's see how much trouble you're going to try to give me."

He turned and walked past the receptionist's counter, and Noah followed him into an office. Roberts shut the door and sat down behind his desk, pointing to a chair in front of it. Noah took the seat he indicated and slouched in it as if he'd prefer to be absolutely anywhere else.

"Let's just cut to the chase, shall we? I understand you're going to be living in Berryville?"

"Yep. My sister lives there, so I'll be staying with her until I find a place."

"Yeah, that's what I got. She lives on Pleasant Street, right?"

"Right. 111 Pleasant Street," Noah said. "Katie Madison is her name, in case you don't have it already."

Roberts grinned at him again. "I've got it. I understand you're coming here to look for work? What kind of work do you do?"

Noah shrugged. "Whatever I need to do," he said. "Katie says there's lots of opportunities over there."

Craig Roberts look him in the eye for a moment, his grin never leaving his face. "There's a lot of opportunities, all right," he said. "The question is what kind of opportunities you're looking for. Berryville is pretty much the center of a lot of the criminal element in this part of Arkansas. You're not looking to get hooked up with anything like that, are you?"

Noah put on an exaggerated expression of innocence. "Who, me? Hell, no, I don't need none of that. I'll probably look for something slinging burgers, maybe washing cars. Ain't no way I'm going to give you a chance to send me back to Beaumont."

"Uh-huh," Roberts said. "Well, here's the deal. I'll be coming over to see you about once a month, and when I do, you're gonna have to pee in a cup for me. As long as you manage to stay out of trouble, you and I are going to get along just fine. Understood?"

"Understood, Captain," Noah said. "Believe me, I don't want any more trouble than you do."

Roberts reached down beside his desk and picked up a urine sample cup and held it out. "Bathroom is around the corner," he said. "Try to get it at least half-full, will you?"

Noah took the cup and got up from the chair, stepped out of the office, and found the bathroom. A few moments later he returned and set the cup on Roberts's desk. It was nearly full.

Roberts glanced at it and then grinned up at Noah. "Okay," he said. "You checked in. That's all till next month. If you move out of your sister's place or change your phone number or get a job, call and let me know. Other than that, you won't have to put up with me at all until I come to see you."

Noah nodded. "That sounds fine to me," he said. He turned without another word and walked out of the office, made his way down the elevator and out the front door, and then around the building to where he had left the Charger. He got back in, started the car, and followed the GPS directions to Highway 45.

The Arkansas countryside rolled past, and Noah thought that the colors of the leaves seemed a little brighter than they did back in Colorado. Highway 45 led him to Highway 412, and he cruised along at just a little over the speed limit until the GPS told him to turn north. He followed its directions for another half hour and suddenly found himself in the tourist town of Eureka Springs.

A right turn put him on Highway 62, and he followed the winding curves through the quaint little town that seemed to be trying to imitate something from the Swiss Alps. There were hotels, motels, and restaurants all along the road, along with dozens of obvious tourist traps, and he found himself feeling slightly relieved when he finally left the town behind him.

The road to Berryville was still pretty curvy, but at least it was open road. He noticed a couple of bed-and-breakfast places along the way, a motel that was specifically designed for bikers, and several antique and junk shops. One spot on the left had about two dozen antique cars in various states of decay, while another seemed to be nothing but a pile of salvaged building materials. Despite himself, Noah found himself thinking about coming to check those places out when he got a chance.

Suddenly the road widened and seemed to level out quite a bit, and he spotted the first sign indicating that he was coming into Berryville. He had put in Kate Madison's address, so the GPS directed him all the way through town. He passed the big Walmart on the right, followed the turns that led to the town square, and then went another mile before he had to turn right to get to Pleasant Street.

He pulled up in front of Kate's house, a little brick house on a dead-end street full of other brick houses. He stopped the car at the curb and shut it off, then stepped out and stretched.

"Rex?" A woman's voice came from the side of the house, and he turned to get his first look at his "sister."

Kate Madison was about five foot six and, as Sarah had said, rather chubby. She was wearing jeans and a flannel shirt and stood with her hands on her hips as she stared at him. Like Noah, her hair was blonde, but while his was short and neat, hers looked like she'd gotten it caught in a blender.

"Hey, sis," Noah said. "You put on a little weight since I saw you last."

Kate sneered at him. "Not that much," she said. "Well, don't just stand there. Get your stuff and come on in." She turned and walked across the front of the house to the front door and went inside without bothering to see if he was following.

Noah leaned back into the car and grabbed his bag, then shut the door and locked the car up. He walked across the yard to the door and pushed it open without knocking. He stepped inside and glanced around as he closed the door behind him.

Kate was standing in the middle of the room, but now she was wearing a smile. "You didn't have to make the wisecrack about my weight, you know," she said. "It was definitely in character, though." She looked him up and down. "Damn," she said, "you really do look a lot like Rex. Sometimes I almost forget about him, but as much as he was a pain in my ass, I always loved the little jerk."

Noah shot her a grin. "I figured if I'm supposed to be your annoying kid brother," he said, "I should let any nosy neighbors catch on to that fact pretty quickly."

Kate walked over and extended a hand. "Well, it's good to finally meet you. I've been briefed, so I know what you're really doing here, and while it seems a little extreme—well, I guess I can understand why the big guys think it's necessary. I've been here going on three years, now, and nobody has been able to touch these people in all that time. Everyone who tries dies, so I can understand why they sent you in."

Noah nodded. "Well, they seem to think I'll be here quite a while. Any idea where I should start?"

CHAPTER SIXTEEN

Kate grinned and motioned for him to follow her, leading him into a small bedroom. There was a single bed in the room, along with a dresser and a small desk. "Start by settling yourself in here. This will be your room while you're with me, but I understand that won't be very long. According to my briefing, you've got a wife coming soon?"

"Yep," Noah said. "Her name is Angie, and she's bringing her little brother with her, too. He's a tall, skinny computer nerd."

Kate looked at him sideways. "And are they—are they like you?"

"Not exactly," Noah said. "Angie really is my wife, and Neil is part of my team. He's my intelligence specialist—that boy can do things with a computer that would amaze anybody."

Kate nodded. "Okay, I just wondered. From here on out, we won't ever discuss your mission unless you need to tell me something or ask any questions. It's safe enough at the moment—I just scanned for bugs this morning—but we need to avoid any risks we can. Go ahead and unpack your stuff, while I put on some coffee. You do drink coffee, right?"

"Yes, and that would be welcome." Noah dropped his bag on the bed and opened it, then started putting his clothes into the dresser. Everything he brought with him fit into the top drawer, and he set the empty bag on the floor beside the desk.

Kate was still standing in the doorway. "Well, that didn't take long. Come on out to the kitchen."

Noah followed her and sat down at the kitchen table while she busied herself with the coffee maker. "Nice little house," he said. "What's it like around here?"

"This is a pretty decent neighborhood," Kate replied. "I guess the whole town is actually kind of nice, and you don't really hear about a lot of what goes on behind the scenes. Morgan, as bad as he is, tends to keep the riffraff out of the area. I mean, don't get me wrong, every town around here has its share of tweakers and drunks, but most of them are more afraid of Morgan than they are of the cops. Unless you get on his bad side, you can leave your door standing wide open while you're gone for a week on vacation, and when you get back, everything will be just the way you left it. Morgan can't stand thieves, unless they work for him. The last guy who broke into somebody's house in Berryville was found beaten half to death out by the fairgrounds. That was a year and a half ago."

"Well, I definitely hope to get on his good side. Any idea how I can do that?"

"A couple," she said. "He hangs out most evenings at a bar over in Eureka, a place called the Barn. It's a pretty decent club, live music and all that, so you should check it out. If you can get close enough to talk to him, make sure he gets a look at that car of yours. He loves cars, and he's got quite a few of his own. I'm pretty sure that one will get his attention in a hurry, and if it's as fast as it looks, he's gonna want you for a buddy."

"Okay, that's one. You said a couple ideas. What else?"

The coffeepot was half-full, so Kate poured them each a cup and then let it finish filling. She set one in front of Noah and sat down across from him. "Well, if you're as tough as you look, then you need to kick some ass. Hang out around him and wait for somebody to start trouble. If you can put a stop to it in a hurry, he's going to start thinking you might be an asset. With your cover story, fresh out of prison and all that, you're probably exactly the kind of man he's looking for."

Noah nodded. "I can handle most people," he said. "Does trouble break out around him often?"

"Hah!" She laughed. "Jimmy Morgan is the kind of guy who likes to keep all the other alpha males close, where he can watch them. He's big enough and tough enough to handle just about anybody, but every now and then there will be some rutting young buck with a few stupid buddies who decide they can make a move on him. When that happens, Jimmy's boys all jump into the fray. He likes to sit back and watch the fight, and anybody who stands out by kicking a lot of ass suddenly finds himself being Morgan's fair-haired boy for a while."

"So, if I can put on a good show in a fight, that could get me in with him?"

"Not just could, it would. Like I said, he likes to keep the toughest guys close. If you can kick the snot out of a few others, he's going to want you right where he can watch you closely. That'll give you the chance to convince him you might be executive material in his organization, and I'm guessing that's part of your plan. Am I right?"

"Pretty close," Noah said. "I don't want to be his right-hand man, but I want to be somewhere close to that. I need to be able to move around inside his mob, get to know who all of the big players are. I'm supposed to take as many of them out as I can, but I have to do it all at once. I can't leave enough standing that they can regroup and keep it together."

Kate was sitting there looking at him, and suddenly she shivered. "My God, you say that so nonchalantly. I can't imagine what it must be like to do what you do."

Noah said nothing, and she finally looked away.

"So," she said, "how do you want to proceed? Do you want me to try to introduce you to any of the locals, or just go out and meet them on your own?"

"We're not supposed to be close, remember? I think we should maintain that act, keep a little hostility going between us until Angie gets here. The plan is for the two of you to become friends, and that's supposed to loosen things up between you and me. Until then, we need to keep up appearances, so I don't think you would be too eager to introduce your black-sheep brother to too many people."

Kate shrugged, but she was grinning. "Makes sense, I guess. Still, we should probably let ourselves be seen together around town a bit. I'll just make sure to be grumpy with you when you take me out to dinner, okay?"

"That'll work. And speaking of that, since your brother just arrived, going out for dinner tonight would probably be in order. Any decent restaurants around here?"

"Not many, at least not here in Berryville. A lot of fast food, a Chinese place, and several Mexican joints. I've gotten pretty tired of tacos, to be honest. If you want anything decent, we need to either go to Eureka Springs or down to Harrison. Harrison is Boone County, and it's not really part of Morgan's territory. The sheriff there has played it smart and managed to keep most of Morgan's people out."

"Really? How did he manage that?"

Kate laughed for a moment, then got herself under control. "Nobody really knows for sure," she said, "but the suspicion is that he uses some of Morgan's own tactics against him. Jimmy tried several years ago to move into Boone, sent some people down there to muscle in. Funny thing, though, several of them never came back. A few were found floating in the river, a couple others turned up as piles of burnt bones. There is no proof the sheriff had anything to do with it, but it's no secret that he and the local militia get along really, really well, if you get my drift."

"You have militia groups around here?" Noah asked.

"Hey, this is the Ozarks," Kate said. "This is the land of rednecks, and Harrison is just about the capital of the Ku Klux Klan nowadays. There are probably a half-dozen different militia groups within thirty miles of us right now. Most of them just sit around and complain about the government, don't really do anything, but there are a lot of rumors about the two in Boone County. They seem to be pretty adamant about keeping the drug dealers and any kind of organized crime out, no matter what it takes."

Noah nodded. "Sounds like the sheriff over there is smarter than the average bear. A properly managed militia group could probably do a lot to keep an area free from crime, provided the local law enforcement doesn't try to lock them up for doing it."

Kate winked. "And there you have the theory behind Boone County." She took a sip from her coffee and gave a deep sigh. "Good thing you drink coffee," she said after a moment, "or nobody would believe you're my brother."

Noah picked up his cup and guzzled it, then got up and poured another. "Tell me about yourself," he said as he sat back down. "Who is Kate Madison, here in Berryville?"

"Well, when I first came here I went to work at the chicken plant, like just about everybody else. If you're working undercover, the chicken plant is a good place to get to know a lot of people in a hurry. My cover is that I came here to get over a bad breakup, so if you hear me mention my ex-husband, just shake your head and pretend you're sick of hearing about it. I told everybody that he used to beat me, so I finally got up the nerve to file for divorce and get away from him. Took back my maiden name and moved halfway across the country, and now I'm happily single and determined to stay that way." She sighed again. "It's about half-true. I really did have an abusive ex-husband, but I wouldn't mind being married again someday, if I can find a decent guy. There are even a few of them around here, but I can't risk getting involved with anyone, not anything serious. Sooner or later, they'd have to know what I'm really doing here, and I don't trust anybody that far." She looked up at Noah and shrugged. "So I deal with the occasional hookup and pretend that's all I want. Maybe after you get done, I can finally get out of this place and stop living a lie."

"So, where do you work now?" Noah asked.

"Oh, sorry, got sidetracked. I'm actually a radio personality. I'm the morning show on the local radio station. I do the news and weather, and run the Swap Shop program, where people call in and talk about stuff they want to sell or want to buy. I play some music now and then and pretend to be a DJ, but mostly I'm just the welcome voice of Berryville. I go in early, about 4:30 in the morning, and I'm usually home by one. It lets me stay on top of what's happening around the area, and I've got half my day free for doing other things." She winked at him again. "The radio station is online, now, so I even have a code I use to report some of the things I hear. Somebody back at Quantico has to listen to me every morning, just to see if I slip in something the home office needs to know about. Isn't that cool?"

"It's brilliant," Noah said. "Your idea?"

"Sure was—I even made up the code we use. If there's a murder that's definitely attributable to Morgan and his people, for instance, I say my feet are killing me. Then I subject my listeners to my own terrible poetry for a minute or two, and the first letter of each line spells out the name of the victim, or gives some other tidbit of information about it. I've got a code for just about everything Morgan does, and nobody's twigged to it yet."

"Obviously," Noah said. "You're still alive. If Morgan ever figures it out, you won't be."

Kate grinned and saluted him with her coffee cup. "Which is why I really hope you manage to pull off your mission. Something tells me I'll live longer if you do."

"I understand Morgan has hooks into the local phone company, manages to monitor phone calls when he wants to. Is that true?"

"Oh, yeah," Kate replied. "You absolutely do not want to discuss anything about your mission on the phone, not with anybody. In fact, if you need to get hold of me by phone to tell me to meet you somewhere, just call me up and say something about aches and pains. If you say your back is hurting, for instance, that'll mean we need to

meet at my place. If it's your feet, that means I should drop by wherever you're living at the time. We'll come up with more ideas like that
as time goes by."

"Good idea. And if I call you up and say I've got a migraine, that
will mean get your ass out of town as fast as you can because I'm
about to light things up. Okay?"

Kate's eyebrows were trying to call over the top of her head. "Boy,
I can't wait for that call. Be a shame to miss out on the fireworks,
though."

"I'd rather you miss out on the fireworks than get caught in the
crossfire. Anybody who can stay in deep cover for three years is an
agent we don't want to lose. If I get a migraine, you get out of town,
deal?"

"Okay, okay, no problem. Should I grab your wife on my way?"

"She wouldn't go. Besides, she's also part of my team. When the
balloon goes out, she'll probably be right in the middle of it with me."

Kate nodded her understanding. "You know what I'd give to have
a team? I've been out here all alone all this time. Kinda nice to have
someone I can actually talk to. Even if it is my annoying kid brother."
She chuckled.

Noah glanced at his phone and checked the time. "Speaking of
your annoying kid brother," Noah said, "it's almost six o'clock. Ready
to go get some dinner?"

"Sure," Kate said. "Just let me go change into something more
presentable, first."

She got up and left the kitchen, and Noah called Sarah. Just like
the night before, she answered on the very first ring.

"Rex? Baby, is that you?" Sarah asked, already in character.

"Hey, Angie," Noah said. "Just wanted let you know I made it to
Berryville. Me and sis have been catching up for the last hour or so,
and we're about to go grab a bite to eat. Just wanted to hear your
voice. Everything okay back there?"

"Hell, no, it's not okay. I miss you, baby, and the geek is driving me crazy. You know how he gets, sometimes. Can't get him off the computer long enough for a decent conversation, and it gets boring just sitting around talking to myself."

Noah chuckled. "Well, just hang in there. I'll start looking for a house tomorrow morning. I looked on the newspaper website and there are quite a few available for rent, even more for sale. I might just buy one, not have to deal with all the landlord problems."

"Mmm, house of our own? Baby, that would be great. Think we could find one out in the country somewhere? I'd love to put in a garden next spring."

"I'll bear that in mind, honey. Maybe I can find something. After my time in Beaumont, I don't really like the idea of having neighbors all up in my business, anyway."

"Neil says hi," Sarah said. "At least, I think that's what he said. He's talking with food in his mouth again."

"He's always shoving food in his mouth. Tell him hi for me, and tell him I said to get off the computer and spend some time with his sister."

"I will. I miss you, babe. I love you, love you."

"I love you, love you more," Noah said, putting a smile into his voice. "Katie's just about ready to go, so I'll call you back tonight before I go to bed. Love you, sweetheart."

"Love you more," Sarah said. "Ha, I got you that time."

"Yeah, you win that one. I'll talk to you later, honey."

"Okay, bye-bye, baby."

Noah ended the call and slipped the phone into his pocket. A moment later, Kate came out of her bedroom. She had changed into a skirt and blouse and had even put on some makeup.

They walked out the front door, and Noah used the remote to unlock his car, then walked around and opened the driver's door. Kate glared at him for a moment, then opened the passenger door for herself and climbed in. "Haven't you ever heard about being a gentleman?" she grumbled as she got in. "You could've at least opened the door for me."

"You're a big girl, you can open your own door," Noah shot back. Kate was stifling a laugh as he started the car. He used her driveway to turn around and then headed back toward Eureka Springs.

Kate pointed out different buildings as they rolled through town. Noah saw the ancient hotel that still stood on the square, and a few of the buildings that had actually survived the Civil War. Berryville had the distinction of being the only town to be sacked and burned by both the Union and the Confederacy during that conflict. It had actually been occupied by Quantrill's Raiders at one point, and several local citizens had been murdered during the occupation.

She had him take a slight detour and showed him the big chicken plant. A large segment of the population worked there, she said, along with quite a large number of illegal aliens from Mexico and South America. ICE raided the place about once a year, rounding up the illegals and deporting them, and then prosecuting someone in the personnel office for hiring them in the first place. That person always got probation and then got a fat severance check from the company. A few months later, they would be working at a different branch of the company, and most of the illegals would be right back at the same jobs they had been taken from.

"There was an incident once that was pretty funny," Kate said. "A whole group of Mexicans, probably ten or twelve of them, got their paychecks and went to Walmart to cash them. Well, it turned out only one of them had any ID, and that said his name was James Baker. None of them spoke any English, so the cashier called one of her associates who could speak Spanish, and he told her to accept that one ID to cash all of their paychecks, which is obviously illegal. She was going to do it, but then some guy standing in line said that if she did, he would post the whole story on the internet the next morning.

Well, the guy who interpreted started to say something back to this other guy, but then all the Mexicans took off running out the door because right behind the guy who was threatening to put it on the internet was a crowd of about thirty local rednecks, all of them dressed in camo. I guess they thought it was about to be open season on illegal aliens, and the looks on their faces made the whole bunch decide they wanted to cash their paychecks somewhere else."

Noah nodded. "I can see how that might be funny," he said. "Did anything come of it?"

"No, of course not. It just kind of illustrates how these companies don't even bother to check whether the people they hire even have identification."

Kate directed him to a restaurant called Grandma's in Eureka Springs, and Noah parked the car as close to the building as he could. They got out, and he followed Kate inside.

"Hey, Kate," several different people called out. "New boyfriend?" one woman asked.

"Bite your tongue, Marge," Kate said. "This is my brother, Rex. He's staying with me for a while to look for work, so I made him buy me dinner. Don't let his good looks fool you—he's an ass."

CHAPTER SEVENTEEN

"**G**ee, thanks, sis," Noah said, sarcastically. He followed her to a table off to one side, and they sat down. A waitress approached immediately and set glasses of water in front of them. Kate picked up a menu that was tucked in behind the napkin dispenser and began looking it over. Noah picked up a second one and glanced through the options, then put it back. "I'll have the porterhouse," he said. "Medium rare, with corn and mashed potatoes on the side."

The waitress scribbled his order on her pad. "Gravy on the taters?"

"Yeah," Noah said. "And give me a Coke with that, okay?"

The waitress nodded and then took Kate's order before she hurried back toward the kitchen. Kate leaned back in her chair and crossed her arms over her chest.

"So, anyway," she said as if continuing the conversation, "your best shot would be the chicken plant. They're always hiring, and the pay isn't too bad. At least you could say you were doing honest work for once in your life."

Noah looked around the restaurant and noticed that several of the patrons seemed to be trying to listen. "Oh, I don't know," he said. "Maybe I'll come work at a restaurant over here. I've always been a pretty good cook; I'm sure I could get a job slinging hash in one of these joints."

"You? A cook? Rex, come on. You never even learned how to make macaroni and cheese, and that came in a box with directions. Somehow I don't think you'd work out very well in a kitchen around here."

"Are you always going to be such a bitch?" Noah asked her.

"As long as you're a jerk," she replied, "I'm gonna be a bitch. Deal with it."

"Wow," said a woman a few tables over. "Can you feel the love?"

"Oh, I love him," Kate said. "I just don't like him."

The two of them continued their act through dinner, and Kate actually did introduce Noah to several people. As a local celebrity, she was quite well-known around the entire area, and it seemed almost everyone in the restaurant knew her. Noah met a doctor, a police officer, and several women, all of whom glanced at his left hand and then got sour faces.

"Why are the good ones always taken?" lamented one woman who was probably old enough to be his mother.

"I don't know," Kate said, "but this isn't one of them. Rex, this is Judy Henson. She owns that little clothing store on the square in Berryville."

Noah smiled up at the woman standing beside the table. "Nice to meet you," he said. "I'll have to come check out your store."

"Not unless you're into cross-dressing, now," Kate said. "It's a dress shop. Your wife might like it, though."

"Isn't she with you?" Judy asked.

"No, ma'am," Noah said. "I came on ahead to find a house, but she'll be here in a week or so."

Judy's eyes lit up. "You're looking for a house? Are you looking to rent or buy?"

"Well, that depends on what I find. Do you know of something?"

"Oh, yes," the woman said. "My husband is a real estate broker." She fished in her purse and came out with a business card. Noah accepted it and glanced at it quickly.

"Henson Realty," he read aloud. "Thanks, I'll give him a call tomorrow."

There were several more introductions, and they spent almost an hour in the restaurant. When they finally finished eating, Noah made a point of saying goodbye to each of the people he had met who were still there, and then he and Kate got back into the car and headed back to her house.

"Watch out for Judy," Kate said. "She may be married, but that won't stop her from trying to get you alone. If you decide to go look at a house they got listed, make sure her husband, Bob, is there. Judy has something of a reputation around here. They call her the Cougar, because she likes her boyfriends young."

"Well, she'd find me to be a disappointment. One thing I'll never do is cheat on my wife."

Kate looked at him. "Well, you were doing good until now. It's a good thing nobody around here ever knew my brother, because he was never known for being faithful to anyone."

They got back to the house a few minutes later, and Kate announced that she was tired and going to bed. She had to get up early for her job, of course, and wanted to get plenty of sleep. She said good night to Noah and went into her bedroom, closing the door behind her.

Noah wasn't terribly tired, but he decided to retire anyway. He went into his bedroom and shut the door, kicked off his shoes, and stretched out on the bed, then took out his phone and called Sarah. This time, the two of them stayed on the phone for almost half an hour, and Noah made a point of telling her again that he loved her before they finally hung up. He plugged his phone in and set it on the dresser beside the bed, then stripped down to his underwear and got under the covers.

Noah awoke when the sun came through the window and went into the bathroom to get a shower. Kate was gone, he knew, but he wanted to start looking for somewhere to live immediately. He took care of the morning necessities, then got dressed and headed out the door.

Kate hadn't given him a key, but he remembered what she said about people leaving their doors open, so he didn't bother to lock it behind him. He got into his car and drove out to the other end of town, stopping at McDonald's to get something to curb the hunger. He ordered their scrambled egg breakfast and sat down to eat.

When he finished, he took out the business card Judy had given him the night before and dialed the number. It was just after eight o'clock, but Bob Henson answered the phone on the second ring.

"Henson Realty," he said. "How may I help you today?"

"Mr. Henson, my name is Rex Madison," Noah said. "I ran into your wife while I was out with my sister for dinner last night, and she gave me your card. I wondered if you might have some time this morning to talk with me."

"Certainly, certainly," Bob said. "Would you care to come by my office?"

"Yes, that will be fine. How do I get there? I'm in McDonald's, right now."

"Oh, that's easy, then. When you come out of the drive, turn right and then take the first left turn. Follow that road about a mile, and you'll come to a little industrial area. My office is actually right beside the entrance. A little bungalow-shaped building made of natural stone. You can't miss it."

Noah smiled into the phone. "Great," he said. "I'll be there in just a few minutes."

Five minutes later, Noah was sitting at a small conference table with Bob Henson. His desk held a very nice computer with multiple monitors, and Bob began asking Noah a series of questions designed to help him choose some properties to present, but Noah decided to just cut to the chase.

"Bob, let me ask you this. I'd like to find something out in the country, something not terribly expensive but decent. A little acreage, maybe, no close neighbors. I like my privacy. Got anything like that?"

The look on Bob's face told Noah that the man was hungry, but also that he genuinely cared about taking care of his customers. He turned to the computer on his desk and started tapping the keys. A second, larger monitor facing Noah showed a number of different properties.

"See anything you like, there?" Bob asked. "Those are just a few of the places we've got listings on right now that might fill the bill, all within just a few miles of town."

Noah asked a few questions about a couple of the properties he saw, but then Bob's face suddenly lit up. "You know what?" he said excitedly. "Rex, I think I might have just the thing." He tapped on the keys again for a moment, and another farmhouse appeared on the screen in front of Noah. "This is the old Howerton farm. It was occupied by one of the oldest families in the county until just a couple of years ago, when Charles Howerton passed away. His children had all moved away, so they put the place on the market. Five bedrooms, three bathrooms, a recently remodeled kitchen, a big living room, and a family room, and both the front and rear porches are enclosed. It sits on fifteen acres, and there are several outbuildings. The house has a two-car garage attached to it, but there's also a barn, a workshop building, and a couple of pretty good-sized sheds. Central heat and air, one of the best wells in the whole county, and it just so happens that the owners put in a new septic tank just six months ago. That won't give you any trouble for at least ten years, maybe even twenty."

Noah looked at the image and nodded. "It looks and sounds good," he said. "Definitely a nice-looking place, and the outbuildings sound good. But I bet it's expensive."

"Actually, it's not. As I said, it's been sitting empty for a little over two years, and the family really wants to get it sold. They've been good about keeping it maintained, but they've reduced the price six different times. They got it listed right now for only $98,000, but I happen to know they would accept any offer over seventy-five." He

gave Noah a conspiratorial wink, then lowered his voice as if someone else might overhear. "Between you and me, they actually put
more money than that into the house after the old man died. He lived
there almost his entire life without any kind of air-conditioning, and
the only heat he ever had was a wood-burning stove."

Noah leaned in and looked again at the image, and Bob reached
over to start a slideshow. Noah saw several pictures of the exterior of
the house, and then the inside came into view. From what he could
see in the photos, the house did seem to be in very good condition.

"Well, that's within my budget," he said. "When can we go see
it?"

"We can go right now," Bob said. "Would that work?"

"Sure," Noah said. "Your car or mine?"

Bob suddenly broke out in a big smile. "Listen, buddy, I saw that
beautiful thing you drove up in. If you think I'd turn down a chance
for a ride in that car, you've got another thing coming."

Noah smiled back, and the two of them left the office. Bob
locked up and hung a sign on the door saying he'd be back in a couple
of hours, and they got into the Charger.

Bob was like a kid in a candy store, looking at everything inside
the car. "Holy cow," he said. "I know these old Chargers are worth
some money. Can I ask how much this one set you back?"

"About a quarter mil," Noah said. "I was lucky enough to make
some good investments a while back, and they paid off recently. Of
course, then I was unlucky enough to run across the guy who wanted
to sell this thing. Well, you know how it is, I saw this car and had
enough money, so it didn't take him long to talk me into buying it."
He looked over at Bob and winked. "But between you and me, it was
worth every penny. There might be a lot of '69 Chargers out there,
but there's only one like this baby. And I've got it."

Bob told Noah to go south on Industrial Park Road and then
take a left onto Highway 221. The Howerton farm was about eight

miles out on a county road, but it was one that had been paved only a year earlier.

"That's one of the reasons I thought it might be the right house for you," Bob said. "I can't imagine you'd want to take this car down any gravel roads."

"You're right about that," Noah said. "And thanks for thinking of it."

They followed 221 for a couple of miles, and then Bob told Noah to turn right. The old county road was definitely in good shape, and there was a nice long stretch of straight road that allowed Noah to give Bob a thrill by opening the engine up and letting it roar. Bob was laughing like a little kid when the speedometer hit one twenty, but then Noah had to just about stand on the brakes to slow it down enough for the curve at the end of the straightaway. Noah laughed right along with him, keeping up his act.

"Okay," Bob said, "it's the next driveway on the left. There it is, see it?"

"I see it," Noah said. He slowed the car down and turned into the driveway, surprised to see that it was also paved. He pulled the car up close to the long, ranch-style house and shut it down, and then he and Bob got out and walked up to the front steps.

Bob unlocked the front door and held it open while Noah stepped onto the porch. Bob had told him that it was enclosed, but it was very nicely done. All three of the outer walls were made of glass, but every section had a window that could open to let air through, and every window had a screen to keep out the insects. Noah admired it for a moment while Bob opened the main door into the house proper, and then followed him in.

It wasn't nearly as luxurious as Noah's house back in Colorado, but it was very nice. The floors were all hardwood and in good condition, the walls were straight and clean, and the ceilings were covered in antique-style metal tiles. There were rugs in each of the bedrooms, which Bob said would be nice during the winter, and the kitchen was very well-appointed and immaculate, with cabinets that appeared to have been custom-built from good hardwoods. The countertops were of composite stone, and all of the appliances—range, refrigerator, dishwasher, and even a microwave—were obviously brand-new. The same was true of the washer and dryer in the utility room, just off the kitchen.

What surprised Noah more than anything was that the house contained a lot of furniture, and most of it would probably have been considered antique. There were beds in all of the bedrooms, while the living room had two large sofas and a couple of chairs. There was an obviously ancient trestle table in the kitchen, and it was surrounded by some of the nicest oak dining chairs Noah had ever seen. While he was no expert on antique furniture, he would have been willing to bet that all of the furniture combined was probably worth a third of the asking price of the house.

Bob was beaming from ear to ear as he watched Noah look over every feature of the house. When they went out the back door and began looking through the other buildings, he seemed to get even more excited. That excitement built until they got to the big barn, and then he handed Noah a key to the big padlock that secured the doors and stood by while he opened it.

"A tractor?" Noah asked.

"Yep. It's an old Ford 9N, but it's in excellent shape. It's got a bush hog mower, and a rear-mount tiller with it, in case you want to do any gardening. Old man Howerton loved that old tractor; I heard he had it rebuilt three different times. The last time was just a few months before he died. The family hired a handyman to make sure the place stayed in good shape, and he uses that tractor to mow the whole place, so I know it'll start up and go anytime you want it to."

Noah looked around the barn for a moment and spotted even more antiques. There were several examples of old farm equipment, and he spied a lot of boxes up in the loft. He walked back out into the sunlight and looked at the house once more, then turned to face Bob.

"They'd take $80,000?" Noah asked.

"I guarantee it," Bob said. "Like I said, they really want to get it sold. Just paying the handyman to keep it up is quite an expense since no one is living here."

Noah looked at the house again as if he were thinking it over, but he had already made his decision. "How soon do you think I could move in?"

"Well, if we write up an offer today, I can fax it off to them and we'll probably get acceptance by tomorrow morning. It'll take a couple of days at least to get all the paperwork done, but I don't think they would object to you moving in once everything is signed. You won't have any trouble getting financing, will you?"

Noah looked at him. "How would you feel about cash?"

Bob's eyes got wide and lit up even brighter than before. "Oh, that would be fine," he said. "We can get everything together while your check clears and..."

Noah grinned at him. "No, I mean cash. Greenbacks, hundred-dollar bills. Would that be a problem?"

Bob's smile turned into an expression of shock. "Eighty thousand dollars in cash? Well, I—normally, the banks get upset when you have a really big sum of cash like that, but I think we can bypass them and work it out. What I mean is, if you give me cash, I'll write the checks to the sellers. Okay?"

Noah nodded. "Let's go write it up," he said. "As soon as we get the acceptance and all the paperwork is done, I'll hand you the money and you can handle it however you want to."

Bob locked everything up again, and they got back into the car to head back to his office. An hour later, Noah handed over $10,000 as earnest money and signed the offer. Bob immediately faxed the offer to the attorney handling the sale for the family, then picked up his phone and called the eldest of the Howerton heirs and told him about the pending sale.

John Howerton, Charles's son, made a pretense of being disappointed at such a low offer but finally admitted that they were ready to get the house sold. He promised to call his siblings immediately and call Bob back within an hour to give him a final decision.

Bob looked at Noah and smiled. "Rex," he said, "I think you just bought yourself a house."

"I guess it sounds that way," Noah said. "We've got an hour to wait. Want to go grab some lunch?"

Bob agreed and they got back into the Charger and drove up the road. Noah had spotted a KFC, and the two men partook of the buffet while they waited.

John called back while they were still working on their first plates and told Bob that they had agreed to sell. John, who had power of attorney over the house, was already on the way to the lawyer's office to sign his acceptance of the offer.

"It's yours," Bob said. "Like I said, it'll take a couple of days to get all the paperwork done. I'll give you a call when it's ready, and we can settle up. You do have the rest of the money available, right?"

Noah nodded. "I do," he said. "It's in a safe place, but I can get to it at any time. Soon as you call and tell me the papers are ready to sign, I'll dig it out and bring it along."

They finished lunch and Noah dropped Bob off at his office, then drove back to Kate's house. She was already at home when he walked in, and was delighted when he told her the news.

"That's a beautiful place out there," she said. "And if you got it that cheap, you stole it."

Noah raised his eyebrows. "That would make me a thief," he said. "And if I'm a thief, then maybe our friend Morgan will think I'm just his kind of people."

Kate grinned at him. "And that's exactly what we want him to think, isn't it?"

CHAPTER EIGHTEEN

Noah called Sarah and told her about the house, and she was delighted. Unfortunately, it didn't change anything in the plan. She still had five more days to wait before she could join Noah in Arkansas, but the prospect of living in the country with him again pleased her a lot, and Noah could hear it in her voice.

Since the house hunting was out of the way, Noah decided it was time to take a step in the direction of the mission. Kate told him how to get to the Barn, the nightclub where he was most likely to find Jimmy Morgan, and he decided to make his first appearance that evening. Kate made dinner for them both, spaghetti and meatballs, and the two of them watched a movie afterward.

By the time the movie was over it was almost 7:30, and Noah decided it was time to make his move. He drove off alone toward Eureka Springs, and the chance to put all their plans into action.

Noah walked into the bar and immediately spotted Jimmy Morgan. The man was sitting at a table with someone who could only be Jimmy's son, Ralph. He made a point of ignoring them and walked up to the bar, then heard Morgan ask someone, "Any idea who that might be?"

A moment later, another man sat down beside him and ordered a beer of his own. "Hey, man," he said. "Ain't seen you around here before. You new, or just passing through?"

Noah shrugged. "That all depends," he said.

"Yeah? Depends on what?" asked the man beside him.

Noah turned and looked him in the eye. "Depends on whether or not I find work. My sister lives here, and she seems to think this is the ideal place for me."

Forney grinned at him. "Really? And who is your sister?"

"Katie Madison," Noah said. "Well, Kate is what she goes by around here, but I've always called her Katie. I'm Rex Madison, by the way." He extended a hand, and the other man shook it.

"Scott Forney," he said. "Kate Madison, huh? I didn't even know she had a brother. Don't think she ever talks about you."

"Yeah, well, there's a reason for that. See, up until about a month ago, I was a guest of the federal government down in Beaumont, Texas. Black sheep of the family, you might say. Katie always tried to keep me under wraps—I guess it doesn't do a girl's reputation much good to have a brother doing time in a fed joint. I've been out a month, but I can't deal with all the probation crap back in Ohio, so Katie suggested I come give it a try here. Just got in yesterday."

"Federal time always has probation attached to it," Forney said. Forney watched his face carefully while he was talking. "Bloody Beaumont, huh? Is it as bad as they say? I heard stories about somebody dying there every week."

Noah shrugged. "Ain't really like that, but it's bad. I've seen both guards and inmates end up dead in the riots, and I saw a guy get his throat slit just for looking into another man's cell. You learn real quick to keep your eyes on the floor right in front of you all the time. Somebody thinks you're looking at him, it's like waving a red flag in front of a bull."

Forney nodded. "So why was you there?"

"Because Uncle Sam doesn't like it when one of his DEA boys gets his head blown off. We had one who got into a little operation we had going back in Cleveland, but he slipped up and got found out, and then he got dead. They couldn't prove who did it, so they just wrapped us all up, conspiracy bit. I did most of five years over that."

"Man, that sucks. What kinda dope?"

Noah laughed. "You name it," he said. "Meth, crack, X, heroin, pot, and anything else you can imagine. As long as there was a market, we were selling it."

Forney leaned close so that their shoulders were almost touching. "So, tell me," he said in a stage whisper, "you have anything to do with that fed? Him getting his head blowed off?"

Noah had his bottle up to his lips, but he turned and glanced at Forney out of the corner of his eye. "Now, come on," he said. "If I did, would you really expect me to admit it to somebody I just met? And would you even believe me if I said I did it?"

Forney shrugged and chuckled. "Hey, man, 's just you and me talking. I ain't gonna say anything to anybody else."

"Cool," Noah said, "and I'm not gonna be stupid enough to tell you anything that could possibly send me right back to Bloody Beaumont, dig?"

Forney laughed and sat up again. "So what kinda work you looking for?"

Noah turned and looked him in the eye. "Kind that makes me a hell of a lot of money."

"Oh, yeah? You looking to get into the same kind of business again?"

"Wouldn't scare me," Noah said. "You know of any openings?"

"Maybe, maybe," Forney said noncommittally. "Of course, I'm kinda like you. I don't trust anybody I just met. For all I know, you could be a fed yourself."

Noah chuckled. "Bet my probation officer would love to hear somebody say that," he said.

"Yeah, probably. Who you got?"

Noah lowered his eyebrows as if thinking, then reached for his wallet and pulled out Craig Roberts's business card. "Roberts," he said, "Craig Roberts. He's out of Fayetteville."

"Yeah, I know who he is. I've known a couple other guys who did fed time. He had one or two of them a while back."

"Cool. So, you really think you might know of some work? What do you need to check me out?"

"Oh, nothing. I know your name, I know you say you did time at Beaumont. It shouldn't be too hard to find out if you're telling the truth." He turned and looked down the bar to where the deputy was still sitting and caught his eye. He motioned with his head for the deputy to come closer, and the man got up and moved to the stool beside him.

"What's up, Scotty?"

"Wanted you to meet somebody," Forney said. "This is Rex Madison. He's Kate's brother."

The deputy reached around Forney to shake hands with Noah. "You're Kate Madison's brother? Kate from the radio?"

"Yep," Noah said, "but don't hold that against me. She and I don't have a whole lot of use for each other. She's letting me crash at her place right now, but only till the paperwork is done on my house."

"Your house? You renting a place around here?" Forney asked.

"Hell, no," Noah said. "Renting is just another way to throw money down the toilet. I made a deal this morning to buy this little farm. The old Howerton place, they call it."

The deputy's eyebrows rose. "You bought Lonnie Howerton's place? Man, that's a sweet old place."

"Sweet?" Forney quipped. "I always heard it was haunted. You do know the old man killed himself out there, right? Stood right there in the kitchen and blew his own brains out with a .45."

Noah looked at him. "You know, the broker never mentioned that little detail. Not that it worries me, you know, just would've been nice to know."

The deputy was grinning. "Scott's just playing with you," he said. "Lonnie died in Mercy Hospital of complications from pneumonia."

"Yeah, sure," Forney said. "That's the official story, anyway. The Howerton family had enough money to cover up the truth, that's what happened. The old man killed himself because it was about to come out that he was behind some of the murders that happened back forty years ago."

The deputy simply shook his head and chuckled. Noah looked from one to the other, but then he shrugged. "I ain't afraid of no ghost," he sang, and both men burst out laughing.

"Anyway," Forney went on, "I just thought you might want to meet Rex. He's moving here to try to start over, on account of he just got out of the federal prison down in Texas."

The deputy kept smiling, but the humor went out of his eyes. "That so?"

Noah looked him in the eye. "Yep. Did five years on a conspiracy rap. I'm sure my probation officer will be letting your office know about me."

"Rex Madison, right? Is there anything in particular I should know about you?"

"I don't know what it might be," Noah said, "other than the fact that I did five years for conspiracy to manufacture and distribute narcotics."

The deputy nodded, and his eyes softened a bit. "But you're here to try to go straight, right?"

"Absolutely," Noah replied. "Let me tell you, one stint in Bloody Beaumont is more than enough. I don't ever want to go back."

"That's good to hear. By the way, Scott told me your name but didn't tell you mine. I'm Billy, Billy Martin. You run into any kind of problems around here, feel free to look me up and let me know. Oh, and tell your sister I said hello, would you? If you put in a good word for me, maybe she'll let me take her out again one of these days."

Noah put a wide grin on his face. "Billy, I'll be sure to do that."

The deputy swallowed the last little bit of his beer and said good night, then got up and walked out the door. Forney watched him go and then turned to Noah.

"Well, we'll know soon enough if your story is true," he said. "I can flat guarantee he's on his way back to the office to check you out." Noah rolled his eyes. "Which is exactly what you had in mind when you called him over," he said. "Don't worry, I don't mind. The way the world is nowadays, you've got to be really careful who you're dealing with. Maybe after he reports back to you, you might tell me more about that possible job opportunity, yeah?"

"Yep," Forney replied with a smile. "And that, my new friend, is why I really called him over. You sound like you might be a useful guy to have around. Anybody who can live through five years at Beaumont is probably pretty tough, and the people I'm thinking of like having tough guys working for them."

"Hey, as long as the pay is there, I'll be as tough as I need to be."

"That's good to hear," Forney said. "Why don't you let me get your phone number? If things work out, I might be able to give you a call in the next day or two, get some money coming into your pocket."

Noah gave him his phone number, and Forney walked away. Noah went back to nursing his beer but took a look over his shoulder and saw Forney leaning down to whisper in Jimmy Morgan's ear.

Noah finished his bottle and ordered another, then sat and sipped at it just as he had the first one. People moved around him, and a few said hello. One girl who looked to be about sixteen sat down beside him and tried to strike up a conversation, but Noah waved his wedding ring at her. She huffed at him and moved down the bar to an older man who seemed more appreciative of her youth and company.

He had just about finished the second bottle when the girl suddenly yelled an obscenity and jumped off the barstool. Every head in the place turned toward her and the man she'd been talking to, as she loudly called him every name she could think of.

"You dirty mother—you piece of crap, I wouldn't touch you if you were the last man on earth! You need to learn to keep your filthy hands off a woman, at least until she lets you know it's okay."

The man appeared to be mildly intoxicated, as he sat there laughing at her. "Screw you, bitch," he said. "Everybody in here knows you're nothing but a whore—why you getting all high-and-mighty? Just like any other business, baby, you want to sell your wares, then you've got to allow the customer to examine the merchandise."

A number of men were getting to their feet and looking at the fellow, but Noah noticed that Morgan's people were staying in their seats. The girl started to turn away, but one of the men who had risen grabbed her arm and spun her back toward the man she had insulted.

"You need to apologize to that man," he said, but the girl spat at him. Before she even realized what was happening, the man holding her arm had punched her in the face. Her head reeled back, and blood began running from her nose.

The man on the barstool had stopped laughing, and he held out a hand and said, "Hey, stop. Leave her alone. She ain't worth it." He turned away and picked up his drink.

"What the hell you mean, leave her alone?" asked the man holding her arm. "This bitch got you scared or something, Cory? You can't take that kind of crap off these whores, man—get up and slap the snot out of her!"

Cory knocked back what was left of his drink and turned to face the girl, now being held by two men while four others stood around them. Noah thought that the man didn't seem all that drunk anymore, nor did he seem nervous or frightened. He kept watching, curious about what was going to happen next.

"Look," the drinker said. "Apparently, I thought things had progressed a little further than the lady did. Now, I don't care if she called me a few names—that doesn't hurt me any. Just let her go so she can go home and clean herself up or something. I think you've already handled the situation well enough, Philip."

The young man Cory had named as Philip cocked his head to the right and stared. "So that's it? You're just gonna let this go?"

"Philip," said a new voice suddenly, "Cory already said to let it go."

Philip turned his head to see Jimmy Morgan's son, Ralph, on his feet and staring directly into his face. "Ralphie, come on," Philip said. "We can't take shit off whores in this town, right? They got to learn their place, right?"

Ralph Morgan looked at the girl's face. "Well, I think you sure taught her. You've done enough damage to her already—she's going to be off her beat for a week or two. Now, you know what the problem is with that?"

Philip looked at the girl and screwed up his face as if confused, then looked back at Ralph. "So she takes a couple weeks off, so what? Booty girl like her can probably afford it, right?"

Ralph nodded slowly. "Yeah, she won't go hungry, nothing like that. Hell, come tomorrow she might even be ready to say thanks to you, giving her a little vacation like this. But, you see, that means two weeks she ain't making us no money, which is why we don't allow anybody to beat up on our girls. Now, here's what's about to happen. Cory, there, he's going to turn around and pay attention to whatever he's drinking. You and your boys are going to let go that girl, and she's going to walk out of here and go on home. After that, your boys can decide just how stupid they want to be tonight."

Philip's grip tightened on the girl's arm. "Ain't none of us stupid," Philip said. "You know, maybe you and your daddy got the whole town scared, but you don't scare us. Y'all hurt one of us, there's twenty more gonna come back on your ass for it."

Ralph shook his head. "Philip, you don't have enough friends to give us any problem. And your friends that are standing there with you right now? I'm looking at their faces, and what I see is some guys who really wish they were somewhere else." He looked at each of those men in turn, and the man holding the girl's other arm suddenly let it go.

"Phil," the young man said, "let's just let this go, okay? Ralphie, I'm sorry, man, we didn't know she was one of your girls. We thought she was somebody new, because your girls don't never act like that."

Ralph looked at him for a moment. "Okay, Billy," he said. "I'll make this easy. The only one who actually did any damage here was Philip. The rest of you can leave, or you can stay and take the same punishment he gets. Better make up your mind right now, though, 'cause time has already run out."

Noah saw several of Morgan's men slowly start to rise to their feet, but then he caught a furtive movement out of the corner of his right eye. The young men surrounding the girl were facing Ralph, so their backs were to Noah. The one farthest in the back was reaching up under the back of his shirt, and Noah saw him wrap his hand around the grip of a small pistol.

No one else in the bar could have seen it, though Noah was sure there were security cameras that would catch it. Noah's mind raced at incredible speed, predicting the outcome of several different choices he might make in the next three to five seconds.

He could easily take the boy down and remove the pistol, but even though he would be attacking in defense of Ralph Morgan, it was highly probable that the others would immediately start swinging at anyone within reach. That would start the very sight Ralph Morgan seemed to be trying to avoid.

He could wait until the gun was being brandished and then attack, take the boy down to the floor and disarm him. That would paint him as a bit of a hero, but it could also result in someone innocent being killed or wounded if the gun were to go off. That could seriously affect his ability to infiltrate the organization.

He could simply sit still and wait until the boy actually fired a shot and then move in. There would be other guns in play, so it would be risky. If the boy managed to kill or wound Ralph Morgan, then taking down his shooter would probably help Noah when the decision was made on whether to use him.

Throughout all of his thinking, Noah had kept his eyes focused mostly on Ralph. When they examined the security cameras later, it would appear that he couldn't have seen the gun being drawn, and if it weren't for his extraordinary peripheral vision, he might have missed it completely.

The gun came out of the back waistband of the boy's pants and was held low for a moment, behind one of his friends in front of him, but then the boy started shaking and simply pushed through between two of the others. His gun came up instantly and pointed directly at Ralph's face for a split second, and Noah lunged. The gun went off just as Noah's hands grabbed the boy by the neck and yanked him back.

Noah spun and threw the boy to the ground, as gunshots rang out in the bar. Noah crouched low over the shooter, his knee in the boy's back and his right hand holding his wrist. He squeezed as hard as he could and the boy screamed, and the gun fell out of his hand without firing again. Noah grabbed it and slid it along the floor until it was out of reach.

Something hit Noah in the back, and he realized that it was one of the other young men, who'd been shot through the chest and had fallen backward. Noah looked around and saw that Philip and all of his friends were on the floor, but he focused on the scene just in front of them.

The bullet had hit Ralph, but Noah couldn't tell where. Five men were crouched over him, and one of them was Jimmy Morgan himself. The shock and tears on his face told Noah that the situation was serious, and the sobbing of the girl kneeling on the other side only served to confirm that opinion.

Noah suddenly felt himself yanked away. He rolled onto his back on the floor and looked up at Scott Forney, who was holding a pistol pointed at his face.

"You in on this?"

Noah shook his head, keeping his hands in plain sight. "No," he said. "When I saw that kid aim his gun, I thought I could take him down before he could fire. That other boy, is he..."

"It ain't good," Forney said. He turned his attention to the boy Noah had taken down, who was trying to turn over and get to his feet. "That's Benny Smoot. Benny, he's a tweaker. A meth head, know what I mean?"

Forney's gun had shifted over to Benny, so Noah got up onto his haunches and yanked Benny back down to the floor. "I know what a tweaker is," Noah said. "That's the gun over there. What do you want me to do with him?"

Forney walked carefully around Noah and Benny, then picked up the gun and looked at it. "A freaking little Ruger 22," he said as he popped out the magazine. It was loaded with hollow-point rounds. "Makes a little bitty hole in your forehead, but then it can make one hell of a mess in your brain."

Noah grabbed Benny by the front of his shirt and shook him. "What was this all about? You got some grudge against that boy?"

Then he looked scared, but he was trying desperately to hold on to his bravado. "Screw you," he said.

Noah looked at him for a second, then reached out and caught the skin on the back of his upper arm between three fingers. He pinched the skin tightly and twisted as hard as he could. Benny let out a scream, and when Noah dragged his face up close again and asked the same question once more, he started nodding frantically. "I got paid, I got paid, man," he said. "Dude gave me two grand, said he'd give me five more if I get a bullet into Ralphie's brain."

Forney stood looking on as Noah held on to Benny. "Who was it?" Noah asked. "Who paid you to try to kill him?"

"I don't know, man," Bennie said. "Big dude, like a pro football player. He handed me the two grand and promised five grand more once it was done."

Noah shook his head. "Sounds like you got sent on a suicide mission," he said. "Why would you be that stupid?"

Benny looked at him for a moment with resignation in his eyes, then turned them down to the floor. "Didn't think," he said. "Just didn't think it through, and I needed the money."

Noah looked around at where Ralph had fallen and saw Jimmy turn his head toward Forney. Forney pointed downward at Benny, as Jimmy got to his feet and started walking toward them.

CHAPTER NINETEEN

A siren could be heard in the distance, but it was rapidly getting closer. Jimmy stood and stared down at Benny for a long couple of minutes, then turned his attention to Noah.

"What happened?" Jimmy asked bluntly.

"Benny says somebody paid him to try to kill Ralphie," Forney said. "He might have gotten it done, if it wasn't for Rex, here. He saw the gun come out and tried to stop it."

Morgan turned to Noah. "Is that true?"

"Yes, sir, and I'm so sorry," Noah said. "I didn't see the gun until it was pointed at that boy, and I thought I could get him before he could pull the trigger. If I'd seen it just a split second sooner..."

"Can't worry about the what-ifs in life," Jimmy said. "Just tell me what you saw."

Noah looked down at Benny for a second, then turned his eyes back to Jimmy as he got to his feet. "I was just watching what was going on," he said, "and then all of a sudden I saw this guy raise a gun and point it at the one who was talking to them. I jumped then, to see if I could get him down before he hurt anybody. I wasn't quite fast enough; I heard the gun go off. That boy—how bad is it? Is that your kid?"

Jimmy stared at Noah's face for a moment, then looked down at Benny again. "Yeah," he said quietly. "He got it along the side of his head, like it took a crease out of the skin just over his left ear, but he's not dead. He just don't have any idea who he is, at the moment. Ain't making any sense."

The sirens had gotten closer, and Noah heard cars screeching to a halt outside the bar. Several officers, including the deputy he had met earlier, came rushing through the door with guns drawn. At a wave from Jimmy Morgan, however, they stood down and put their weapons away as three teams of paramedics came racing through the door. One of them hurried over to where Ralph was lying, and a woman began barking out orders. The others began checking the rest of the bodies on the floor.

A couple of the deputies gathered around Jimmy, but Billy Martin took one look at Noah's face and beckoned him off to the side, while Forney stood over Benny.

"Are you in the middle of this somehow?" Martin asked.

"Kinda. I was sitting at the bar when this boy"—he pointed at Benny—"suddenly had a gun and pointed it at that boy who was shot. I jumped and tried to get him before he could pull the trigger, but I was a split second too late. Damn gun went off as I grabbed him, and I couldn't reach it to try to make it deflect upwards."

Martin looked into his face for a moment, then slowly nodded. "Who shot you?"

Noah looked confused for a moment, but then Martin pointed to his left shoulder. Noah looked and suddenly realized he had been nicked by one of the flying bullets. There was a hole through the fabric of his shirt, but a quick glance inside showed him that the blood leaking out of it was from a simple flesh wound.

He looked back at the deputy. "No clue," he said. "It ain't as bad as it looks, though. I didn't even feel it until you pointed it out."

"Yeah, probably nothing compared to what happened to you in that last big riot at Beaumont, right? Yeah, don't look so surprised. I checked your story out, and you're telling the truth. According to your records, you were one of the inmates who got shot up by accident when the federal marshals went in. That right?"

"Wrong place, wrong time," he said, remembering what he'd been trained to say. "I wasn't in one of the gangs; I rolled solo. Me and a bunch of other independents were just trying to stay down and out of the line of fire, but one of the marshals got a little trigger-happy. It was touch and go for a little while there, but I made it. Some of the others didn't."

Martin nodded, then looked over to where the other deputies were talking with Morgan for a moment. He turned back to Noah. "Listen, Rex," he began, "this could go about either way for you. That's Jimmy Morgan's boy, Ralph, laying there. Just a little while ago, Jimmy was talking to him about taking over some of their operation. If his mind is all messed up, Jimmy could blame some of it on you, or he might respect the fact you tried to stop it. Just keep your cool, no matter what happens, all right?"

Noah looked over at Jimmy, who was standing over the paramedics. He could catch snatches of the conversation, just enough to know that the paramedics were saying Ralph had a chance of recovery. They got him onto a stretcher and wheeled him past Noah on the way to the door, and Noah saw that the boy's eyes were moving wildly around. Jimmy Morgan was clutching his left hand as he hurried along beside him. The girl that had started it all was holding on to his right.

The bandage on his head told Noah that the bullet had grazed the right side of his cranium. That meant it had probably not penetrated or damaged the frontal lobes, but there was no way to be certain of that. That area of the brain controlled planning, social interactions, and logical thought. If he suffered any serious damage there, there was no way he was ever going to be capable of stepping into his father's shoes.

Noah considered for a moment the incredible possibility that one of his targets might have been taken off the list on the very evening that he made his first attempt at contact. The odds against something like this had to be unbelievably high, and yet it had happened. Ralph might survive and recover, but there was a possibility he would no longer be part of the organization, in which case there was no longer any reason for Noah to terminate him. All Noah could do was wait and see.

He had gone through all of those thoughts in a matter of seconds but suddenly returned to the present. "All I know," Noah said, "is I tried. I didn't know who any of these boys were, but when I saw a gun come out, I figured I should do what I could to stop it." He shrugged. "All a man can do is try, right?"

Deputy Martin had taken out a notepad and was scribbling down notes to remind himself of Noah's statements. He'd have to write it up later, but the notes would also serve to help when he spoke with Morgan. He personally thought Morgan ought to be grateful to this new guy, because it was very possible that his interference is what kept the shot from being fatal.

That was how he planned to pitch it, anyway. While it wasn't officially known, Billy Martin was one of Jimmy Morgan's people, and he had built himself a position that was strong and enduring. All of the deputies working under the already corrupt sheriff were useful to Morgan, but Billy had taken things a few steps further. With careful thought and planning, and by making sure he often brought news to Morgan before anybody else could, he had gradually risen to a position of trust and delegated authority.

Billy Martin would enforce the laws, but he wouldn't hesitate to break them, as well. Billy was one of the lieutenants in the Morgan Mafia, and he personally thought this new guy might have potential.

"Okay," he said after a minute, "just stay here. The sheriff is on his way here now, and he'll probably want to talk to you."

Noah pointed at Benny, who was still sitting on the floor. "What about this scumbag? Is somebody going to arrest him?"

Martin looked down at Benny, and his face became a grimace. He looked back up at Noah, and it didn't improve.

"Rex, you're in a different world now. You need to understand that the things you saw here tonight may not be quite the way you hear about it tomorrow on the news. Don't make waves, man—that's the most important thing to remember right now. Do not argue with anybody about what happened here tonight. Got it?"

Noah made his eyes go wide. "Hell, you're going to kill him?"

Martin breathed out a sigh and shook his head. "You ever heard of something called the Morgan Mafia?"

Noah nodded. "Yeah, Katie told me about it. I gather that's the Morgan?"

"That's him. Now, imagine for a moment that you run your own little, oh, let's call it a syndicate, right? Somebody, some punk kid hopped up on meth, shoots your son. How would you feel about letting the cops haul him off to jail, where it's always possible he'll end up walking away with probation or an order to spend some time in drug rehab?"

Noah grinned. "I'd feel like I didn't want him to get that kind of opportunity."

Martin grinned back. "It was a pity all these boys got killed in a shootout with a rival gang, wasn't it? Poor old Ralph—did you hear about him getting caught in the crossfire?"

Noah nodded once again. "I sure did. Damn shame, that."

Martin patted him on the shoulder. "I think you might end up doing well, here. You seem to have a real ability to grasp what's going on around you and adapt to it."

"How do you think I survived Beaumont?" Noah asked. "When you're a kid growing up on the street in a two-bit city like Zanesville, Ohio, you have to learn how to make yourself fit in. A guy can get anything he wants if he knows how to ask for it."

"That's true," Martin said. "Okay, just wait right here. I'll get back with you in just a bit."

Noah sat down at the bar and picked up the beer bottle he had been drinking from. There were still a couple of swallows in the bottom, so he tipped it up and drank them down. He turned around on the bar stool and leaned his back against the bar.

A noise behind him made him glance around, and he saw the bartender standing there. She had just set another beer beside his elbow. "On the house," she said. "I saw what you did. You tried to stop this, and I appreciate that."

Noah picked up the beer and saluted her with it, then took a long pull. "I just did what I thought I had to do. Hope that kid lives."

"Yeah, don't we all," she said. "Morgan's bad enough when he's in a good mood. God only knows what things are going to be like around here for the next few weeks."

"I was just hearing a little bit about Mr. Morgan," Noah said. "I guess he pretty much runs the show around here?"

"More than you can imagine. I'm Amber, by the way."

"Rex," Noah said. "Rex Madison. Kate Madison, the one on the radio? She's my sister."

"I know Kate," Amber said. "She comes in here every now and then and usually sits up here so we can talk. She never mentioned having a brother, though."

Noah shrugged. "I guess I'm the black sheep of the family," he said. "I just got out of federal prison a few weeks ago. Katie wasn't ever very happy about that, and we never were really close. I just got to talking to her a couple weeks ago, and for some reason she suggested I come here and try to get a job and settle down."

"And how does your wife feel about that?" Amber asked. She grinned when Noah looked up at her. "Hey, when a good-looking man walks into a bar, every woman in the place checks out his left hand. You got a wedding ring on."

Noah smiled at her. "It's so new that I almost forget it's there. Angie and I were high school sweethearts, and it just carried on. She must really love me, because she waited the whole five years I was gone. We got married not long after I got out, and she'll be coming here next week. I just came ahead to find us a place to live."

"And did you find one?"

"Yep. Bought the old Howerton place today."

"Lonnie Howerton's old place? Wow, I didn't think they'd ever get that sold." She suddenly got an odd look on her face. "You did hear about Lonnie killing himself there, right?"

Noah nodded. "Yeah, and I heard it's haunted, but then I heard that story is not true. According to the sheriff's office, Lonnie died in the hospital."

Amber shrugged and rolled her eyes. "Believe whatever you want," she said. "My dad went out there and thought about buying the place, but when he went into the kitchen he said it was like walking into a refrigerator. Spooked him so bad he just turned around and walked out."

"Was that before or after they redid the kitchen? It's all brand-new in there, now."

"It was before," Amber replied. "My dad said he could still see bloodstains on the floor and the cabinets around the sink. He said it got so cold he could see his breath, and that's why he decided to get out of there."

"Well, I'll be moving in within a couple of days. Next time I'm in here, I'll let you know if I have any spooky experiences, okay?"

The bartender nodded as she wiped down the rest of the bar, but then a voice beside him said, "Rex Madison?"

Noah turned the barstool around again and found himself looking into the eyes of the sheriff. "That's me," Noah said.

"I'm Dan Redford," the sheriff said, "County sheriff. Everybody here tells me you tried to stop this, and I wanted to tell you how much we appreciate that." He glanced over at where the paramedics were still working on two of the other boys who had managed to survive. "I also heard a lot about some of your earlier experiences. Billy says he checked out your story and it comes back true. Are you the kind of man who can do what needs to be done and keep his mouth shut about it?"

Noah lowered his eyebrows and looked hard at the sheriff, feigning confusion. "Keep my mouth shut? I'm not sure I know what you mean, Sheriff. All I did was try to keep somebody from getting killed, you know?"

The sheriff turned back to him and grinned. "I think you know exactly what I'm saying," he said. "But maybe this badge is making you nervous. Guess I can understand that. Don't worry, I'm pretty sure you'll catch on right away."

The sheriff touched the brim of his Western-style hat and then turned and walked back over to Morgan's men. Noah couldn't hear the conversation, but each of the men glanced his way more than once. It lasted a few moments, and then the sheriff and one of the men turned and walked out the front door of the bar.

Scott Forney came walking toward Noah, and he had an unusual look on his face. He almost looked like he was trying to decide whether to stand or run, but he didn't hesitate. As soon as he and Noah were face-to-face, he took hold of Noah's arm and pulled him to a spot where they were unlikely to be overheard.

"Listen, Rex, I'm not sure what's going on," he said. "Seems like everybody in this thing suddenly thinks you're some hero they been waiting for, something like that. Your sister ever tell you about the Morgan Mafia?"

"Yeah, she did," Noah said. "I understand that was Morgan himself whose son got shot?"

"That's right," Forney replied. "Everybody who was watching pretty much agrees that Ralphie would be dead if it wasn't for you, and I guess the doctors at the hospital think he's going to be back to normal pretty soon. Somebody checked the security video footage, and it looks like you yanked him backward just as he was about to fire, and that's what brought his aim up so the bullet only grazed Ralphie's head. If you hadn't, that bullet probably would have gone through one of Ralphie's eyes."

"Any idea why he pulled a gun? I mean, that seems like a pretty stupid thing to do in such a simple little argument."

"I agree with you, but you just never know with a tweaker. He might have had a grudge against Ralph, or maybe he was just at that stage where he was in a rage at everything and everybody. I've seen that in meth heads many times."

Noah shrugged. "Well, if I helped, I'm glad. Maybe the word will get around and it will help me get that job you were talking about."

"Well, actually," Forney said, looking around once more to make sure no one could overhear them, "that's what I wanted to talk to you about. Billy talked to Morgan about you, said he thinks you'd be a good addition to our little organization. The sheriff got here after they had left, but Billy got to talk to him and he thinks the same thing, so I got sent over to try to recruit you. If you're interested, the pay is good—you start out at two grand a week—and you don't have to worry about going to jail, because the cops all take their orders from the same people we do."

Noah had let his eyes go wide and was grinning. "Two grand a week? Who do I gotta kill?"

"That's the kicker," Forney said. "If you want the job, the first thing you gotta do is finish off Benny Smoot."

Noah feigned an expression of shock. "Do what? This is BS, man—I just met you and you want me to kill somebody for you?"

"Hey, like I said it wasn't my idea. Jimmy called, he said he looked into your eyes and saw a killer. You do this, you kill Benny, and you're going to end up eventually riding high in the organization. Everybody starts at the bottom, but if you do this you won't stay there very long."

Noah looked around. "Geez, man, there's still a half-dozen cops in here. If you're playing me, they can haul me off to life in prison, or worse, if I do that."

Forney turned and waved a hand until he caught the attention of one of the deputies. "Hey, Collins," he yelled. "Come on over here for a minute."

The deputy named Collins turned and came their way, and Noah was surprised at the size of the man. He probably stood six foot eight and would've easily weighed three hundred pounds, but there wasn't an ounce of fat on the man anywhere. He walked up to them and looked down at Noah and Forney.

"Hey, Scott," he said. "This the new guy?"

"I'm trying," Forney said. "I told him what Jimmy wants, but he's a little nervous about doing anything with you guys standing around."

Collins looked at Noah. "Here's what you need to know right now," he said. "Jimmy Morgan runs everything around here. If he wants you to do something, you can either do it or suffer the consequences. As far as illegality and all that, that's not really stuff you need to worry about. Jimmy is the law, as far as we're concerned. Now, I know he wants you to snuff out Benny. If you do, that will prove to him that you're the man he thinks you are, and you will be well rewarded. If you don't, that's fine, but don't ever be stupid enough to talk about it." Collins patted him on the head like a little kid and then turned away. He walked back to the other deputies and said something, and then all of them walked out the front door.

Noah looked over at where Benny was sitting, his face ashen and his body trembling. All of the anger that seemed to have triggered the shooting appeared to be gone, and he was realizing what he had actually done. Sure, he had managed to wound Ralph Morgan, but he had also signed his own death warrant. It didn't take a genius to figure that out, and Benny was no fool.

"You want it done right here?" Noah asked Forney.

"Probably be better if you take him out in the middle of nowhere. Make it someplace where he'll be found, but not necessarily right out in plain sight. As soon as the body is discovered, we'll be in touch." Forney looked at him for another moment, then turned and walked away.

Noah walked over to Benny and reached down to grab his arm. "Come on, Benny," he said. "You and I have to go take care of some business."

The skinny drug addict whimpered as he walked along beside Noah, but even as scared as he was, the big black Charger caught his attention. Noah put him into the passenger seat and then walked around to get behind the wheel.

When the engine fired up, Benny smiled. Noah put the car into gear and drove out of the parking lot, made his way through the eastern end of Eureka Springs, and followed Highway 62 toward Berryville. He remembered seeing a spot with a lot of old cars on the side of this road and drove directly to it. He turned in and cut his lights, glad that there was no other traffic on the road at that moment. He slowly cruised the Charger around behind the big garage and got out, then walked around the car and opened the passenger door.

Benny looked up at him. "This is where you're gonna do it?"

Noah nodded. "It's nothing personal, Benny," he said. "Just something I have to do."

Benny started to cry, and Noah reached in to take hold of his arm. He halfway expected a fight, but Benny didn't have it in him. He got out of the car and let Noah lead him around behind an old '47 Cadillac that had seen better days.

Noah put him into a sleeper hold and choked him out, then snapped his neck while he was unconscious. Benny would never awaken from this final nap.

Noah got back into the Charger and waited until there was no traffic in sight before he started the car and pulled out onto the road. He didn't turn his lights on for a quarter mile.

CHAPTER TWENTY

Since it was already four in the morning, Kate was up when he got home. She was in the kitchen drinking coffee and smiled as he walked in.

"Hey, bud," she said. "You look like you had quite a night. Is that blood on your shoulder?"

"A bit," Noah said. "There was a bit of a fracas at the bar tonight, but I think it accomplished what I was out to do." He told her the story of what had happened and watched her face as he did so. When he finished, she was already shaking her head in disbelief.

"Do you have any idea how many federal agents have come in and tried to get into that organization? Nine—the answer is nine—and do you want to guess how many of them are dead?"

"Nine?" Noah asked.

"Exactly. And here you come—you just waltz in and stumble into just the right circumstances. I don't know whether to laugh or cry. I mean, I've heard rumors about you, how you pull off absolutely impossible missions, but I never believed I'd actually see it happen. Good Lord, Rex, this is incredible."

Noah nodded. "I agree with you," he said. "I was planning to spend weeks trying to find a way in, and nobody could have predicted that something like this would happen. Now all I have to do is wait until the body is found, and then we'll see what happens."

Kate shivered. "You just said that like it was no big deal. 'All I have to do is wait till the body is found.' You really don't feel anything when you kill somebody, do you?"

Noah shook his head. "No," he said, "I don't. That part of my psyche is somehow shut down. It's because of something that happened when I was a little kid."

Kate's eyes were big and round. "I really don't think I want to know," she said. "Look, I gotta get to work, and you need to get some sleep. Sleep, they used to tell us in the academy, is the most important weapon in any arsenal. The more rested you are, the more effective you can be."

"I think they stole that from the Jason Bourne stories," Noah said. "But that doesn't make it any less true. I'm headed for bed, now."

"Good idea. I'll see you this afternoon, if you're awake."

Noah nodded and headed for his bedroom. He lay down on the bed and closed his eyes, and a minute later he was sound asleep.

He had The Dream again. He woke up in his own bed and rolled over, to see a beaten and bloodied Sarah sitting up and staring at him. "Noah, you have to find me," she said. "You have to save me."

"But I already did," Noah replied. "I found you in China and brought you home."

Sarah stared at him, with blood running from her nose and mouth. There was blood all over her clothing as well, and she simply shook her head. "No," she said softly, "you didn't."

As always, that was the moment when he awoke for real. He sat up in bed and drew a deep breath, and instantly realized where he was. It had only been The Dream again, the one he had over and over since he was able to bring her home. No one knew about the dream, not even Sarah, herself, and Noah was keeping it that way. He knew enough about dreams in psychology to realize that this dream must represent something in his subconscious, some knowledge he had that he was not aware of. He suspected that his subconscious mind was trying to tell him that there was some part of Sarah that didn't get away from the torture and interrogation in China, some part that he still had to save.

He shook it off and picked up his phone to check the time. It was only a little after six, so he rolled over and went back to sleep.

He was awakened again at nine by the ringing of the phone. He picked it up and saw that it was Scott Forney calling.

"Hello?" Noah said.

"Jimmy wants to see you," Forney said. "Meet me in the front corner of the shopping center parking lot, the one next to Walmart."

"What, now? Man, I'm trying to get some sleep."

"Sleep when you're dead," Forney replied. "When Jimmy calls, nobody sleeps in. Meet me in twenty minutes." The line went dead.

Noah stood and checked himself over, decided he didn't have to have a shower right that moment, and went to the bathroom to take care of other morning necessities. A quick shave made him look presentable, so he pulled on some clothes and transferred everything from the pockets of the pants he'd worn the night before.

The big black Charger pulled into the parking lot of the shopping center right on time, and Noah had no trouble spotting the one car sitting alone at its farthest edge. He pulled up beside it and powered down his window, and Forney smiled as he looked the car over.

"Holy she-it," he said. "Man, what a car. You build 'er yourself?"

"Nope," Noah said. "Some of the investments I made before I went to prison paid off. I bought this and a few other things, and just blew the rest of it on that haunted house."

"Well, it's way cool. Listen, when we get to Jimmy's place, just be sure to be respectful to him. Trust me when I tell you that's not something you want him upset about. He's going to probably tell you what a good job you did with Benny and offer you some kind of position in the organization. It won't be quite at the bottom, but you'll have people over you to answer to."

"Okay, no problem," Noah said. "Why couldn't you tell me that over the phone?"

"Because if anyone finds out I gave you a heads-up on this, I'm going to get my own ass in the sling, and Jimmy's got somebody who listens in on phone calls around here. Don't say anything on the phone that you don't want Jimmy to know about. Trust me, sooner or later it'll come out."

"Gotcha," Noah replied. "So, how do I get there? Do I follow you?"

"That's the plan. Just follow me and we'll be there in fifteen minutes." He powered up his window and started the car, a late-model Buick. Noah put his own window up and turned the car around, ready to follow.

The ride actually took about twelve minutes, and they came to a guard shack that seemed to be in the middle of nowhere. Forney stopped and spoke with the guards inside, who then motioned for Noah to go ahead and follow Forney. He eased past the guard shack and followed Forney's Buick for another three minutes before they came to the house.

It was large, but not the kind of place you would expect some self-proclaimed king to occupy. This looked more like a large farmhouse, built to accommodate a family with a dozen or more children. Noah parked his car beside Forney's in the large gravel driveway, then stepped out and followed him up to the front door.

Two men opened the door, and Forney stepped inside. Noah started to follow, but the men stopped him.

"Need to put your hands on the wall," one of them said. "Nothing personal—we just got to make sure you're not carrying."

Noah shrugged and put his hands on the wall indicated, then ignored the indignities of being frisked. A moment later it ended, and the same man told him to come on inside. Noah followed him and found Forney waiting to lead them farther into the house.

The entry foyer led into a hallway, and then another hall crossed it. Forney took the one to the right and then immediately stepped into a nicely appointed office with Noah on his heels. Jimmy Morgan sat behind a large oak desk, and he looked up as the two men entered.

"Scott," he said, "shut the door and bring our guest on inside. You boys want a drink? I got cold beer, I got whiskey, I got vodka, you name it. If I ain't got it here, won't take me five minutes to get it."

"Beer's fine," Forney said, and Noah echoed him. Morgan passed them each a bottle of the most popular local brand and motioned for them to take seats in the big chairs facing his desk. When they were settled, he turned and looked at Noah.

"Rex Madison," he said. "Twenty-six years old, grew up in Zanesville, Ohio. Several minor skirmishes with the law during your teenage years, but then you hit the big time just a little while before your twenty-first birthday. You were one of five people named as suspects in the death of DEA agent William Prior. The feds couldn't come up with enough evidence to prosecute any of you directly for murder, so the best they could do was a conspiracy charge. I guess they thought it was going to put you away for a long time, but some federal judge decided five years was enough on a conspiracy beef. That sound about right?"

"Close enough," Noah said. "The judge wasn't trying to give me any leniency, though. There was some error in the paperwork when they filed the charges against me that limited the sentence to not more than five years." Noah shrugged. "Sometimes I think I got a little angel up there somewhere, just keeping an eye on me."

"From everything I read about you today, Rex, you must've been a model prisoner in Beaumont. Says the only thing you ever got into any trouble over was sneaking food out of the chow hall. I've known a couple people who did time at Beaumont, and they were always in some kind of trouble."

Noah looked him in the eye. "Not sure where you're getting your information," he said. "I got hit up four different times and did a total of nineteen months in the SHU. First time was for insubordination when I told their psychologist she was a fat ugly cow who had no idea what was going on in the minds of men who were locked up away from society. Second time was for refusing a work detail. The job was going outside the prison to do highway maintenance, and somebody had put my name down. I didn't have enough time in to qualify for off-site work, so I refused. I got a shot and was sent to the hole. It took them almost a month to figure out I was right and they were wrong. The third time..."

Morgan was grinning as he waved a hand to stop Noah. "Yeah, you're right," he said. "That was a test. I just wanted to see if you really were Rex Madison, or maybe just somebody using his name. We can't be too careful, you know what I mean?"

Noah nodded and shrugged. "Yeah, I get it," he said. "I think I already proved myself, though, don't you? Or doesn't murder qualify?"

Morgan kept grinning, but a steeliness came into his eyes. "You seem just a little bit bitter, Madison. Something you want to say to me?"

Noah locked eyes with Morgan for a moment, but then slowly lowered his own eyes. "No, sir," he said. "I'm just a little shook up over it. It was the first time I ever killed anybody who wasn't trying to kill me."

"And yet you did it," Morgan said. "Scott, here, tells me you want to get into some good paying work, and that he thinks you might be an asset. I've had several other people tell me they agree with that assessment, so I decided to give you a chance. Naturally, I wanted to make sure the test was something that would show me how far I can trust you, and I think you passed with flying colors."

Noah looked up again. "Thank you, sir," he said. "If you have a job for me, I can promise you right now I'll do everything I can to do it for you and do it right."

"Cheer up, Rex," Morgan said. "You don't mind if I call you Rex, right? And I'm Jimmy—none of that 'sir' stuff. Everybody calls me Jimmy, you got that?"

Noah grinned sheepishly. "Yes, s... Yes, I get it."

Morgan leaned back in his chair and steepled his fingers together as he crossed his legs. "Rex, I'm always in need of good people," he said. "The thing is, I've got plenty of people who will kill somebody if I tell them to. What I don't have enough of is people who can think and react quickly. Now, last night, you were on your feet and had grabbed that stupid kid before my guys even saw there was a gun out. It wasn't until you took the boy down that they realized something was going on and jumped up. Now, considering that they're supposed to be on top of things every second so that they can keep me alive and healthy, I'm starting to wonder if I'm working with some modern-day version of the Keystone cops." He grinned and watched Noah's face, but there seemed to be no recognition. "Is that too outdated for you? You don't know who the Keystone cops were? Bunch of silly characters that ran around like their heads were up their butts. Never could get anything done. What I'm saying is that I'm starting to feel like my personal security people are about that useless."

"That's not good," Noah said. "I'm sorry to hear that—Jimmy."

Morgan nodded, then leaned forward again and put his elbows on his desk. His fingers were intertwined with one another as he looked across the desk at Noah.

"Rex, you moved faster than most people could even dream of, and you realized what the threat was long before anybody else. I've even looked at the security tapes, and you reacted before anybody else. If you hadn't jumped and grabbed Benny when you did, he might have gotten off a clear shot, or more shots, and managed to actually kill my boy. It certainly appears that I have you to thank for the fact he's still alive, and likely to recover completely. Doctor says once the swelling on his brain goes down, we'll know more, but at this point it doesn't look like there's any serious damage."

Noah shrugged but added a grin. "I just did what I felt I needed to do," he said. "I'm glad your son is gonna be okay."

"Me, too," Morgan said. "Rex, like I told you a few minutes ago, I got several people telling me I should try to keep you around. I think they're right. I was already planning to offer you a job, but I've been thinking about this and I think I know just the spot for you. Rex, how would you feel about being in charge of my boy's security detail? He's going to be a lot more visible, now, and that naturally means he's going to be more at risk. I don't know what kind of insanity got hold of Benny last night, but it made me stop and think about the fact that there are people out there who would love to use my own son against me, if they ever got the chance. I don't intend to ever let them have that chance, so that's why I want to offer you this position. I'll pay you five grand a week, and you can handpick your team from all the people I've got. You can take them out of my own detail, if you want."

Noah pretended to be overwhelmed by the offer for a moment but then looked at Morgan. "Jimmy, the only problem with this is that I can't even have a gun. I got a felony on my record, and that's not even taking into account the fact I have to report to a federal probation officer every month. I mean, I'd love to take the job, but..."

"Apparently you don't know as much as I thought you did," Morgan said. "Federal probation, right? Who you got?"

"Craig Roberts," Noah replied. "I just met him a couple days ago. He seems pretty cool, but this..."

Morgan picked up a cell phone and scrolled through its contact list for a moment, then punched one of the icons with a finger. He held the phone up to his ear for a moment, but then apparently someone answered.

"Craig Roberts? Yeah, this is Jimmy Morgan. I'm thinking about hiring one of your people and putting them on my security detail.

Yeah, he actually helped keep my boy from getting killed last night, so I think he might be useful. Yeah, I didn't think you'd have a problem with that. Let me hand him the phone so you can explain it to him."

Morgan leaned forward and passed the phone to Noah, who took it nervously and put it to his ear. "Hello?"

"Hey, Rex, it's Craig," he heard, and he recognized the voice of his probation officer. "Jimmy Morgan is looking to put you to work, huh? I was kinda hoping you'd get in with him. As long as you do what he wants, you don't have to worry about me or anyone else coming down on you. Fact is, law enforcement around here pretty much does whatever he says, you know what I mean?"

"So, you mean it's okay to take this job? I mean, I might have to carry a gun."

"Yeah, I imagine you would. It won't be a problem, don't worry about it. Just do a good job, and good luck to you. I'll see you next month, on schedule."

The phone went dead, and Noah tried to look amazed as he passed it back to Morgan. "He says there won't be a problem," he said. "So the only thing I can say is, I'm in."

Morgan stood up from his chair and came around the desk to shake Noah's hand. "Damn glad of it," he said. "I got people watching Ralphie while he's at the hospital, but he's likely to be released tomorrow morning. I want you ready to go ahead and take over now, though. Is there anything you need for this? I mean, do I need to advance you some money or anything?"

Noah shook his head. "No, no, I'm not hurting for money at the moment. I guess what I'd like to do is find out where I can buy some weapons, someplace that won't ask questions?"

"Let me give you a head start on that," Morgan said. "I've got a pretty good selection just down the hall." He led the two men out of the office and a couple of doors down, then opened a steel door with a key. When it was open, he invited them inside, and Noah let out a low whistle.

The room was filled with guns. Three of the walls were lined with rifles, shotguns, and assault rifles, along with several that Noah was certain were full automatics. The fourth wall held pistols, and there were probably three hundred of them there.

"This reminds me of a gun shop I was in several years ago," Noah said. "Are any of these for sale?"

"You need a pistol, right? Well, you pick any one you want, it's on me. The piece, holster, your first box of ammo, I'll give it all to you as a bonus."

Noah stared at him for a moment, then looked around the room carefully. He saw several that he knew were good weapons, but then he pointed at a particular weapon. "That's a Springfield Armory XD(M) with a five-and-a-half-inch barrel. Nine-millimeter version, right?"

He picked up the gun and checked, then nodded. "I was right, yeah, it's a nine mil. How about this one?"

Morgan grinned. "For a guy who's been away for a while, you sure know your guns."

"First Amendment, freedom of the press," Noah said. "They can keep us from having guns, but they can't stop us from ordering *Guns and Ammo* or any other good gun magazine. And if there's one thing I love to do, it's read about guns."

Morgan laughed, then busied himself finding a holster and a box of 9 mm hollow-point ammunition. Once he had Noah outfitted, they went back to his office to talk a bit more.

"Like I said, you can take your pick of my men. My boy is the most important thing in my world, so I want the best I can get taking care of him. Right now, you're at the top of that list. I need you to add more people to it. And the first one you should add is the one sitting right there beside you."

CHAPTER TWENTY-ONE

"The first thing you need to understand about this is that it's a job," Forney said, "just like any other job. You know what you're supposed to do, so you do it to the best of your ability and that's all it takes."

"That's BS, man," Noah shot back. "My job is to keep his son safe. How am I supposed to do that? I can't be with the kid twenty-four hours a day."

The two of them were sitting in Noah's car, which was parked on a back road. Noah had told Forney to follow him, but a mile later he had suddenly pulled over and waved out the window for him to come up to the Charger.

"That's not what Jimmy was saying," Forney said. "Remember he said you can take as many of his men as you wanted? He knows you can't be on the job 24/7. He wants you to be chief of security for Ralphie, not his babysitter. That means you pick the guys who will be with him when you're not. It's not as bad as you think, trust me. You got me, already. Believe me, I can show you a few others you can really trust. We can build a team in no time."

Noah shook his head and pulled on his lower lip, as if he was nervous. "Okay, okay, I get it," he said. "So you're like my assistant, right? Well, then, I guess it's time you start introducing me to everybody else."

"Not a problem," Forney said. "Let me set something up for tomorrow morning, okay? I'll bring a few with me when we get with Ralphie." He opened the door of the car and started to step out.

"That'll work," Noah said. "And, hey, Forney? Thanks, man."

Forney gave him a thumbs-up sign and closed the door, then walked back to his own car. He started it and drove away, turning around and heading back the way they had come. Noah started the Charger, but then this phone rang suddenly. He pulled it out and saw that the call was coming from Bob Henson.

"Hello," he said.

"Rex? Bob Henson. I'm calling to tell you that all the paperwork is done, and the house is ready to be yours. Incidentally, I took the liberty of having all of the utilities turned on in your name. I hope that's all right?"

"Hey, that sounds great, Bob," Noah said. "Listen, I've been talking to some people around town, and I keep hearing this story about that house. Do you know what really happened? Did the old man commit suicide in the kitchen out there?"

Henson sighed. "No, he didn't," Henson said. "Believe it or not, I had forgotten all about this issue. Here's what happened: Lonnie Howerton had emphysema, real bad. Everybody knew it was only a matter of time. Poor old guy couldn't even leave his house, because he had that big oxygen tank he had to carry around. Well, then I guess he got pneumonia or something, and he started coughing up blood. From what I understand, it was so bad he was spraying blood everywhere every time he coughed. He dialed 911, but the operator couldn't understand him because he was coughing so much, so she just sent the paramedics out. They found him in the kitchen floor, and they said it looked like somebody had been hacked to death, because of all the blood. They took him to the hospital, and it actually looked like he might pull through, but then I guess the pneumonia got worse and he died pretty suddenly. The story about him killing himself came from rumors about the people who went out to clean up the blood."

Noah chuckled. "Okay, so the house isn't haunted?"

Bob laughed. "Well, I've never spent a night out there to find out, but I can say I've never seen or heard or felt anything strange when I've been there. I've probably been there more than anybody else since Lonnie died."

"That's good enough for me," Noah said. "How soon can we get this done? I've gotten a job and I'm going to be pretty busy, so I need to get settled in as quickly as I can. I miss my wife, but she can't come until I get moved in."

"Rex, I've got it all ready right here on my desk. You can stop in whenever you like and we'll get this done. Oh, and by the way, I've solved that problem about payment. I just transferred money from my personal account to my escrow account. When you give me the cash, I'll issue the check from the escrow account to the sellers, and then I can deposit the cash over time. Save us all a bunch of headaches with the banks, right?"

"It'll save you one," Noah said. "I don't trust banks. I'll be there in about thirty minutes, Bob."

Noah started the car and headed out, then punched the icon on his phone that would dial Sarah's number. She answered even before he heard the ringing on his end.

"Hey, baby," she said. "How's it going down there? Do you miss me?"

"I do miss you," Noah said, carefully leaving any feigned emotion out of it. He wanted Sarah to hear the words from Noah, not from Rex.

She was silent for just a couple of seconds, then said, "I miss you so much. Everything okay?"

"Everything is great," Noah said, now slipping into the Rex personality. "I've got a great job as a bodyguard to the son of a big rich guy, and I'm on the way to close the deal on our house right now. Sure will be glad when you get here."

"Well, I've got some good news on that score," Sarah said. "I finished my classes a couple days early, and Professor Gary went ahead and gave me my certificate. You say the word and I can pack my clothes and help Neil pack up all his junk, and we can be on the way."

Reading between the lines, Noah knew that she was telling him she had absorbed all of the information about Angie Madison that Gary Mitchell had wanted her to learn. That meant, Noah was sure, that he had managed to use hypnosis on her despite her objections. He didn't ask about Neil, because she wouldn't have suggested coming unless Neil was also ready to go.

"Baby, that's awesome," Noah exclaimed. "Yeah, come on. I can't wait to see you. Hell, I can't even wait to see that nerdy brother of yours. Maybe the Ozarks will get him out of his room once in a while."

"Ooooh," Sarah squealed in delight. She turned away from the phone for a moment and called out to Neil. "Hey, Rex says he's ready for us to come on down. Start packing your crap." He heard an unintelligible response from Neil, and then she was back on the phone. "It'll take us a few hours to get packed, so we'll probably have to stop somewhere tonight. But that means we'll see you sometime tomorrow, so that won't be too bad."

They talked for a few more minutes as Noah drove, but then he arrived at Henson Realty and Sarah wanted to get on the road as soon as they could. They said their goodbyes, and Noah put the phone back into his pocket as he got out of the car.

He opened the trunk and pulled out the rest of the money from the safe, then carried it inside. The weight of the pistol in its holster on his belt felt good, and it was the first thing Bob Henson noticed when Noah walked into the office.

"You got that to keep people from trying to steal your money, right?" Henson asked nervously.

"No, it's actually for my new job," Noah replied. "I got hired as chief bodyguard for Ralph Morgan."

Bob's eyes went wide. "The kid who got shot last night? How in the world did you end up with that job?"

"I just happened to be in the right place at the right time. I saw the guy who tried to shoot him and jumped to stop it, but I was a split second too late. They're saying I kept the shot from being fatal, though, so Jimmy Morgan offered me the job this morning and I took it."

Bob was smiling broadly. "Rex, if you got in with Jimmy Morgan, you got it made. I'm not asking, but I bet your pay is probably pretty good?"

Noah put a grin on his face. "Let's just say that, by the end of the year, I could afford another house like this. Maybe two of them, come to think of it."

Bob grinned and nodded, and then they turned their attention to the business at hand. It took about twenty minutes to fill out all of the paperwork and sign it, and then Noah handed over $70,698, which included all of the fees required for transferring property in the state of Arkansas. Bob had already gotten the termite inspections and surveys done the day before, so in return for that much cash, he handed Noah a certified copy of the deed and a ring full of keys.

"I suspect they'll be calling it the Madison Place before too long," Bob said. "Believe me, it won't be long before the whole town knows who you are and pays attention to what you're doing. Between you and your sister, I suspect the name of Madison is going to make an impact on this town."

Noah thanked him, picked up all the paperwork, and took it out to the car. He shoved it into the safe in the trunk for the moment, then got into the car and drove to Kate's house. It was close to noon, so he wasn't surprised to find her at home, awake and drinking coffee.

"So, what's the latest?" Kate asked as he poured himself a cup.

"Well, I got the house—and why didn't you tell me it was rumored to be haunted?"

"To tell the truth, it never occurred to me. I'd heard those rumors once or twice, but I guess I just put them out of my mind. I don't believe in ghosts, do you?"

"If there were actually such things as ghosts," Noah said, "I'm fairly certain I would have been visited by some of the ones I've created."

Kate looked at him for a moment, then asked, "And how many have you created?"

"Truthfully? I don't actually know, but it would be well over a hundred. I'm pretty sure at least one of them would've found me by now, so I don't worry much about the afterlife. I stay busy enough with this one."

Kate shuddered. "I don't know how you live with it," she said, "but I guess that's what makes you the kind of specialist you are. Anyway, are you moving out today?"

"Yeah, I think I am. I told my wife about the house a little while ago, and she's got all her classes finished up so she's heading here this afternoon. I want to get myself settled into the house and start getting it ready for her."

Kate sat there for a moment and looked down at her cup, then popped her eyes back up to Noah's. "You want some help? You said the place was furnished, but you're going to need a lot of things before you can actually live there. I mean, does it come with dishes, pots and pans, brooms and mops, and all that stuff?"

Noah shook his head and remembered to put a grin on his face. "No, I checked all the cupboards and cabinets and they were bare. You want to come out and see the place? Maybe we can hit Walmart and get some of the stuff it needs before Angie gets here."

Kate's eyes lit up. "Thought you'd never ask," she said. "Trust me, the place is going to need a woman's touch before your wife sees it."

They got into Noah's car, and he drove her out to his new house so she could start making a list of what it might need. He unlocked the outer front door that led onto the enclosed porch, then unlocked the main door that led inside. Kate followed him and was slightly overwhelmed by how nice the place really was.

She was even more amazed at all of the antique furnishings. "Rex, do you realize you got a small fortune sitting here? I know a little bit about antiques, and some of these are quite valuable. And just look at the condition—they look like they're either brand-new or they've just been freshly redone. Are you going to hang on to them or put them up for sale?"

"I thought I'd let Angie decide on that," Noah said. "That way, if we need to go buy new furniture, she can pick it out. Right now, I'm more concerned about getting the things we need so we can live here for a while. You know, the dishes, pots and pans, cleaning supplies. I think maybe we ought to buy new sheets for the beds, don't you think?"

Kate agreed and started making a list. The bed in the master bedroom was a queen-sized bed, but the rest were simply full-size, or what were once called double beds. She noted the sizes and then checked the pillows. "Pillowcases, too," she mumbled as she scribbled on her notepad.

Each of the bathrooms, both spotlessly clean, got several notes. Toilet tissue, soap, shampoo, toothbrushes, and toothpaste... Noah admitted to himself privately that he would never have thought of putting such things in bathrooms that no one was using at the moment.

And then they entered the kitchen. Kate looked around for several minutes, then turned to Noah. "Rex, are you sure you got enough money? If you want decent stuff in here, I'm about to set you back several hundred dollars, and that's not even counting some basic groceries and staples."

"Have at it," Noah said. "I've got a little extra stashed away."

"It's a good thing. There is absolutely nothing in here. I found one old pie pan, but it was so nasty you wouldn't want to try to cook anything in it." She started adding to her list, and Noah told her he'd be back. He walked out the back door and around the house to his car, then headed back toward town.

There was a farm supply store not far from where he turned onto Highway 221, with a nice convenience store built on to it. Noah went in and ordered two large coffees, dumped a lot of sugar into Kate's cup, the way he'd seen her do back at her house, then grabbed a big box of the fried chicken they offered. It came with fried potato wedges, so it would be fairly easy to eat and clean up after.

He paid for it all and ended up introducing himself to the guy running the cash register, who seemed pretty excited to be meeting Kate Madison's brother. Noah smiled and promised to have her stop by sometime, then managed to escape with his purchases.

Kate was still making notes when he got back, but she was delighted to declare herself finished when she saw the food and the coffee. They pulled out the old oak chairs and sat down at the table to eat.

"I found something for you while you were gone," Kate said. She pointed to the counter, where a pair of garage door remotes were sitting. "I already tested them and they work. They were hidden in the back of the little cabinets over the refrigerator. I had to stand on a chair to look in there, but something told me I'd find a surprise."

"Cool," Noah said. "It'll be nice to be able to put the Charger inside."

"I'm amazed that this is so good," Kate said, after biting into a piece of chicken. "I've seen the sign for their chicken a thousand times, but I never got up the nerve to stop and check it out. This isn't bad at all."

"Yeah, you ought to stop in there and get some now and then," Noah said. "The kid who works there seems to think he's your biggest fan. I told him I'd try to get you to stop by and give him an autograph."

"Be glad to," Kate said. "You always have to take care of your fans. The more they like you, the better your ratings, and the better your ratings, the better and longer your pay keeps coming. I like to get to know as many of them as I can."

They chatted while they ate and then cleaned up the best they could. Noah used the bag he'd carried everything out of the store with as a trash bag and took it out the back to where four steel panels with holes in them had been set up as an incinerator. There was nothing inside it, but Noah tossed the bag in.

"That'll be gone by the time you get around to looking at it again," Kate said. "Raccoons, possums, even wild house cats—they all run loose around here. Something will climb in there and eat what they can, and drag the rest back to wherever they keep their nest."

"Everything's gotta eat," Noah said. They climbed into the car, and he headed back into town toward Walmart.

Kate had been somewhat optimistic on her estimate of what Noah would spend. After two hours in Walmart, the grand total came to just over twelve hundred dollars. Noah simply pulled a wad of hundred-dollar bills from his pocket and peeled them off as if it were no big deal.

Kate watched hungrily as he did so but said nothing until they were back in the car. Once he had driven away from Walmart and was on Industrial Park Road, she finally couldn't hold it in any longer.

"Are you just naturally rich?" she asked. "Or does your outfit give you an unlimited budget?"

"It depends on the mission," Noah said. "For this one, it was decided that I should look like I came to town flush, but getting to the bottom of my cash stash. Buying the house definitely put a dent in my reserves, but I thought it was a logical move. If it took me some time to get in with the Morgan people, I could always work at the chicken plant. Owning the house means no rent or mortgage payments, so my cost of living would be lower."

Kate shook her head. "I guess that makes sense. I have to live on my radio salary, and trust me, it ain't much. I shouldn't gripe, though, at least it keeps me out of the chicken plant. I worked a while there in deboning, and I've got so many scars on my hands it's ridiculous."

Noah looked over at her. "I can help, if you need a little extra cash. That would be in character, since I'm supposed to be your brother. Do you need a few hundred right now? I can spare it."

Kate shook her head. "No, goodness, no," she said. "For one thing, I don't need my bosses wondering how I'm spending more money than I'm making, but I also don't want to get dependent on you. I hate to be this blunt, but every other agent that has gone after the Morgans has ended up dead. If they figure out who you are, they're going to be coming after me, too. Bear that in mind, okay? If you blow your cover, you've blown mine, as well."

"Relax," Noah said. "I don't plan on blowing anything."

They got back to the house and carried everything inside. Kate set to work changing the bedding while Noah began opening boxes in the kitchen. It wasn't difficult for him to figure out where to put the dishes, and the pots and pans went into some of the lower cabinets near the range. Brooms and dust mops and cleaning supplies went into the hall closet, along with the vacuum cleaner and hardwood floor system he had bought. He even managed to set up the coffee maker they had purchased by the time Kate got done in the bedrooms and bathrooms.

"You surprise me, little brother," Kate said. "I wouldn't have thought you could organize things so well."

"It's that thing we talked about that happened when I was a kid," Noah said. "It left me with an extremely logical mind. I had a friend who actually used to call me Mr. Spock, because I had no emotions and thought everything through to its logical conclusion. Logic dictates that certain things need to be in certain places, so putting all this away wasn't that big a deal."

Kate nodded and smiled at him. "Rex," she said, "it's—it's good to have you back."

CHAPTER TWENTY-TWO

Noah's phone chimed, and he glanced at it to see that it was a text message from Neil. He opened it up and read, "I need rest. Just keep looking at the new moon, and we'll be there before you know it."

The message meant that the mole had been in contact through the car forum's email system, and it had been relayed into the game that Neil was playing as part of his cover. Neil and Noah had devised a simple code that would allow him to send Noah the phone number that always appeared in the messages. The first seven words of the message would start with a letter that corresponded with the correct number on a telephone dial pad. Noah's mind read the message and instantly translated it to 467-555-2866.

"Kate, I've got to step outside and make a phone call," he said. She only nodded, still checking the cabinets and drawers to make sure he had put everything in its proper place.

Noah stepped out the back door and walked far enough away to be sure she could not overhear him, then dialed the number. It rang twice, and then the distorted voice answered.

"I wanted to tell you that you were quite effective in Odessa," the mole said. "I also wanted to discuss something else with you, if you have a moment."

"I'm all alone," Noah said. "Just spit it out, will you?"

"I get the impression, Mr. Wolf, that you are not entirely happy in your present employment, and yet it seems perfectly suited to you. May I ask what the problem might be? Oh, and that was a polite way of saying tell me what the problem is."

Noah hesitated for a moment, then let out a sigh. "You already know so much about me, so I'm sure you know I just got married, right?"

"Of course. Go on."

"We both know, my wife and I, that our lives aren't likely to be very long in this business, and one of us is going to end up alone, sooner or later. I don't like the fact that my wife has to be part of my team. I know we both got recruited because we were looking for a way out of the penalties we were facing, but I just wish there were a way I could get her out."

"I actually thought that might be part of the problem. Tell me something, Mr. Wolf, what would you say if I told you I could accomplish that? That if you were to agree to work exclusively for me, I can make it possible for the two of you to be certified dead and then give you new identities. I have it within my power to completely erase you from the system so that your fingerprints, your DNA, no matter what system might be used, will not come back to you. I could pay you very, very well to handle situations for me, and you would be sleeping at home with your wife most nights. Considering your skills, I suspect you will survive any mission I might send you on. You could give your family a normal life, Mr. Wolf, even have children if you wish."

Noah was quiet for several seconds, but then he spoke rapidly. "Don't play with me," he said, "don't tempt me with something you can't deliver. If I tried to cut out on the outfit I work for now, they would never give up trying to hunt either of us down, not me or my wife. I won't even listen to any idea like that unless you can guarantee they will consider us dead. Can you do that? Can you really do that?"

"Of course I can," the mole said. "All I would need is to know the location and nature of a mission that requires your entire team. I know that she'll be joining you in a couple of days, so it might even be possible to use this particular mission that you're on at the moment."

"Holy crap," Noah said. "Geez, man, this is outta left field, you know?" He made a point of stomping around in the gravel for moment, holding the phone down so that the mole could hear his footsteps. He put it back to his ear a moment later. "I've gotta think about this. Hey, what about—there's another kid in my team, Neil, the computer guy. What if I wanted to bring him out, too?"

"Could you honestly trust him? If he made any contact with his past, it could lead back to you and Sarah. I think you should consider carefully before risking your lives for a third party."

Noah sighed deeply. "Yeah, I guess you're right. I just hope they reassign the kid; he's pretty good at what he does." He stopped talking for a couple of seconds, then went on. "You said I'd be home most nights. What's the risk rating on the missions you would send me on?"

"Rarely higher than a four. Most of the time it will be like Odessa, simply applying persuasion. Occasionally, I may need to take advantage of your skills as an assassin, however. I manipulate powerful people, Mr. Wolf. You can't always do that without applying the most personal form of warfare."

Noah crunched around in the gravel for a few more seconds, again holding the phone away from his ear. When he put it back, he said, "Okay, let me get this straight. You want me to let you set it up so that E & E thinks we're dead, and then I have to work for you. In return, I get to give my wife a chance at a normal life, maybe even to the point we could have kids. Now, here's my question: what happens if, somewhere down the line, you get really pissed at me and decide to let my former employers know where I live?"

"As long as you do the jobs I ask of you, there's no risk of that. Mr. Wolf, this is simply a business proposition. It gets you what you want, and gets me an asset that I desperately need. If you need to think it over, I understand. I'll be in touch again in a few..."

Noah cut him off. "The only part I need to think about," he said, "is how far I trust you. Remember that I'm out here in the cold, and if we do this, that means my wife will be out in the cold as well. I have absolutely nothing to convince me you won't cut my throat sooner or later. Toss me a lifeline, here, would you?"

There was silence on the other end of the line for a few seconds, but then: "What kind of lifeline are you looking for?" asked the distorted voice.

"A meeting," Noah said. "Face-to-face, you and me. You can take any security precautions you want, bring me in blindfolded, whatever. Before I can agree to this, though, before I can agree to put my wife's life on the line, I want to look you in the eye. If I do, I'll know just how far I can trust you."

The silence lasted longer this time, and Noah began to wonder if the line had gone dead. Suddenly, however, he heard the distorted voice again. "No one sees me face-to-face, Mr. Wolf. Even if I were inclined to do what you asked, I don't have anyone who could blindfold you and bring you to me. The fact is that this is how I have remained in operation for more than five years. I understand your need to know if you can trust me, but you must understand that I do not trust you, or anyone else."

"You're offering me the only hope I've ever got of having a family," Noah said quickly. "I want to take you up on it, I really do, but I don't want to put us at even greater risk than we already face. If you really want me as badly as you say you do, you find a way for us to meet. That's all I'm asking."

"As I said, Mr. Wolf, I understand. I will be in touch." The line went dead.

Noah put the phone back into his pocket and went back inside the house.

"Everything okay?" Kate asked as he stepped back into the kitchen.

"It's my wife," he said, smiling. "She's pretty impatient about getting out here. They're getting all packed up and ready and will be on the way shortly."

"Well, I'm looking forward to meeting her. She must be quite a woman if she can put up with you."

Noah grinned. "I'm pretty sure you won't be the first person who ever told her that."

Kate glanced at the watch she wore on her wrist. "Holy smokes," she said. "I know we had a late lunch, but it's almost six o'clock. I need to get home and have some dinner and then get to bed. I have to get up awfully early in the morning to go to work, you know."

"Then let's get out of here and I'll buy you dinner," Noah said. "You pick the place."

"Just run through one of the fast-food joints," Kate said. "I don't have time to go out. I've still got to get a shower and everything."

They got back into the car and headed out, and Noah made a stop at the burger place. They got their order at the drive-through, and Noah drove on to Kate's house. "I need to gather up my things from here, anyway," he said as they went inside.

"No problem," Kate said. She grabbed some napkins from the counter and put them on the table, then sat down and ripped open the bag. "Forgive me, but I'm starving. I'm a creature of habit, and it's my habit to eat my dinner at six o'clock. That habit is probably why I have this waistline, but oh, well. There are some curses in life we just have to learn to live with."

Noah raised one eyebrow at her as he sat down and unwrapped his own sandwich. "I know the plan calls for you and my wife to become friends, but I think she's honestly going to like you. You talk a lot like she does."

"What can we say? Great minds think alike, right? Don't worry, she and I will get along just fine."

They finished eating and Noah went to gather his things out of the bedroom he had been using. He hadn't completely unpacked, so it only took him a few minutes to shove everything back into his bag. The only thing that didn't make it was the dirty clothes he hadn't had a chance to wash, yet. Kate stepped in and handed him a plastic trash bag for those, then reminded him that they had bought laundry soap. "You do know how to use a washer and dryer, right?"

"I do," Noah replied, "and I even know how to fold my clothes when they're done." He shoved the last of his dirty clothes into the bag and then turned and smiled at Kate. "Listen, thanks for everything," he said. "We've got to keep up this act for a while, so we'll be seeing a lot of each other. I just want you know I really appreciate what you've done, both for the mission and for me personally."

Kate started to speak but looked flustered for a moment. She closed her mouth and then opened it to start again. "You really are a lot like my brother," she said. "This is probably as close as I could ever get to having him back, even for little while. I should probably be the one thanking you."

Noah carried the bags out to the car and found several teenage boys standing around it, staring. Their tongues weren't exactly hanging out of their mouths, but the overall visual effect was about the same.

"That's your car, man?" asked one of the boys.

"It is," Noah said.

"Is that a General Lee car?" another asked.

"Yeah, it is. It's a 1969 Dodge Charger, but the General Lee wouldn't have been able to keep up with this one." He slid in behind the wheel and watched the boys as he started the big engine. Their eyes, already wide, got even bigger when the 540-cubic-inch hemi engine roared to life. The whining of the blower drive system could just be heard over the rumble from the exhaust system, and when Noah revved the engine once, the boys looked like they were about to jump out of their skin.

He tapped the horn once and put the car in gear, backing out onto the road and then starting the twenty-minute drive to his new and temporary home. He got there without incident, used the remote on his sun visor to open the garage door farthest from the house, and tucked the car inside. He closed the garage door, grabbed his bags, and carried them in. The door from the garage entered through the utility room, so he dropped his dirty clothes bag onto the washer as he walked on toward the master bedroom.

He tossed his bag onto the bed and then opened it to put his things away. There was a beautiful old dresser, which he planned to leave for Sarah, so he took the four-drawer chest that stood on the other side of the room for himself. He didn't have that many clothes with him, so it only took a few minutes to put everything away. His bath and shaving kit went into the master bathroom, and he was suddenly glad Kate had thought to buy towels. He took a long shower and then wrapped a towel around himself and sat down on the bed.

He took out his phone and dialed Sarah, and she answered quickly.

"Hey, babe," she said. "We still haven't gotten on the road. All the stuff we have to bring with us won't fit into my car, so we have to get a trailer. Your buddy Wally is putting a hitch on my car for me tonight, but I won't be able to get a trailer until tomorrow morning, about eight o'clock."

"That's okay, honey," Noah said. "It's actually only about a nine-hour drive. If you leave there by noon, you'll be here by ten o'clock, local time. I'll text you the address so you can come straight to the house. My sister, Kate, helped me get some dishes and stuff, but if you don't like what she picked out we can always go get more."

"Oh, come on, Rex, you know I'm not that picky. I'm sure it'll be fine. I'm just excited that we're finally going to have a home together."

"Me, too, babe. Is Neil giving you any trouble?"

"Not really," Sarah said. "He's just got so much computer junk that he has to bring along. If it wasn't for that, we'd already be on the way."

They talked for several minutes and then said good night. It was only a little after eight, but Noah planned on being up bright and early. His new job would actually begin in the morning, when Ralph Morgan was released from the hospital, and he planned to be there long before that happened.

"HOW IS HE DOING?" NEIL asked. "Everything going okay over there?"

"Seems to be," Sarah said. "That sister of his is being awfully helpful. Apparently she helped him pick out dishes and such for the house today. She and I might have to have a little talk when I get there."

Neil just looked at her for a moment. "Please correct me if I'm wrong," he said, "but isn't that something a sister would do?"

"Yeah, but... Okay, fine, you're right. I'm just a little jealous, okay? Now that he's mine, dammit, I have a right to be jealous."

Neil, his eyes wide, held up both hands and surrendered. "Did I say you didn't? I'm quite sure I never said you didn't have a right to be jealous. You can be as jealous as you want to, I don't mind a bit."

Sarah burst out laughing and threw a couch pillow at him. "Knock it off," she said. "Don't ruin my mad when I'm just getting it going. Besides, when I finally get to meet this 'sister,' I'm probably going to like her. From everything I've read about her, she seems like a pretty good person."

"She's a fed," Neil said. "There's no such thing as a good fed."

"You butthead," Sarah said. "Remember something—we're feds, too."

"Yeah? And your point is? But at least we're better than FBI agents. All we do is kill people; those bastards ruin their lives and then make them keep living."

Sarah stared at him for a moment. "Neil, what on earth soured you on the FBI so badly?"

Neil grimaced. "Who do you think came after me when I hacked the bank back in high school? I'll never forget how they marched right into school and took me out of my twelfth grade English class. I was handcuffed and dragged out like I'd murdered someone, right in front of everybody I knew. I was railroaded through court, tried as an adult, and sentenced to ten years for something they called 'digital bank robbery.' I hadn't actually stolen anything."

"But you did hack the bank, right? I mean, if you committed a crime, why were you so surprised when you got arrested?"

"Because I thought I was too good to get arrested, okay? I thought I had outsmarted everybody, but my whole life went down the tubes when they arrested me. The only good thing was when one of the agents on my case, a woman, said she didn't believe I was a danger to anybody, so they sent me to a federal prison camp, instead of putting me into one of the actual prisons. At a camp, you have to go out and get a job, and as long as you're back on the premises of the camp when you're supposed to be, you don't get hassled. I got hired on at Geek Squad, and that's where I met Rafael."

"Rafael? I don't think you ever mentioned him before. Who was Rafael?"

Neil grinned. "Rafael was the guy who showed me the mistakes I was making as a hacker. He taught me some tricks I'd never even dreamed of, but once he opened my eyes to what was possible, I suddenly started seeing new ways to use computers against themselves. Since I wasn't allowed to drive, most days it was just me and Rafael in the office, helping people with their computer problems over the phone or dispatching the house call crews. When things were dead, he would show me all sorts of things I'd never heard about before, but by the time I'd been there a year, I was teaching him things. The trouble was that he couldn't quite understand a lot of what I was saying."

"You're saying, he was smart, but you were smarter?" Sarah asked.

Neil shrugged. "Yeah, I guess so. He told me he wasn't surprised, that he had figured out right from the get-go that I'd pass him up in no time." Neil looked thoughtful for a long moment, then turned back to Sarah. "You know, it turned out Rafael was the one who put Allison on to me. She actually went after him first, but he told her that I was better, and that I deserved the second chance more than he did."

Sarah cocked her head at him. "Why? What was he in for?"

Neil looked down at his lap for a moment, then turned his face up to look into her eyes. "He had hacked into the traffic control system in San Francisco about eight years ago, and accidentally—which the court believed, by the way—set every traffic light to green. Over three hundred accidents happened over the span of twenty minutes, and a hundred and fifteen people died. He was still trying to fix the problem when the cops tracked him down and arrested him."

Sarah looked at Neil's face for a moment, then picked up the remote for the TV. "Let's find a movie," she said. "Real life is too depressing."

CHAPTER TWENTY-THREE

N oah was awake at six and was shaved, dressed, and out the door by six thirty. Morgan had told him the day before that Ralph's doctor was supposed to see him around eight thirty or nine, but Noah wanted to be there early and talk to the men who were already watching over the boy. There were two sheriff's deputies at the hospital when he arrived, but one of them was Collins. Noah walked up to him boldly, and the deputy cut off his conversation with his colleague.

"Deputy Collins," Noah said, "I've been hired..."

"Yes, sir, I already know," Collins said. "The sheriff briefed us this morning, and we're supposed to assist you in any way you need us to."

Noah had expected it, but a part of him was almost surprised. "Okay," he said. "I'm going up to talk to the people on duty now, but I may be letting some of them go. Scott Forney should be here about any minute with a few potential new people. Would you send him on up when he gets here?"

"Yes, sir, Mr. Madison," Collins said. The other deputy nodded to Noah with a smile, and he turned and walked into the hospital.

Morgan had told him that Ralphie's room was on the fourth floor, and it took Noah only a couple of minutes to find it. A large man with missing front teeth tried to stop him from going into the room, but Noah simply stared at him. "Do you have any idea who I am?" Noah asked, and the big man shook his head. "My name is Rex Madison," he said. "Jimmy Morgan hired me to take over as chief of security for Ralph. Now stand aside so I can go in and make sure my charge is okay."

Missing Teeth stepped aside, and so did three other men with him. Noah entered the room to find Ralphie sitting up in the bed, his tray table pulled up close and holding the remains of his breakfast.

"So you're Rex Madison, are you? Pa told me you'd be taking over today. I guess I owe you a big thank-you; Pa says if it wasn't for you, that dweeb Benny might've actually managed to kill me."

Noah shrugged. "I can't say for sure. All I know is that I saw a gun come out and get pointed your way, so I tried to stop anything bad from happening. Couple of deputies told me that the security tape looked like he had a good bead drawn on you, and that when I grabbed him and threw off his aim."

Ralph grinned at him. "Well, thanks, whatever you did. All I remember is seeing that gun barrel appear in front of me and realizing that I was looking straight down it. I'm smart enough to know that means it was aimed right at one of my eyes. I'd much rather have this concussion than be blind or dead, right?"

"I'd have to agree with you on that," Noah said. He turned and looked at the men who were standing around the room, staying out of his way. "These were your bodyguards?"

"Yeah," Ralph said. "That's Ronnie and Billy Jim and..."

"I don't care who they are," Noah said. "Not one of you had seen a picture of me, had you?"

All of the men in the room, including Ralph, shook their heads. "No," said one of them. "Why? Was we supposed to see one?"

"Not necessarily," Noah said, "but you should never have taken my word for the fact that I was supposed to be taking over today. All four of you stepped out of my way on my say-so and let me walk right up to Ralph, who's laying in his hospital bed and completely vulnerable. If I were somebody other than who I am, then maybe whoever hired Benny to try to kill Ralph could have gotten to me, too. If that were the case, Ralph would be dead already, and I probably could have killed all four of you before you could react. You're all fired. Get out of here now, before I really get pissed off."

"Hey, wait a minute," said one of the men. "Who do you think you are? You can't..." The man fell suddenly silent as he dropped his eyes downward. Noah had drawn his pistol and pointed it directly at the big fellow's groin.

"Care to bet?" Noah asked. "If I had been a killer, I could have shot Ralph as soon as I walked in and then taken the four of you down with a single shot each. Firing five shots and having to spin around once would take me about 1.3 seconds. It would take any one of you more than two seconds just to draw your weapon, and another 1.5 seconds or more to aim it at me. I'd even have time for a second shot if I missed a couple of you with the first. And even if one or two of you survived, would you really want to? Ralph would be dead; would you really want to face Jimmy?"

All four of the men were staring at Noah, and all four of them swallowed hard as they considered his last question. One by one, without another word, they walked down the hall toward the elevator and left the hospital.

"Wow," Ralph said. "You were a little rough on them, don't you think?"

"Not nearly rough enough," Noah replied. "They let a perfect stranger walk into your hospital room without even checking to see if I was armed. What I said to them was true. If I were hired to finish what Benny Smoot failed to accomplish, you would already be dead. Your father has hired me to make sure you stay safe. I'm not going to have idiots like that working your security detail. As far as I'm concerned, kid, you're more important than the president of the United States. That means I want a security detail on you that's every bit as good as the one on him."

Ralph let out a sigh. "Okay, look, Rex, let's talk. See, Pa thinks I can't take care of myself, but there's a lot of things that I like to do where I don't want a bunch of freaking babysitters around, know what I mean? That's why I kinda like the guys I had, because they knew how to get lost when I wanted them to. Now, if you're taking over, you and me got to work this out."

Noah looked at the boy for a long moment, then shook his head. "What part of 'I'm going to keep you alive' do you not understand? I'm going to put together a security detail that is going to shadow you twenty-four hours a day. There will be men standing outside your bedroom door and under your bedroom window all night long, and when you get up in the morning, at least two of them will be at your side from the moment you roll out of bed until you turn out the lights again. I don't care if you and your girlfriend are doing the horizontal hula—there will be at least two armed men within three feet of you at all times, do you understand me?"

Ralph's face fell. "Aw, c'mon, man," he said. "I gotta have a little bit of privacy, know what I mean? Me and my girl, we like to—you know? I can't have a couple of goons standing around when I'm trying to get her in the mood, now, can I?"

"Sorry, Ralph," Noah said. "But this is how it's going to be."

"How what's going to be?" Jimmy Morgan asked as he entered the room, Scott Forney right beside him.

"Pa, you gotta talk to this guy," Ralph said to his father. "He's saying he's gonna have bodyguards standing over me every minute of the day. Come on, Pa, I don't need no babysitters. Hell, I already pack a gun of my own. I don't need somebody like this goon standing over me all the time."

Morgan smiled at his son, but then his hand flashed out and slapped the boy across the face. "You let me tell you something," he said. "Somebody tried to kill you a couple nights ago. Now, maybe it was just Benny getting his tweak on, or maybe somebody paid him to try to take you out, like he said. Either way, we now have a situation where we can't take any chances. We've got to make sure you're safe, because you're the next generation of the Morgan empire. What that means is, if this man right here says he's going to have somebody standing next to you while you take a dump, you might as well just ask the guy to hold the toilet paper for you. Rex has already been through some pretty bad stuff, and he's managed to survive it. That tells me he's a man who can think on his feet, and that means he's probably a man who can keep you from getting killed. He's going to be in charge of your security from now on, and if I hear of even one time you try to give him or his people the slip, you're going to answer to me. You got that, boy?"

Ralph's eyes were wide and locked on his father. "Yes, sir," he said shakily. "No problem, Pa."

"There'd better not be," Jimmy said. "After what happened the other night, I'm not taking any chances with you. You might not understand it, son, but you're the most important thing in the world to me. All the rest of this could go to hell in a hand basket, but if anything happened to you I'd be destroyed. Now, Rex is the kind of man who can figure out pretty quickly what to do to keep you safe, so I don't want to hear any more talk about you not doing what he says."

"Yes, sir," Ralph said. "There won't be any." He looked up at Noah. "Rex, I'm sorry about all that. We got no problem, I promise you."

"We're good," Noah said. "I just want to do my job, that's all."

"And on that note," Forney said, standing behind Noah, "I've got a few people waiting in the hall for you to meet. Ready?"

"Jimmy?" Noah looked to Morgan for permission, and Morgan nodded. He turned and followed Forney out into the hall, where four large men were waiting.

"Guys," Forney said, "this is Rex Madison. Like I told you, Jimmy just put him in charge of Ralphie's security, and he's looking for a few good men." A couple of the men snickered at the Marine Corps reference. "Rex, this is Jake, David, Brendan, and Shawn. I've been knowing them pretty much all my life, and they're not only pretty stout, every single one of them has a brain in his head. I thought they might be useful to you because you could put one of these guys in charge of a crew and then relax."

Noah looked them over and nodded. "That would give me one for each shift, and two guys to cover days off. Good thinking, but don't expect to get yourself out of this."

Forney laughed. "Thought never crossed my mind, boss," he said. "I'll do whatever you tell me to do; I just thought these guys would be beneficial."

Noah smiled at him. "Okay. For today, I want two of these men—Jake and Shawn—with me on the day shift. David, we'll find a couple of guys to put with you for the evening, and Brendan can run the graveyard shift." He gave each of the men his cell number and make sure they all had one another's. "David, you call me at four, and I'll let you know where to meet up and take over. Brendan can call you at midnight, and I'll find him in the morning."

"Sounds good, boss," David said.

Brendan extended a hand, and Noah accepted it. "Thanks for this, Rex," he said. "Scott's been trying to get me moved up out of the grunt department."

"Well, I'm giving you the chance because of his endorsement. The job description is very simple: we don't let anybody hurt the kid. If that means you have to take the bullet, you do it. I suspect that would be better than trying to face Jimmy if anything happened to Ralph, anyway."

Brendan chuckled. "I can personally guarantee it," he said.

The two men left to go and prepare themselves for their shifts, and Noah beckoned Jake and Shawn into the hospital room. Just before he followed them, he turned to Forney.

"Think you can find a couple of reliable guys to put under each of them? And we'll need people for off days. The last thing I need is for security guys to get exhausted, so I don't want anybody working more than five days straight."

Forney grinned. "Other than yourself, you mean?"

Noah shot the grin back at him. "Comes with the job, man."

"I know a few guys," Forney said. "I'll have to steal them from other crews, but Jimmy won't mind. I'll get them all gathered up, and you can meet them this afternoon, okay?"

"Sounds good," Noah said. "Let me know where and when." He turned and walked into the room, while Forney started down the hall.

Jimmy was joking with the two new men when Noah got inside. "Rex, you're already stealing some of my best guys," he said gruffly when he saw Noah, but then he cracked a smile. "Relax, I'm yanking your chain. I told you to pick whoever you wanted, I meant it. These are good boys, here."

He turned around and looked at his son, then slapped him gently on the cheek. "I'm gonna go," he said. "I'll see you at home tonight?"

"Sometime," Ralph said. "I want to see Darlene tonight, too. She was going to come up and see me yesterday, but I told her to wait. Didn't want her to see me looking weak, you know?"

"Damn right," Jimmy said. "Never let them see you in a moment of weakness. You just behave yourself, and make sure you don't give your security any problems." He patted Noah on the shoulder and walked out of the room.

It turned out that Ralph already knew both Jake and Shawn and grudgingly admitted that he could stand having them to hang out with. "At least they're not assholes," he said. "I just don't want anybody hitting on my girl or making nasty comments when we—do the horizontal hula." He threw a grin at Noah.

Noah nodded and grinned back, then turned to the other men. "I'll make that an order," he said. "When Ralph and his girl are together, I want you paying more attention to what's going on around you than to what they're doing. Okay?"

Both men were stifling grins of their own, but they solemnly promised not to try to watch.

"Good," Noah said. "What you carry for hardware?"

Jake swung his jacket out so Noah could see the nickel-plated Glock 40 on his belt, and Shawn did likewise, displaying a pair of compact revolvers.

"Thirty eights," he said. "I just do better with revolvers, but they don't hold as many rounds, so I carry a spare."

"Fine by me," Noah said. "Just as long as you know how to use them." He turned to Ralph. "I'm planning to keep three men on you at all times. Two will be your shadows, and the third will be in charge but somewhere out of sight most of the time. During the daytime, I'll be with you most of the time, as well."

Ralph shrugged. "Ain't like I get a say in it, right?" He tried to sound cheerful, but Noah detected a hint of resentment in the comment.

"Probably no more than I do," he said. "Look, Ralph, this is just a job to me, but I'd really prefer if we get along. It'll make both our lives easier, don't you think?"

Ralph rolled his eyes but managed another grin. "Yeah, that makes sense. It ain't like I got nothing against you, not really, I just never thought I'd be having to have babysitters again. Know what I mean?"

"We'll do our bests to be unobtrusive. Now, you're supposed to be getting out of here today?"

"So they told me yesterday," Ralph said. "Doc usually comes through here around nine, so it shouldn't be much longer."

"Cool," Noah said. "Meanwhile, I need a cup of coffee." He turned to Shawn and handed him a ten-dollar bill. "They've got some kind of a cafeteria downstairs; I saw the sign when I came in. Go fetch us each a cup. Ralph, you want one?"

The boy shook his head. "No, but I can sure stand a Mountain Dew."

"And a Mountain Dew," Noah said. Shawn nodded, took the money, and left the room.

The next ninety minutes were spent just waiting for the doctor, and he finally showed up at just a little past nine. He talked to Ralph for a couple of minutes, then told him he could start getting dressed and ready to leave. "I'll sign the release, and the nurse will be in in a few minutes. I'm giving you something for the headaches you're bound to have, but other than that you're good to go."

"About time," Ralph said. He threw off the sheet and climbed out of the bed, digging in the little nightstand for his clothes, then carried them into the bathroom to get dressed. He was out a few minutes later, just as the nurse entered the room.

"Doctor says you're supposed to take it easy for couple of days," she said, "and he gave you a prescription for a mild painkiller. Sign here, and here, and then you can leave."

Ralph signed where he was told, and Noah sent Jake out ahead of them. He made a mental note to purchase some radios, the type used by other security teams, and train the men in their operation. For the moment, he just had to count on hearing any gunshots if Jake ran into a problem.

Shawn had driven his own car to the hospital, so Noah told Jake to ride with him while escorting Ralph to the Charger. The boy's eyes grew wide when they approached the car, and he just about fainted when Noah started it up.

"Man, this is awesome," he said. "You want to sell it?"

Noah grinned at him. "You don't have enough money," he said. "This is my baby."

"You sure about that?" Ralph asked with a laugh. "Money isn't exactly a problem for me."

"Just trust me on this." Noah cruised through town at normal speeds, then looked over at Ralph when they got to the town square. "Anywhere in particular you want to go right now?"

"Yeah, home," the boy said. "I need to get changed. This shirt still has blood on it."

"Cool. Where is home?"

"Go out to the Outpost and hang a right. I'll show you from there."

The Outpost was a service station and convenience store almost a mile out of town toward Eureka Springs. Noah opened the car up a little bit when they got outside the city limits, and Ralph laughed with delight. He slowed again to make the turn, but the two-lane county road was almost perfectly straight for quite a way, so he punched the accelerator and the car leaped forward, rear tires screaming.

The acceleration slammed them both back into their seats, and Ralph gripped his armrest. "Holy shit," he yelled. "This is incredible. What's under the hood?"

"Hemi," Noah said. "Five hundred and forty cubic inches and over nine hundred horsepower." He shrugged. "It does all right."

"All right? Dude, you gotta take this out to the drag strip. You will mop the floor with everybody else!"

Noah laughed. "Maybe someday," he said. "Might be fun."

"Yeah, okay, but slow down. That's my turn up there. Hang a right."

CHAPTER TWENTY-FOUR

Noah turned where the boy had indicated and saw the house they were headed to off in the distance. The driveway was almost a mile long and looked like a nicely paved road. He pulled up in front and got out, with Shawn's late-model Camaro parking right behind him.

"You guys can wait out here," Noah said. "He's just going to change, so we shouldn't be long."

"Yes, sir," Shawn replied, and Jake echoed him.

Noah followed Ralph into the house, and they were instantly greeted by a small, gray-haired woman. "Hey, Marlene," Ralph said. "Just running in to change clothes."

Marlene caught him before he could get to the stairs and grabbed him by his shoulders. "You just hold on a minute, young man," she said. "What you mean, giving an old woman a scare like that? That isn't good for me, you know."

Ralph smiled and gave her a hug. "I'm fine, Marlene." He turned her so she was facing Noah. "This is Rex—he's the guy who saved my life. Pa hired him to run my security from now on, so you might as well get used to seeing him around."

She let go of Ralph and instantly threw her arms around Noah. "I heard about you, I heard what you did," she said. "Thank you, thank you so much. I've been taking care of this boy since he was a baby; I don't know what I would do if something happened to him."

Noah smiled and returned the hug. "I was just in the right place at the right time, ma'am," he said. "But now it's my job, so I'll make a point of taking care of him for you."

The short little woman squeezed him tighter for a second, then patted him on the shoulder as she let go. "Thank you," she said. "Thank you so much."

She turned and headed into another part of the house, and Ralph started up the stairs. Noah followed, looking around at the grandeur of the mansion. It appeared to be relatively new, but the architecture was impressive. The house was built almost entirely of stone, and there was a small waterfall flowing down the wall opposite the stairway.

"Nice place," he said.

"Yeah, Pa built it back when I was little. It's pretty nice, I guess."

They reached the top of the staircase, and Ralph entered the first door on the left. Noah followed him inside, and the boy turned and looked at him.

"You really gotta stand here while I change?"

"Your dad said I'm not supposed let you out of my sight," Noah said, "but you can step into the bathroom if you want. Just don't try going out the window. I'm pretty easygoing, but I can get awfully pissed if I feel like I'm being played."

Ralph grinned ruefully and shook his head. "Okay, okay," he said. "Be right back." He grabbed some clothes out of his dresser and stepped into the bathroom that was attached to his room. Noah could hear him moving around inside for a moment, and then he was back. He pulled his belt out of the pants he had taken off and threaded it through the loops, then looked up at Noah again.

"So, I'm supposed to be taking over from Ronnie Sneed," he said. "I figure we might as well go on out and talk to him today, start the whole transition thing, right?"

Noah nodded. "If that's the plan," he said. "Tell me about Sneed."

Ralph led the way out the door and started down the stairs. "Ronnie's been with the old man probably longer than anybody else," he said. "Back in the day, he was part of how everything got started.

That was with him and some others boosting cars and bringing them into the yard to cut up. Him and Pa got to be good friends, and Pa put him in charge of running the drug operation when he took it over. That was before my time, of course, but I've heard the stories over and over."

Marlene was nowhere in sight when they got to the ground floor, so Noah followed Ralph out the door. Jake and Shawn had been leaning against Shawn's car, but they snapped to attention as Noah came out the door.

Noah looked at Shawn. "Ralph needs to go see Ronnie Sneed. I want you to lead the way, and we'll follow."

"Yes, sir," Shawn said, and he and Jake got back into his car as Noah and Ralph climbed into the Charger. Shawn pulled out and swung around, and Noah fell in behind.

"IS THAT EVERYTHING?" Sarah asked.

Wally looked at the two men who were loading the trailer, and they nodded. "Looks like that's all of it," he said. "Just be sure to drive carefully. Have you ever pulled a trailer before?"

Sarah chuckled at him. "I've driven a Freightliner with a fifty-seven-foot trailer," I said. "My dad taught me when I was fifteen. I'm pretty sure I can handle a sixteen-footer."

Wally grinned back. "Yes, I'm sure you can. I'm also sure you're ready to get on the road, so don't let me keep you. I just want you to drive safe and be careful."

"I will," she said. She looked around at Neil, who was already climbing into the passenger seat, and slid in behind the wheel. She powered down the window and smiled up at Wally one more time. "I guess we'll see you when we see you," she said.

Wally waved as she drove away. He was sure she wasn't terribly happy with the car they had provided, but his understanding of the character of Angie Madison was that she was a simple type of girl. Sarah was leaving her Camaro behind and driving off to Arkansas in a ten-year-old Ford Explorer.

Of course, Wally's automotive crew didn't leave anything to chance. While the SUV looked like a typical one, it had been built to crank out well over six hundred horsepower. If it came down to it, the little SUV could probably outrun most late-model Corvettes.

Sarah looked over at Neil. "You got everything? We need to make any other stops before we leave?"

"I'm good," the skinny kid said. "Jenny left this morning on a mission of her own, so I'm ready to hit the road."

Sarah smiled and tapped the horn twice as they passed at the security gate, waving at the guard on duty. Most of the guards at R&D were familiar with her by now, and this one smiled and waved as they drove past.

The R&D center was on the north end of Kirtland, but there was a bypass road that took them around the city and straight to the interstate. It added about ten miles, but the lack of traffic lights made it popular. Sarah chose it and watched the trailer in her rearview mirror as she pressed down on the accelerator.

"It tracks pretty well," she said. "Doesn't wiggle around; that's a plus."

Neil had been looking down at the computer on his lap, and he looked up into her face with an expression of confusion. "Wiggle?"

"The trailer," Sarah said. "A lot of smaller ones like this tend to wiggle around a bit. Sometimes it's because of the way they get loaded; sometimes it's just because there's something not balance right in the load. I think we've got everything loaded properly, though."

Neil looked over his shoulder into the back window. The covered trailer was just a normal rental unit, the kind you see at dealerships all over the country. Sarah had gone and picked it up that morning, using her new ID and credit cards to pay for it.

"Looks fine to me," Neil said.

"That's what I said, it's fine. It shouldn't slow us down at all."

Neil grinned at her. "Aww," he said, "are you missing your hubby?"

Sarah grinned, but there was a slight pinkish tint to her face all of a sudden. "You bet your ass," she said. "Noah—I mean, Rex—isn't going to know what hit him when I get there."

"Good grief, he hasn't even been gone a whole week yet."

"Yeah, well, after the last few months even a day is too long. Now that he's mine, I want to take advantage of it every minute I can."

"Speaking of which," Neil said, "aren't you going to call and tell him we're on the road? As you just sort of pointed out with the name slip, we're supposed to be in character now. Wouldn't it be normal to call and say, 'Hey, lover boy, we just got on the road?' I'm pretty sure that would be normal, don't you think?"

Sarah stuck her tongue out at him. "Yes, and you're definitely in character. You're already being the annoying kid brother." She picked up her phone off the console between the front seats and hit the icon that would call Noah directly.

The answer on the second ring. "Hey, Angie," he said. "How's it going?"

"About sixty-five at the moment," Sarah said. "Just wanted let you know that we are on the way. It took a little longer to get the trailer and loaded than I thought, so my GPS says we wouldn't get there before about two o'clock in the morning. I'm thinking about driving straight through, what you think, babe?"

"That sounds like an awfully long drive," Noah replied. "Don't you think you ought to stop and get a room somewhere on the way?

Maybe Kansas City—you could be there by ten o'clock, probably. Get some sleep and come on down tomorrow?"

"I can't wait till tomorrow to see you," Sarah said, putting a bit of whiny sound in her voice. "It's been too long—I need to be with you."

Noah chuckled. "Okay, but just be careful. If you start feeling too tired, you stop and get a room somewhere. Understand me?"

Sarah laughed. "Yes, Daddy," she said sarcastically. "Come on, Rex, you know I can drive. How many times do I drive all the way to Texas to see you?"

"About twenty," Noah said, the answer instantly coming from the backstory he had been given. "But that was an even longer drive, and you always stopped about halfway. I just don't want you to overdo it and end up in an accident."

"I'll be careful. How's the new job going?"

Noah made a coughing sound. "This kid can be a royal pain in the ass," he said. "I've been driving him around all morning, and now it's getting close to lunchtime, so we're on the way to pick up his girlfriend at school. I guess he wants to take her out to lunch."

There was a burst of laughter and a protesting sound that came through Noah's phone. "I gather he's in the car with you now?" Sarah asked.

"Yep. I can't escape the little jerk, but at least his daddy is paying me very well." He laughed again. "Actually, Ralph isn't that bad. Pretty smart for only being nineteen years old."

"I seem to remember you being pretty smart when you were that age. You guys probably ought to get along pretty well, then."

"We actually do. Although if he tries to buy my car one more time, I may just stuff him in the trunk. Other than you, Black Beauty is my number one pride and joy. I've been trying to explain to him that she isn't for sale, but he doesn't like taking no for an answer."

"Yeah, well, I expect he'll lose that attitude pretty quickly with you around. Tell him I said to be glad he is married to you. You tell me no a whole lot more than I like."

"I only have your best interest in mind," Noah said. "You know I try to give you whatever you want, within reason. I mean, I even went out and bought you a house. I'm afraid you're going to get spoiled."

"Hey, spoiling me is your job, now. Don't act like it's such a burden—you love it and you know it."

"I do," Noah said with a chuckle. "And I love you."

"I love you more," Sarah said. "Ha! Gotcha!"

She could hear the smile in his voice. "Yeah, you got me that time. You win. Listen, babe, we're about to pull up at the school. I'll give you a call this evening, after I get off duty."

"Okay," she replied. "Talk to you then. Love you."

"Love you more," Noah said, and then he ended the call before she could reply.

In the Charger, Ralph was looking his direction and grinning. "That your girlfriend?"

Noah shook his head. "Wife," he said. "We've been married a little over three weeks, now. She was my girlfriend in high school, and when I went to the Fed joint, she waited. Used to drive all the way down to Texas to come see me every couple of months."

Ralph gave him a lascivious smile. "Federal prison, huh? Did they give you like, conjugal visits, that kind of thing?"

Noah rolled his eyes and laughed. "No, you don't get that in the Fed. At least, nobody I ever heard of did. Maybe that's something you only get if you're a snitch."

"That could be right," Ralph said. "Wouldn't surprise me, anyway. Here, turn in here." He pointed to a driveway that pulled in behind the school. It led to a parking lot filled with cars, and Noah drove the Charger off to a fairly empty area, off by itself. Shawn pulled in beside him and powered down his window.

"I want you and Jake to get out and stand either side of us," Noah said. "Look for anything out of the ordinary, but don't open fire on anybody unless they fire first. Just watch, and be ready for anything."

Both men nodded as they got out of the car and took up the positions Noah had indicated. He watched them until he was satisfied that they were able to keep most of the area under observation, then turned to Ralph. "Call your girl and tell her to come over here," he said. "I don't want you getting out of the car with so many hiding places around us."

Ralph rolled his eyes but took out his phone. "Hey, Darlene," he said when she answered. "Come out to the back parking lot. Look for the most incredible black car you've ever seen, and that's where you'll find me." He listened for a moment, then chuckled. "Trust me, baby, you'll know it when you see it. And hurry up, we don't want you to be too late getting back to class."

He put the phone back into his pocket and turned to Noah. "She'll be here in about three minutes," he said. "You care if we get into the back seat?"

Noah grinned. "I don't mind, but keep your clothes on back there. I don't want to have to disinfect it."

Ralph burst out laughing. "Man, you're cool," he said. "If I gotta have a babysitter, I'm glad it's you."

"It won't be me all of the time," Noah said, "but I'll be with you a lot during the day."

Ralph nodded, then pointed out through the windshield. "There she comes," he said. Noah looked in the direction he was pointing and spotted a pretty blonde girl. She looked young, and Noah turned his eyes back to Ralph.

"How old is she?"

"Sixteen," Ralph replied. "Her daddy is the mayor. We've been dating for about a year and a half now, though. It's cool."

Noah shrugged and said nothing. When the girls got close, Ralph stepped out and flipped the back of the front seat forward, then offered her his hand as she climbed inside. A moment later he was settled in beside her and made the introductions.

"Rex, this is Darlene," he said. "Baby, this is Rex Madison. He's my new bodyguard."

"Security chief," Noah corrected. "I run the security crew that is charged with keeping Ralph alive and healthy."

"That's awesome," the girl said. "I couldn't believe it when they said somebody tried to kill him. Why would they do that?"

"Somebody's apparently afraid I'll be even bigger and tougher than my dad," Ralph said. "I guess they figure if they take me out now, it'll save trouble for later."

"That's terrible," Darlene blurted out. "My daddy says your dad is what keeps this whole area running smoothly. This used to be the kind of place where drug gangs kind of ran everything, but since your dad took over all that stuff, we don't have the kind of crimes we used to get. Daddy says we're lucky to have Jimmy Morgan, so I think we'll be even more lucky to have you running everything."

Noah grinned. This girl was obviously full of hero worship, and Ralph was the target. Either that, or she was shrewd enough to know that getting her wagon hitched to the rising star was the smartest way to make sure she came out on top in local society. After a quick glance into her eyes through the rearview mirror, Noah began to think the latter was closer to the truth.

"Where to?" Noah asked.

"Someplace we can get out of the car," Ralph said. "I don't even care if it's burgers. I just don't want to eat in here."

Noah nodded. "No problem with that," he said. "I'm not really a fan of having food in the car."

He started the car and headed out of town, making the turn onto Highway 221. The farm supply store was only a couple of miles away, and they had picnic tables outside. The weather was balmy, so Noah decided it would be an appropriate place for a lunchtime rendezvous.

"OH-OH," NEIL SAID. "Rex just got a message from that other guy."

Sarah looked over at him. "Great," she said. "Better send it to him now."

"Doing so as you speak," Neil said. He composed the coded message that would give Noah a number he was supposed to call and then typed it into his phone.

NOAH'S PHONE BEEPED, signaling an incoming text message. He took it out of his pocket and read it quickly, then looked at the other two bodyguards.

"I need to make a phone call," he said, then got up and walked over to sit down inside the Charger. As soon as the door was closed, he dialed the number. The familiar distorted voice came on the line almost instantly.

"How is your mission going?" the voice asked.

"It's going," Noah replied. "You figure out how to set up our meeting yet?"

"That's exactly why I'm calling," the mole said. "I'll be very close to you tomorrow evening. Have you seen the town of Eureka Springs yet?"

"Yes, I've been over there."

"I'll be attending a function there tomorrow at seven. At 8:05, I will be finished and will call you. I am going to meet with you, as we discussed, but I want you to understand that I am not coming alone.

When I call, I'll tell you where we can meet, but if my people or I were to see any sign of a problem, I can assure you that you will never leave their alive. Immediately afterward, your wife would become a target. Do we understand one another?"

"Perfectly, like crystal. As I told you, all I want is for you to convince me this is a legitimate offer. If you can get us out, I'm all for it."

The line went dead, and Noah put the phone back into his pocket. There was no safe way for him to let anyone know what was going on, not until Neil arrived with his computers. He sat there for a moment, then took his phone back out and dialed the number that rang through to Sarah.

"Hey, baby," she said as she answered. "Miss my voice already?"

"Yes," Noah said. "And the kid is busy munching on chicken with his girlfriend, with the rest of his security team keeping watch. I figured I had a couple of minutes alone, so I wanted to give you a call."

"Aww, that's so sweet. We're just barely on the interstate right now, got on a few minutes ago. I've got my cruise set at eighty, just a little over the speed limit. Hopefully all the cops will be too busy to pay much attention, and I'll get there a little earlier. I really don't want to stop anywhere tonight."

"Well, I admit I hope you don't have to. Can't wait to see you, sweetheart. How's Neil doing on this long ride?"

"Like always," Sarah said. "Playing games on his stupid computer."

"My computer is not stupid," Neil said in the background. "It's just not quite as smart as I am."

Noah chuckled. "Maybe I'm just getting horny," he said. "Been away from you too long, and I can stand to kick his butt in another game of chess."

"That'll be the day," Neil said loudly. "She's got the volume turned up so loud I can hear you crystal clear."

"Shut up," Sarah said. "Ignore him, baby. I'm horny too. If I didn't have this trailer hanging on the back, I'd kick it up another five miles an hour."

"No, don't do that. I just hope you manage to make it in tonight. I really can't wait to see you, baby."

The reference to a chess game was a code that Noah and Neil had worked out before Noah left. It meant that there was a development in the mole situation, so Noah was confident that Neil would relay that information back to Allison. Once they arrived, Noah could fill him in on the details about the meeting, and Neil would be able to transmit that information to one of the gamers back at Neverland.

CHAPTER TWENTY-FIVE

It was almost three in the afternoon before Forney called. "I got you some guys," he said. "Where would you like to meet up?"

"Take them out to my place," Noah said. "We'll be there in about fifteen minutes."

He and Ralph were in the car at the time, so Noah made a couple of turns to get back onto the highway and headed for his new house. Ralph looked over at him, and there was a nervous glint in his eye.

"You really bought the haunted place, right?"

"That's the rumor," Noah said. "I haven't seen any sign of ghosts, though. To be honest, I think the whole story is bogus. Apparently the old guy had something wrong with his lungs and coughed up a crap ton of blood all over his kitchen. The story about him killing himself there came from the people who went to clean it up, but I checked and double-checked. He died in the hospital of complications from emphysema. Don't think there's any haunting going on out at my place."

The kid smiled, but the nervousness didn't quite fade away.

When they got to the house, Forney and the others had not arrived yet. Noah parked in the driveway and led Ralph inside, leaving Shawn and Jake out in the yard. The boy was looking all around as they entered, and made a point of poking his head into every doorway for at least a few seconds.

"I think you're right," he said, visibly relaxing. "I think I'd feel it if this place was really haunted."

Noah shrugged. "I don't feel anything. I've got root beer and cola. You want something?"

"Got any beer? The real stuff, I mean?"

Noah grinned. "Sure," he said. He went into the kitchen and came back a moment later with two bottles of Bud Light and passed one to the boy. They sat down, Ralph on the couch and Noah in a recliner, to wait for Forney and the others.

They didn't wait long. They arrived a few minutes later, and Noah invited them all inside.

Forney made the introductions all around, and Noah spoke with each of the new candidates for a few seconds. As far as he could tell, all of them were serious about their willingness to take the job, so he agreed to taking them on. Two of them, men named Chuck and Riley, he immediately assigned to the afternoon shift with David, whom Forney had also brought along. David took his new subordinates outside to talk, and it appeared they were going to get along well.

Noah delegated the responsibility for scheduling to Forney and then told him to take over running the day crew. Noah would also be present, he said, at least most of the time, but with his wife coming in late that night he would probably be late in the morning. Having Forney in charge, however, would make it possible for Noah to move himself around, get a little rest when he needed so that he could pop in on the other shifts and see how they were doing. Forney shook his hand and left, taking all of the other men with him.

At four, Noah told Shawn and Jake they could go off duty, then offered each of them a beer. They hung around for an hour or so, then headed for their homes. Each of them seemed surprisingly proud of his new job, and Noah suspected they had wives or girlfriends they wanted to brag to for the evening.

David and his men took over then, and Ralph left with them. Noah was finally alone and allowed himself to relax for a bit. He picked up the satellite TV controller and turned on the television, then kicked off his shoes and put his feet up. A moment later he sat up again, took the pistol off his belt, and laid it on an end table beside his chair, then leaned back once more.

He caught the local news programs and paid particular attention to a couple of stories about murder in the area. It seemed the local sheriff's office was having a hard time finding clues in the recent murder of a local thug named Benny Smoot, but they were confident they would make an arrest sometime in the next few days. The other murder had happened a few months earlier, when a homeless man had apparently been robbed and then beaten and set on fire. He had not died at the time but had suffered burns over most of his body and passed away almost a week later in the hospital.

In this case, there was genuine outrage in the sheriff's voice when he appeared on camera. Apparently the old fellow had been a veteran, a local fixture around town for several years. He had never been known to cause any problems or hurt anyone, and the sheriff was determined to find his killer. A reward of almost $10,000 was being offered by local businessmen.

The weather followed the news, and Noah noted emotionlessly that it was supposed to rain the following day. Weather was something he rarely thought about, unless it was going to interfere with his mission. In this case, rain simply meant that he would want to put on a light, waterproof jacket. This mission was not going to be over soon, and he didn't want to start planning for its conclusion just yet. It was now that he was beginning to meet a number of the people he would have to take out.

Ronnie Sneed, for example, was the type of person Noah would expect to find on his target list. The man could laugh about people who died from overdose, and didn't seem to care at all about the families who were hurt when drug abuse struck them. While Noah could not feel compassion for these people, his own personal moral code required him to consciously abhor their deaths and suffering. He would never, even if he had a conscience, lose any sleep over killing a man like Sneed. It would fall under the heading of community service, as far as he was concerned.

He had met others, as well. There were at least a dozen lieutenants under Morgan, each of them responsible for overseeing one of the many divisions of his criminal empire. Noah filed each name and face away in his memory and reminded himself constantly to be alert for any further information he might pick up on them. The Morgan Mafia was a hydra, with many, many heads. When he struck, it was his intent to eliminate all of them so thoroughly that none of them could grow back.

This led into thinking about Ralph. Other than being the son of a criminal boss, he seemed to be a fairly typical teenager. Unfortunately, he had been groomed all his life for the day when he would take over the illegal enterprises his father had founded. His elevation to running the drug operations was a step in that direction, and Noah had no qualms about him being on the target list.

The trick, he knew, was going to be figuring out how to take them all out at around the same time. If any of them survived for any length of time—more than an hour or so—it would give them the opportunity to regroup and possibly even resurrect the organization. This was something Noah did not intend to allow.

He cleared his mind and turned his attention back to the television, flipping channels until he found a movie he wanted to watch. Strangely enough, he felt very comfortable in the house, and it wasn't long before he dozed off in the recliner.

The sound of tires crunching on gravel woke him, and Noah was up out of his chair instantly, the pistol snatched off the table and out of its holster without him even thinking about it. A quick look out the window, however, showed him that it was very dark out and the vehicle coming up the driveway was towing a trailer. He put the gun back in its holster and onto the table, then shoved his feet back into shoes and stepped out the front door.

Sarah had made good time. It was actually just a little after two in the morning, even though she had lost an hour on the way due to the time zone change. Noah stepped off the front porch and walked quickly out to where she parked, right beside the Charger.

She jumped out of the SUV quickly and ran to him, throwing her arms around his neck and kissing him passionately. Noah returned the embrace, surprising even himself with the relief he felt at having her back in his arms.

When they finally broke for air, Neil was standing close by, a silly grin on his face. "I thought she was going to smother you to death for a moment there," he said. "Good to see you again, Rex."

"You too, punk," Noah said. "Come on in, we can unload that tomorrow."

"Sounds good to me," Neil said. "Just let me grab my computer. That's all I need for tonight."

He reached back into the SUV and grabbed the case that contained his laptop, one he had been given by Allison when he had first been recruited and which had been upgraded several times since then. It was capable of reaching the internet through cell towers or by direct satellite uplink, all with the built-in, internal antenna system it contained. It also held more computing power than all of the computers NASA used during the Apollo and space shuttle programs. He carried it up onto the front porch, then stopped and giggled when Noah swept Sarah up into his arms and carried her across the threshold.

"You already did this once," she whispered into his ear.

"But this is the first house I ever bought for you," he replied. "We can't let an opportunity go to waste, now, can we?"

She burst out laughing and threw her arms around his neck. She smothered his cheek with kisses until he dropped her suddenly onto the couch, then sat down beside her.

Noah looked up at Neil as he set his computer case down beside the recliner. "Why don't you check the place out? Never know what you might find that I missed," he said.

Neil grinned and opened the case. Besides holding the computer, there were several other items of electronic equipment inside. He picked up one of them, a small silvery box with a digital meter, and turned it on. It was marked as a signal strength meter, but it had another purpose.

It took him about five minutes to walk all the way through the house, watching the readout the entire time. When he was satisfied, he returned to the living room and put the box back inside the case.

"All clear," he said. "No microphones, no cameras, no bugs of any kind."

"Good," Noah replied. He was leaning back on the couch, with Sarah's legs thrown over his lap. "That last call from our mysterious friend was the one we've been waiting for, I think. He's coming to this area tomorrow—later today, I mean—and is willing to meet with me. He's trying to talk me into leaving E & E and going to work for him directly, baiting it with the idea that I'd be able to have a normal life."

Sarah's eyebrows went up. "A normal life? You're not actually considering this, are you?"

"No. I'm just pretending to be interested in order to secure this meeting. He made quite a point about the fact that he won't be alone, however. It may be impossible for me to take any action against him this time, so I may have to keep up the act a while longer."

"And of course," Neil said, "he's not going to give you any advance notice on where to meet. That'd make it too easy to set up a hit, or try to take him into custody."

"Right. I'm planning to go to this one unarmed, just try to establish an atmosphere of trust. My idea is to try to convince him that I'm the jealous type, that if he wants me, then he's got to make sure I'm number one. I won't answer to anybody but him, and I've got to have enough access to make it certain that I could burn him if he betrays me."

"Honor among thieves," Sarah said. "My dad used to deal with the people he sold cars to the same way. Make sure you got enough on them to hang their butts out to dry if they ever turn on you."

Noah nodded. "Exactly. It's the only kind of trust model that could work in a situation like this. He has to be just as concerned about what I'll do as I would be about what he might do."

"I like this place," Sarah said suddenly. "But I have been driving all day and I'm tired. Can we discuss these things tomorrow?"

Without a word, Noah pushed her legs gently off and stood up, taking her by the hand and leading her toward the master bedroom. "I'll let you sleep in," he said as they walked down the hall. "I have to be on the job at seven in the morning."

"Sleeping in is good," Sarah replied. "And is it only me, or is this all antique furniture?"

NOAH ROSE AT SIX, QUIETLY made his way into the bathroom and took a shower, then slipped into his coat and shoes. Sarah was sprawled across the bed when he came out, and he leaned down to kiss her cheek before slipping out into the hallway.

Neil was up sitting at the kitchen table. "I made coffee," he said. "Couldn't sleep, so I thought I'd try to play the game a bit. I relayed the situation back home, and you're supposed to proceed."

"I was planning to," Noah said. He poured himself a cup of coffee and sat down across from Neil. "So how does the game work?"

"It's an espionage game, one of those where players have to follow clues and track down a target, then eliminate the target. I'm a game master, which means I'm sort of like God in the virtual world of the server. Molly is one of the players on my server, and she runs a team that's made up of people from Neverland. She and I worked out a code so that we can send just about any kind of information back and forth, simply by embedding it into screenshots I attach. It's pretty so-phisticated; NSA might crack the code if they knew about it, but it would take them a couple of months."

"Sounds excellent. And you actually get to interact with real play-ers?"

Neil snorted. "So far, I haven't found half a dozen that could be called real players. There are a few thousand in my group that are rank amateurs in this game, even though they may have been pretty good at some of the others out there. Almost everything else is sim-ply a battle game, where you build your army up until he can kick the ass of somebody else's army. This is entirely different because they have to understand the politics of this virtual world in order to ac-complish the missions assigned to them." He grinned and winked at Noah. "I've already based for the missions on some of the real ones we've already pulled off."

Noah raised one eyebrow. "You might want to be careful about that," he said. "If the mole is aware of how this mission runs, he may be watching what you do in the game. If he figures out that some of the missions in the bio he's got on me are not real, it could blow the whole operation."

"Relax, Noah," Neil said. "Like I said, I only based the missions on some of our real exploits. There aren't enough similarities for any-one to put them together, I promise you. Different names, different locales, different reasons for the mission, everything." He waggled his eyebrows at Noah. "I'm not stupid, remember?"

Noah simply stared at him for a moment. "A high IQ doesn't nec-essarily mean a lack of stupidity. Some of the most intelligent people in the world have made stupid mistakes."

Neil stuck his tongue out at him.

Noah finished his coffee and walked out the door. A moment lat-er, Neil heard the Charger start and then the crunch of gravel as he drove out of the driveway.

CHAPTER TWENTY-SIX

One of Brendan's crew was standing in front of the Morgan house when Noah pulled up, and he stood facing the Charger until he saw who was driving. As soon as Noah stepped out of the car, the man almost came to attention.

"Relax," Noah said. "I'm just checking in on the kid. Everything go okay last night?"

"No problems since I've been here," the guy said. "Nice and quiet all night."

"Good. I don't really expect anything to happen around the house, but you just never know. You're Al, right?"

"Yes, sir, Al Spencer. We met briefly yesterday."

Noah nodded. "I remember. The day crew ought to be here in a few minutes—just let them know I'm inside." He walked up the front steps and knocked on the door.

Marlene opened it a few moments later and smiled when she saw him. "Come on in," she said. "We're having eggs and bacon, would you like some?"

Noah put his big smile on his face. "If it won't cause any problems, I couldn't turn it down," he said. "For some reason I can't figure out, there's not a restaurant in this town that serves a decent American breakfast."

Marlene laughed and patted him on the shoulder. "Come on into the kitchen," she said. "There's plenty."

Noah followed her and found Ralph, Brendan, and Jimmy Morgan sitting at a big table inside the kitchen itself. The Morgans were eating breakfast, and Brendan was drinking coffee. Jimmy looked up and smiled, then waved him over.

"Sit your ass down," he said. "We're having breakfast, and there's plenty."

"I already told him," Marlene yelled. Noah slid into a chair, and she set a plateful of scrambled eggs and bacon in front of him. "Dig into that. You want some coffee?"

"I'd love a cup," Noah said. She was back a moment later with a mug and then pushed the sugar bowl toward him. "You need cream?"

"Nope, I'm fine." He added a couple of spoons of sugar and stirred, then picked it up and took a big drink. "Okay, now that is some very good coffee. Can I ask what brand?"

"I don't know what it's called," Jimmy said, "but it's imported. I tried some once when I was on a trip and liked it, so I have a standing order in all the time. Comes in these big three-pound bags. I'll give you one."

"See?" Ralph said. "This job comes with perks, man."

Noah had just shoved a forkful of eggs into his mouth, so he chewed quickly before answering. "I'll say," he said. "If you guys eat like this every day, I'll show up for breakfast all the time."

"Marlene wouldn't mind," Jimmy said. "She seems to think she needs to cook for a small army every day, anyway. I hate to think about how much food gets thrown out this house every week."

"Not very much at all," Marlene said loudly. "How can it, with you guys here? Jimmy, you could eat more than most baseball teams all by yourself."

Jimmy laughed and slapped his belly. "That must be why I've got this," he said, still chuckling.

Noah laughed along, keeping up his act. "Ralph," he said a moment later, "what's on your agenda for today?"

"I'm going down to see Ronnie," the boy said. "We talked a little bit yesterday about some of my ideas, especially about liquid pot and things like that, so it's time we decide how we're going to handle the transition. He'll be introducing me to his crews today, letting them know I'm taking over."

Noah looked over at the boy's father. "Anybody on that crew I need to be aware of? Anybody you don't trust?"

Jimmy shrugged. "The way this bracket works," he said, "is you put your lieutenants in place, and then you trust them to do their jobs. I don't know who Ronnie has working for him, but I've never heard of any issues. I'm thinking that Ralphie will have to make some of those decisions on his own."

"I can handle it, Pa," Ralph said. "Anybody working under me will understand real quickly that I don't play games. It's my way or the highway, nothing in between."

"That's good," Noah said, "but I don't want you alone with any of them until they've proven themselves. You keep Forney and one of his boys with you at all times today, okay?"

Jimmy Morgan looked up at him. "What are you going to be doing today?"

"My wife and her brother got in at two o'clock this morning," Noah said. "There are couple of things I need to take care of today, but I'll be with Ralph and Forney most of the time. Is there anything particular you want me to do?"

Jimmy shook his head. "Nope. Just wondered where you'll be. You know, if the wife just got in and you need the day off..."

"I don't," Noah said. "I made sure to get some sleep before they arrived last night so that I'd be all right for today. The job comes first, and Angie understands that."

Jimmy grinned at him. "I do like a man who knows where the bread comes from." He swallowed his last swig of coffee and scooted his chair back. "Well, you boys have a good day. I've got some things I need to attend to, so I'll be tied up for a good part of it. Call me if you need anything." He rose and turned, then stalked out the door without another word.

"Don't let him get to you," Ralph said. "He likes to give the impression he's some kind of badass, but the truth is that he just likes power. If he's got something to attend to, it's probably something to do with one of the dozen or so women he keeps on the string."

Noah met Ralph's grin with one of his own. "Rank does have its privileges," he said. "It's good to be the king."

"That's what he always says," Ralph said, chuckling. "And now he calls me the crown prince. I guess it's good to be that, too."

Noah smiled. "I guess so. I know I'm glad to be the prince's guard. Best job I've ever had, I can tell you that."

A sound behind him made him turn his head, and Scott Forney walked into the room. "Hey," he said. "How's it going?"

"Going great," Noah said. "Got here in time for breakfast, and it's good."

Forney smiled. "I know, I've had Marlene's cooking before. Hey, Marlene." The housekeeper came to him and gave him a hug.

"Sit down, Scotty," she said, "and I'll bring you a plate."

"Oh, no, Marlene," Forney said with a grin, "I'm already full. Janet fed me waffles this morning." He leaned close to her and stage-whispered in her ear. "But I'll make sure I save room tomorrow, okay?"

"Tomorrow we're having pancakes," Marlene said with a grin. "Janet will get jealous if you start eating here every morning."

"And you think that'd stop me?" Forney let her go and stood facing Noah. "Anything special today, Chief?"

"I might need to do some running around sometime today," Noah replied, "but not a lot. He's planning on spending time with Sneed, and I want you to watch all the guys on his crew. If anyone seems nervous or fidgety, get 'em away from Ralph. Nobody new, either, nobody gets close to him without you knowing who they are."

Forney nodded. "You got it. I know most of his people, anyway, so if I don't, they get patted down before they come in."

"Right," Noah said. "We still don't know who paid Benny for the hit. Until we do, and he's dead, everyone is to be considered a potential threat. No exceptions."

"No exceptions," Forney repeated back. "Best way to handle things. Hey, did the wife make it in?"

Noah grinned and nodded. "Yeah, about two this morning. She's sleeping in today. That's one of the things I need to take care of today. She's never met my sister. Katie was gone before I met Angie, and I need to get them together and see if they're gonna get along."

There was a bit more small talk around the table, but finally Ralph was ready to go. Forney relieved Brendan, and he took his men with him as he left.

"Ralph," Noah said, "you'll be riding with Scott today. I'm going to follow along, but I'll just be watching from the car."

Ralph shrugged. "Don't make no never mind to me," the boy said. "I just think it's cool I get my own personal chauffeur out of this deal."

Noah chuckled, then walked over to his car and climbed behind the wheel. He waited until Forney started his own and fell into line behind the two men he had brought along. The three-car convoy moved along the driveway and out onto the county road, then headed toward Berryville. Ronnie Sneed conducted his business from an old used-car dealership on the east end of town, and Noah kept a close eye on surrounding traffic until they got there. The place still sold cars, mostly cheap ones such as Ronnie's primary clientele could barely afford the weekly payments on. In fact, most of them came from those same clients when they were desperate for the money to conduct the other sort of business.

No one seemed to pay any attention to the little motorcade, however, so he simply parked near the entrance of the lot, facing the main road. In his rearview mirror, he watched Ralph and Forney enter the brick office building. The other two men sat on the hood of the car they had ridden to the place in, one of them facing the road and the other facing the building's door.

A moment later, two men came out, both of them looking angry. Noah tensed slightly as they stomped past the two bodyguards, but neither of them said or did anything alarming. When they drove away, Noah took out his phone and dialed Forney.

"Couple of guys who owe money," Forney said as soon as he answered. "I told them to come back later; we had other things to occupy us for now."

"No problems?" Noah asked. "They looked pretty pissed."

Forney chuckled. "They were only pissed because Ronnie's been letting them have some stuff on credit, and Ralph told them that's all over. Cash and carry, no charge accounts anymore. Ronnie and Ralphie are arguing about it now."

Noah let a chuckle of his own escape. "Ralph is in charge now," he said, "so he's probably gonna start out by showing everyone who's the boss. If he looks like he's going to make new enemies, try to steer him a bit, but don't piss him off."

"Will do," Forney said, and Noah cut the call off. He settled back in his seat and contented himself with watching the traffic go by.

It was almost three hours later when Ralph came out again, and he walked directly to the Charger. Noah powered down his window and looked up at the kid. "How'd that go?" he asked.

Ralph grinned at him. "Old guys like Ronnie—he's as old as my Pa—they don't like it when the kid comes in and starts giving orders, but we got through it. He's calling all his people now, to come in after lunch so we can meet. I'm thinking of going over to Eureka for lunch, that cool?"

"Sure," Noah said. "I'll follow you guys." He sat up and started the car as Ralph walked back toward Forney's Buick and got in. The bodyguards were already in their own car, and Noah fell in at the rear of the line once more.

They were almost to the edge of town when his phone rang, and he saw that it was Sarah calling. "Angie, baby," he said. "You decide to get up at last?"

"Ha-ha," Sarah said. "I'll have you know I've been up for more than half an hour. How's your day going?"

"Pretty decent," he said. "All I've been doing so far is sitting in the car. Chilling and taking it easy."

"Must be nice. Neil and I are about to start unloading the trailer. Don't suppose you want to come home and help, do you?"

"Leave the heavy stuff for me and Neil. I'll probably be home around four, but I've got another appointment later, remember that."

"No problem, babe. Hey, who picked out the dishes and stuff?"

"That was Katie. She helped me figure out what all we'd need."

"Yeah, I remember you telling me that. I was just surprised that they're so nice. I was pretty sure you didn't pick them."

Noah laughed. "No, the ones I wanted were big and heavy and looked like they were meant for a campfire. Katie reminded me that I had married a girl, so I let her use her own judgment. I'm glad you approve."

"And speaking of your sister," Sarah said, "when do I get to meet her?"

"Tell you what. After lunch, I'll run by her place and get her and bring her out. I can help unload the heavy stuff then, that work?"

"Awesome, baby. Can't wait."

"See you then," Noah said, and then he ended the call and put his phone back into his pocket. He followed the others all the way to Eureka Springs and was surprised when they stopped at a little place called Carol's Kitchen. He parked the car away from most of the others and got out, locked it, and followed them inside.

With the waitress's permission, they pushed a couple of tables together, and the five of them sat down. Ralph seemed to know the place pretty well and ordered a buffalo chicken sandwich without even looking at the menu. Noah picked one up and glanced at it, then decided to try the same sandwich.

A few of the customers recognized Ralph, and one or two knew Forney. Noah was introduced—as Rex, of course—to several new people. Ralph referred to him as "my new babysitter," while Forney simply said he was "the new guy." Apparently, most people understood that being "the new guy" meant working directly for Jimmy Morgan.

The sandwich wasn't bad, and they were finished at just a little after twelve thirty. Noah had told them he had to run home for a little while after lunch, and Forney had assured him that everything was under control. He paid his tab and left them standing at the register, walked out, and got into the Charger and headed back to Berryville.

Kate was home and still up. When Noah tapped on the door, she yelled for him to come in.

"Hey, bro," she said. "Angie make it in?"

"Yep, and she sent me to kidnap you and drag you out of the house. Something about making you help her unload the trailer."

Kate rolled her eyes. "Yeah, I'll be right there. Tell her not to wait, though—it's okay to go ahead and get started."

Noah grinned. "Actually, she wanted me to bring you out so the two of you could meet. Are you busy?"

Kate smiled back at him. "Give me ten minutes to change," she said. "There's coffee if you wanted, or there's pop in the fridge."

Noah opened her refrigerator and took out a bottle of orange-flavored soda, then twisted off the cap and took a big drink. He licked his lips and looked at the label, but it wasn't a brand he recognized. By the time she came out of the bedroom again, he had finished it and set the bottle on the counter.

"Okay, I'm ready," Kate announced. "I'd better just follow you out; I don't need to get stuck out there all afternoon. Some days, I go in for a little while in the afternoon to help the programming manager. I'm supposed to be there about three thirty, today."

"No problem," Noah said. He went back out to his car and got behind the wheel as she backed her own out of the driveway. Noah had to pull into her driveway to turn around, and then he actually followed Kate's car out to his place.

Sarah and Neil were standing at the back of the trailer when they pulled in, and Noah quickly made the introductions. It took less than two minutes for him to realize that the two girls were going to get along quite well, so he let them go on inside and start getting to know each other while he helped Neil carry some of the bigger boxes and packages into the house.

"Rex, you just wait into you see this new 3-D printer I've got," Neil said. "It is absolutely awesome. With a little bit of work, I could actually 3-D print entire pieces of furniture."

Noah grinned at him, conscious that Kate could be looking their direction at any moment. "I think I've already got enough furniture," he said. "What do you need something like that for, anyway?"

Neil pretended to be shocked. "Are you kidding? The stuff this thing uses for raw material doesn't cost nearly as much as you'd think. Say I wanted a bicycle, I could either go out and buy one for a couple hundred bucks, or I can print out the frame, the wheels, just about every single part, and then all I've got to buy is a couple tires and a seat. It'll be lighter than what I could buy and won't cost half as much."

"I see," Noah said. "And how long would it take you to print it out?"

"Couple hours, maybe three. But if I was using a bicycle for an example, I could literally make just about anything. You've heard of nanotubes?"

"Yeah, makes a super strong material, right?"

"Yep. Well, this stuff takes that several steps further. It uses something called nanosheets in a polymerized matrix to transfer all the strength of the nanotubes into the entire object it makes."

Noah raised his eyebrows. "And this is important because..."

Neil chuckled. "That means I could print out a razor blade with this stuff, and you could shave with it. The funny thing is that you could probably shave with it a hundred times before it got dull enough to throw away."

"Cool," Noah said. "That'll save me a lot of money buying razors."

Neil leaned close to him. "And, of course, we have the added advantage that the stuff makes incredibly fine shrapnel when we use it in our own special ways."

Noah nodded but said nothing. They carried the large case into the house and down the hall to the room Neil would be using for his office.

"What happened to the bed and stuff that was in here?" Noah asked.

"I took it down and carried it out to the storage building," Neil said. "But don't worry, I wrapped it all in plastic real well."

CHAPTER TWENTY-SEVEN

By the time Neil and Noah were finished, Sarah and Kate were comfortably sitting on the couch and talking like old friends. Noah kissed Sarah goodbye and promised that they would have Kate over for dinner soon, then said he had to get back to work and left. He called Forney while he was leaving the driveway and was told that they were back at Sneed's office, but that everything was going well.

"Either Ralph or I know all of these guys," he said. "I'm not going to argue with the kid when he says he can trust these people, but unless it's somebody I know well enough to trust in myself, I'm not going to let my people relax around them. Oh, and by the way, Billy Martin called a while ago. He thinks they may have a lead on whoever it was that paid Benny. I told him you might want to talk to him about that, was I right?"

"Damn right," Noah said. "Text me his number, will you? I want to call him now."

"You got it." The line went dead, and a moment later Noah got the chime that signaled an incoming text message. He opened it and tapped the number it contained with his thumb, and the phone dialed it automatically.

"Billy Martin," the deputy answered.

"Deputy, this is Rex Madison. Scott Forney said you may have a lead on the person who hired Benny?"

"Hey, Rex. Yeah, there's a guy named Justin Haggard who's apparently been heard saying that something is going to happen to Jimmy and Ralph. Don't have anything concrete, yet, but word on the street is that Haggard's been working with some out-of-towners with a lot of money."

"Out-of-towners," Noah repeated. "We talking about the mob, here? Like in New York and Vegas?"

"That's kinda what it sounds like," Martin said. "At the moment, though, that's all we've got. We're looking for Haggard now but haven't found him yet."

"I don't suppose you could send me a picture of him, could you? I'd like to make sure my guys all know who he is."

"No problem at all," Martin said. "Give me just a few minutes. Can I send it straight to your phone?"

"Absolutely. And I appreciate it."

Noah ended the call and held the phone in his hand as he drove. It chimed again a few moments later, and he found himself looking into the face of a man who reminded him of Schwarzenegger, when he was younger. The same iron jaw, the same emotionless expression; if Hollywood ever went looking for a new Terminator, Noah would have happily nominated this guy.

He got to the car lot a few moments later and shared the photo with Forney and his men. He forwarded it to Forney's phone, and Forney sent it on to all the rest of the crew and then started calling them to explain. Within a matter of minutes, all of Ralph's security team were aware of Haggard and why he was not to be allowed near the younger Morgan.

Noah sat in on some of the meeting for a while and got to shake hands with a number of Ralph's new drug dealer employees. He listened to a lot of talk about the logistics of the drug trade and recognized a lot of the terminology. Part of his preparation for the mission had been a crash course, under hypnosis, in how the illegal drug trade worked. In theory, he could manufacture methamphetamines with the best of them, and understood exactly what they meant when they referred to "pilling it out," or talked about drying it on a sheet of glass. To stay in cover, he even told a few stories about his own fictitious time in the business.

It was just after four, and Noah was about to head for home, when his phone rang. He didn't recognize the number, so he answered it by saying, "Joe's Pizza."

The distorted voice on the line. "That's funny," it said. "I arrived earlier than I expected. Are you free at the moment?"

"Yeah," Noah said. "You want me to come now?"

"Yes. Do you know where the Passion Play is held?"

"Yeah, I've seen the signs for it."

"There's a statue of Jesus north of it a little ways. Christ of the Ozarks, they call it. Meet me there in forty-five minutes. Come alone."

The line went dead. Noah put the car in gear and pointed it toward the west.

Forty-five minutes was not a lot of time, not with the twists and turns on Highway 62. Likely, the Charger didn't let the curves slow it down much. Noah got to the intersection of the highway and Passion Play Road in just over twenty minutes, then turned right.

The Christ of the Ozarks statue was built in 1966 and stands sixty-five and a half feet tall. It resembles the famous statue of Christ at Rio de Janeiro, but looks out over the Ozark Mountains around Eureka Springs. Tourists flock to it every summer, and to the Passion Play that runs almost every day when the weather is warm.

This road had its own share of twists and turns. By the time Noah arrived at the parking lot for the statue, forty-three minutes had elapsed since he got off the phone.

There were four other cars in the parking lot, and each of them was occupied by two or more people. He parked his car to one side of the lot, then tucked his pistol under the seat, got out, and sat on the hood.

No one moved for several minutes, so he simply sat there and waited. He kept his face turned toward the statue, as if he were simply admiring it or trying to commune with God.

One of the cars started suddenly and drove slowly toward him. There were two men in the front seat, and he could tell that someone was sitting in the back but couldn't see who it was. When it stopped, ten feet away and facing him, the back door opened. Noah turned his face toward the car to see who might be getting out, and his eyebrows rose slightly when he saw that it was a very small woman.

She looked like she might be just shy of five feet tall and was probably in her late thirties or very early forties. Her hair was blonde, but it had the kind of sheen that he associated with hair that was not naturally that color. She closed the door and walked directly toward him, a broad smile on her face.

"Hello, Noah," she said. "You can call me Monique."

"Monique," he said. "So it's you, is it?"

"Am I the one you've been speaking to on the phone? Yes, I certainly am. Technology, of course, allows me to hide my gender as well as the actual timbre of my voice, but I am the one who made the offer to give you back a normal life. I am also the one who sold your Sarah to the Chinese and set all of this in motion. I'm quite certain that you have entertained thoughts of what you would like to do to me when we finally came face-to-face, but I would advise you against trying to carry out those thoughts. I can assure you that you would never leave this place alive if you were to do so."

Noah simply stared at her for a few moments, his thoughts taking shape. "What do you actually want with me?" he asked her. "You know what I am—I'm an assassin. Do you have that many enemies you want eliminated that you need a specialist like myself?"

"Sometimes I think so," she said. "That's not all I would want you doing for me, however. In fact, you would probably go months without ever telling anyone. There may be stretches as long as a year when the most strenuous activity you would face would be something like what happened in Odessa. You'd be at home with your wife most of the time, and I would see to it that you could live quite well."

"And you could honestly make it look like we were dead? You could guarantee that no one would be hunting us?"

"Allison isn't the only one who has talented people. Could I make it appear that you were dead? Quite easily, and I could even provide them with bodies to bury. With a little preparation, even your doctors wouldn't be able to tell the difference." She took a couple of steps closer. "Noah, you could keep Sarah out of the line of fire. You could have children, if you so choose. Would that be so bad?"

Noah took a deep breath and then sighed. "You're right," he said. "I had a lot of ideas on what I'd like to do to the person who put Sarah through that. Unfortunately, you don't have the right anatomy for me to carry out those ideas even if I had the chance. Somehow, I really thought you would be a lot bigger."

She burst out laughing. "I'm sure you did," she said, "and I'm sure you expected me to be older and have bigger balls than you." She glanced down at her chest. "I've got those, they just hang a little higher than yours."

Noah grimaced. "Well, you're as crude as any man I've ever met. So, how would this work? How do we actually make this happen?"

Monique smiled then, a genuine and radiant smile. As small as she was, she was actually a rather attractive woman. "It will require some planning," she said. "I'll have to make arrangements for your apparent deaths, and if you still insist on bringing the other boy along, that may take a little longer. I'm guessing it would take a couple of months to get set up, and then I would simply need to know about your next mission. All three of you would apparently die in a terrible attack, something that would leave your bodies burned beyond recognition and require medical and dental records to sort you out. After that, though, you would be free. Oh, we might resort to a bit of cosmetic surgery just to be safe, but it won't be much." She reached out and laid a hand on his knee. "Are you interested, Noah?"

Noah looked at the other men in the cars. "Who are these people?"

"They work for me the same way you would work for me," she said. "They don't actually know who I am, which is why they are simply sitting in the cars and watching this conversation rather than getting the opportunity to hear it. As far as they are concerned, I am the representative of their employer, and they are charged with my safety. They don't know that I'm the one who could actually give the order to kill their families, or they might decide to eliminate me themselves. We couldn't have that, now, could we?"

"I'm sure that wouldn't be anything pleasant for you," Noah said. "The thing about me, though, is I don't play second fiddle to anybody." He turned his eyes back to focus on her own. "If I work for you, I work only for you. Nobody else tells me what to do, and I only answer to you. Who I am, where I came from—all of that stays entirely between us."

She tipped her head slightly to one side, acknowledging his statement. "I can agree to that. The only caveat I would add would be that any disobedience, any refusal to follow my orders, would unleash a terrible retribution. I'm sure you don't need me to spell it out."

Noah nodded. "I don't do what you want, Sarah suffers. I think you already know I do whatever it takes to keep her safe, so I doubt you really expect that circumstance to arise."

"Oh, I can see that we understand each other quite well. Do we have a deal, Noah?"

Noah stared into her eyes for several more seconds, then slowly nodded. "We do," he said. "Make your preparations. Give me some way to let you know when that next mission begins, and I'll have everything ready on my end. I'm not going to let Sarah or Neil know what's going on, because I can't take a chance that one of them might slip. When it happens, we'll make it happen all at once. I'll explain it to them then, when it's already a done deal. Sarah will be okay with it, I know. As for Neil—I think he'll be okay with it, but if he's not, I'll deal with him."

Monique looked into his eyes and nodded once. "I'll be in touch." She turned and walked back to the car, got into the back seat, and said something to the driver. The car started again and drove away, down the road Noah had just followed to get there.

The other cars stayed where they were for at least five minutes, and then all of them started up and drove away at once. Noah waited until they were out of sight and then got back into the Charger, started the engine, and put it into gear. He drove slowly down the road, and all of the other vehicles were gone before he got back to the highway.

He turned left and headed toward Berryville, driving sedately and thinking over the conversation he'd just had. He was almost halfway back by the time he realized that his thinking was becoming cloudy, and it was at that point that his vision began to blur slightly. He shook his head to try to clear it, but it didn't help. He saw a gravel parking lot ahead on his right and slowed the car quickly so that he could turn in. He got it stopped and parked, then opened his door to climb out, but his legs seemed to be weak. He couldn't manage to get up out of the driver's seat, so he simply sat back and took out his phone.

His eyes would not focus, as he tried to find the icon that would ring through to Sarah. He shook his head again, desperately trying to think, but it only made him dizzy. The phone slipped from his hand as he fell back against the seat.

The last thing he managed to see was another car pulling in just in front of his own, but then everything went dark. His thoughts continued for a few seconds more, as he realized that she had somehow poisoned him when she touched his knee.

Noah Wolf, who had never experienced any kind of regret, suddenly wished he had called Sarah before attending the meeting. He would have liked to have been able to say goodbye.

HE WASN'T DEAD. NOAH knew that he was alive because the dead can't hurt that badly. Something seemed to be running around inside his head, smashing on his brain with a large hammer. In all of his life, he had never felt a headache like this one.

He opened his eyes, but it was dark wherever he was at. The darkness was complete, and he could tell no difference with his eyes open, so he closed them again. It didn't help with the pain, but it allowed him to concentrate just a bit more of his attention on his other senses.

He was lying on something hard, he could tell that. He tried moving his hands and found that they were not restrained, but he was too weak to attempt getting up. The surface under his hand felt like wood, and he suspected that he was lying on the floor.

He breathed in quickly through his nose. There was an odor, something familiar, but he couldn't quite place it. He stopped trying to recognize it and simply thought about what it might remind him of. By letting his thoughts run free for a moment, he glimpsed a quick mental image of a flower garden. He suspected there were either flowers growing nearby, or else he was in a funeral home.

He turned away from that line of thought and listened, straining his ears for any sound. There was something, some kind of rhythmic noise, and it dawned on him that he was hearing the sound of an electric motor. It sounded like a big one, but he couldn't be sure.

A wooden surface, the smell of flowers, and an electric motor. He tried desperately to put those things together into something coherent, but nothing would come. He decided it was time to force his body to cooperate, so he began to struggle up to a sitting position. A wave of nausea struck him, and he fell back. His head hit the floor, and he was gone again.

A loud creaking invaded his consciousness and forced him to wake. The pain was much less, now, and bearable. He opened his eyes and saw that light was coming through a doorway some distance away, and someone was walking toward him. From the shape and stature, he knew that it was Monique.

"What..." His voice cracked, and he worked his tongue a bit to generate some moisture in his mouth. "What the hell is going on?" It still sounded rough, but he got the words out.

"There's a reason," Monique said, "why those few people who know who I am have never betrayed me. Would you like to know that reason? Well, I'm going to tell you anyway, so you might as well just listen." She knelt down beside him and put a hand on his left arm. "There's an amazing bit of technology that's out there today, something most people would never have heard of. You know how they can inject a microchip into you, something that can carry a lot of information about who you are, your finances, your medical records, all that stuff? Well, that's not the only thing that's been developed for injection. Do you feel the soreness in your armpit? If not, don't worry, it'll come. We just injected you with a little insurance. The needle was kind of large, almost two millimeters in diameter, but it allowed us to implant something into your muscle. It's lodged right beside the artery that comes through your shoulder, the one that feeds all the blood to your arm. It's a very tiny but very powerful explosive device, and it contains a microchip that can receive a radio signal from any of a number of satellites overhead. If it receives that signal, which is heavily encrypted, then it will detonate. The force of the explosion will tear most of your arm off and will rip that artery to shreds. You would bleed to death within barely over a minute, and nothing anyone could do would save you."

"I thought we made a deal," Noah managed to croak out.

"Oh, we did," Monique said. "Let's just say that I like to have a bit of insurance. There are only two things that could set off that device and kill you. One would be if I enter a certain code into the computer that holds the encrypted signal. Should I do so, it would explode within three seconds. The other is the one I'm particularly proud of, though. You see, there is another little device implanted inside of me. It measures my heart rate and keeps track of every beat. Should my heart suddenly come to a stop, it would wait about fifteen minutes to see if it was merely some sort of glitch, but if it hadn't detected my heart beating again during that time, then it would instruct that same computer to send that signal out. That way, it becomes just as important to you that I survive as it is to me."

Noah looked at the dim image of her face and licked his lips. "Pretty smart," he said. "You drugged me?"

She waved her fingers in front of his face. "Some patches on my fingers. I put them on just before I got out of the car, because that stuff is extremely potent. It contains a natural solvent, so it passed right through the fibers of your jeans and into your skin. Once it got there, it was absorbed into the capillaries and carried into your bloodstream. We knew how long it would take to act and simply followed you. I was confident you'd pull over once you felt it start to take effect, and I was right. Then all we had to do was help our poor, inebriated friend out of his car and into our own. I had this little place prepared in a hurry after I knew we were going to meet. If you agreed to my offer, then I knew that I'd have to bring you here to put my insurance policy in place. If you had not agreed, then we would've simply killed you where you sat."

She stood up straight again. "We didn't leave your car," she said. "It's sitting right outside the building. You might have to use your

GPS to find your way home, but you'll be fine. The effects will wear off the rest of the way within the next twenty minutes or so, and you'll be able to get up and walk out of here. As for our arrangement, I'll get everything sorted out, and then I'll be in touch. As I said, it might take a couple of months. Until then, just keep doing your job so that no one suspects anything."

Monique turned and began walking toward the doorway, but then she stopped and came back to him. "Can you believe I almost forgot? There's one other little thing you need to know about that device in your armpit. It measures the amount of pressure that your tissues put against it. If that pressure drops significantly lower than it was in the beginning, it will also cause the device to detonate. That pressure can only drop if someone is trying to take it out of you, though, so it probably isn't a good idea to go looking for a surgeon. Believe it or not, that little sucker has enough power that it could probably kill the doctor as well. You wouldn't want to do that, now, would you?"

She turned again, and this time she walked out the door and closed it behind her. Noah heard a car start and drive away, and then he began forcing himself to get up. He made it, but he was so dizzy that he had to stumble into a wall to stay on his feet.

Although it was dark inside the building again, he was certain that the doorway was off to his right. He felt along the wall until he came to the corner, then followed that and found the door. It had a simple doorknob, and the door opened when he turned it.

The Charger was sitting there, just as she had said. He staggered over to it and leaned on the front fender for a moment, then managed to get the door open and climb inside. Once he was there, though, he simply leaned back in the seat and waited for the worst of the nausea and dizziness to pass.

And then he started the car and went home.

CHAPTER TWENTY-EIGHT

I t was just past seven thirty by the time Noah got home, but Sarah hadn't been excessively worried because she had known he was supposed to meet the mole that evening. When he pulled in, she stepped out onto the porch with a big smile and waited for him to climb the stairs.

He smiled and pulled her close to kiss her, then kept an arm around her as they walked inside. At that moment, though, he dropped the act.

Sarah had made beef stew for dinner, and they sat down at the table while he told them both what had happened. Sarah swallowed hard several times as he related the story, and Neil simply sat there and stared with his eyes wide.

"There has to be some way to get it out," Sarah said. "Some way that doesn't kill you. There simply has to be."

"I agree," Noah said, "but it'll have to wait. For now, I've got to stay in character on this mission and make sure Monique thinks I'm going along with our agreement. I can't risk blowing either end of this thing, not right now."

Neil shook his head. "The thing is, that gadget's got to have a disarm code. If we could figure out what it is, we could simply shut the damn thing off, and then any doctor can take it out."

"Yes, but how do you figure it out? I thought about that on the way back here, but what if putting in the wrong disarm code simply tells it to explode?"

Neil scowled. "And that's exactly how I would design it, if it were me. Dammit, Noah. This just can't be happening."

Sarah reached over and touched Noah's hand. "So we just act like it's not there?"

"For the most part, yes," Noah said. "The only thing I want to do is try to keep you on my right from now on. If it does go off, the rest of my body should protect you unless you're right there under my left arm."

Sarah just looked at him. "Do you think I'd want to live if that thing goes off?"

"It doesn't matter," Noah said. "I just can't risk you getting hurt or killed at the same time. From now on, you walk on my right, you sleep on my right—we usually do it that way anyhow, but I'm going to be a lot more conscious of it from now on."

"Oh, damn," she said. "How can you be so freaking calm about this? Noah, I know you well enough to know you're not going to let this stop you from killing her the first time you get the chance. You understand that that would be suicide for you? Right?"

"Again, it doesn't matter. Eliminating the mole, eliminating the risk that she represents to America, is far more important than my life."

Sarah looked into his eyes for another moment, then got up and stormed down the hall. Noah heard the bedroom door slam shut as he turned to look at Neil.

Neil put up both hands in a defensive gesture. "Hey, I get it," he said. "Thing is, that's not just part of your team that stomped off down the hall. That's your wife, Noah. She's not going to take this logically, no matter how you try to explain it. All she sees is the fact that if you kill this woman, she ends up a widow."

"I understand that," Noah said. "Her emotions aside, it doesn't change the fact that Monique's death is still a necessity."

"Okay, fine, I get that. The only thing I want to say is that we've got a little bit of time. You said it's going to take her a couple months to get this set up and get back to you, right? Well, I'm going to encode this whole freaking disaster and send it off to Molly. I figure, between me and her, we're bound to come up with some way to either shut that thing off or get it out of you without it blowing up."

"I'm counting on it," Noah said. "Despite the fact I'm willing to do whatever it takes to accomplish the mission, I don't have a death wish. I've always said that the world is better with Sarah in it; I assure you, I'm fully aware that she feels the same way about me. Maybe even more so, she feels things that I don't. Believe me when I say I'm holding out a lot of hope that you geniuses can come up with an answer before I have to put a bullet in that woman."

Neil just stared at him for a moment, and then he put his head in his hands and looked at the table. "Geez, Noah," he said. "Why do you have to give me headaches like this?"

Noah said nothing but got up and walked down the hall. He tapped on the bedroom door and then tried the knob. It turned, and he opened the door and stepped inside to find Sarah lying on the bed, sniffling as tears soaked into the pillow she had shoved her face into.

"Neil thinks he and Molly can come up with an answer," Noah said. "I think they can, too. Until then, I simply want to take some sensible precautions. Okay?"

Sarah didn't move for a few seconds, but then she rolled over and looked up at him. "Don't ask me not to be close to you. Don't ask me not to put my arms around you and hold you close. Don't ask me not to make love to you—don't ask any of that. I don't know how, but somehow we're going to beat this thing." She wiped the moisture away from her eyes. "And then you're going to kill that bitch, and I'm going to watch when you do it."

Noah looked at her, and then he nodded. "Okay," he said. "Can we go eat dinner now?"

To be continued...

SPECIAL OFFER

Building a relationship with my readers is the ultimate goal with writing. At least, it should be. Without you guys, us writers would just be making up stories for ourselves...which would be weird. That's why I like to connect with my readers in a way many big name authors don't.

I occasionally send newsletters with details on new releases, special offers and other bits of news relating to Sam Prichard, Noah Wolf, and the other varies series and stand alone novels that I write.

And if you sign up to the mailing list today, I'll send you this free content:

- A free copy of the first Sam Prichard novella, FALLBACK (plus the audiobook version)

- A free copy of the first Noah Wolf novella, THE WAY OF THE WOLF (plus the audiobook version)

- Exclusive content and pricing to my mailing list – you can't get this anywhere else. Every book launch I set a discounted price for my mailing list for a couple days. This is exclusive to my list *only,* and something that isn't publicized anywhere else.

You can get the novella's, the audiobook's, and the exclusive discounted pricing **for free,** by signing up here.[1]

NOTE FROM THE AUTHOR

If you enjoyed this adventure, would you please consider taking a moment and leaving your thoughts for others who might also enjoy this book?

It takes only a handful of seconds to leave a review, but can literally make or break a self published career. Please don't feel any obligation to do so, but if you had fun, or perhaps enjoyed yourself at all, then I'd sincerely appreciate it!

Thanks so much,

David Archer

BOOK EIGHT COMING SOON...

Made in the USA
Coppell, TX
05 June 2022

78497775R00173